RAIN FALLS ON EVERYONE

CLÁR NÍ CHONGHAILE

Legend Press Ltd, 107-111 Fleet Street, London, EC4A 2AB
info@legend-paperbooks.co.uk I www.legendpress.co.uk

Print ISBN 978-1-7850790-1-6
Ebook ISBN 978-1-7850790-0-9
Set in Times. Printed by Opolgraf SA
Cover design by Anna Morrison www.annamorrison.com

Clár Ní Chonghaile was born in London but grew up in An Spidéal, County Galway. She left Ireland aged 19 to join Reuters in London as a graduate trainee journalist. Clár has been a reporter and editor for over 20 years, living and working in Spain, France, the Ivory Coast, Senegal and Kenya.

She now lives in St Albans, England, with her husband and two daughters. Her debut novel, *Fractured*, was published by Legend Press in 2016.

Visit Clár at
clarnichonghaile.wordpress.com
or on Twitter
@clarnic

To David, Lucy and Rachel

CHAPTER ONE

Theo ran. Feet pounding, arms pumping, chest heaving, heart racing. In this frenzy of motion, the only still thing was his mind. He had to get away. That was the only goal: to put as much distance as he could between him and the pebble-dashed house where a man he knew little, but enough to hate, lay in a pool of sticky, gold-flecked blood. He had to get away from Deirdre's terrified eyes, from her outstretched hands with the grazed knuckles. He sped through the estate and out onto the main road, his open anorak flapping behind him like the clipped wings of a giant crow.

He didn't stop until he was heading west on a country road. He had covered miles, at first frantically and then steadily with his long, loping stride. He stopped, bent, placed his hands on his knees, and still his brain did not engage. He saw the road, noted its silvery greyness, looked up to the half-moon and then over the stone walls, across the fields. He registered the absence of cars. No surprise there at 2 am on a minor road leading out of Dublin. To his right, a two-storey house – a relic from the austere Ireland of the 1950s – loomed like a sentinel, marking the boundary between the sin-filled city and the countryside, where legend had it, maidens once danced at crossroads while boys played hurling without helmets.

He needed transport. It was his first clear thought since the gun went off. He would never make it on foot. Deirdre might not set the Gardaí on him right away but it'd surely happen. He'd done her a favour, no doubt about that, but sometimes people didn't want favours. In those first, freeze-framed moments after the sharp crack that marked the beginning and the end, no one had moved, no one had said anything. Deirdre was the first to react.

"Go, go now!" she hissed, grabbing a notebook and writing furiously. "Go to my father. He will look after you until you can get out."

She pushed the paper into his hands. Did her fingers flinch as they touched his? She had written her father's address, just a few lines of scribbled instructions, a list of villages to pass through, a left and then a right down a lane. A roadmap to oblivion. Before he left, he tried to read the moral relativities in her eyes but he found only fear. It hurt him then and the memory stung now but there would be time for a reckoning later.

He checked his phone. The battery was nearly dead but who would he call anyway? He clambered over the nearest wall, dislodging the top stone in his wake. It clunked dully onto his toes. He cursed, but in Kinyarwanda. The words had the force of a Taser, freezing him to the spot. He hadn't used his own language in years. The last time was when he was around sixteen and went to a meeting for African immigrants in a church near his home in Clontarf. Teenage identity crisis, he supposed. He never returned. Instead of feeling at one with the other young men, who sat awkwardly on squeaking plastic chairs in the echo-filled basement down below the world, he felt more like an outsider than ever. The social workers – a pudgy woman in a tracksuit and garish pink lipstick and a man in the kind of jumper most of the young black kids wouldn't be seen dead in – were kind and well-meaning and utterly clueless about what made the lads around them tick. It wasn't their fault. They were offering practical solutions – language classes, dole forms, counselling services – when what the young men wanted was someone to wave a magic wand over their heads to make them the same as everyone else. All teenagers need to comply with the pitiless rules that govern their world and they were no different. But because they were black, and had funny accents, and strange, sometimes tragic, tales of foreign lands, they would never fit in. The boys knew it but they didn't get this far by respecting the limits of the possible. The social workers, who might well have had teenagers at home with their own hang-ups about belonging, didn't recognise that same desperation in the boys around them, though it was in every snazzily trainered foot, every awkwardly mumbled Dublin colloquialism, every too-sharp haircut.

There was one other Rwandan, like him but not. His name was Patrice but he called himself Paddy. It made Theo laugh. Patrice was nineteen and had arrived two years before. He was still illegal and still unemployed. During a short break for weak tea and Jaffa cakes, they spoke together in Kinyarwanda, the words dropping thick and clumsy from Theo's lips. They only talked about Dublin and they kept their voices low, as they had been taught by those who first gave them these words. They did not speak of that which was unspeakable. Patrice was clearly a Tutsi and Theo knew that it was just as clear that he himself was not, or at least not just. He'd no idea if Patrice had been in Rwanda during the killing, he'd no idea where he was from, and he did not want to know. In this new world, Patrice was no more like him than Bono. That awkward evening in the church basement was the last time he'd spoken his language, until now, until the curse words burst from his lips as the jagged stone fell onto his foot. Half-formed anamneses crept upon him – other feet slapping other roads, other mouths panting, a remorseless sun – but he hadn't come this far to let the feckers in. *Anam* – soul in Irish. *Anamnesis* – Greek, but so perfectly expressing itself through another language. Theo had always loved words because of what they showed and what they hid, and how they could, by their very existence, create new worlds, new thoughts, new possibilities. Of course, he knew only too well the flip side of this power. Words could also obliterate.

He levered the stone off his toes and stumbled through the reeds and grassy hillocks that stippled the field. He vaulted another wall, careful this time, and emerged onto a narrow country road in front of the house with its lightless window-eyes. He crouched down by the front wall, hidden still by the bushes that swayed like tipsy Wombles in the cheek-clipping wind.

There was a light over the door and another on the side of the breezeblock garage. Leaning against the garage wall, there was a high-seated black bicycle that must belong to someone who had grown up with the house. An old man with a flat cap, maybe, who cycled these lanes straight-backed, spitting curses at the pace of change. Theo unlatched the small gate quietly, slipped across the front garden, grabbed the bike, lifted it smoothly onto his shoulders and returned to the road. In a few breath-starved seconds, he had left the house behind and was speeding down a hill into the safety of a nave of trees. He could feel the house's blank gaze on his back and it quickened his big feet on the pedals. He cycled without caution, eyes down, the up-and-down of his knees anaesthetising his brain until he was spinning down a different road, red dust rising beneath the wheels of the wooden scooter that Shema had made him, wind making him cry, going so fast even the sun couldn't lay its heavy hand on him, sweet breeze filling his flaring nostrils, and his own shadow struggling to keep up. He laughed suddenly and lifted his feet from the pedals, thrusting his legs to the side. Then he wobbled and he was back and there was no sun now. The swollen sky was already paling. When the road forked two kilometres later, he set his face to the darker West, heading towards the bogs of the mid-country and beyond to the Atlantic.

He cycled until an invisible sun finally managed to poke straw rays of light through the sullen clouds. He knew now he was on the R446 beyond Tyrrellspass. He came off the road and found a stone shed with a balding thatched roof. One corner was dry and there were bags of cattle feed stacked by the wall, as well as two empty sacks. Theo lay on one of the sacks, putting the other on top of him, his right arm under his head. He slept quickly. He had done this before, slept on other floors on another continent, and he was tired.

An hour or so later, he woke suddenly and got on the bike again, his mind numbed by cold and hunger. He kept heading west, cycling through towns and villages where another day was stirring for people who knew who they were, and where they were going. He cut a strange sight, weaving through Monday morning mini-jams on streets made for donkey carts not cars, but he didn't slow down long enough to see the eyebrows raised above suspicious squints.

In Kilbeggan, he stopped at a petrol station and bought a coffee and a bun with thick icing. He went outside to where he had put the bike by the front wall, and stood drinking and smoking. A red-faced hook of a man got out of a battered cream Mazda and as he filled the car, he looked at Theo openly, brazenly, the way old men in small places will do. Even when he'd put the nozzle back in the machine, he pushed his hands into the pockets of his cords and stood staring. There was neither anger nor compassion on his face. He was just looking and when he was satisfied he walked into the shop, fumbling for his wallet in sagging pockets so that he looked like a hunchbacked sailor, unused to land.

Theo didn't care. The looking was nothing, less than a nuisance. Things had changed since his arrival in 1995. Then, he was a curiosity to everyone, the freakish survivor of what the 'blue babies' got up to when they grew up.

He'd always thought it was funny that the Irish language described black people as blue. *Na daoine gorm*. Black and blue. Bruised. Damaged. His Irish teacher in secondary, Máistear Burke, said it was because whenever the first Irish met the first Africans, they didn't want to offend them by calling them black, or *dubh,* because that colour was associated with the devil. Theo had liked Burke, even though

11

he was a nutjob with a dangerous habit of picking up chairs and waving them around students' heads while demanding they conjugate the conditional tense properly. By the time Theo came to him at the age of twelve, his foster parents had mostly managed to piece together the broken child they'd been given. There were still a few bits missing but mostly people didn't notice. Máistear Burke did but in his gruff way he treated Theo both the same as everyone else and differently. He never spared him, he never excused him, but there was the odd hand-on-the-shoulder, or chat after class that made Theo think the crazy bastard was looking out for him. In any case, Theo loved learning Irish. He was good at it. Better than the Irish themselves, Burke used to joke. Unlike the other kids, Theo didn't feel it was a burden. They all moaned about learning a 'dead' language, but Theo, who had grown up speaking Kinyarwanda, French, Swahili and some English, didn't see the problem. He liked adding another window to his house of words.

It was Máistear Burke that Theo was thinking about as he ate his chips on the banks of the Shannon near Athlone. It was mid-afternoon and the pubs were already filling but he was well out of the way of any troublemakers and he would be on his bike in a few minutes. From a little hillock covered with scratchy brown pine needles, he could see over the sluggish water to the town and beyond. No grand vistas here. Just a heatless sun skulking behind flat clouds skimming monotonous estates of identical houses, all satellite dishes and twitchy curtains. He'd better not hang around.

"Howya? Nice place for yer tea. Might be a bit cold for my liking though. Gonna be a chilly night, I reckon."

The voice was to his left, on the other side of the bushes that hemmed the spindly trunks of the trees behind him. A rustle, and a man appeared. Stocky and short, he wore a surprisingly bright blue hat above a thin face and there was a cigarette hanging out of the corner of his cranky-looking mouth.

"None of my business, of course, but I was wondering what you might be doing here? Not my land, don't worry. It's all public property here by the river but other side of the trees, now that's my field and I like to keep an eye on things round here. You'd be surprised what goings-on you'd be getting at night; kids drinking, smoking drugs, laying into each other. Not like when I was a young one."

The man squeezed around the bushes, moving closer with every word. Theo wasn't frightened; he was far bigger than this red-neck and look what he'd done last night, for Chrissakes. But he didn't want any trouble here. He nodded vacantly at the man, then returned to his chips.

"Visiting are ye?"

Jesus, this guy wasn't going to let up.

"Jus' down to see me mam's folks, maybe you know them? The Connors?" He laid on the accent.

The man's face was a picture. For the first time since the night before, Theo allowed himself a secret smile. To hide the twitching of his lips, he furrowed his brow and then slowly pulled his hoodie over his head.

"The Connors? Mikey Connor's lot?" the man said.

"Naw, Séamus. Maybe you don't know them. You haven't been living here long yourself?"

The man glared at Theo through slitted eyes. He pulled the fag angrily from his mouth, choked a little as he swallowed some smoke, and flung the butt into the water beyond Theo's feet.

"Coupla years," he said sharply. "My family's from Oranmore."

"Ah, right."

The man flinched and Theo knew he'd got the dismissive tone just right. His years of being an outsider were paying off. He knew just which buttons to push.

Theo picked the last chip from the packet, balled the paper and put it in his pocket. He rose to his feet, grabbed the bike and pushed it past the man, back towards the road.

"Nice talking to ye. Have a good one!" he said.

He was still chuckling as he rode into the town.

He parked the bike carefully outside the stone bus station with its vast glass windows. He wondered how long before someone would see their lucky day and grab it from the rack. What an adventure for the black iron horse, galloping across Ireland, free at last. *Trup, trup a chapaillín*, he muttered, the words of the nursery song echoing across the years from the start of his story in this place. But the image that came with it was from over there and it wasn't a horse: it was a donkey, grazing by the side of a mist-wreathed track as a little boy with a big belly jutting over a pair of dirty shorts waved a long stick around its arse to get it moving again. Fuck, the walls inside me are coming down, Theo thought, shaking his head as if that could straighten out the tangled mess inside.

He bought a ticket from the driver and sank into a seat, his whole body fluttering into softness like a shirt dropped from a hanger. He no longer had the strength to hold himself up. He melted into the upholstery. He'd have to change buses again in Galway but at least this way he would definitely get there by nightfall. The bus pulled out, wheezing and chuffing as though it too had struggled even to get this far.

There were plugs for charging phones so Theo asked to borrow a charger from a stringy guy with a beard and a barbell through his eyebrow, who was chatting to his mate about some 'deadly' gig they'd been to in Limerick.

"Sure, gimme a second. I'll get it for you."

The guy rummaged in his battered green rucksack, handing over the charger with a smile so big and sincere that Theo, after the argy-bargy at the river, felt like bursting into tears. That was the thing about this place: you just never knew which kind of Irish you'd be getting on any given day. The postcard Jekyll or the dark-veined Hyde.

As soon as the screen lit up, the phone beeped. A message

from Cara. One from Deirdre. Both punctuated by question marks.

He dialled Cara's number, squeezing down into the seat as far as he could go. He turned his head to the window, to the fields running by jauntily outside and crows wheeling backwards across the grey sky.

"Hey, it's me. Yeah, I'm okay. Shush, it's fine. Really. I can't talk now. I know, I know. Sorry, my phone died. I'm on my way to Deirdre's dad. I'll be there tonight. Don't cry, Cara. Don't cry. It'll all be okay. I just need to be away for now. I'll try to call tomorrow. No, I don't think so really but better to be safe than sorry. Listen, I'd better go. Yeah, me too. Sorry, Cara. I didn't mean… Me too. Bye."

He hung up. The lads on the other side of the aisle were talking too loudly, trying to give him the pretence of privacy even if they all knew everyone nearby had listened to every word. He texted Deirdre, told her where he was. Then he switched off the phone, closed his eyes and sat there wishing there was a button he could press to switch off his mind too. At this stage, he'd take the risk of it never coming on again, of the battery running down to beyond empty.

It was almost dark when he arrived, stomping through molten grey puddles under a granite sky of pregnant clouds, the air salty on his lips. The sky and sea formed a symphony of greys, reminding him of a few lines from one of the only Yeats poems he'd taken to or, to be honest, even half-understood: *"Imagining a man, and his sun-freckled face, and grey Connemara cloth, climbing up to a place, where stone is dark under froth."* The lines were fresh in his mind because one of the last podcasts he'd listened to had been about Yeats. Was it just a few weeks ago? It'd been before his life veered off its tracks again anyway. There were too many damn 'befores' now. His 'afters' had no staying power.

He paused at the top of the hill and looked down at the blue bungalow, too big now for one man, with its green-grey roof tiles weathered by the spray and the grasping winds that smashed onto this shore after weeks frolicking across the white-tipped Atlantic. The house seemed to be crouching on the soft ground, poised to strike. It radiated tension. Or maybe he just thought that because of what Deirdre had told him about her father. It didn't matter. He was cold and tired and there was nowhere else to go.

He paused at the rusty gate set in the wall. Twisted branches splotched with red berries rose above the stones and a light in the front room cast a weak glow onto the patch of grass out front. A shadow passed across the net curtains. The silhouette paused, the head turned. For a second, they looked at each other – a faceless shadow, a shadowy man, white eyes shining in black faces, two men with no connection at the end of the world.

The shadow disappeared and the light above the door with its peeling grey paint came on. Theo opened the gate. Behind him, the wind and the sea wrestled. He could hear the waves sucking pebbles down the shore. The dull grind of stone on stone set his teeth on edge. The door opened.

"Shema!" The name jumped from his lips like a forgotten prayer. What the hell was going on in his head today? It was as though the walls he had built between his worlds were crumbling, sending shredded memories hurtling into each other, a Big Bang of the brain. Of course, it wasn't Shema. It couldn't be Shema. Shema belonged to the 'there' with all the other dead. He started to stammer an apology, cursing his unreliable memory and treacherous eyes. The old man cut him short.

"Don't fecking stand there all night. Get inside. Look at the state of ye. C'mon now."

The voice was harsh, impatient. Theo hesitated but where else was he to go? By now, everyone in Merrickstown would know what he'd done. In the end, Dublin was not much different from the village outside Kibungo where Shema would hear from raisin-faced old ladies how Theo had stolen roasted corn from their yards even before the yellow beans

16

had begun to digest in his guilty belly. If he didn't want to end up chopped into bits and spread across the Wicklow mountains, he'd better stay away and stay quiet. Maybe this was the penance he deserved. Crimes of the father, crimes of the son. The mark of his people. The mark of Cain.

"Jesus, are you thick as well as violent? I said get inside!"

Deirdre's father was tall and thin and wore old-man tartan slippers. As he edged past him, Theo chanced a quick glance. Hooded eyes chiselled into a broad face, white stubble around his chin and mouth, thin lips sucked clean of smiles, wispy grey hair rising like a halo in the door's light. Was this his saviour? He looked like a witchdoctor, a man more used to cursing than curing.

"Take those mucky shoes off, then down the hall to the kitchen. I'll make us some tea. Then you can tell me yerself what this is all about. Deirdre's called but she's in a right state and I can't make head-nor-tail out of her blathering. So you'll have to tell me exactly what happened."

Theo bent to unlace his trainers. What happened? Good question, he thought. The furniture shop closed, that's what happened, and that's why he ended up working at The Deep, and that's where he met Deirdre, and Cara, and that was the start of it all.

CHAPTER TWO

He noticed her eyes first, or rather he noticed the lurid, purple lids and thick eyeliner that made it look like she was peering at him from behind a carnival mask. Her cheeks were Barbie-pink and her whole face was pancaked with flaky, slightly too-orange powder that ended in an obvious line below her ears. A tideline of desperation. He thought of the ads he had seen some time after arriving in Ireland: *You've been Tango'd!* He'd assumed the sketch had something to do with him. The guy was a different colour and disrupted everything, just like him. Everything was so confusing in those first years. He didn't have the tools, in any language, to describe what had happened to him or to reason his survival. No surprise there. His own people had had to make up a word to describe the killing. It went beyond language.

She had to be around forty, he thought, taking in the fine wrinkles cradling her brown eyes and bracketing well-defined if slightly thin lips. Her gaudy, over-painted face sat uneasily with the rest of her body, which was hunched over the enormous sink. Her dark hair was scraped carelessly into a low bun. She wore a shapeless grey cardigan under her blue apron but her jeans were tight, moulding a trim arse and shapely calves. She wore black-and-white hi-tops, too cool for the rest of her outfit.

"Théoneste, this is Deirdre Walsh. Deirdre, Théoneste – sorry, I just can't manage your last name – what's it again?" asked Desmond Fahy, The Deep's manic owner.

"Mukansonera." Theo said the word slowly. He always did.

He could've taken Jim and Sheila's last name after he moved in with them. Clifton. A solid, rounded word, no worries there. But in a rare display of stubbornness and pride, as inexplicable to little Theo as it was to his foster parents, he'd insisted on keeping Mukansonera. Maybe he hadn't wanted to betray his dead family, or at least not add any new betrayals to that ultimate sell-out: his survival. He took the decision before his memories started reforming – fragments coming together in agonising slow motion after the explosion that was April 1994 – and before he knew the truth of that name. He'd stuck with it though, reasoning that he could always change it later if shame overwhelmed his conflicted sense of loyalty to the ghosts of the time before.

"That's it, ah yes, good lad. Anyway, Dee, Théoneste is starting today. He'll help you on the wash-up for now but we're planning to eventually put him on the veg with Jason."

Deirdre wiped her hands on her apron and extended the right one, red and hot from the water.

"Hello, Théoneste. Welcome to Merrickstown's finest."

For once, Theo experienced the aural double-take that his thick Dublin accent usually inflicted on others: he'd expected a high-pitched voice sharpened on Dublin's tough grindstone. Instead, her voice was deep and husky, the words soft and elongated. She should have been working on one of those sex hotlines that used to be advertised on pink and green flyers in phone boxes. When he was younger, he collected the flyers and drew pictures on the backs: huts, trees, monkeys, bicycles and stick-men farmers. At the time, he didn't understand what the flyers were going on about. He knew the skimpily clad women were somehow up to no good; he could read the words but couldn't seem to put it all together. He knew about sex, of course. He had learnt the basics at home, watching the goats and the sheep in the fields around the village. Shema had filled in the blanks, barking out the details with a loud cackle after each sentence. Theo collected the flyers because he liked the bright colours. He couldn't recall ever seeing paper like that in Kibungo but the brassy greens reminded him of the hills rising above the village, eternal sentinels with their heads in the clouds, whispering to the gods who must've been dozing in 1994. During his first year with the Cliftons, his year of living dangerously, of almost sinking out of himself, he papered his wardrobe with these crude pictures so that his confused eyes would have somewhere to rest. Later, he took the drawings down, replacing them with posters of his favourite Man United players: Cole, Giggs, Beckham and Scholes. By then, he was desperate to hide his difference, insofar as that was possible. Which of course it wasn't.

When he first arrived in Ireland, the counsellor he'd been assigned, a bearded man with lavender socks and a lavender disposition, encouraged him to put what was in his head on paper but he didn't want to trivialise those events. How could he 'draw what happened'? What if someone found those pictures? What if an Irish child found them? Their head would explode.

"Howya?" he said, grabbing Deirdre's hand in his own big one. She started, eyes widening, and he grinned even wider. Even now, people did not expect a big, black guy to speak with such a heavy Dublin accent. He was still something of an anomaly, although Dublin was more 'United Colours of Benetton' now than ten years ago, for sure.

"So, Deirdre, could you show young Theo – d'you mind if I call you Theo? No? Good stuff – show him the ropes today, will you?" Desmond said, his grey eyes bouncing between the two of them. He was a man of constant movement. His hands fluttered and darted like fish in a tank, his eyes flickered, always seeking out hidden enemies poised to destroy him and his restaurant. Theo liked Desmond. He looked like Jim, but on steroids. They'd the same 1970s haircuts, unkempt sideburns defying changing times, paunches telling of kebabs drowned in beers, squat bodies that might have proved deadly on the rugby pitch but were never tested. But Jim was of average height, while Desmond was six-foot-two, a restless giant. Theo felt he'd be a fair boss and that was the best kind when you didn't really want a boss at all.

Three weeks before, Theo had lost his job when the furniture store out on the N4 shut down, another victim of a recession that Theo was beginning to take personally. He'd gone to college in 2006 and by the time he came out of Dublin's Institute of Technology with an electrical engineering degree three years later, everything had changed. There was bugger-all chance of a job. Turned out the Celtic Tiger was a shyster, conning people into maxing out their credit cards and piling up the loans with his tall tales of boom, boom, boom, only to haul tail when the wheels came off the world in 2008. Theo thought the damn Celtic Tiger was a bit like the Cat in the Hat: he came in, said 'let's party', and then wrecked the place. But unlike the Cat, he didn't stay and tidy up before mother came home.

So Theo ended up in the furniture shop, but then when the economy hit the bottom below the bottom, people didn't want big sofas for the big houses they could no longer afford, or fancy garden furniture to sit rotting in the rain. At least the coke business had held up. It was one addiction the country couldn't seem to shake. There'd always be money for drugs, and booze, and fags, thank God.

He was already earning a fair bit nixing – and that's how he saw his drug dealing, just a little nixing, nothing serious – but when the furniture store closed, he needed another source of income, not so much for the money but for Big Brother. He didn't want too many questions asked about how he made ends meet. Precious would definitely disapprove so she needed to believe he was working somewhere legit. He also needed an answer for when Jim called asking, "What are you at these days, lad?"

"So, I'll leave you to it," Desmond said now, stumbling over the words. Even his voice was in a hurry. "I'm expecting a supplier any minute now. In fact, he's probably out back already, creaming off a tin here and a packet there. Jeez, you'd need eyes in the back of yer head with that lot."

He flashed a glance at the cheap watch flattening the ginger hairs on his wrist.

"I'll pop back in a while."

The 'pop' exploded like a magician's puff of smoke as he raced off through the red doors to the back. They clattered together noisily.

"So, Théoneste, do you live around here?" Deirdre had turned back to the sink and was scrubbing a blackened pot with a scraggly Brillo pad. She was left-handed and married. She caught her tongue between her lips as she scrubbed.

"Yeah, I live just around the corner from the Methodist Church. With my girlfriend. And, Theo is fine."

"Right, sorry. Ah yeah, I know it. How did you end up in Dublin then?"

Theo watched Deirdre's hands in the suds. She rubbed fiercely as she talked but now she switched the Brillo pad to her right hand. It looked awkward and just below the elbow of her left arm, half-hidden by the sleeve of her cardigan, Theo noticed a red mark, shiny, silent and sore. None of his business. There was plenty of that around.

Deirdre turned to face him, her face flushed.

"Oh God, I'm sorry. I didn't mean to imply anything. Sure, maybe you've been here all your life. Why not? I'm being old-fashioned and stupid. My daughter, Grace, she's eighteen, she'd kill me. Tell me to move with the times."

Theo realised his silence had made her think he was offended. No harm in that. In his fifteen plus years here, he'd learned never to look a gift act of mild racism or stereotyping in the mouth, especially not the inadvertent ones. You never knew when you might need that guilt in a country that thrived on equal measures of xenophobia and an ages-old, finely tuned sense of culpability. No smoke without fire, he often thought.

"S'alright," he muttered. "I'm from Rwanda. Came here when I was a child. Grew up in Clontarf. My foster parents used to live out by the GAA club. They've moved to Donegal now though. I came to Merrickstown after college. For a job but that didn't last."

There was silence. He was used to that as well. Too many questions, so people usually didn't ask any.

"So you must be, what, twenty-one?" Deirdre asked, rinsing the saucepan one final time and clanging it onto the draining board. She kept her head down now. "Bit older than my three. Grace is doing her Leaving next week, God help us. She's at the Mercy College, I've one boy in Mount Temple secondary, and Kevin, my youngest, he's in St Joseph's."

"Tough time for Grace then," Theo said. "I'm twenty-two, so that was a while ago for me. Did an engineering course at the DIT afterwards but haven't been able to get a proper job since then. Looks like the Celtic Tiger's lost some of its roar."

"Isn't it desperate?" Deirdre said, pausing to look up at him. "Fergal, that's my husband, and funnily enough he's an electrician too, he says the work is falling off a cliff. All those new houses that were built, sure no one has the money now to put lights up in them. Never mind live in them. Thank God, he's still got a job though. His company, well it's not his but it's where he works, they've got a couple of good industrial clients, so… that's something. We haven't had to pawn the flat screen yet anyway."

She laughed and grabbed another massive pot from the floor beside the sink. Theo leapt to help her although she could certainly manage. She had that sharpness that defined a lot of women in this part of town. Gimlet-eyed, good-looking in a brash way, hard-living and hard-working, but sometimes you'd see them sipping takeaway coffees and crying quietly on benches in Stephen's Green, or at discreet corner tables in Bewleys, or down by the canal. Sheila wasn't like that. She and Jim had always had enough, they were what people here called comfortable. That's why they could afford to take him in after Sheila's sister Cath, who worked for Trócaire, found him sitting on an upturned red bucket like a mud-encrusted statue in a smoke-filled, stinking camp in Tanzania and resolved to save him, and maybe a bit of herself, from that end-of-times. But to say they fostered him because they could afford it was not fair, or at least it was not the whole truth. Theo knew that but the disloyal thought slid through his brain anyway. Sometimes the monologue in his head was crueller than he wanted it to be. He guessed it was the same for everyone.

"That's some pot," he said now, stepping back again.

"Yeah, not as bad as the ones we use to cook the lobsters. Now, there's a dirty job," Deirdre said. She turned to look at him. "Good job the lads paying twenty euro out there for their thermidors don't see behind the scenes. You know what I mean? Like you should never see what goes into black pudding."

She laughed again and dried her hands on her apron.

"I'll show you around before the rest of them come in. You've been into the restaurant before?"

He shook his head.

"I'm more a Supermac man, to be honest," he said, smiling despite himself.

He didn't usually warm to strangers. Warming led to talking and that always led back to the what-happened-to-ye question, and he was buggered if he was going to tell that sorry saga to every Tom, Dick and Harry. He knew he often came across as a standoffish black bastard but he didn't care. He'd enough friends, and besides, it was good to have a little man-of-mystery thing going, especially in his real line of work. But there was something about Deirdre, something about that mix of tough and vulnerable. He liked it and it stirred a memory, warm and soft. He let the sensation flit through his brain, happy to let it be, knowing he might never capture it or label it. It would land if it wanted to but then he didn't always want these butterflies to stop flying.

"Alright, we'll start in there and work back," said Deirdre. "The way customers never do. Then you can help me finish this lot. Best way to learn where everything lives is to put it away."

"Spose so," he muttered.

His mood darkened as he realised he would actually be washing dishes in a restaurant. Fair enough, he might not have been destined for much growing up in a village of mostly mud huts in the heart of Africa, but surely he didn't survive for this?

"Where are you from? You don't sound like you're from Dublin," he said as they headed for the short corridor that led out to the restaurant.

"The Wesht," Deirdre said with a deliberate slur. "I grew up in Connemara, County Galway. So yeah, I'm a right culchie but I've been living here over twenty years now. Came up to study nursing, and then I worked here for a while and met Fergal. He's a real Dub. The rest, as they say, is history. I was doing some part-time nursing until recently, but it seems healthcare is a luxury we can't afford any more. The nursing jobs have dried right up. That's why I'm here. But I'll hopefully get back into it when things pick up. We'll always have the sick and eventually the powers-that-be will have to realise that. Unless people dying is part of the whole recovery plan."

She laughed, turning back to him and lifting her head slightly so her face caught the gleam from the over-bright strip lights on the ceiling. Now the bruise around her eye, sloping to her cheekbone, was all too clear. She'd done a good job with the make-up but it wasn't enough. She caught Theo gawping and stared defiantly back, her head still raised. She didn't want his pity. And in any case, he didn't really feel inclined to give it. None of his business. Everyone had their own problems.

He stepped around her. "Through here then?" He pushed through the swing doors, keeping his eyes firmly forward.

Later, after they had toured the dimly lit dining room with its red velvet curtains to shield diners from the dispiriting sight

25

of rain and wet, miserable people, and visited the cold toilet cubicles that Theo would be expected to clean, they tackled the dishes left over from the previous night's service.

"Here we go. Lobster thermidor dishes. The worst of the lot, after the lobster pots. That sauce dries so hard, it'd take your fingers off," Deirdre said as she lifted four or five heavy clay-fired dishes from the trolley. One of the sauce-smeared plates slipped and she stumbled, flailing to catch it as it slowly slid off the top and thundered onto the floor. Theo bent to pick up the unbroken dish. Deirdre's jeans were speckled with yellow globs.

"At least it didn't break. That would've come off my pay and God knows I get little enough as it is," she said, offering him a weak smile. Her hands were shaking.

"Sorry, I'm a bit on edge today. Didn't get much sleep."

Her attempt at bravery, her trembling hands and the sauce teardrops on her smart jeans made Theo sad in a way he couldn't explain.

"Let me take those," he said, reaching out for the stack of dishes still in her hands.

"Thanks. Put them over there. Okay so, I'll wash if you dry and then I'll show you where to put them. We could pop them in the dishwasher there, but honestly, it's not up to much and definitely not dried sauce. We'd only have to do them again," she said, turning on the tap and squirting washing-up liquid into the sink.

Theo watched the bubbles form and burst. Little things like this could still sometimes thrill the young Théoneste silently peeking out from below big Theo's hard-man veneer. A liquid just to wash dishes. The extravagance still gave him a thrill. He remembered once, when he was about nine, he went to a kids' party where the birthday boy was given a bubble machine as a present. An orange-and-yellow gun-type thing that shot bubbles up into the sky and into delighted faces. He didn't remember anything else about the party. He stood for ages watching the bubbles fly out of the 'gun'. After a while, he went closer to try to touch them. It was a wondrous thing. Bubbles from a gun! What would happen if all the guns in the world only fired bubbles? Surely, even the haters would smile. Just imagine: they shoot, bubbles fill the air, then everyone tries to catch them and laughs. It was an exquisite, extravagantly stupid idea. But then, he had remembered, there were still the knives, the machetes, the axes and nail-studded clubs they called masu.

The rest of the crew began to drift into the kitchen. Deirdre introduced Theo to them all: Jason, a puffed-up peacock of a teenager wearing baggy, low-slung jeans and wreathed in the herby smell of recently smoked weed; Siobhán, only half as pretty as she thought with a loud voice and brilliant red nails; Cathal, a thirty-something moustachioed gouger who was, somewhat surprisingly, the chef; Barbara, a fragile mother-to-them-all who must have been in her fifties; and Cara, who was at the same school as Grace, Deirdre said, and who looked at Theo seriously as she twisted her hair around her fingers. Deirdre said there were two waitresses but they wouldn't be in until later.

"Ladies of the night," she whispered, winking at him. She'd recovered her poise but he noticed that she introduced the others a little deferentially, as if she was afraid she was wasting their time. Theo tried to reconcile this with the hard look she'd given him when she'd caught him staring at her face. Clearly, there was some kind of caste system here, based on how close to the customer you were. He and Deirdre were at the bottom of the pile, along with Barbara who did the cleaning: Kitchen Untouchables.

The grassy smell lingering around Jason gave Theo a longing, though he hadn't smoked pot for years now. He said he was going out the back for a smoke. More than a nicotine hit, he needed a few minutes to form his opinions without them all gawping at him. He went out the back door, which gave onto a classic restaurant yard – skips, pigeon shit, skittering cans, and a cold breeze worrying discarded plastic bags in the corners. They must sell these yards in flat packs in Ikea, he thought.

He lit up, dragging gratefully on his fag and wrapping his other arm around his body as the wind bit through his faded, knock-off Levis t-shirt. He was right feeble when it came to the cold, he blamed his early years in Rwanda, but Jesus, it was supposed to be summer anyways. His phoned hummed. It was Precious.

"How is it going?" she said in her sing-song voice.

She was trying to get the intonation right, to get it more 'Dublin', but in the two years since she'd arrived from Nigeria to study business, she hadn't managed to shake off her Lagos lilt. She pronounced the 'is' and the 'it' entirely separately. She might never get it right, he thought, and that was fine too.

"S'alright. Haven't done much yet. Just having a fag outside now. What's up?"

"Nothing. I'm in the library, swotting. I'm bored. Do you like the place?"

"What's to like?" Theo dragged deep and gave a tiny jump to warm himself. "Hopefully, this is just short-term, babe. I have other plans, you know."

"Yeah, like living off your sexy, smart Nigerian mama!" Her giggle was infectious.

Precious often made him smile. She didn't do sad. Demanding yes, furious yes, but never down. She was his bit of African sun. They'd met last Christmas in Spirals, a dive of a nightclub near her college. She didn't know he was there to sell pot and yokes to the pretend-broke students from the posher colleges, the nobs from Dublin 4 who fancied a bit of rough now that they were living away from Mammy and Daddy's six-bedroom gaff. They might whinge loudly about being skint but they'd cash for drugs, and that's why he was there.

Precious was with a bunch of girls in a corner – all tortuous cornrows, cloth handbags and colourful earrings. He was not a fan of ethnic chic but he thought one or two might be buyers and if not, they were good cover so the bouncers didn't wonder what he was doing mooching around the club on his lonesome. He sauntered over for a chat. He didn't like this part of the business but he was smooth, fairly good-looking when he smiled, and most girls seemed to like his mix of confidence and charm. Not to mention the exoticness of him.

"Hello ladies, mind if I join ye for a bit? Ye seem to be having great craic over here but why are ye hidin' yerselves away in this dark corner?"

He squeezed onto the bench beside them before they had a chance to say a word. Precious arched one of her meticulously drawn eyebrows. Another girl, prettier than the rest, smiled warmly at Theo. She had a gold tooth. Africans, he thought, probably students, they won't want the stuff. He was right but by now he was committed and sure, what harm?

"So, what're ye all doing here tonight?" he'd said. "Hen party?"

"I hate that." This came from Precious.

"What?" he said, wrong-footed and suddenly worried he'd said something stupid but at the same time noticing and liking her soft drawl.

"Hen party. It's demeaning," she said, enunciating each word carefully.

He looked properly now, taking in her full lips, the delicate shape of her head under the cornrows, the long nails painted with hearts and butterflies. In that moment, he decided he wanted to sell himself for once. He forgot the gear. There'd be takers later for what he had to offer, no doubt.

"It's demeaning of a party of women hitting de town before de marriage," he replied, laying his Dub accent on thick.

"Aren't you the sharp one-oh?" she'd said.

Her tone was dismissive but her lips were twitching. She waited a heartbeat and then smiled. An hour later, the bored friends had reluctantly moved on and then a couple of weeks after one of the worst nights for sales that Theo had ever had, Precious moved into his little flat behind the church. They were still there together. And for all her smarts, she still didn't

29

know he sold drugs. She'd kill him if she found out. Precious was a weird mix of uninhibited sexuality, boundless ambition and a kind of, in Theo's opinion, bogus morality that she attributed to the hard hand of a devout mother.

"I forgot to say. Michael texted. He's coming round to see me tonight, so like, if you want to go out with the girls, maybe?" he said now.

Her anger rang like the end of an echo in the silence that followed.

"Why's he coming round Theo? He's no good." She stopped herself but Theo could feel the unspoken Lagos 'oh' in the air. Her accent always came a cropper when she was mad.

"Sorry. Last minute thing. He might have news of a job. Ah, Precious, he's not that bad. You know, he's got connections in construction and in the whole import thing. Could be good for me. For us, right? I don't want to be washing dishes all my life."

"You haven't even started yet, you fool! Today's been so boring with the studying. I thought we could go out together, I'd love a night in the pub. I've been studying all week."

"We will. You go first, meet your friends, and I'll be along later. It shouldn't take long with Michael. You're right, he's a pain in the arse but he could be useful."

Precious didn't answer. In the pause, he could imagine her studying her long nails, crimson red this week with a blue eye in the middle. He didn't like this style but like most Nigerians in Dublin, or the ones he met anyway, she was obsessed with her nails. She'd found a lady, originally from Port Harcourt, who did it well cheap in a small shop off Grafton Street. But this new design freaked him out, especially when he saw the eyes caressing his chest, snagging in his hair. Bad omens.

"Fine," she eventually said, the word clipped and ominous. It was as good as he was going to get.

"I'd better get back inside," Theo said. "See ya later."

He hung up, took another look around the bleak,

slash-your-wrists yard, sighed and pushed open the red fire door, gasping slightly in the already cloying heat of the kitchen.

Deirdre was still at the sink.

"Good, you're back. You know smoking will kill you. You should give up the fags. It's the one thing I tell my kids: don't smoke. Mind you, I'm not sure how much notice they take of me, especially with their father lighting up out the back all the time."

Theo looked around. Jason was chopping red, green and yellow peppers in the corner, each strike of the knife managing to convey just how fed up he was. Siobhán was polishing a tray of wine glasses. She caught his eye and gave him a grin, all teeth and attitude. She was pretty in a brittle way. She had a strong chin, hair scraped off a face of angles, sharp nose, tight mouth, defiant freckles. She probably called them beauty spots.

"Don't just stand there with one hand as long as the other." Deirdre was at his side again, holding out worn yellow rubber gloves. "Here, take over here from me. You can wash these pots while I go do the loos. You can have the pleasure tomorrow."

She pushed past him and for a second he was unbalanced by her smell, oranges or something citrusy anyway. Then he remembered. She must be wearing Anais Anais, the perfume Sheila used. When he first moved into their house, Sheila's smell became his comforter. It reminded him of the flowers at home, and how their sun-filled, rainbow scents drenched the air after the heavy April rains. Of course, his Mama never wore perfume, although they were not poor, not there. Their house was built of bricks, not mud. His father, Thomas Mukansonera, was the village teacher and they lived well. They had Shema to work their three fields and his mother, Florence, did a bit of sewing as well. Buried in Sheila's arms in those first weeks, crying endlessly, he would try to push deeper into her chest, losing himself in her perfume, drifting into dreams of home, of his mother walking with him along red dirt paths through banana plants and head-high maize, of playing under the bougainvillea bush with his older brother Clément, building mud towns, catching ants, scratching pictures in the dirt.

"Theo, can you wash this glass again for me, please? It's still all smudgy."

Siobhán crooked her head at him in a way she clearly thought was winning but which actually gave her the look of a pointy-nosed witch.

"Sure," he said, reaching out to take the glass. Her red-talon nails brushed his arm. Her hands were also very freckled and tiny.

"It's good to have a new face in here," she said, perching on the side of the sink and leaning in beside him. He could smell nicotine on her breath, acrid beneath a minty top note. He flashed her a smile but didn't say anything. With girls like this, he thought, less was often more. Better to leave them room to make up a more exciting version of yourself.

"We've all been here since about April. Well, except for Cara. She only does a few hours at the weekend and afternoons sometimes cos she's still in school. So how come you ended up here? Dream job?"

She giggled, a deliberately girlish sound but with an edge. He'd have to watch her, he thought. "Yeah, I've wanted to work here since I was a wee lad. I used to stand outside looking in through the windows, dreaming of this day. This is such a great opportunity. Delira and excira, I am."

Siobhán laughed too loudly, flicked her ponytail and mock-slapped his arm.

"Sure, that's the case for all of us. Isn't that right, Jason?"

"You're full of shite, Siobhán," Jason muttered over his shoulder, his knife clunking steadily through the peppers. "You'd be better off getting those glasses inside to the tables."

Siobhán muttered "Wanker", flicked her ponytail again – that hank of mouse-brown hair had a life of its own – and sashayed to the counter, picking up the tray of glasses and stomping out to the restaurant, her purple-skirted rear snaking provocatively.

"She could wiggle for Ireland, that one," said Barbara, who had just come out of the huge, walk-in freezer, rubbing her hands on a grey cloth and shaking her head.

"Y'alright there, Theo? Getting the hang of things?" Her voice was brusque, as if she didn't want to seem too concerned, as if that might seem a weakness. Another story there, Theo thought.

"Not much to get the hang of really," he said.

"Too good for the place, are you?" side-mouthed Jason, who either suffered from a permanent humour deficiency, was not a fan of blacks, or was dying for a quick puff. Most likely the latter.

When his shift was over, Theo went to get his coat from the back room. He found Cara, sitting on the threadbare, 1970s-reject sofa, hands between her knees, staring into space.

"You alright?" he asked. Her blue eyes focused on him slowly. He wondered if she was slightly dim. A lot of that around as well.

"Grand," she said.

Her voice was clear and light, not fake girly like Siobhán's, just young. It was the first time he'd heard her speak all day. She was like a kitchen mouse, scampering around, staying out of people's way, getting on with her crumb-collecting and hoarding while trying to avoid the heavy tread of those around her.

"Going home? Want some company? I'm heading down towards Hannigan's, beside the church. I live just behind."

"Thanks, but I'll probably hang out here for a little while." She smiled uneasily. "I live down on Leitrim Street."

"I know it. A guy I know lives on the same road. Ronan Patterson?"

"He's my brother." Cara's eyes were wide but there was something other than surprise there. "How d'you know Ronan?"

33

"I see him down the pub sometimes," Theo lied, trying to cover his shock.

Sometimes, this city really was too friggin' small.

"I'm often at Hannigan's with my girlfriend, Precious. She's Nigerian, a student. Saw him there a few times with some other lads I know."

He took a breath. He was starting to ramble and it was not like him.

"So he's your brother? Right. Small world."

He attempted a laugh but Cara was staring at him now. She was making him uncomfortable but at the same time, he couldn't tear his gaze away. She'd fierce pretty eyes, he realised. Surely to God, Ronan, a fat-faced, twenty-year-old with a horsey laugh and badly bitten nails, hadn't told his wee sister about the drugs, but you never know. Theo had learned, the hard way, that making assumptions about anyone in this town was a mug's game.

Theo first met Ronan – a gobshite he would never have given the time of day to if it weren't for the drugs – through Neville, who had bought some pot off him after the guy they used when they were at school in Clontarf got nicked. God knows how Neville had found him but Theo's best friend was the kind to have both quills and knackers in his circle. There was something about his poshness that made him more 'of the people' than the most bum-crack-showing builder. At the time, Neville was studying in Trinity, Theo was in DIT, and Ronan was one of the ranks of lads feeding the habits of students across the city. Somehow they all ended up in a pub near Merrion Square one night, and Ronan went on and on about how good 'business' was, telling Theo he should take the whole thing more seriously and offering to hook him up with 'some of the serious lads'. Until then, Theo had mainly stuck to selling weed – he'd started when he first was smoking himself, just after doing his Junior Cert. Then, when he went to DIT, he kicked the habit himself but kept using the same dealer and selling on to friends and other students. Word got out and his stash started moving faster and faster. The dealer gave him some yokes, and a little coke one time, and that's when, Theo supposed now, he became part of the loose network of sellers that made Dublin bump and grind.

It'd been something of a rough start. He'd had to prove himself on the streets a few times and he'd the scars to prove it. The usual crap – 'What ye doin' here? Go back to your jungle!' – but in some ways, the lads and ladies who surfed chemical waves through Dublin's looking glass were less worried about difference than the people on the other side of the mirror. At least no one ever roared at him that he was taking Irish people's jobs. In Dublin's dingy underworld, the colour of his skin was less of a problem. And so when he couldn't get an engineering job after college, Theo moved to Merrickstown because by then he was working regularly with Ronan and besides, rents were cheap.

"Where d'you go to school again?" Theo asked now, trying to steer the conversation away from Ronan.

"I'm at the Mercy, same year as Grace, Deirdre's girl. But we're in different classes, so I don't really know her so well."

"So you've got the Leaving coming up then?"

"Yeah. I'm terrified. My parents say they expect big things from me. Ronan didn't do well, he's on the dole now, so I'm their last chance. Me ma'll go mad if she can't boast to the other mothers. Especially if they're already crowing bout their kids, which most of them are."

No flies on this one, Theo thought.

"Most important exam of your life," he said.

"And was it? For you?" she said.

He'd a feeling she was smiling at it all – her job, his job, this place, and the whole maxed-out country. Definitely not dim, he realised.

"Ah yeah," he smiled back. "I wouldn't be where I am today without it."

She gasped a laugh and quickly swallowed its tail. Her face was different when she smiled. He could see no resemblance to Ronan. He'd known Ronan had a sister, but that was all. Their pub talk, which was always an obligation for Theo, never went beyond football, commenting on the tits on the girls nearby, or Ronan's passion for fast cars. Ronan was what Theo liked to call a spacer – all space, nothing inside. He knew that wasn't what the word really meant but nobody used it much any more so he felt it was alright to make it his own and graft another meaning onto it.

Theo remembered that Michael was coming round and that he'd better get a move on if he didn't want Precious to eat the head off him.

"You on tomorrow?"

"Yeah," Cara said, the shyness and hesitancy creeping back into her voice. "I think we're all in at midday, that's usually the way on Saturday. That'll be my last day for a while though. Gotta hit the books. See ya then."

Theo was surprised at how happy it made him to know that he would.

CHAPTER THREE

It was drizzling outside. Funny word that: drizzle. It was one of the first new words Theo learned in Ireland. It was a perfect word, holding within it the soft sound of the almost-rain while also managing to suggest this rain was not really serious. Frivolous, fizzle rain. Still, he squinted at the sky, it might get heavier later. He walked briskly down the street, past pubs that were beginning to hum ahead of the Friday night rush. He pulled his earphones from his pocket.

This week, he was listening to a podcast about Patrick Kavanagh's poems. This was Theo's greatest secret – bigger than the fact that he dealt reasonably small amounts of coke, yokes and pot around Dublin, bigger than the fact that his teacher father had also been a murderer, even bigger than the fact that he drank vodka like a girl. He was hooked on the magic that happened when a set of words came together perfectly – meaning, metre and melody fusing to make something that opened a door through which he could sometimes, almost, see everything.

It all started with Máistear Burke, of course. He'd given him a book of poems by Yeats, then one by Paul Durcan, Séamus Heaney and so on. It was after Theo got an A in Irish in his Junior Cert. Burke was there when they were handing out the envelopes and gave him a spontaneous hug, which seemed to embarrass them both mid-embrace. Overwhelmed by the screechy frenzy exploding all around him, Theo had haltingly tried to explain how he felt about Irish, and really any language. He'd said something lame about words being like keys, helping him unlock the Irish and Ireland, and all the other things he had to unlock because of who he was and where he came from. It was like he was drunk on all the pimply potential in the noisy school hall with its climbing frames, basketball hoops and gamy air.

Burke's eyes had teared up – some sensitive eejits did that when he so much as hinted at his past – and he said Theo should consider going to uni to study literature. But by the time he did his Leaving, two years later, Theo had messed up and a whole set of doors had slammed shut on him. There were no excuses but if he were to look for triggers, there was the pot he'd started smoking, and the way that led to his schoolyard dealing and everything that followed. But it wasn't just the pot. A kind of lethargy settled over him as he hit his late teens. Ennui: another wonderful word. He couldn't say it right, but when others said it, it sounded so ace. It even looked the part: downturned mouths in the middle. Some words were like that. One-of-a-kind, whatever the language.

It was as though, having finally realised he had survived the end of his world, he hit a reality wall and couldn't see past it. Until then, survival had seemed so precarious. He was never sure he could really cut it. But after the Junior Cert, he knew he'd done it. He was as Irish as anyone. And he didn't know what to do with that. Having worked so hard to belong, he no longer knew what that meant. It was also around then that he started to have flashbacks to what really happened at the roadblock where they hid from the red-eyed, blood-stained *men with the single purpose*. He began to remember what he saw his father doing. Maybe it was the pot, loosening the screws on the box where he'd hidden these things. Or maybe it was because of the mud on the rugby pitch that sodden winter, or maybe it was because of the butterflies that descended in droves on Dublin one summer during that time. One or all of these things flipped a switch, and he couldn't find it again to turn off the light spearing holes into the corners of his mind.

Theo turned onto Raymond Street, taking the corner recklessly and then swerving to avoid an old lady bent like a question mark, pulling one of those cloth shopping baskets on wheels. We should've had one of those when we ran, he thought idly. You could fit a whole life into one of them. The woman tut-tutted laboriously, swaying towards him, slow like an old clock's pendulum. Theo scattered a load of 'sorrys' towards her and pulling his hood lower over his forehead, he legged it, eyes down. There might be more colour on Ireland's streets now than the original forty shades of white, but it was still best to keep a low profile. Tolerance was a real fair-weather friend on this island and now that the party was over, it was slinking off home for a good long sleep. It wasn't as bad as when he first arrived but you still never knew when you might be looking around at the flowers-and-the-bees and find your eyes stuck on a tosser in a trackie who'd be after you for looking at him strange. De Niro moments, Theo called them. In some ways, Dublin, or at least his Dublin, was as divided as the place he'd come from. Just that the violence here was mostly suppressed, behind closed doors, or rising, like bubbles, from the bottom of a glass, sharp and sudden and soon over. People rarely went the whole hog. They'd more to lose, he supposed. That must be the difference.

As he turned into his own road, the presenter in his ears was reading:

I have lived in important places, times
When great events were decided: who owned
That half a rood of rock, a no-man's land
Surrounded by our pitchfork-armed claims.

Michael's silver BMW was parked outside the flat. Leaning against the wall was one of the boyos from the high-rise across the street. A pimply strip with a fag hanging out of his mouth and dirty blonde hair sticking out from the Man U cap pulled low over his forehead. Watch duty. Michael always made sure someone had his back. Theo made a note to keep well clear of the kid in future. He was obviously another one on Michael's expanding pay roll. And that essentially meant he was part of the Gerrity empire. It'd be a couple of quid now, maybe a yoke or two on the house, but in a few years he'd be climbing the ranks, hoping for the moment when he'd be able to pay someone to mind his own bike. Theo kept his eyes down. After he'd stormed up the stairs to the flat, he paused, and ran his sleeve across his face to wipe off the mix of drizzle and sweat. He didn't want Michael to think he was in any way worried or harassed. Michael had a short fuse, a vicious temper and a suspicious mind. No need to give him a reason to start fretting. Especially if he had a new delivery stashed somewhere, ready to be doled out. That always made him skittish and that had to be why he was here. Michael didn't do social calls any more – not since he'd become someone in Gerrity's crew.

The man himself was sitting on the sofa, legs stretched out like he owned the place. Precious was in the kitchenette, making tea. Her face was blank but she was dressed to kill. She looked up when Theo walked in, made a face and pointedly glared at the clock over the TV. He shrugged and did the dickhead sign. Her lips twitched but she refused to smile and went back to shovelling sugar into the chipped mugs.

Michael swivelled on the sofa but didn't get up. He acknowledged Theo with a slight lift of the head, like he was some kind of royalty and Theo just a bogtrotter. Theo took a breath. No point in it.

"Howya?" He stood above Michael for a moment, just for the kicks and to remind the jumped-up chancer that this was *his* flat. And that he was taller.

"I'm good, man. I'm good," Michael said, reaching up to fist bump Theo. He was wearing a new gold chain, this one with a shiny dollar sign hanging from it. He wouldn't be able to stand up soon for the bling. New jeans too and black-and-gold trainers. Things must be good in Barry Gerrity's world.

"I hear you've a new job. Nice. My neck of the woods so let me know if you need anything or have any issues, like, with the owner or pay or hours or what have ye," Michael said.

Theo stifled a smile. 'Issues' must be Michael's word of the week. He might've left school after his Junior Cert but he was always trying to talk posher than the street cur he was. Theo supposed it fit the image Michael had of a proper boss man, like Gerrity, who was no slouch and spoke like a teacher in a quiet, measured voice. Boss men always spoke softly – all taking their cues from *The Godfather*. Theo could just imagine Gerrity, with his round, friendly-butcher's face, using the word 'issues'.

He'd only met him the once, when he started dealing for Michael exclusively this year. Five minutes of chat in a near-empty pub early on a Sunday in Sandymount. It was said Gerrity's Sandymount pad was just one of five houses he had in the city. Not to mention the villa in Spain and, if you believed Michael, who was equal parts lick-arse employee and the one man most terrified of Gerrity, a loft apartment in Amsterdam. Theo had met Michael, who spent his early years in the badlands between Ballymun and Finglas and now lived with his mother in Merrickstown, through Ronan, who treated Michael with a cloying, poodle-eyed respect. It drove Theo mad. He wondered if there were actually any dealers in Dublin who weren't thickos or wankers, or both.

"Thanks, man," Theo said. How the hell did Michael know bout the job? Ronan must've told him, he was worse than an old lady for gossip. Michael would be even more unbearable now. He'd probably waltz in one evening for a lobster whateveritwas, just to prove some kind of point.

"Seems alright so far and I'm just washing dishes. It's not like I'm gonna be there long. It's just to tide me over, like, until I find something else."

Precious sauntered over and handed Michael his tea.

"Thanks, love," he said, his smile a little too friendly. But the flash of yellow teeth below his patchy blonde moustache was wasted on Precious.

"Right, I'm going out now," she said flatly, plonking Theo's cup on the low table by the sofa.

She grabbed her leather jacket off the back of Theo's chair, taking care not to touch him in a way that made him know he'd not been touched. He'd be for it later, he thought, watching her ample rear stalk out of the door – like a cat's raised tail, it left him in no doubt about her mood. He turned back to find Michael giving her arse an eyeful too.

"Keep your eyes to yourself," Theo growled, his anger besting his characteristic caution.

Michael laughed, too loud, like he was one of the Sopranos about to take out the piano wire.

"Easy, Theo. Sure, looking never hurt anyone. You've got a good one there. Park a bike in that."

"So, what's the story? Good stuff coming in?" Theo said, mainly to stop himself from saying or doing anything else. So much of his interaction with Michael involved fighting the urge to smash his fist into the spanner's face. It was a battle he knew he must always win. Michael might be a little younger but he was a rising star in Gerrity's world. His mother was the big man's cousin or something, and he'd been dealing drugs since he was fifteen. Done jail time too and there was talk that he'd had a hand in Billy Mannion's disappearance late last year. Billy, a ferret of a man who had driven for Gerrity, was said to have lifted a bag or two off one of the loads of coke. Word was that he was nabbed one night as he walked home from the pub. Never seen again but Neville had heard that he was in the Wicklow mountains. In bits too small for the plodding Gardaí to find, even if they did ever chance to look in the right place.

Michael sipped his tea slowly, taking his own sweet time. He's watched too many episodes of *The Sopranos* for sure, thought Theo, resisting the urge to get up and grab a beer from the fridge. If he had a beer, he'd have to offer Michael one and, as well as being vicious and easily riled, the man was a piss-poor drinker.

Michael swallowed and set the cup down on the ring-marked cheap table, alongside Precious' *VIP* magazines. Probably fancies himself in the society pages, Theo thought.

"It's better than good. It's fucking A-1," Michael said, leaning back and spreading his legs wide. "All the way from South America via the muchachos in Spain. But it's a lot. Ten kilos. Top drawer stuff. Himself wants us to look into new channels of distribution." The last words came out in an American drawl.

Theo had to physically stop himself from rolling his eyes. No wonder Precious despised Michael. What did she call him? *Agbero*. It meant some kind of street thug in Lagos. He looked out the window to hide the smile that was forming on his lips. A crack opened in the clouds and the evening sun hit the window, electrifying the dust mites. Precious wasn't the world's best housekeeper, it had to be said.

"I have never cleaned," she'd declared shortly after she moved in, her emphatic tone suggesting this was the end of a long-running and dull discussion.

She explained that, in Lagos, an elderly lady from the delta had managed her parents' house. Precious had not moved to the developed world to start cleaning, she said. So Theo had taken on the role of housekeeper. But he had to admit he was no great shakes as a cleaner.

"Gerrity wants us to hit some of the swankier clubs, round Jarvis Street, Temple Bar, and then out to Drumcondra and Clontarf. He's thinking of heading into Maynooth as well but that's a ways down the road yet. Need to get the supply regular first, iron out any issues. We'll need new lads though, drivers, proper crews, the lot." This last was said with a touch of pride.

"This is it, Theo. This is the big time. Gerrity says this supply line is a dead cert, proper pros. We've cut the first batch already. Wouldn't want to blow the heads off the punters now, would we?"

Theo nodded, wondering again how he had got in so deep, so fast. If only he'd stayed in that night, instead of going for a few scoops with Neville, who'd introduced him to Ronan, who'd introduced him to Michael. If only he had done better in his Leaving. If only the bottom hadn't fallen out of the economy right when he'd got out of college. But none of those things were really reasons and in any case, if he was playing the blame game, he should really go back even further: if only Juvénal Habyarimana's plane had not been shot out of the sky above Kigali; if only the Belgians hadn't divided Hutus and Tutsis to play them off each other in the first place; if only his father hadn't killed Shema, which surely he wouldn't have if that roadblock hadn't been there. If only. The two saddest words in the world.

He wondered, as Michael kept up his blather about 'expansion' – another Gerrity word for sure – if the cops would start to watch him now. He wasn't the only black in the village these days, so he didn't stand out as before, but ever since Operation Clean Streets in the late 90s, the Gardaí had been cracking down on everyone. Not that it worked. There was more stuff coming in everyday and more lads trying to get in on the act. Drugs were probably the only growth industry around at the moment. That and the violence that came with the trade; turf wars started by tanned gangsters in Spanish villas and ending with dead bodies on damp Dublin streets. Still, he was probably just under the radar for now, and that's the way he wanted it to stay. Rumour was the cops didn't care about the little lads anyway. It was the big guys with the foreign villas they really had their eyes on. The Gerritys. Mind you, if the boss was looking to expand, it might be time to think about getting out. Who knew who Gerrity might piss off, and it wouldn't be him facing the barrel of a gun on a dark street. It'd be lads like Theo.

"Anyway, we need to shift these 10k first. I'll leave ye this to get ye going." Michael dug into the pocket of his bomber jacket and threw six plastic bags onto the couch beside him, with a piece of paper. "There's loads more where that came from. Gerrity wants you to try around Jarvis this weekend – ye know what he thinks about open markets and selling on the streets. Not happening. So get a gang together, friends, no one in the business, and go to the clubs I've written down there. On the QT, like. As far as we know, there's no one else selling snow in those places for now, so just take it easy and see what the craic is. Can ye do that, Theo?"

Theo guessed the tone of this last sentence was meant to be sinister but Michael's nasal whine couldn't really do sinister. More Daniel O'Donnell than Marlon Brando. The thought amused him. Michael didn't like that.

"Will I take Ronan Patterson?"

Theo threw the question in quickly, without really thinking. He had seen the gleam of umbrage in Michael's eyes and he didn't fancy a row. Precious was in the pub down the street, waiting and getting fiercer by the second, and Theo was all too aware of the fine line between a make-up ride and no sex at all. Ronan might be useful in any case and he was part of the Gerrity crew already. The only other dealer Theo knew, in fact. Michael didn't sell any more. He was more like a manager. That was the way things were now: the big guys liked to keep the small lads on their toes, not really knowing where they fit in the grand scheme of things. Ignorance is bliss. And potentially a shorter jail term. He wasn't sure why Gerrity had wanted to meet him out of all the others. Maybe because he was a foreigner, he wanted to check him out himself. Boss men could be curious too.

Michael frowned, diverted from falling into a sulk.

"Yeah, why not? Not the brightest but he'll do. Tell him it's an important job though. Don't want him messing it up."

Theo let the irony light up his mind with fluorescent laughter waves. He'd ask Cara to come too, he thought. She looked like she could do with a last night on the lash before the exams, and it'd back up his story that he was just friends with Ronan. Maybe he'd ask Jason and Siobhán. He was sure Jason's friends would be up for chemical enhancements. They could all go together after the restaurant closed – it'd help break him into the new job too. Precious might fancy it, although she didn't mind him going out now and then with other mates and she wasn't that fond of Jarvis Street.

Shit, Precious.

"Listen, man I've gotta go. Herself is waiting for me." Theo spread his hands, layering the 'sorry' tone on thick, knowing it would appeal to Michael's big man psychosis.

"Alright so, she's got you where she wants you, that's for sure. I'll be off. Gimme a shout and let me know how it goes. You can drop the money to us at the usual place on Monday, and I'll have more for you then if ye've moved it all. Come round bout midday."

Theo nodded. He followed Michael to the door.

"Gerrity's in town just now, ye know," Michael said as he passed into the hall. "So watch your backs. The cops'll be on the lookout to pin stuff on him so no screw-ups. And pass that on to your mate Neville too. I'm hearing he's getting careless, his take is down, and if he doesn't pull his socks up, I'm gonna have to take action. We don't want an Apache on the crew. Tell him I said so."

Theo nodded vaguely, did the obligatory fist bump and gratefully shut the door. Only then did he let his shoulders sag. Neville? What the fuck was he doing working with Gerrity's crew? He hadn't mentioned a thing. Theo'd thought he was still just selling part of his own stash of weed and coke around the campus, small-time stuff. This was no world for Neville. Everyone knew a dealer-client was a liability. Always but especially when it came to Neville, Theo thought.

For some reason, the world was never enough for Theo's friend. Not shiny enough, not real enough, not big enough. He needed his highs and his new lands, just like it said on the tin. Name the man, make the man, Theo thought, remembering what Neville had said when he asked him where his name came from. "Apparently it's French. Means new town,"

Neville said, shrugging his shoulders. "No idea why they called me that. Probably had notions," he laughed.

Neville was also soft. He'd lend a fiver to a stranger, no questions. Not for the first time, Theo wondered if Neville was deliberately trying to spin himself out of orbit and into freefall.

CHAPTER FOUR

These days, the news would make you cry, thought Deirdre as she sipped her rum and coke. Spending cuts, unemployment up again, expenses scandals, priests up to all sorts. The trouble was the misery was becoming boring. This meltdown was so long in the making that even the presenters and reporters looked bored. Ireland was bored. Nobody ever wants to talk about the cleanup after a party.

Still, it was nice to be on the sofa on her own, feet tucked in beneath her, glass in hand.

The presenter was now talking about the World Cup in South Africa. It was starting next week and Deirdre wondered fleetingly if she should call Kevin who was upstairs somewhere, but in the end, she couldn't be bothered to move and she was also reluctant to give up this rare moment of peace. Grace must be studying. She was up in her room anyway, door closed as usual.

When Deirdre went up earlier, she didn't dare even look in. Instead, she'd listened, head cocked, thinking what an eejit she was to be too afraid to go into her own daughter's room. A fine state of affairs for a grown woman, skulking around her own house. These days, she spent hours preparing sentences in her head before speaking, terrified of waking the stressed teenage beast through a misplaced word, pause or implied question. Jesus, it was exhausting. Grace was a lovely girl, really. It was just that she seemed to be constantly at war with her mam. It wasn't just the eye-rolling and door-slamming that the parenting magazines talked about. Grace's anger seemed to be fuelled by Deirdre's very person, the actual fact of her, something that kicked in even before she opened her mouth. Still, could she blame her with everything that was going on? She'd ask Pauline for advice but she only had the one lad, and God knows, she had enough trouble of her own with Michael.

The Leaving was making things ten times worse, of course. The final exam couldn't come soon enough for Deirdre. She'd never say it, because despite all the mess with Fergal she'd quite like to live into her fifties, but Grace had put her head down too late. She barely did any work until a couple of weeks ago and then she'd met your man with the posh name at some library in the city and since then she'd been hanging out with him all hours of the day and night. Deirdre took another sip.

"I'll turn into an alkie myself at this rate," she muttered. "And one in the house is enough."

It felt good to say it out loud, even if it was just a whisper to an empty room.

She should call her dad. He'd have watched the news and would probably be thinking about getting ready for bed now. She preferred to ring him around this time. There was always something to whinge about on the news so that gave them something to talk about without having to say anything. She couldn't be doing with the kind of awkward pauses that left too much time to think.

Her father had never been much of a talker. He wasn't around much when they were young anyway, always off driving his loads around the country, and then, after her mam died when she was twelve, he was moody and abrupt, treating her and her brother Cian like nuisances. They were all marked by that terrible absence, the unexpectedness of it. They hadn't realised that a clock deep inside their mother's body was speeding up, ticking out the days faster than anyone could've imagined. How could they have thought she would die at forty-five? There was no imagining such a thing, even as a child when everything was imaginable.

Cian didn't have anything to do with their dad now. He'd put as much distance as he could between them by settling in Melbourne five years ago and he'd never visited since. She missed Cian and her mam. All she had left now was her dad, still stuck in that house out by the Atlantic where she grew up, rushing through the years so she could get the hell out.

She picked up the phone and dialled his number. At least it would take her mind off the time. Fergal should've been here by now. That meant he was in the pub. She felt her stomach twist and for a moment, her brain froze, too scared to think beyond the fact that her husband was out on the lash. Her fingers went automatically to the bruise around her eye. She patted it gingerly, soft touches like you were supposed to use when applying those eye creams she could never afford. There was no bloody cream for this though. She took a breath. It would be okay tonight, surely?

"Hello, Dad."

"Ah Deirdre, it's yourself?"

She wondered who else he thought it might be.

"How are you?" he said.

"Good, good. Getting ourselves ready here for Grace's Leaving and Conor's Junior Cert. It's all kicking off next week. It's a quiet house these days. They've got their heads down at last."

"'Bout time, I suppose."

There was a pause. They were still not good at this.

"How's Fergal?" he said.

"Okay, he's not in right now but work seems fine. No talk of any redundancies yet anyway. Mind you, looking at the news tonight, you'd not hold out much hope of things getting better. Did you see the protests up at the Dáil the other day, against the cuts? There was an old lady there looked just like Mrs McClusky up the road from you. D'you think she made the trip up to raise a racket?"

Her dad laughed, a thin, skeletal sound. Still, it made her smile. Ever the child trying to make Daddy happy. Her dad, as she knew he would, launched into an expletive-laden rant against 'those bastards in the Dáil', and as he railed, she tried to remember if he'd laughed more when her mother was around. Maybe. He must've but so few of her memories of him had survived the cataclysm of her mother dying. She had a picture in her head of her dad sitting behind a table laden with pint glasses, head tilted back, mouth wide. But she couldn't remember the context and how would she have seen him in a pub? They weren't at all that kind of family. Must be an old photograph she had come across – maybe when she was clearing out her mam's things after the cancer took her? But without the context, it was hard to give the memory credence. And wasn't Grace blathering on the other day about some article she'd read that said each time you recalled a memory, you actually distorted it, just by thinking of it. Grace had said it was like changing the shape of a coat a tiny bit every time you put it on. Because getting older wasn't depressing enough without knowing you were losing your past just by thinking of it, Deirdre thought grimly.

Still, she didn't want to dismiss the pub image, false or not, out-of-hand. She didn't want all her memories to be dark ones. She'd need balance one day. She'd need to be able to remember a flesh-and-blood man when she buried her father. Not just a morose, angry figurehead with, as they said admiringly back in the day, links to the Provos.

He had segued into his favourite subject now – 'the bloodsucking bankers'.

"Cheats and traitors, the lot of them. They sucked this country dry, buying themselves yachts and villas and fancy cars. And they're still swanning around in their millionaire mansions while we're stuck here in this god forsaken drenched hole with nothing to show for all those years of plenty. They should all be lined up and shot. There was a time, I'm telling ye, when we would've put a bullet in their heads, no question."

Deirdre wondered if he still had a gun, if indeed he'd ever had one. She assumed if he had, he'd kept it, probably hidden somewhere in the shed where he kept the bales of hay for the three or four cows he had in his fields. They were not his cows. The few fields he had now he leased out to local lads looking for a bit more grass for their animals in that desolate land of stones. Despite being born in the area, like his father and father before as he was fond of saying, he was not a son of the land. He'd driven trucks, carrying chocolates, canned food, appliances, beer and the occasional gun, it was said, up and down Ireland and across the border for years. She didn't know much about his time with the IRA. She didn't think he did much other than ferry stuff around but you never know. He definitely had the coldness in him to use a gun. She'd probably never know for sure. That time might well be past, and many of the players might be dead, but the fanatical Irish version of omerta was still in force. Sure, they hadn't even found all the bodies yet and those who knew, like her dad maybe, were not telling. It was a heartless thing to keep a body from its loved ones, Deirdre thought. It was the kind of thing she could well imagine her dad doing, God forgive her.

She tuned back in. He'd asked a question.

"How's that job of yours going?"

"Sure, it's grand. I go in, I get on with it, I don't do many weekends and we're all happy with that," she said.

"I wish you'd give it up," he grumbled, his voice taut and low like a cat ready to pounce.

If there was one thing Deirdre Walsh née Flaherty had learnt over the years, it was how to read voices. It was her top survival skill, she would joke to Pauline when they'd had a few. Gauging someone's mood by the tone of their first word could get you a crucial couple of seconds, enough time to get to the bathroom and bolt the door. She would laugh as she said this and Pauline would laugh with her, and sure it'd be laughs galore until the next time she really had to do it. And it was no laughing matter then.

"I'd wager you're only earning peanuts, and it's… it's dirty work. Not for you," her dad was saying.

"I don't mind it, Dad. It gets me out of the house, I get a few pounds so I don't always have to be asking Fergal for money for myself or the kids and it's not like there are millions of options for women my age right now. It'll get me through the summer and then, I promise, I'll look for something else. There might be some nursing jobs then, you never know. Things have to pick up at some stage. Surely they can't break anything else and there can't be anyone left to steal from, so I guess the TDs and the bankers and the tycoons will have to start putting it all back together again. They'll want new toys to play with and they've smashed their old ones, so they'll have to build some more."

"But sure, doesn't Fergal make enough for ye all? And if he doesn't, he bloody well should. Anyways, where's he tonight? Out drinking again, I suppose."

"No, no. He had to go see a supplier in Kildare." Deirdre lied smoothly.

Another survival skill. Her dad had never liked Fergal much anyway. There was no way she was telling him the truth now.

"Anyway, like I said, I'm only going to be in the restaurant for a few months. I want to get Grace something really nice after the exams. I was thinking I might even buy her a ticket to go over to England. And then Conor will need a present too after the Junior Cert. Every little helps, as they say."

"I suppose, you've got a point," he grunted.

Deirdre smiled into the phone. Her dad might believe washing dishes was below his daughter – and the thought made the child in her feel warm again – but he couldn't argue with her financial logic. And at least she'd gotten him off the subject of Fergal. If he knew her husband beat her, he'd very likely kill him, old man or no old man. She'd always bet on her dad versus her husband. Fergal might be handy with his fists but he was a child compared to Séamus Flaherty.

After she ended the call, she topped up her glass, put the rum bottle back in the press under the telly and tried to relax back into the sofa. There was a Will Smith film on and she loved the lazy ease of the man but the moment for mindless watching was gone. She put her feet back into her slippers. She got a coaster for her glass and made sure the curtains were closed properly, even though it was still light out. She ran to the front door to make sure her keys were not in the lock on the outside. She'd been doing that a lot lately and it made Fergal lose the block altogether. She poked her head around the kitchen door to give the small room a once over. One of the kids had made a sandwich, it seemed. When was that? She hadn't heard them. She put the dirty knife in the sink and cleaned the crumbs off the counter. She switched off the light. Then put it on again. He'd probably want some light when he came in but the bulb in the hall was very bright and he'd see that from the van and be mad at the waste before he even entered the house. The kitchen light would have to be the Christmas candle tonight, guiding the weary to shelter. If only there was no room at this inn.

She settled again on the sofa, but this time like a teenager at a job interview, arse clenched, leaning forward. She looked at her watch. Already gone 10. She should check if the boys were at least getting ready for bed. Upstairs, Grace's door was still closed but she could hear music inside. She said it helped her study but Deirdre couldn't see how. They did say today's kids were better at multi-tasking because of all the technology. But then there were the experts who said their attention spans were shrinking. Maybe they were two sides of the same coin. She should Google the whole music/homework thing, she thought.

Kevin was in his pyjamas already, brushing his teeth in the bathroom.

"Good lad," she said, wrapping her arms around him from behind and holding him fast. He nodded, his mouth full of frothy toothpaste.

"We'll do something nice tomorrow, maybe go for a walk by the sea?" she said. "The other two will be studying, so it'll just be us. Would you like that?"

"Yeah, Mam. Can we skim stones?" He spoke wide-mouthed, trying to keep the toothpaste in. Then he spat.

"Yeah, why not?" she laughed.

"And have ice-cream? And a slushie?" His voice had gone small, beseeching.

"Now you're pushing your luck, you cheeky so-and-so. Get off to bed with you. We'll see about the rest tomorrow."

For the briefest of moments, Kevin snuggled into her chest, turning his face up for a kiss. She held him tight. Her last little baby. She was probably six months out from a total ban on this kind of sloppiness. She knew better than to hug him in the street nowadays, or touch him at all actually since he gave out to her about ruffling his hair at the school gate last month, but at ten, Kevin still allowed her to cuddle him at home. She breathed in his smell, deeply, deliberately like she was choosing a bouquet at a flower shop. One day, this would be a memory, this feeling of holding the world in her arms. Her heart gave a little jolt. Pleasure and pain; it all got so mixed up as they got older. The ache of letting your kids go was like a series of small deadly shocks, a years-long, slow-mo earthquake. She wouldn't shy from the reality, she would face it head on because maybe then she would be ready, maybe by taking it on the chin every day, it would hurt less when they did leave her. But deep down she knew it was a hopeless strategy. Nothing would lessen the pain that was coming. It was not either/or but and. It was always the way.

She followed Kevin into the bedroom, past Conor's stubbornly closed door. She wouldn't dream of hugging her eldest son now. Fifteen and so angry with her, with the school, with the world. Like his father, he'd a massive chip on his shoulder all the time. That was an ugly thought but it didn't make it less true.

In Kevin's room, she fiddled with the curtains and picked up some dirty football socks from the floor. Kevin was already under the covers in the bottom bunk. Ever since Conor had moved out to set up camp in the little study, Kevin had slept in the bottom bed. "I feel safe here, Mam," he'd said. Conor had teased him for being a Mammy's boy, too frightened to sleep up high. When Kevin came to her crying about this, Deirdre felt another heartstring fray and then snap, twanging out its pain in the dark place where she kept her soul. Kevin *was* scared but not of heights. He, more than anyone, soaked up all the anger in the house, like a little sponge that could not bear the weight of all the tears.

She bent to kiss him. He was nearly asleep already, wrecked by playing football all afternoon on the patch of green that had notions of being the estate's park. He loved football but she was pretty sure he also wanted to make himself scarce. He was no fool, she thought. Between the hormones, the exams, and all the rest, this was a right madhouse at the moment. Better off out of it altogether, my darling.

"Goodnight, Mam, love ya."

For the umpteenth time, she marvelled at how different Kevin was from the others. What did that mean? Was it her fault? Did she treat him differently because he was the youngest? Was she stupid enough to love Conor less because he looked more like his dad, while Kevin was definitely from her side, with the straight hair, wide eyes and the Flaherty lips? Surely to God not.

As she turned to blow Kevin a kiss from the door, she thought of Theo, the new lad at work. If parents were responsible for the way their kids turned out, who was responsible for Theo? The parents he'd had there in his own country or his foster parents? During their break today, she'd stepped outside to keep him company as he smoked and he'd told her a bit of his story. She'd had to press him a bit, and he didn't seem over the moon about talking, but there was something about him that made her want to know more. To look after him somehow.

"My parents were killed in the genocide," he'd said.

The word sounded ludicrous in the scuzzy yard. It was too

big for the small space, too big for her. She wanted to say something back but what? What did you say for a genocide? Sorry for your troubles wouldn't really cut it. She should ask Grace, she would know more about what happened in Rwanda. Deirdre herself knew the basics, of course. She was pregnant with Conor around then, and out of her skull with tiredness, but still she remembered being yanked out of her personal fog by the pictures on the telly – a church in the middle of nowhere, all around it quiet apart from the chirping of insects, and then bodies, everywhere. The images were fuzzy, faces and injuries blurred out, but they couldn't kidglove the scale. She remembered in one news report the bodies were barely there. Just the clothes left, and the bones, as though the people had just oozed into the ground.

"I remember the pictures on the telly," she'd said finally. "All those poor people killed in the churches. Aren't humans just terrible? Mind you, we've had our own horrors here." She was rambling, she knew. "But tell me, Theo, what was it all about then?"

He told her of the plane crash and the radio messages that told people to 'clean up the dirt and clear the brush', and then explained that in his language, those 100 days – and she was shocked to learn it took so little time but then, how long could you keep killing? – were called *itsembabwoko* from the words for exterminate and clan. She tried out the long word with her clumsy tongue, and maybe it was something about the way she mangled it, but suddenly, Theo threw down his half-smoked fag and stomped back inside. She felt foolish as she stood there shivering in the cold wind that seemed to always be whipping round this yard, even in August. She should leave the poor boy alone, instead of sticking her nose into things she didn't, and couldn't, understand.

She knocked like a supplicant on Conor's door.

"What?" Her hackles rose. The tone on him. Still, now was not the time.

She popped her head in. He'd go ballistic if she actually

walked into the room. Her son was sitting at the computer, his back to the door. He didn't even bother to turn round. The window was open and she thought she could smell just the faintest whiff of nicotine. God help him, wait 'til he finished the exams. She would be on his case then. If it weren't for the fact that Fergal might rock up any moment now, she'd give him a piece of her mind. He knew damn well he wasn't allowed to smoke, especially not in the house. Tomorrow. She would give him a right earful tomorrow. She took a deep breath.

"Can you finish up now, Conor? You need to get your sleep ahead of the exams. No use getting too tired. There'll be time enough to study again in the morning."

She said it all in a rush because she knew she'd only get the one chance. He never turned, much less acknowledged what she said. She waited, sighed loudly, a teenager again herself, and closed the door quietly.

Lights flashed onto the wall downstairs through the glass panes of the front door. The van was turning, too fast, into the drive. He was back. She hurried past Grace's door. She could just about hear her music but was that her daughter's voice buzzing underneath? She was probably on the phone to that bloody boyfriend. She'd have to talk to her about that. Tomorrow again.

She slipped into the sitting room, picked up her glass, put it down again, and waited. Shit, her heart was beating like a drum, her hands were shaking.

"Pull yourself together, woman," she muttered under her breath. "He's just a man."

It didn't comfort her as much as she had hoped.

She'd always known Fergal was easily wound-up. Pauline used to say he was a bit of a headcase and that was even before they got married. It wasn't until after they'd walked up the aisle – him with a monumental hangover, of course – that she realised he was prone to slapping. She supposed it was that peculiarly Irish code of silence that made violent men wait until they were hitched to lash out, knowing full well that their bruised wives would keep quiet. What woman would want to be hearing whispers behind her back as she went up to communion on Sunday, or see heads tilted knowingly her way in the shop? Better to suck it up.

They weren't stupid, the violent men.

It had started with the odd slap, not too bad though he'd string them together when he was particularly langered. But the beating he'd given her this week had stunned even him, she thought. Apart from the pain, that was the worst thing: realising he wasn't in control of whatever rage was eating him up like a cancer. Later, when she was in the bathroom, cleaning the blood from the inside of her nostrils after dabbing witch hazel around her eye, he'd come in, guilty-looking as a rat.

He hugged her and she suffered his embrace, even though every single part of her wanted to grab his hair and smash his face, teeth first, into the ceramic of the sink. Even as he whispered beer-breath 'sorrys' into her ear, the fear she had of him flowed like venom through her stiff shoulders and clenched fists, deactivating her rage so that she was a hollow nothing.

The door slammed and she heard the keys clang onto the small table in the hall. Then silence. He was waiting, standing there, swaying, trying to get his bearings, no doubt. The whole house seemed to hunker down in the silence. Deirdre realised she was barely breathing. She forced the breath out. She heard his heavy, fumbling footsteps in the hall. Please God, let him go straight up to bed. I won't drink for a week, she promised, remembering the bargains she tried to strike as a girl with whatever was up there dealing out the cards. Let Mam live and I'll never pinch Cian again. I'll never swear again.

The sitting room door creaked. God was always out when she called.

Fergal came in, tripping on the mat in front of the fireplace, lurching towards the sofa. She tensed, half-rose, but he collapsed beside her. He stank and there was a dark stain on the front of his light blue shirt.

"Jesus, I'm wrecked," he said. "What a shaggin' day."

She chanced a look at him. He'd thrown his head back and his eyes were closed. He had the beginnings of a dark beard around his chin and the drinking seemed to have sucked the moisture from his skin so that the wrinkles around his eyes and mouth were deeper.

He was still a handsome man – a fine, straight nose and the cheekbones of a squire, but his cheeks were sunken now from the late hour. He was deadbeat drunk, she realised. There'd be no flying fists or filthy words tonight. She felt her whole body relax, her muscles aching in the release.

"Y'alright love?" she said. "What happened? Was it fierce busy?"

He didn't answer and she thought he might be asleep. She was just rising to get a blanket and cover him up but then his eyes flickered open, he grabbed her hand and she saw, to her horror, that he was crying.

"God, Fergal, what is it? What's happened? Did something happen to your mam?"

"I lost me job, Deirdre. I lost me job. They've only gone and laid off five of us. Jesus Christ, what the fuck are we going to do, Deirdre? What are we going to do?"

He was sobbing now, all tears and snot, head on her shoulder and hand clasping her arm, just below the bruise he'd given her. His fingers hurt but she didn't move. She just rubbed his head, like she would with Kevin.

"Shush, shush now, we'll be okay, we'll be alright, love. You'll find something else. Come on, now. It'll be fine."

Meaningless, automatic comforts like kisses on grazed knees. But she felt no real sympathy. All she felt was relief. Tonight the drink had lost. She'd won this round. Then slowly, she let herself take in what he'd said. No job. He was right. What the fuck were they going to do?

The door creaked again. Grace looked in.

"Is everything okay, Mam?"

"Ah yeah, love. It's grand. Dad's just tired."

Her daughter's eyes flickered to her father's slumped form.

"Will I get ye a blanket from the room? So ye can cover him up. I suppose he's going to sleep here."

Deirdre ignored the tone.

"That'd be great, love."

She heard Grace head upstairs. Fergal was sleeping proper now. His head was a deadweight on her shoulder. She eased herself out, prised his fingers from her arm and let him slump the whole way down. She managed to put a cushion under his head and took off his trainers and socks. His toes made tears rise in her throat. When she met Fergal all those years ago, she fell for the sharp look of him, the pretty face, the banter, the way he made a crowd laugh and then looked for her eyes, to give her a wink, all for her. But now, these knobbly toes, with the slightly too-long nails, owned her heart more than all the rest. In the toes, she saw the young man he had been, all that promise, all that hope they'd had together. Toes never aged.

Grace came back and together they laid the blanket over Fergal. Grace's touch was light but her face was dark, and there was a briskness to her hands. She'd make a great nurse, Deirdre thought.

"Cup of tea, Mam?"

"Yeah, love."

She followed her daughter into the kitchen, switching off the light and shutting the door softly behind her. She felt like dancing down the hall, and crying, and collapsing into the deepest sleep.

Grace put a cup of tea in front of her and they sat facing each other at the tiny table by the window that looked onto the small back garden.

"Pissed again, I suppose."

It wasn't a question and Deirdre didn't answer.

"I don't know why you put up with it, Mam. Look at the

state of your face today. You have to do something about this, or God knows where it will end."

Grace's voice was full of righteous anger and tears, and it hurt Deirdre more than the bruises on her face and the red mark on her arm, which had started throbbing again.

"Ah love, don't worry. It's the drink. We know that. He isn't always… like that. Look, tonight, he's like a baby. He'll sleep it off and be grand in the morning."

"Yeah. 'Til the next time. And the time after that. I swear to God, Mam, if I catch him at it again, I'll swing for him."

Deirdre had to smile but that just infuriated Grace. Of course, it would.

"Jesus, Mam, it's no laughing matter. There's words for it – domestic abuse. It might've been okay in the old days but it's not now. You could have him locked up for what he's done to you."

"And where would we be then, love?"

Deirdre took another sip of her tea and looked straight at Grace. Her daughter's pale face was even whiter than usual, apart from the two spots of rage staining her cheeks.

"I've made my bed and I have to sleep in it. Anyway, I think it's just a phase. A kinda mid-life crisis, maybe. You know, maybe for men like your dad, men who can't afford the Ferrari and can't pull the young ones, maybe they have to find other ways to deal with the whole getting older thing?"

"That's rubbish, Mam, and you know it. It's a crime and I'm telling you, if he lifts a hand to you again, I'll shop him to the Gardaí myself."

"Shush now, you'll wake him and then we'll both be for it. Forget about it."

Deirdre reached across to rub her fingers down Grace's cheek and smooth the hair from her creased forehead. She had an urge, almost a physical need to tell her that Fergal had lost his job, but she wasn't so far gone that she didn't see that burdening her daughter, just days before her exams, was the move of a weak woman. Her eyes welled. I'm not that desperate, she thought. Jesus, it was bad enough that her teenage daughter was having to comfort her over her marriage. How the hell did she fuck things up so monumentally? Married to a violent drunk, washing dishes in a kitchen. She felt the self-pity rise in her but she blinked hard, looked across at Grace and thought of Conor and Kevin sleeping upstairs.

They are reason enough for this poor life. Now today, they are enough and they always will be, she thought.

"How's the studying going?"

Grace grimaced. "I'm absolutely bate," she sighed. "I never want to see another book again. I'm going to burn them all after this and my highlighters. Especially the highlighters."

She narrowed her eyes. She'd bloody do it too, Deirdre thought and swallowed a smile.

"Just a few more weeks now and it'll be over," she said. "You won't feel it."

"Of course I bloody will. A few weeks is a… lifetime. Anyway, I'm taking a break tomorrow and going out. And don't even start with the lecture. I'll go mental if I don't take some time out. Nothing big. Just me and Neville and a few friends, down the pub for a couple of hours."

"Now is that wise, Grace?" Deirdre couldn't help it. "There's only a couple of days left and God knows, you started on the books late enough. Yes, you *did*," she said as Grace rolled her eyes, picked up her cup and stomped to the sink.

"Anyway, ye can't stop me. I'm going off out and that's that."

"Well, it's alright for Neville," Deirdre persisted. "He's well past all this – what's he? Twenty-three? Twenty-four? I've told you before, Grace, and I'm telling you again: that boy is too old for you." And too posh and too smart, she added silently. Not that her daughter wasn't smart but Deirdre had taken an immediate dislike to Neville when she bumped into him and Grace at the Jervis shopping centre last week. He was charming, for sure, but there was something doomed about his easy ways, something that raised goose bumps on her arms. Maybe it was the way Grace had looked at him, up at him despite her own height. There was adoration there and Deirdre did not think he was worthy. That was probably all it was, nothing more and nothing less than a mother's natural jealousy.

"He's twenty-two, Mam, and you've got it all wrong. *He* told me to stay in. He's only coming because I told him I was going out anyway, with or without him. Jesus, you really don't get anything at all, do you?"

She dropped her cup into the sink and legged it up the stairs.

Deirdre got up, took her own cup to the sink, rinsed both, wiped down the table, and switched off the light. She had messed that up alright. Time for bed.

Fergal would be fine where he was and there was no way she could move him in any case. He might whinge in the morning but he was never violent when he was sober so he could moan all he liked. No skin off her nose. The light was on under Conor's door but she was dead tired, she'd nothing left to give, and no patience for treading on teenage eggshells.

She lay for a while worrying over Fergal's news. What the hell would she do with him at home under her feet all day long? And how would they pay the bills? She could take more shifts maybe at the restaurant, if Des would let her, but there was Theo to do the weekends. Would Fergal drink more now? Surely there'd be no money for it. Or for his fags. She'd better hide the cash she'd saved to spend on Grace and Conor. It was all in an envelope at the bottom of the shell-studded jewellery box Conor had brought her from Nice after he went there on a school trip. She'd better find a new, safer place.

What an almighty mess. It'd make you want to cry. Or drink.

Well, if Grace could go out just days before her exams, she would bloody well go out too. Tomorrow, she'd call Pauline and they would head out together. A last hurrah before things went to rack and ruin. Pauline would be just the tonic with her donkey's laugh and total understanding of how easy it was to screw up your life even when you were trying really hard to do everything right. Fergal would be mad but too bad for him. He'd just have to deal with it. She didn't care what he thought.

As she slid into sleep, she knew she was lying to herself but sometimes that was the only way forward.

CHAPTER FIVE

"Sorry I'm late, Pauline. Some young eejit drove his car into the wall, down near the church, you know, just past the roundabout, and the bus couldn't pass. The Gardaí were there and the young lad was standing on the path, trousers at half-mast, boxers out for the world to see. I nearly got out and walked but sure, I forgot my umbrella. Y'alright there? Ah, and you got me a drink. Fair play to you, love. I'm gagging now."

Deirdre collapsed into the chair, raised her glass to her friend, and took a deep slug. She was going to enjoy herself tonight. To hell with the consequences, she would max out the fun to make sure the hangover and whatever else came her way were worth it.

"Not a bother," said Pauline. "I'm only here a few minutes myself. We're lucky to have the seats, it's jammers already."

Her thirst quenched for now, Deirdre took a closer look at her friend. Pauline had done a good job with the contour brushes and the foundation, and her blonde hair had been blow-dried but she still looked tired.

"Everything alright? Only you look a little... well, wrecked, if I'm to be honest."

Pauline laughed grimly.

"Sure, say what's on your mind, why don't ye? I've not been sleeping great. It's that Michael. I tell ye, Deirdre, I'm going to have to throw in the towel with him. And I'm not lucky like you. I've no others to fall back on. This is it, my one child and he's the bane of my life."

Deirdre's lips tightened. Pauline's son Michael had been in and out of trouble for years. He'd been inside for drug possession when he was sixteen and served six months. At the time, Pauline was devastated. A few years later, she'd confessed to Deirdre that she wished they'd kept him in longer and knocked a bit of sense into him while they were at it. She said it quietly and then cried for an hour, spilling her grief onto her friend's shoulder, and not for the first time.

Pauline and Deirdre met in nursing college and hit it off straightaway with Pauline enthusiastically taking on the role of the country girl's streetwise guardian angel in the big city. Deirdre caught the bouquet at Pauline's wedding – everyone said it was a fix because she was head bridesmaid – and then spent hours comforting her friend when her good-for-nothing husband, Peter Clancy, left her when Michael was twelve. When they were kicked out of their house in Finglas, Deirdre came with her car and drove Pauline and Michael and their boxes back to Merrickstown, to a poky flat not far from Deirdre's own place. Peter never contacted Pauline again, never even sent so much as a birthday card to his son. Everyone was surprised, none more so than Pauline. Peter'd been quite the catch back in the day: good-looking in a stocky sort of way, a handy dancer, and he always had cash. Rumour was he had a friend in the city council who'd give his firm contracts for building work. But it turned out he couldn't hack the real world when the dancing was over and the confetti had been washed away. At some point, his friend must've left the council and the bills started pouring in. There were too many men like that – fair-weather Charlies, Deirdre called them. At least Fergal had stayed. At least she didn't have to do everything on her own. Up until now, the bargain had worked mostly in her favour. A few slaps, the odd punch, but she wasn't alone, like Pauline, and Fergal wasn't always a brute. They had good craic together too. Less so nowadays but they'd had their moments.

"So what's Michael gone and done now?"

Deirdre didn't hide her impatience. She didn't like Michael, never had. The feeling was mutual and Pauline knew it. He'd had a go at Deirdre one night after they came back to Pauline's from the pub, making snide comments about her 'skivvying' in a kitchen.

"Good enough for a culchie, I suppose," he'd said.

Pauline had cuffed him around the head for that – "this is still my house and you'll keep a civil tongue in yer head when my friends are round" – but Deirdre never forgot the sullen, dark look in his eyes. He might be dumb as a box of nails but she had a notion he could be dangerous. A fool to carry out fool's work for wiser men.

Pauline took a long glug from her rum and coke, as though she was steeling herself.

"It's just he's become so stroppy. I told ye he bought a motorbike after Christmas. It's like he thinks he's a big man now. He can say what he wants, do what he wants. No respect, Deirdre."

"Why don't you kick him out? He's clearly got money."

"Yeah, he's got money alright but where's he getting it from? That's what I'm worried about. He never tells me anything. Last time I got anything even close to a straight answer, he said he'd got a job driving for delivery companies. But that was months ago now and ye can't buy a BMW bike on that, can ye?"

Deirdre held her tongue. Pauline knew as well as anyone what Michael was up to. She was no stranger to the drugs trade or Dublin's wider interlocking criminal circles. Her cousin, Barry Gerrity, was one of the biggest dealers in north Dublin. Everyone knew that Michael was somehow involved in the same trade, even if Pauline's own ties to Barry were decades-old, consisting mainly of patchy memories: playing football together during family visits or eating ice-cream once on a chilly beach when they were kids. She had no contact with him now. Pauline's own father and his two brothers were also well known back in the day for flogging stolen goods and occasionally doing the stealing themselves. But if Pauline wanted to fool herself, that was her own business. Let her have her drink in peace. No need to state the obvious and anyway, the problem would still be there when the drinks were finished.

"No, you can't," she said. "But d'you know what, Pauline? He's a big boy now and if he's making mistakes, that's his business. There's not much you can do about it."

"I'd throw him out in a heartbeat only I'm that scared he'll go off the rails completely if he doesn't have to come home the odd time. He only stays a couple of nights during the week now and never on the weekend. I've no clue where he is the rest of the time but if I didn't see him at all… that'd be another one gone, Deirdre. Another person I thought I had in my life, walking out on me."

God, she must've hit the drink before she came out, Deirdre thought, as Pauline's voice trembled and her eyes filled with tears, threatening to undo all the hard work she'd done with the mascara brush and the eyeliner. Her friend's strong, wide face looked like it was about to collapse in on itself. This was no good.

"I'm getting another round and then we're going to pick something on the jukebox and do a bit of singing and dancing. Right, Pauline?" she said firmly.

Her friend sniffed, pulling a wad of tissues and a mirror from the pocket of her sequined jacket.

"Jaysus, look at the state of me. Sorry, Deirdre. Yeah, get 'em in. I'll be alright in a sec. It's just everything this week. There's been fights in the nursing home, staff off sick, Mrs Quinn went missing again, in the middle of the night mind, and I haven't seen Michael for two days. Then, someone said Barry was back in town and you know how nervous that makes me. When that man rides into town, trouble's not far away."

Deirdre shook her head sympathetically and put her hand for a second on Pauline's shoulder as she headed to the bar.

She had to push her way through the crowds. When did I become so invisible? Not one of the young lads gave her a second glance as they grudgingly inched sideways to let her through. Mind you, she was wearing her skinny jeans and a shimmering gold top, sleeveless too. Her arms were still firm, and so was her arse by the grace of God and good genes but she'd clearly lost that something. Potential possibly. Maybe it was her face that said, 'here is a woman who decided to give her best years to a worthless man, with fast fists and a temper to match'. She furtively slid her hand across her forehead, just in case there was something written there, some mark of a fallen woman. It took her an age to get served.

But Pauline cheered up after that. They took control of the jukebox, laughing like hyenas at the faces of the teenagers who'd been playing endless Rihanna and Kesha songs and who Pauline easily elbowed aside, with a jaunty: "Step back girls, let the *real women* have a turn."

"Oy, do you mind?" said one girl, flicking her glossy black hair, squaring her tanned shoulders and jerking her head towards Pauline.

"Not at all, love. Now, why don't you be a good girl and go and sit down with yer friends?" Pauline threw this over her shoulder as she rummaged in her purse for coins.

Deirdre grinned. Pauline was back on form.

The younger woman stood for a minute with her mouth hanging open. She shared a look of disgust with her already retreating friends but decided in the end that she was no match for Pauline's girth and the pure steel of her couldn't-care-less back. She stomped off, her heels hammering an outraged clickety-clack.

Smarter than she looks, thought Deirdre.

"Right, let's have this then. Alright, Dee?"

"That's the one, let it rip, Pauline."

For the next hour, Pauline and Deirdre hogged the jukebox, dancing on the spot, shaking their shoulders and gyrating their hips, sometimes deliberately towards the teenagers who had

70

gathered in a perfumed cloud of fury in a corner. Of course, their interest didn't last long. They'd better things to talk about than the two middle-aged women making eejits of themselves by the jukebox. They only looked over now and then to jeer, especially when Pauline, who always said she'd curves and bumps to bate the Wicklow mountains, started strutting to Betty Boo. But Pauline in her black leggings, wedge heels and sparkling jacket, didn't stop. She sashayed right up to them, turned on her heel like Michael Jackson, and shook her ample arse at them. They tutted but a few young lads at the bar cheered and whooped. They were seeing them now, alright. Deirdre had tears running down her face and she was laughing so hard her ribs hurt. Deep in the rum-bubble, she was still young, still happy, still with Pauline. No one knew them here and no one ever would. They always made sure to travel afield when they wanted to let their hair down. Too many spies in their locals, people who might know their kids or, in Deirdre's case, Fergal. He'd say she was making a show of herself. She was.

Later, they bought curried chips and sat spent on a bench by the canal. The rain had cleared and the sky was a deep navy, stars spangling the gaps between the inky clouds. There must be a moon somewhere, thought Deirdre. You just couldn't see it from here. There were stars dancing in the still water too. Heaven and earth coming together, just for a moment. The trees grooved gently back and forth overhead, the water was swaying, and with the rum-fizz still buzzing in her head, Deirdre felt like the whole world was rocking her, like a baby in a cradle. Her legs were wobbly from all the dancing and she suddenly felt dog-tired. She kicked off her shoes and flexed her toes.

"Fergal's lost his job," she said.

"Shit," Pauline managed through a mouthful of chips. "When'd that happen?"

"He told me Friday, came in langered from the pub, of course."

"Did he have a go?" Pauline asked sharply. "Ye know, if

he goes for ye, you've to leave. I'm not saying forever, but ye have got to walk yourself outta that house. Look what happened to me mam. She didn't have the gumption to get out and he broke her nose. Twice."

"Nah, Fergal was too shagged last night to do anything. Anyway, I can't walk out, Pauline. The kids are there. What if…?"

"You don't think he'll go after the kids? Surely Conor's big enough now to keep him off and protect Kevin. Grace can also probably handle herself. She's got the look of a tough vixen about her. Just like you used to have, before ye went soft in yer old age."

She paused, ate a chip thoughtfully.

"You're right though. I was being unfair to me mam. I'm sure that's why she stayed too, at least some of it." She shook her head.

"The tears, blood and bruises that go into a marriage here. Doesn't happen anywhere else, but here, oh yeah, one false move and it's the fists."

Deirdre had started giggling.

"Pauline, you're gas. It's not everyone here, you know. Your Peter never hit you."

"No," said Pauline, clearly outraged at the very idea. She didn't *really* understand, Deirdre knew, but then it was like swimming in the sea. How could you know what it was until you were in it? "But he left without a backwards look and not so much as a tenner in support," Pauline continued. "Honestly, I'd rather take my chances with a beater. Although I don't think they'd be around long if they raised their hands to me." She chuckled darkly.

"Yeah, pity the man who'd take you on, Pauline. Maybe I should call you instead of the guards if he comes after me again?"

"Do. Call me." The laughs were gone from Pauline's voice now. "Or call someone but don't just take it. You're better than that Deirdre and well you know it."

They watched the water stars fracture as a moorhen swam by. Of course, she was better than that but Deirdre had long ago dropped the idea that you got what you deserved.

"How's Grace now? She all ready for the exams?"

"Not at all," Deirdre said, grateful for the change of subject, even if talking about Grace would be no picnic either. "All she does is hang around with her new boyfriend. I told her to go down the Liffey Valley centre and see if any of the shops were hiring summer staff so she could earn a bit after the exams, but oh no! 'No time for that, Mam. Going to see Neville, Mam'."

Pauline pulled a packet of Rothmans out of her pocket and lit up.

"Neville?" she said, raising her eyebrows. "Sounds posh. Not from our neck of the woods, then?"

"Nah, I think he grew up round Clontarf. She doesn't tell me much about him but she said his parents are doctors."

"Oh, well done Grace," said Pauline. "If ye can't get a teacher or shag a priest, and Lord knows they don't seem to be into women these days, then a doctor's the next best thing. And a doctor's son is the best thing after that."

Deirdre laughed.

"He's a good-looking lad, I'll give him that, but Pauline, he's twenty-two and Grace's only eighteen. That's a big difference at that age. He's very charming, well-spoken, Dublin's answer to Hugh Grant in fact, but there's something dangerous about him. Not like the lads round here, not like guns and knives but... I know he smokes dope, could smell it off him, but it's not even that exactly. Even when he was talking to me, I felt like he was somewhere else, not off with the fairies exactly, but not totally with it. Sorry, I know I'm talking shite but I just can't put my finger on why he gives me the creeps."

"Sure none of them will ever be good enough for your Grace, will they now, Deirdre? Is that not maybe a big part of it?"

Deirdre had to laugh. And maybe Pauline had a point.

"I'm freezing my tits off here, girl. Shall we head?" Pauline said.

By the time Deirdre got home, it was well after midnight. They'd walked some of the way back and the air had done her good but she was still a bit unsteady and her feet were killing her. Once inside the door, she bent down to take off her high heels. She was fiddling with the slender clasp, cursing her drunk-dumb fingers, when she was pitched forward. She slammed her head into the door she had tried so hard to close quietly behind her. She slumped to the ground and he kicked her right in the stomach. The air rushed out of her. I'm going to die, she thought, struggling to breathe. He's going to kill me this time. But she was so dazed, so in pain, she couldn't do anything about it, and this helplessness terrified her.

"Get up, ye slut! Get on yer feet. Stumbling in at all hours like the hussy you are."

Fergal was towering over her but she couldn't see his face. He was silhouetted against the faint light on the upstairs landing. His voice was low and for that she was thankful. She couldn't let the children see this.

"Where were ye? Out hooring 'til all hours. You're a disgrace."

He grabbed her hair and pulled her into the sitting room, flinging her onto the sofa like an empty packet of fags. Then, he turned and shut the door.

Still struggling to catch her breath and clutching her stomach, Deirdre forced herself to sit upright.

"What the fuck do you think you're doing, Fergal?" It came out like a whimper. Where was the rage she was feeling? Why was her voice letting her down as well?

"Teaching ye a lesson." He came towards the sofa.

She fumbled in her pocket but her phone must've fallen out in the hall. The house phone was there too.

Deirdre felt a cold fear spreading through her body. Her

heart was racing. He was going to properly hurt her this time and there was nothing she could do. She couldn't even bloody scream. She stared at his contorted face, all throbbing veins and hate. She did not recognise this man. He slapped her hard so that her head twisted, her neck muscles screeching. Then, he was on top of her, pinning her to the sofa, his face in hers. With a start, she realised his breath was clear. He was stone-cold sober and he was straddling her and whispering the most dreadful, vicious things. But she barely heard his insults, just the blood rushing in her ears and her own anguished voice, ringing inside her head, saying again and again: he's sober.

Then, suddenly, it was over. He delivered one final cuff to the side of her head and marched out, switching off the light so that the dark hid her humiliation. She heard him go upstairs and slam the bedroom door. That's when she started crying and that's how Grace found her when she came home an hour later.

Deirdre didn't hear the front door but something made Grace come into the sitting room and when she switched on the light, she gasped and rushed to the sofa where Deirdre was still curled up, knees to chest, head buried in her arms.

"What's happened, Mam? What's wrong?"

Deirdre could hardly bear to look at Grace, so flushed and beautiful and hopeful and everything that she herself had once been. For her to find her mother like this. That hurt more than anything he could do. *He* was nothing but Grace was everything – a justification for her past, the fuel for her future, absolution for her mistakes. Deirdre felt sorrow wash over her. After everything I wanted for my girl, I have trapped her right in the middle of my nightmare. We are killing her dreams.

She watched pity and anger ripple across her daughter's face. There were no answers to the questions that would come. And those questions – of why and what – were not interesting to Deirdre. She was too ashamed to even look for answers and she was beyond reasoning this now.

I just wanted the fairytale for her, she thought. She deserves the fairytale. I swore my home would be different, full of love. We were going to be better parents, the best. Now, we have shot the prince and burnt down the happily-ever-after castle. What kind of dreams can she have now? She swallowed a sob so deep she felt it twisting her insides. She had to pull herself together.

"I'm alright, love. I was just a bit sad and I must've conked out. Too much Bacardi with Pauline." She tried to smile. "You alright?"

"Don't bullshit me, Mam. What happened to yer face? Was it Dad again? I thought he was staying in tonight, minding the boys?"

"He's here, don't worry, love. It's all fine. He was a bit upset but he's gone to bed now and I think I'll just sleep here tonight. You go up to bed now, you must be knackered."

"It *was* him! What the hell is wrong with him? Is anything broken?"

Grace was looking her over now, her hands caressing Deirdre's arms, as though she was afraid to break her.

"No, no. It's grand. Go to bed, Grace. There's nothing you can do."

It was no good. Deirdre started crying again, and then she couldn't stop.

Grace left the room quietly but came back with two cups of tea and a folded blanket under her arm.

"I don't know what to say, Mam. You can't let him do this. You have to talk to him, or get someone to talk to him. What about Grandad?"

"No, no."

Deirdre forced herself to sit up. She took the tea and looked Grace straight in the eye.

"You can't tell him, Grace. He'll go mental and do something stupid. No, leave him out of it."

Grace started to protest but she cut her off, too harshly she knew but this was important.

"I mean it. I don't want him to know about… this. Not him of all people."

Grace glared at her but Deirdre met her look head on. She would control this as much as she could. Fergal might think he had the upper hand but he would not bring her down to that level. They would not talk of her as the beaten woman. She would keep her public dignity at least and her place in her father's eyes.

But Grace deserved something, sitting here beside her, face like thunder, the essence of life itself, all bright cheeks, and perfume, and the fresh scent of youth, of a future yet to be past. She took a deep breath.

"I know it looks bad but he's just frustrated. I can handle this, pet. And I promise, if the day comes that I can't, you'll be the first to know. And anyway, what would I do, Grace? I'm not young, I'm not you, I don't have anywhere to go. I don't want to lose you kids. No, this is my life. This is where I am."

I got myself into this, she thought, imagining what her own mother would have said. Sarah Flaherty had been a tough woman even before her epic battle with the cancer that colonised her ovaries. Sarah didn't do self-pity and she didn't encourage it either. She'd been a teacher down at the primary school before she fell ill and even today, her former pupils would sometimes come up to Deirdre when she was home to say what a good influence Mrs Flaherty had been. Firm but fair, that's what many of them said.

"Will Dad get another job?"

The hard edge of the almost-woman was gone from Grace's voice. Now, it was the voice of a child, confused, needing comfort. Damn Fergal for telling the kids. Deirdre had wanted to wait until after the exams but he just blurted it out at breakfast, needing the pity, she supposed. He was always like that.

"Of course, he will. He'll have to find something. Don't worry, Grace. This is just a blip."

Grace kissed her on the forehead, picked up the cups and headed for the door. Then she turned.

"I'll head down the Liffey Valley after the exams, Mam. I promise. I'll find something for the summer."

She tried to smile and then walked out.

Deirdre curled up under the blanket. Jesus Christ but how many more times could one heart break?

Fergal left early the next morning and it wasn't to Mass either, Deirdre thought as she heard the door slam behind him. When he came back for his tea, he kept a civil tongue in his head but the house was heavy with words that weren't said so that the very air around them felt thick and sluggish. Grace was out and Deirdre blessed her daughter again. There would have been a scene for sure if Grace had been there but as it was, Fergal just asked where she was and Conor piped up: "Out with her poncy, posh boyfriend."

"Who asked you to pass comment on her boyfriend?" Fergal snapped. "I don't see girls lining up outside to go out with *you*."

Conor flinched at the contempt in his father's voice, then his shoulders slumped and Deirdre knew there'd be silence now for days. What was going on with Fergal? He was usually nice to Conor. Why was he so bloody angry all the time? She was so cross she dared not raise her head, fearful of catching Fergal's eye and triggering an explosion. Instead, she poked viciously at her peas and carrots. How did it get like this?

Kevin was quiet too. She'd taken him to Claremont beach out at Howth yesterday. Before the day had fallen off a cliff. They'd walked for ages – the water was still too cold to really swim although a few brave souls were bobbing up and down. Old lads and ladies with nothing better to do, she'd thought, and then immediately berated herself. Sure, weren't they the only ones with the gumption to brave the water? Just cos they had grey hair didn't mean they were washed up. You'd think she of all people would know not to judge the book by the cover. Would she never learn? Kevin tried to skim stones and peppered her with all sorts of questions about seagulls and fish and cruise ships. Then he listed the places he was going to visit when he was grown up.

"You can come with me, Mam. It'll be great craic. We'll go to see the windmills in Holland and the icebergs in the... is it the Arctic, Mam?" She nodded. "And we'll go to Pompeii to see all the burned people."

"I don't think those people were burned, Kev. I think they were smothered in ash, or something. You know, you always see the pictures of them in terrified poses. Like this."

She threw her hands in front of her face, opened her mouth and eyes wide in horror, and let everything out in a silent scream. Then Kevin struck his own pose and she took pictures on her phone, and then they had ice-creams on a low wall at the edge of the sand, and everything was so wonderful she could see again the point of being alive.

Now, at this table of razor-edged silences and scraping knives, she wondered if those moments would be enough.

CHAPTER SIX

The track was narrow and so Theo's world at that moment was nothing more than the green stalks rising above him on either side, the blue sky that wouldn't dull its light for them, and his mother's back ahead of him, with Angélique's head bobbing above the red-and-green wrap that held her between her mother's shoulder blades. He looked down and there were his feet but they were little feet and they were different – callused and dust-covered, and he was wearing green flip-flops. He could hear Clément's soft breathing behind him. He wanted to say something – where am I? Where are we going? – but his father, who he knew was up ahead although he could not see him, had said not to talk, that they were playing a special game where they had to move silently, like snakes, through the fields, as far as they could, as quickly as they could. It wasn't much of a game, Theo thought, but he would never argue with his father. Where was Shema? Was he ahead or behind? Theo wanted to turn around but for some reason, he couldn't. His head seemed to be stuck, facing forward. Now, they were in a ditch, all of them crouched down together, even his father. Theo couldn't understand why his father, so tall, so strong, was hunkered in a ditch, among the plant roots, discarded corn husks, and the beetles. But still he couldn't speak. Now the sky was darker, finally, and they were running. The air was full of panting and feet slapping the ground and he could still just see Angélique's head bobbing ahead of him, as though it was its own source of light. The track was getting narrower, the rough grass scratching his legs, fear crushing his chest. And still he couldn't speak. And now there was noise, and screaming, and he could see his father's silhouette against the light – where was the light coming from? – and his arm was raised and he was holding a machete, and Shema was on the ground, and for some reason, even though it was dark, Theo could see Shema's terrified eyes, boring into him, begging him. What did he want? Theo still couldn't speak. And then his father's arm fell and Theo screamed and screamed. And then someone was calling his name, and he looked around, and his mother wasn't there any more and Clément was gone too, and he was alone, but someone was calling him from the deep grass beside the track, and he wanted to go to them, but he was scared, and he didn't like this game, and he wanted to go home.

"Theo, Theo! Baby, wake up. You're having a nightmare. Baby, it's okay, shush."

Precious was cradling him in her strong arms, stroking his head.

"Hush. You are crying, my darling. Was it the same one? The same nightmare?"

Theo nodded, then whispered, "Yes."

He was shaking, all of him, his body, his brain, his blood. It'd been a while since he'd had such a vivid one. Mostly his nightmares were collages of disjointed images: bodies flashing across his eyelids just before he dropped off, slashed, broken, like grotesque parodies of the human form; the snarling faces of men with knives at roadblocks; or sometimes it was just the screaming, echoing through the darkness he'd worked so hard to nurture in his mind. Sometimes he was back in the mud, among the papyrus, everything buried except for his eyes. He could feel the sludge moving around him, stirred by unseen creatures; he could smell the dank air in his nostrils; he felt again the fear that kept him and all the others submerged in their mucky shrouds all the hours of the day. In other dreams, about other things, he would suddenly find himself in a gigantic field full of head-high grass and he would watch the grass bowing down, starting at the edges and moving in to where he was, so that he knew that soon he would be left standing with no cover in the middle of the field. Sometimes he saw the field but sometimes he just felt that pure, naked fear, something he couldn't control. It set his heart racing, he couldn't breathe and when that happened, he got up and walked.

He would do that now. He gently lifted Precious' arms from his shoulders.

"Do you want to talk about it, sweetness? Would that help?"

He could see her eyes in the feeble light from the street lamp outside. He raised his shaking hand to her cheek.

"Nah, there's not much to say, babe. It's what I told you before. I just keep seeing my father killing the old lad who worked for us. It's always the same shit. And I can't stop him, there's never anything I can do."

"You were only seven."

She said the words slowly as though she had never said them before, as though she could make them new so that this time he would see the truth of them.

"I know, I know. I don't blame myself, not really. But I won't be able to sleep now. I'm going to go for a walk. That alright?"

Precious sighed and slumped back on the pillows. He kissed her forehead. He'd had to tell her his story after she moved in – he hated rehashing the whole thing but she demanded to know why he screamed in the night, why he called out 'Shema, Shema' in the voice of a terrified child, why he woke with tears on his face. So he told her some of what he remembered, unearthing only the barest bones, brushed clean of all the flesh and blood. Still her hands flew to her mouth, the universal sign for crimes so terrible they could not be named. He faltered a little in the telling. It'd been a while and he'd forgotten, to be honest, how many gaps there were. It was like pulling a pair of old trainers from the back of the cupboard only to realise they were green, not blue as you'd remembered, the brand was different, and you couldn't for the life of you remember where you'd bought them. And then you started to question if they were really yours.

He'd told Precious he was Rwandan that first night they met in Spirals but he hadn't felt the need to go into the whys and wherefores of how he got to Dublin. She never asked until after she moved in and realised that sharing his bed meant sharing his nightmares. Precious, who sank easily into the deep sleep of the righteous, definitely picked the short straw on the bed-sharing, even if she did snore like a congested Darth Vader.

By the time he got outside, it was 3 am. He walked along the deserted streets as quietly and quickly as he could. He always walked silently. He didn't get those people who stomped through life, all noise and clatter. Michael was like that. All heels ringing, jewellery jangling, and general all-over creaking and squeaking. Maybe it was a sign of insecurity – whipping up a personal storm just to make sure you were really here.

He popped in his earphones but turned the volume down. These could be mean streets and he didn't want any lively lads sneaking up on him. He was well in with Gerrity's crew now but that was a double-edged sword. Protection, maybe, but also risk. He'd earned a bit of a name for himself in those shadows on the dark side that most people never saw but he was still small fry in the grand scheme of things. Michael had said Gerrity was pleased with him, with how much cash he was bringing in. It made no difference at all to Theo what Gerrity thought. But it amused him that Michael thought this kind of sweet-talking would somehow make him happy.

He was listening to a podcast about Yeats this week. He'd come across a fair few of the poems before, mostly at school, but it still wasn't an easy listen – a lot of the images were fierce complicated. All those gyres, and circles, blather about Byzantium, and roses; what was with the roses? But he liked Yeats' use of folklore, tales of brave men fighting epic battles. Shema used to tell him stories like that about their own heroes and ancestors. He'd forgotten most of them but he did remember the tale of how Gihanga, the founder of Rwanda, followed a gazelle through deep forests to find a wife. He tried to remember where they'd been when Shema told him that story but he could only call up the old man's last face, eyes bulging, lips twisted. Theo quickened his pace but, of course, he couldn't outrun himself. He'd learned that from Shema too. "Theo, you can outdistance that which is running after you but not what is running inside you," he'd said one day. Theo couldn't remember why – had he fought with Clément? Was he mad about something? – but he did remember where. They were sitting together under a mango tree at the edge of a field of sweet potatoes that Shema had been weeding.

Theo often went looking for Shema when he came home from school. He would help him with whatever he was doing in the two fields where they grew plantains, sweet potatoes and beans. Or sometimes, he would watch him pick tea. They had one large field of tea plants, a brilliant green diamond on the hillside. Shema would push slowly through the dense foliage, gently plucking the leaves and dropping them over his shoulder into the basket on his back. Theo would trot behind him, the tea reaching as high as his head so that it was like walking on the bottom of a green sea. But he wouldn't have thought that then because he'd never seen the sea. How many of his memories had he remade in that way, rebuilt with new information? And were they still true if he was seeing them through a different prism?

Sometimes his father would come to the fields too after he finished at the school. He would not pick the tea – that would have looked weird – but he would talk to Shema, about the crop and the price they could expect per bag, and then catch up on the day's gossip from the village.

At times they would all sit together under the mango tree

and his mother would join them, with Angélique nodding to the world from her sling, her small eyes squinting in the sun. Clément would come too if he'd finished his homework. They would drink milk and, if it was the season, they would eat ripe mangoes, tearing off the skin and biting into the firm flesh so that juice ran thick down their chins. His father and Shema would sometimes drink banana beer, *urwagwa*. Theo must've tried it at least once because in his head the word had a taste. It was sharp, sweet, strong. Shema, who brewed the beer behind his hut, drank from a calabash – he cackled that that way he couldn't see how much he was drinking and so didn't need to worry – but Theo's mother usually brought his father a cup. Shema would say that Thomas was a schoolteacher, an important man, and so he could not drink without measure, like him. His father would laugh, sipping delicately, exaggerating the gesture to make Shema laugh even more. Theo could still almost taste the happiness of those afternoons but in the end, Shema had failed to see that the man he trusted would turn out to be nothing more than a conduit for the blood-lust of his tribe. Did that mean that the warmth Theo remembered was just the sun and the beer in their bellies?

"Get offa me! I said, get off!"

Theo stopped, the yelling wrenching him out of his reverie and away from the poems slipping softly, almost unnoticed, through his ears. He pulled out his earphones and realised where he was. He'd walked in a circle, his usual night route, and was a few streets from home. The shouting sounded like it was on the same road, just around the corner. It was a girl. Probably just a lover's tiff. He should leave well enough alone. None of his business. He started to turn around, thinking he could get home another way.

Then a slap rang out and the scream that followed set his teeth on edge.

He hesitated. He really shouldn't get involved.

"Ye're comin' with me, ye bitch. Whether ye like it or not. Now, get moving or I'll belt ye again."

Now, he could just make out a soft sobbing: "No, no, no. I didn't mean…"

Theo ran towards the noise. They were standing at the corner. The lad had hold of her arm and was trying to drag her across the street. She had her head down but she was not budging and for a second, they looked like dancers – his arm stretched out, holding hers, his foot reaching behind him, her leaning back, all spotlit by the street lamp above. But Theo had seen this kind of dancing before and it never ended well.

"Hey, what's going on here then, lads?"

They both looked up but the boy didn't loosen his grip. Theo recognised the pimply git who had been minding Michael's bike outside the flat a few weeks ago. No big surprise that that gobshite would be wreaking havoc at this hour. He probably wasn't carrying a gun yet, though the little upstart might have a knife. He'd take it easy. But then he saw the girl's face. It was Cara. A wide-eyed, tear-stained Cara and she was looking at him like he was God, Jesus and Justin Timberlake rolled into one.

"Howya, Cara? Is this lad causing problems?"

"Mind yer own business and feck off."

Theo had to hand it to the little gurrier. He had balls. He was half Theo's size but had no fear on him. Theo saw his hand edging towards the pocket of his sagging trackies. So he had a knife then. Alright so.

"Leave her be and go home to your mammy. This lady is out of your league. So get out of here."

"Who's gonna make me?"

Theo felt like he was back in the playground but he didn't need Neville to help him now.

"I'll make you if I have to but I don't think any of us wants that so why don't you be a good lad and head off to your bed. This lady is not interested and to tell you the honest to God truth, I'm not that surprised."

The lad dropped Cara's arm and launched himself towards Theo, the knife in his hand flashing in the light of the street lamp. Theo stepped back as the blade sliced towards him. It was just a penknife. Out of the corner of his eye, he saw Cara slump down by the wall, head in hands. Too many rum and cokes there, for sure.

As the young lad came towards him again, he moved sideways, grabbed his scrawny wrist and squeezed until the knife clattered onto the path. He yanked the lad's arm behind his back and leaned in as the little rat twisted and turned, trying to break free.

"Now, what did I say? Feck off out of here."

Theo wrenched the lad's arm a little more and then shoved him roughly into the road. He picked up the knife.

"And you're not getting this back until you learn manners. And how to treat a lady. Now, go home before I really hurt you."

The lad stood in the road. He was all rage and hurt pride and, for a moment, Theo almost felt sorry for him.

"Why don't you fuck off back to yer own place, ye savage monkey? What ye doin' here, anyways? I seen you around. You think yer all that now cos you're with Michael. But you'se a liability. Can't trust your lot. Fuck off back to Africa!"

Theo feinted a move towards the lad and at last he had the sense to retreat. He walked backwards at first, across the street, flipping the bird as he went. Theo just shook his head, watching him until he got to the path on the other side and slouched off round the corner. He'd have to watch himself now, even more than before. That kind of weasel would bear a grudge. He'd have a word with Michael about him. He might well be a savage but he was Gerrity's savage now. The little shite would be sorry yet.

He knelt by Cara who was still sobbing, still hunkered down on the path.

"What was that all about then, Cara? Never mind. None of my business. C'mon now. Let's get you home. You're nearly there anyways."

Gently, Theo lifted her up, holding her under the arms until he got her onto her feet.

"Sorry, sorry. I feel like such an eejit."

The words came out like a child's – hyphenated by hiccups and thick with tears. Her face was a mess: mascara running down her cheeks, a red mark where the tosser had whacked her, her nose running. She reeked of spirits and cigarettes. The straps of her deep-blue top were half off her shoulders, so that the middle sagged, showing the cups of her black bra. She straightened her clothes, and lifted her wide blue eyes to Theo.

"Thank you," she whispered. "I dunno... I was so stupid... I just wanted to... I didn't mean him to think... but I should've... Oh God, I'm mortified."

Even with the face on her, she was a good-looking lass, Theo thought. Those eyes would make the hardest man talk. *Dathúil*. That was it, she was *dathúil*. The Irish for pretty but really it could be translated as colourful. She was full of colour and life, even with the marks of tears on her cheeks.

"Don't worry about that now. Let's get you home. Is your face okay?"

"Yeah, it smarts a bit. I know how to pick 'em, eh?"

She tried to smile and, in that instant, Theo wanted to wrap his arms right round her so that pimply gits never got to touch her again. It was more than a conscious feeling, it was pure instinct and it was pulling him back to a place he didn't want to go. With an arm firmly under hers, he led her along the road. She stumbled a little but that might be the heels on her black, buckled boots. She seemed to have sobered up pretty fast.

"Thank God you came along. I don't know what... What are *you* doing out in the dead of the night, though?"

Theo smiled down at the top of her head.

"Ah didn't I tell you? At night, I'm a superhero. A big, black, savage superhero."

She giggled and the sound lit up his brain like someone was playing the steelpans in there.

"D'ye get a lot of that, like, racism? Tommy's so ignorant. Never been further than Howth and he thinks he's something."

"A little," Theo said.

How to condense more than a decade of insults, big and small? The lukewarm shame of spit running down his face as punk teenagers jeered, a banana thrown on the path in front of him by a bunch of kids as he walked to school, rants from red-cheeked, slurring women on buses, the n-word that he still couldn't bring himself to say. He'd grown up afraid to put a foot out of place – ridiculous when he was already, feet, arms and every little piece of him, out of place. He supposed every teenager felt the same fear of ridicule, of standing out instead of fitting in, but few white Irish teenagers grew up terrified that standing out could literally mean being knocked down. Some people called it Afrophobia, like it was some kind of cool crossover music genre. No point burdening Cara with this. It was his reality not hers. Why darken her view of her city any more than tonight already had? Wouldn't change anything. Preaching to the converted.

"It's better now though. Sure, there's all sorts in Ireland now: Asians, Africans, Iraqis, Serbs. You can't move for us 'savages'," he said, laughing.

"There's the Nigerian guy, whatsisname? The one who became mayor of Portlaoise a few years ago, and your man, the guy who's half-Indian, who's a big cheese now in Fine Gael. It's just the low-lifes who are not moving with the times, like your Tommy there."

"He's not *my* Tommy."

She was hurt and Theo felt bad. She'd been through enough and she'd have to do her own reckoning of what happened in a few hours, and with a sore head to boot. He should leave her alone. She was only eighteen, she'd a lot to learn.

"Mind you," she said, "there was that terrible case of those poor Polish guys, you know, one of them got a screwdriver through the head. That was a disgrace."

"Yeah, that was a shocker, alright," Theo said. "I remember

it. All those people saying it wasn't racism, that the lads were just off their heads. What did they call it? 'Mindless violence'. My arse, it was mindless violence. Too much mind in it, in my opinion. And the lad who was killed there in Tyrrelstown on Good Friday. That wasn't because he was playing for Shelbourne's youth team either."

They were silent for a while. Theo reckoned it was about 4 am. They could've been the only people left in the world. On this back street, there were no buses taking weary night-time workers home and nobody here was up yet, though a few birds were starting to chirp and the stars were fading like the dreams in the houses all around them.

They had nearly reached Cara's house and were passing the little patch of green where teenagers drank cans of cider in the evenings, clustered on a bench under a single willow tree, raucous and seemingly oblivious to tutting passers-by but at the same time acutely aware of the impression they were making.

"Can we sit for a minute? I just need to get my head straight before I go in."

Theo led Cara to the bench, pushing the strings of soft leaves out of the way.

"Are you going to get a scalding from your mam?" he asked. He vaguely remembered meeting Ronan's mother once before when he went round to fetch him out for a drink. A small, fairly young woman in jeans and one of those off-the-shoulder tops came to the door, big eyes wide in a closed face. She gave Theo a good once-over after she'd hollered for Ronan, keeping him waiting there on the doorstep. A good Dub mother, he thought. Sheila would've done the same to any stranger looking for him. Still, he'd leave Cara at the gate tonight. He didn't want to take the fall for Tommy and sometimes there just wasn't enough time to explain before judgment was delivered.

"Yeah, for sure. But not 'til tomorrow. She takes pills to sleep, says she'd never shut her eyes otherwise what with worrying about Dad working out on the oil rigs and everything. And Ronan'll be dead to the world." Cara sighed. "It's not that. I just don't want to go in yet. I'll not be able to sleep now."

Her teeth were chattering. She was not dressed for the outside. Irish girls never were. All bare-bellied, bare-shouldered optimism as though the evening would never end, the pub would never close and there'd be no queue at the taxi rank.

"Here."

He stood up, took off his leather jacket and held it out. He didn't want to put it round her shoulders, that felt too much like a cheesy gesture that would put him somewhere he didn't want to be. She took it gratefully.

"Thanks a million. I'm freezing."

"So are you still celebrating the end of the Leaving?" Theo asked. "That's a good few weeks ago now? Some fierce stamina you young ones have."

"No, I just… I just wanted to get out of the house, to have some fun and forget the Leaving, the results, all that shaggin' pressure to do well in something most people say is a waste of time anyways." The words exploded from her like water from a busted dam. He'd forgotten the sheer, overwhelming enormity of being a teenager. It made him want to smile but it also made him sad. We're always being ambushed by the things that we've lost, he thought.

They fell silent again, listening to the willow branches whispering above and around them, swapping whatever secrets they'd overheard during the day. Theo was just beginning to think he'd better get back to Precious when Cara spoke again. Her voice was calmer now.

"We talked a bit about Rwanda at school. Turns out our religion teacher was there as a volunteer with, I can't remember now, Trócaire, or Concern, or Goal, one of those lads. Anyway, she was very worked up about… what happened. Said it was a stain on the consciousness of mankind. S'that what you think too, Theo? I'm supposing that's why ye left?"

Theo said nothing for a moment. Wouldn't it be great to have a past you could banter about, a past you could sum up in a few jokes, wisecracks about your parents' car, the desperate choice on TV then, the awful clothes, the immersion? His past was so embarrassing, so unacceptable.

"Yeah, that's why I left."

"D'ye ever want to go back? D'ye have family there still?"

"No, there's no one now. I think they're all dead. They must all be dead."

"You don't know for sure?"

Theo took a breath. He should stand up, take her back, go home to Precious, who might already be stirring and wondering where the hell he was. But there was something out-of-time about this moment, sitting here under the willow, curtained from the sleeping world, with this girl with her tear-stained face and wide eyes, looking up at him and seeing him and wondering about him. He didn't want to break the spell – and his nightmare was still flitting around the corners of his brain, goading him to catch it with his net of words.

And so in the nowhere, no-time moment, he started to speak.

"I was seven and they were coming for us – me, my mother and my father, my brother Clément, and baby sister, Angélique. You probably know this already but they were killing Tutsis, that's one of the main tribes, and I think they didn't trust us. My father was a Hutu and a teacher but my mother was a Tutsi. And I think now my father, his name was Thomas, I think he must've said something against it all in the weeks before. Because they'd been getting ready for a while to do… the killing. They'd been training militias and all that. A lot of people don't realise how organised it all was. I didn't either then but I was only seven. A lot of this I've learned since by reading books about it. Isn't that mad? Anyways, we ran from our house and we had another Tutsi with us, the guy who

92

worked on our farm. His name was Shema. I'm not sure where we were going, I was only a kid. We must've come across some of the *Interahamwe* – that means men with a single purpose in my… in the language they use – and then I suppose… Well, I can't really remember everything but I saw my father kill Shema, and then… I dunno… everyone disappeared and I was alone and I ran. I was in the bush for a few weeks, I think. Alone mostly but then I met another group and they took me in. They were Tutsis but they took me with them anyway. I ended up at, like, a refugee camp. I didn't know then where I was but it was in Tanzania, next-door to Rwanda. The border was not too far from where I grew up. I mean it was a bit of a way. You wouldn't walk it here – you'd end up in Wales. Anyway, I was waiting outside that camp, hoping to see my family, and this white lady came by in a big white car and she took me inside the camp and… I dunno why… but then she kept an eye on me and I guess she liked me, or something, because when they couldn't trace my family she arranged for me to come here. That was my foster mother's sister, Cath, and so I was fostered by Jim and Sheila and that's it really."

He said all this staring into the dark but now he sneaked a sideways look at the girl beside him. She was also looking away, across the patch of green. Maybe she didn't understand or he'd spoken too fast. He did that sometimes when he was telling the story – there was always too much and, without all the details, it sounded so banal, like a lesson he'd learned off by heart, so he tended to run through it, as though he was summing up a particularly dull weekend. But he couldn't inflict the real details on anyone because those pictures had to stay in his head. He was the custodian of that horror, like a male Pandora, and if he let it out, he couldn't know what it would do. If he started telling the full truth of those weeks, he would never stop talking.

Then her hand was on his, small and very white and totally unexpected so that he curled his fingers around hers, almost without thinking.

They sat like that for a while longer and then, as if a bell had sounded, they stood up, dropped each other's hands, and walked back to her place.

She didn't say anything until they got to the gate in front of the shabby two-up two-down.

"Sounds like ye should find out what happened to yer family. S'always better to know, otherwise ye won't be able to shake it off. That's what me mam says. She always sees the glass half-empty so she likes to know what's coming up, the better to dodge it, ye know? But I think she might have a point: knowledge is power, isn't that what they say?"

She took the jacket off her shoulders and handed it back. She looked tiny again, newly frail and vulnerable.

"Ah I dunno. They also say too much knowledge can be a dangerous thing. Sometimes it's best to leave these things alone," Theo said, smiling so she knew he didn't think her advice was stupid. He didn't but it was an idea for here, not for there. It was an idea that could only exist in a well-ordered world like this, not in the chaos he'd left behind. She didn't understand and why should she? It was alright.

"Thanks again, Theo. I don't know…"

"Don't worry 'bout it. Sure it was just good luck I came along. I guess the god of nights on the lash was looking out for you. But stay away from that Tommy in future. I've seen him around before and he's a bad one, getting worse all the time."

He guessed he sounded like her dad might've, if he'd not been off working in the North Sea, but Theo didn't care. That lad would break Cara's future into tiny pieces and stamp on them, without a thought. Theo had met plenty of Tommys along the way.

"See ya at work."

She walked up the path, put the key in the lock, turned, smiled and then was gone.

Walking home, Theo realised the 'Tommys' he was warning Cara about included himself. There was no point denying it

94

any longer. Somehow over the last few months, he'd crossed some kind of line so that he was definitely no longer a nixer. He was just a little higher up the ladder than Tommy, which, if anything, made him worse. The thought made him walk faster, anger pushing him back towards Precious.

His phone rang. Neville. What the hell did he want at this hour?

"Theo, thank God. Listen man, I'm in trouble. I... I... need somewhere to stay tonight. Are you at home?"

"Where else would I be at this hour?" Theo said. "Jeez, Neville, what's up?" He stopped outside his building so he wouldn't wake Precious. Neville, usually so calm and quiet, was nearly shouting. He could hear his footsteps down the line. It sounded like his friend was running.

"It's too complicated to go into now but I think I fucked up, Theo. I need somewhere to keep my head down for a while. I'm coming to yours. I'm about thirty minutes away. Is Precious there?"

"Yeah, she's here but she's sleeping, at least she was. I nipped out for a while but I'm back now. Text me when you get here and I'll let you in. Alright? Don't ring the bell and don't knock. I don't want to wake her again, she'll go mental."

"Fine." And Neville was gone.

Theo let himself in quietly. He stood in the hall for a second after he clicked the door shut. There was no sound from the bedroom so he took off his shoes and padded into the living room with its tiny built-in kitchen. He poured himself a glass of water and sat on the couch, suddenly dead with exhaustion.

What a night. He leaned back and closed his eyes. His head was spinning, like one of those sparklers kids carried at fireworks, only instead of flashes of light wheeling off, there were images – dead bodies in fields, his father in that eternal killer's pose, Cara's tear-stained face, the sneer of disgust on Tommy's face, and now Neville, an image from a better time, his floppy fringe falling over his face as he punched Theo playfully on the shoulder. What the hell had Neville gotten himself into now?

After Michael's warning a few weeks ago, Theo'd told Nev to be careful. But Neville had laughed at him. They were sitting together in a corner of the pub down the road, waiting for the girls to turn up. Neville hadn't said much about the new girl he was going with, just that they'd met at the library a couple of weeks ago. That was Neville for you, alright. Picking up birds in bars was not his style.

"Don't be such a mother hen, Theo. Things are fine. Alright, a couple of lads asked me to give them some gear on tick but they've paid up now. I was just a bit short for a couple of weeks and I think that dumbass Michael told Gerrity I might be skimming the product. But I've sorted it now. I'm not scared of Michael, he's a right Mickey Dazzler. Wants to make you feel that he owns you and him nothing more than a lackey himself. Don't worry your pretty black head there. I've got it under control."

"And you're sure you're not nicking the stash for yourself? I'm finding you very perky this evening, Nev."

Theo was only half-joking. Neville was not stupid, far from it, but sometimes he did things that only made sense in his own fired-up brain where neurons and synapses snapped and sizzled thanks to the weed and coke pumping up the base all around his body.

Before Neville could answer, a tall girl with a fine pair of legs poured into tight jeans was leaning over the table, giving Theo's friend a nice, warm kiss on the lips.

"Theo, this is Grace Walsh."

She was a good bit younger than both of them, Theo realised as he nodded to her and pushed back his chair to let her onto the bench beside Neville. Couldn't be more than eighteen. She was wearing heavy eyeliner and too much foundation but she was pretty enough and, when she smiled, there were dimples in her cheeks. There was something about that mouth too.

"Have I seen you around somewhere? You look awful familiar," he said as Neville went to the bar for another round.

"Nah, don't think so," Grace said. "I think I'd have remembered ye if we'd met before."

She smiled to show there was no harm meant. Theo liked that.

"Are you in school?" he said.

"Just done the Leaving. I guess I'll be able to answer that question better next month when we get the results."

And that's when Theo realised who she was. Walsh. Of course, this was Deirdre's girl.

"Small world," he breathed.

"What?" she said.

"I've just realised I work with your mam, down in The Deep. Your mam's Deirdre, right?

"Yeah. Okay, so *you're* the lad from Rwanda, the one who grew up here? I didn't know yer name. Mam might've told me but I forgot. And Neville's been on about his friend Theo, but he never said… I mean, I didn't know…"

Theo smiled. "Yeah, Neville never tells anyone that I'm black. He likes them to meet me fresh the first time. He says it's his fight against racial stereotypes. I think he's onto a loser there but he likes to watch people do a double-take when they have to match what he's told them about me with what I look like. He says he can literally see the wheels in their brains whirring." They both laughed although Grace was blushing too. "Mind you, it was different when he met me for the first time," Theo said.

And he told Grace the story. Well, some of it. He didn't mention that he'd only been in Ireland for four months, or that he was sniffling with fear and clinging to Sheila's arm when he'd arrived in Mrs Newton's class on a wet, spring morning in 1995.

He glossed over all that. He'd leave mixing tragedy with comedy to Shakespeare.

"So anyways, Mrs Newton, she was nice, not the smartest

but nice enough, says, 'This is Theo, from Africa. Now everyone say a big hello to Theo.' Of course, nobody did because I was the first black person most of them had ever seen. She sent me to sit by Neville, he was at the back. He never said a word that whole morning, just stared at me. Finally, just before lunch, he said, 'D'ye not like washing, then?'"

Grace laughed. And so did Neville who had joined them again now.

"I was eight!" he said and he feigned a punch at Theo, pulling Grace to him with his other arm so he could kiss her head.

Later that night, as Neville left to see Grace home, always the gentleman, he again told Theo not to worry, everything was cool, everything was under control.

Now, sitting on his couch, the sky pinking over the high-rises across the street and the night flashing through his brain like lightning, Theo knew with a dull certainty that everything was very much not under control. It was as though the sofa under him was drifting towards the wall, towards the window, leaving the apartment behind. Wouldn't it be great if he drifted right up out of the window into the sky, away above the city, across the sea? Maybe he would land in his childhood and Shema would be there, cackling, and his father, all of them sitting under the mango tree, all of them together, untainted by the future. Before. As he slumped further into the sofa, Theo felt a lump in the pocket of his jeans. Tommy's knife. He chucked it beneath the settee. Fat lot of good a scrawny penknife would be to him. His eyes closed and when he jolted awake again, he'd been out for an hour. It was nearly 6 am. He checked his phone. No missed calls. No texts. Where the fuck was Neville?

CHAPTER SEVEN

When Precious stumbled into the room a few hours later, Theo was still on the sofa but he was no longer tired. He felt wide awake, jittery, like that time he took a yoke, just to prove to Michael that he wasn't a wuss. He'd never taken one again. He didn't want to be the dealer with the habit, like Neville. It was too much of a cliché. And he was already a cliché. The tragic, black African, family wiped out by the mass slaughter that exploded when the 'savages' went mad, a bereft child with bare feet taken in by white saviours. No, if he was going to fuck up the life that had been so inexplicably saved – and today it felt more than ever like he was – then he'd decided he was not going to be another stereotype while doing it. He checked his phone again. He'd texted Michael an hour or so ago but he hadn't replied. Theo was sure the jackass knew what was going on. Maybe he could call him now? It was after eight. He might be up.

"Have you been awake since you got up?"

Precious fell on the sofa beside him, her head dropping onto his shoulder.

"More or less, couldn't sleep. I went for a walk, like I said, and… then I sat here. I think I dozed a bit."

Theo didn't want to go into the whole Cara story with Precious. She'd met the younger girl the night he went to the Warwick on Jarvis Street with the restaurant crew as he scouted for new clients for the coke Michael had raved about. He'd sold a fair bit, word got round the club quickly that the silent black in the corner was the one to see, which was just as well as that supply line from Spain was really coming into its own now and Gerrity was gaining a rep for dealing in weight, cementing his place at the top of this particular pyramid. At some point during the night, Theo was chatting to Cara when he caught Precious giving him the dirty eye. He wasn't up to anything; she just happened to come along as he was standing alone, eyeing the room for potential buyers. He was only half-listening to her, to be honest, but Precious didn't like it. He'd taken his arm from the wall where he'd put it as he leaned in to hear Cara over the music, straightened up and flashed Precious a smile, but her face remained stony and she was quiet on the way home.

No point now going into what happened on the street. Precious'd be mad and suspicious and it would only give her another stick to bash Cara with. For some reason that was not quite clear to him, Theo didn't want her going on again about how Cara was 'like a skinny little dog, all wanting and needing', as she'd done when they got home that night, before he managed to caress her anger away. Anyway, he'd no time to think about all that now.

"Listen, Precious, I've to go out and then I'll be off straight to the restaurant. I know, I know," he said, as she lifted her head and opened her mouth, "I said we could go down to Temple Bar and get breakfast before I went to work but something's come up. Neville's got a problem and I need to… to go see that he's alright. Sorry, love."

"Bloody Neville. He's always up to something," Precious growled as she heaved herself off the couch.

She slammed on the kettle in the tiny kitchen area. The crockery was going to get it, Theo thought.

"Is it drugs? Is that the trouble he is in? Are you going to bring him money again?"

She was standing at the edge of the kitchenette now, one hand on her jutting hip. Even in his baggy Cure t-shirt, with a face on her that would sink ships, she looked like a ride.

Her breasts, like buns with cherries on them, were rising and falling as she puffed her anger and he felt himself getting hard. She looked fine, her stance brazen, her hands twisting elegantly from the wrists at the end of each sentence, like flesh-and-blood question marks.

"No, nothing like that. I mean, I don't think it's cash. It's…"

"What, Theo? What has he done that you have to go out at the crack of dawn at the weekend, leaving your woman alone?"

"Precious, I'm trying to tell you if you'll give me a chance."

Theo was on his feet now. Somewhere in his brain, below the hum of anxiety about Neville and the unsettling sense that gravity was getting loose, there was a throbbing that said, 'a shag is probably just what you need right now'. He made a move but she was onto him.

"You can wipe that look off your face too. There is no way you're getting any of this now."

Theo sighed and went to grab his jacket from the chair. "I just think he's in trouble. He called me last night, this morning really, and I can't reach him now. It's probably fine but I've got to go and check on him, to be sure. I'll text you later."

"You can text all you like."

But as he opened the door, she came to him.

"Theo, I know Neville is like a brother to you. I know he was good to you when you were new here but he's like quicksand. He'll drag you down and me too. He mixes with a bad crowd and he's stoned out of his head most of the time."

Despite the harsh words, her face was soft. Theo bent and kissed her hard and long on the mouth. She cared about him more than anyone, except perhaps Jim and Sheila. And, of course, Neville. And those ghosts in his head, if you could fool yourself into thinking love kept going when the body stopped. He cared about her too, had told her more secrets than most, and she was the best ride he'd ever had. He should just drop this whole drug thing, get her up the duff and settle down, move to another city maybe, in Ireland or somewhere else. But he'd never dared speak to her of these wild ideas and he never would because he knew that, despite what they had here in this Dublin bubble, she was going home one day. Her family was rich and he knew, as well as he knew his name, that they would not want her to be with a Rwandan orphan. That's why he never talked of the future. She was a swallow, her migration route was sure. He was like those parakeets that Neville told him had settled in English parks, lost, out-of-place and never going home to the foothills of the Himalayas where they had first come from years ago.

"I know that, Precious. I know Nev's a mess. But he's my mess." He smiled down at her, fishing for forgiveness. "I have to see if he's okay. I'll tell you all about it later. I'll be finished around 10. Will I see you here then?"

"You might."

But she was smiling too now because his right hand had found her breast and that pert nipple. She stood on her toes and put her mouth over his, nipping and biting and squeezing and sucking so that for a rainbow-behind-the-eyes moment, he was gone from himself. Then his phone bleeped.

That'd be Michael.

"I'll see you later. Stay hot for me."

On the street, he read the text.

Ha'penny Bridge. 10 am.

At least that was something. He'd run over to Neville's place first on the off chance that he might be there, then walk into the city through Phoenix Park. He had time and the walk might calm him. He tried Neville's mobile again. Still nothing. He headed down the street, pulling his earphones from his pocket. He needed someone else's words in his ears to silence everything else. There was nothing he'd not thought of that could reasonably explain Neville's silence. If he kept thinking, he'd only end up scratching the same scab he'd been picking at since the phone call and then he'd be no use to anyone.

There was no answer when he hammered at the cracked red door to Neville's basement flat. Theo wasn't surprised. If he was honest with himself, he'd admit it was a dead cert that Gerrity's crew had taken Neville. What else? But he didn't want to be honest yet. Not even with himself because once he accepted that as fact, he'd have to do something and then there'd be no going back.

He climbed the steps back up to the street and pulled out his phone. He couldn't do Yeats today – he'd get lost in all that mysticism and oblique imagery. Then he'd be back on the where's-Neville mental merry-go-round and until he met Michael, there was nothing else he could do, was there? No point calling Grace. Neville never told her anything about dealing drugs. He'd said that dragging her into it would be the real crime. Theo knew what he meant.

He scrolled through his podcasts. He'd downloaded a weekly arts show after he'd heard a bit of it while he was washing up last weekend, before the rest of the team came in and turned the radio over to Kiss FM. He might try Heaney. He hadn't listened to this one yet and they'd studied some of Heaney's poems at school. He'd liked them, especially *Digging*. That one reminded him of Kavanagh's work. It was the same kind of 'old world' poetry, harking back to a different Ireland, not this one of hard eyes, quick money and broken dreams. Okay, so maybe that old Ireland was no utopia either – no joke to be scrabbling for mould-covered potatoes in a cold field, however beautifully it was described – but these poems evoked a simplicity that, however phony or manufactured it might be, made Theo feel like he could see above the clouds. Some of the poems also made him think of his own childhood, as though where he grew up was not just in *his* past but in *The Past*, further away than linear time and geography could account for on their own. Something about these rose-tinted visions of rural life in pre-boom Ireland spun him back to Kibungo. He called them wordy worm-holes.

He decided to walk straight through the Park – up Acres

Road and then down Chesterfield. It was a beautiful morning, light soft as a lullaby, easy breeze, a curtain of mist rising off the grass. There were a fair few joggers out and the odd horse-and-cart, looking for early-bird tourists. The trees clutched pockets of shadow to their trunks. If only he was just taking a walk. Or going for a run. Then, this would've been a great start to the day.

As he moved deeper into the park, he started to feel a little calmer. He used to roam the city a lot when he was younger, sometimes with Neville but mostly on his own, on a mission to discover his new Dublin. Sometimes the things he found helped him remember old places, old ways, so that the unfamiliar became a lens through which he could look back.

The first time he'd come across red deer in Phoenix Park, it was a frost-edged winter's day and he was stunned. He nearly missed them because the wind was pinching his face so hard he'd buried his chin deep in the collar of his duffle coat and had his eyes on the ground. He hadn't expected wild animals to be roaming free in the heart of the city. He stood watching them, his mind rushing back to Kibungo, that lost world where shy duikers would dart out of the bushes as he sped by on his scooter and where colobus monkeys hooted in the trees in the morning. He'd not thought of these things for years – it was just because of the deer. He supposed his walks around Dublin were really a kind of therapy, reviving memories that his mind had put to sleep.

He got to Ha'penny Bridge way too early so he thought he'd take a wander to the south side of the Liffey. He wasn't really paying attention to where he was going and found himself back in Harry Street, in front of Phil Lynott's statue. He checked his phone again. Still nothing. Still early. He'd have a coffee. There were a few young lasses, sounded like they were from Cork, taking photos with Phil. One girl put her hand on his forever-frozen Afro, another stood mimicking the singer's stance, one leg out, thumb hooked in the pocket of her denim shorts, another girl gave him a hug. They were all long hair, endless bare legs and giggles. They were too young to have really known the music and too white to understand what Phil Lynott meant to someone like Theo. But they were having a good time and Theo felt sure Phil would be loving it, wherever he was.

He'd discovered Phil through Neville, of course. Neville was comforting him after some lads in the playground called Theo a monkey and threw banana skins at him. Again. They must've been about twelve because they were still in primary school and it was before the joints, and then the powder, started to blur Neville's sharp edges.

"They're eejits. They don't know a thing," Neville had said after the arrival of a teacher sent them scattering. He didn't reach out to comfort Theo – they didn't want to add 'fag' to the other boys' lengthy list of insults – but he stood close so that no one could see the sheen in Theo's eyes.

After school, Neville took him back to his house, letting him in with his own key, and then leading the way up the stairs to his room. Neville was an only child and he had the run of the place because his parents were both doctors and out all day. He was like an older brother to Theo – his saviour, friend and role model.

"Listen to this." Neville pulled a video out of a pile by the side of his bed and pushed it into the player. "But first close your eyes."

"Why do you want me to close my eyes? It's a video."

Theo remembered feeling very confused and a little scared. He was still haunted by irrational fears: he was scared of the dark, he hated being alone, the sound of metal scraping against metal terrified him, ditto balloons popping or cars backfiring, and it was all he could do not to cower and cover his eyes when he heard screaming, even that high-pitched, mostly happy playground screeching.

But this was Neville asking, and so, reluctantly, he closed his eyes, putting his hands over his face as well. He didn't want to let Neville down by peeking.

"The minute I went solo, people started offerin' me deals," a man said on the telly.

"Where's he from?" Neville asked.

"I dunno. I can't see him."

"Take a guess. Go on, guess, Theo."

"He talks like you so he must be from here, right? He's a Dubliner."

"Yeah, good. And so, d'ye think he looks like me?"

Theo hesitated. He didn't know what Neville meant. To him, everyone in Dublin looked like Neville in that they didn't look like himself, or at least not many did. So surely the answer must be yes. He opened his mouth but Neville was too excited to wait.

"Look, Theo. Look, he's black. Well kinda. Definitely not white. He's Phil Lynott, he was a massive rock star, and he was black and he was Irish."

He was almost hopping with excitement over by the TV, smiling delightedly, his eyes glittering, all the enthusiasm that would later push him to seek out every kind of high, chemical and emotional, directed at Theo. He looked like he had discovered the secret to eternal youth, the Titanic shipwreck and where Shergar was hidden all at once.

"See?"

Theo didn't know exactly what he was meant to see. But he nodded anyway because Neville seemed to need him to understand so very badly.

They watched the full interview. Theo was hypnotised by the soft lilt coming from the almost-black man's lips. And he thought his Afro looked really cool though Theo would never then, or now, let his hair grow that long. There was something in the back of his mind, some flicker of his mother rubbing her hand over the top of his head, and saying, "It's too long. I will take you to Mama Solange."

But that was all he got. A fragment. He couldn't remember who Mama Solange was or where she lived. Already, even at twelve, he could barely remember his mother's face. He could

106

just about picture it in its entirety but he couldn't break out the individual features. He didn't have any photographs, of course.

"And then, there was Paul McGrath, he was a footballer and he was great in the World Cups in 1990, and 1994, before you came here. There was a song about him and everything. Ooh, ah, Paul McGrath, I said ooh, ah Paul McGrath."

Neville was jumping around now, pumping his fists in the air. He looked so happy that Theo got up and joined him and they both leapt around like eejits until the door banged downstairs and they realised Neville's mother was home. They fell onto the floor, still laughing, still gasping 'oohs and ahs'.

Later that week, Theo bought his first Thin Lizzy tape. It was *Vagabonds of the Western World*. They'd loads of their albums in HMV but he liked that one because the cover was so bonkers with its psychedelic colours and the rocket and the planets. Later, over time, he bought them all and they were still in a cardboard box in his flat. He hadn't kept much from home – he'd gone through his stuff when Jim and Sheila moved to Donegal – but that box he kept, even though tapes were about as useful as floppy disks nowadays. He loved the music but he also loved the legend of the man and his contradictions. Lynott was proof that you could be all and everything, and perhaps dying young was the price he had to pay. Or maybe that was just hype and it was nothing more than an accident. That was the thing about legends – you could hang your opinions on them and they were strong enough to bear them.

That day at Neville's, Theo made up his mind to speak like Lynott. It amused him now to think that what everyone thought was his obvious, ultimately hugely successful, attempt to fit in by speaking like the natives was really a secret tribute to someone who was, superficially, as little like the natives as possible, at a time when that really was a thing.

He swallowed down the last of his coffee and stubbed out

his fag. Right, Michael better have some good news. Still no word from Neville and Theo had a bad feeling that he just couldn't shake. In the best of all worlds, Neville was going to get a hiding. But Dublin wasn't anywhere close to being the best of all worlds and Theo couldn't help thinking about the stories he'd heard when Billy Mannion disappeared. Most of the rumours had been put about by Michael, a smug grin on his stupid face as he swore he didn't really know the details while at the same time slyly hinting that he'd personally had a hand in poor Billy's fate. As he hammered it back to the bridge, Theo wished he'd taken Ronan up on his offer to source him a gun.

"Ye never know when ye might need it," Ronan had said in the pub a few weeks ago, talking as if he were someone. He'd said he could get Theo a tasty 9mm. Theo said thanks but no thanks and drained his pint, desperate to get away from the little git. Ronan was clearly trying to impress, hoping that Theo, whose star was on the rise with Gerrity, would put in a good word for him. Theo could've told him he was pissing in the wind: Michael didn't like Ronan, didn't trust him much and there was no way he was going to give him a bigger role. He should be happy with his lot, not sniffing around for more trouble, Theo thought at the time. He should've taken his own advice.

Michael was leaning on the cast-iron rail in the middle of the bridge. Even though it was a warm day, he was wearing a dark overcoat over baggy jeans and trainers, sunglasses and a beanie, for Chrissakes. Big coat for the big man, Theo thought as he walked onto the bridge.

The Council wasn't having much luck persuading people to stop putting padlocks on the railings. There were still loads, some decorated with little red ribbons, or paper hearts, or just your bog-standard padlock with some names scrawled in marker. To Theo's thinking, the padlock was a bitter symbol. Did love always have to be a burden, a weight, something to stop you being free? Maybe. Then, did hate set you free? But maybe the padlocks were to hold love together, to keep it safe. Maybe the Council should leave well enough alone.

"Howya, Michael?" Theo said.

Michael didn't answer. He didn't turn around either.

Stifling a groan, Theo leaned up against the railing, leaving a good few feet between himself and *Mr Big* so that the gobshite didn't accuse him of being an amateur. He waited. If Michael wanted to play at being in *The Wire*, then they would play at being in *The Wire*.

"I'm only gonna say this once, Theo. Forget about Neville. He's fucked things up and he has to pay."

Theo grasped the railing tighter. Here it was but he hadn't expected Michael to be so bloody blunt. He stared into the Liffey's dirty waters and somewhere deep under the fear and panic rising in his chest, he felt a bone-deep sadness. This was the moment when his train was going to come off the tracks. Again.

"That's just not good enough, Michael. What'd he do? If he's short this week, I'll make it up. I can get the money. Just gimme a coupla days. I'll come good, you know I will."

"It's not the money, Theo. If it was just the cash, do you think Gerrity would be involved himself?"

Theo turned to look at Michael. The waste-of-space was smiling.

"Wipe that smile off your ugly gob," he muttered. "What d'you mean, Gerrity's involved? Is he back in town again?"

"Yep, came in two days ago from Spain. And then, he heard about Neville and he's taking it personal, like."

If he rushed Michael now, he could flip him over the railing and into the water, Theo thought. But the damn Liffey probably wasn't deep enough to drown him. Maybe it would poison him to death.

He spoke slowly, trying to think of the best words, the most meaningful words. There must be words to sort this out.

"What's Gerrity taking personal? For God's sake, will you speak straight and drop the bad-guy act?"

Michael flinched, his smile fading like an Irish summer. Good, the jibe had hit its mark.

"Neville's been ratting to the cops."

Theo almost laughed. It was so ridiculous. But Michael was smirking again.

"Neville, a rat? Don't be an eejit, Michael. He's a user, can barely get through the day without a coupla hits. Why would he grass ye up and muck up his supply?"

"I dunno the details. All I know is someone saw him being taken by the cops the other day, down where the yobs sell their trash round Blanchardstown. Fuck knows what he was doin' there. Not our turf. And ye know what Gerrity thinks of open markets. Anyway, that's on top of him not delivering his money last week. Like I said, I don't know the details of it all but don't you worry, Theo. Gerrity'll find out."

Theo struggled to take it all in. No time to figure out the truth now. He had to keep talking and he needed to get Michael on his side. No use flying into a rage with the tosser.

"I've known Neville nearly all my life, Michael," he said, spreading his hands to show he wasn't pissed at the younger guy. "There's no way he'd talk to the cops. You've made a mistake."

"Well, if that's the case, he'll have a chance to explain himself. Gerrity's having a wee chat with him today."

Theo turned away again and grasped the railing harder. He was feeling dizzy. The light suddenly seemed too bright, the water too shiny, the people too loud. This happened sometimes when he was stressed. Everything overwhelmed him, as though his whole system was starting to shut down. He took a deep breath.

"Where? Where are they? I want to be there."

"No way, big man. We don't need you gettin' mixed up in this," Michael said. "We'll handle this the same way we always handle all these things."

The smug tone, and that ridiculous 'we', finally tipped Theo over the edge. He leaped across to the smaller man, grabbed him by the lapels of his stupid coat, and pushed him hard against the railing.

"If anything happens to Neville, I swear I'll get you, Michael. You think you're God's gift but you're just a low-life wannabe. Gerrity'd cut you loose tomorrow. You're nothing, Michael, and I promise you, you'll be less than nothing if anything happens to Neville. You might think you're the boss of me but you know nothing. And you can take that to Gerrity too. Anything happens to Neville and you've got a big problem with me. I know things."

Michael glared at him, his face tightening so that for a moment he looked almost smart, almost deadly.

"First, Theo, you're the one that knows nothing. That's why we do things the way we do."

Was the tosser really stressing the 'we' again?

"You know me, you've met Gerrity once, and ye hang around with that waste of space, Ronan Patterson. But for the rest, you know nothing. You've no information to trade, and the sooner ye get that into yer thick black head the better. Or is your English still not good enough for you to understand what I'm tellin' ye?"

Theo pushed him away. To his horror, he thought he might cry. Michael was right. He didn't know anything. What would he go to the cops with? 'Hello Garda Plod, I've met Gerrity, he's the leader of a gang selling bags of brown, bars of coke and yokes across Dublin'. They knew all that already and the bruiser was still on the streets, still going after people like Neville who'd done nothing wrong, who were just too trusting to play this game.

Theo rubbed his hands over his head. What *could* he do?

"Tell Gerrity to call me."

When Michael just grinned and shook his head, Theo grabbed him by the neck again, this time pressing his thumbs into the soft flesh around his windpipe. That wiped the smile off his face. A few passers-by sidled their eyes over to them but hurried on past, staring resolutely at their shoes.

111

"You've no idea what I really am, Michael. Things I've seen. Things I could do. You think I'm frightened of you? Don't be a gobshite. Tell Gerrity to call me," he said, each word slow and sure. "Tell him I'll vouch for Neville. I know he's not a grass. Tell him."

He dropped Michael and spun away, heading back across the river, back to the north of the city. He was shaking and his mind was racing. He wasn't interested if Neville had grassed to the police or not. It didn't matter now. They were going to act like he had anyway. It might already be too late. Jesus, what was he going to do?

Theo couldn't bear feeling this helpless again. He stopped, leaned against a wall, tried to calm his breathing. He hadn't been able to stop his father, he hadn't been able to save Shema, and he'd lost the rest of his family by sneaking off like a mongoose through the bush. He couldn't let that happen again. He couldn't still be that powerless, could he? What was the point of everything if he was just going to let things happen around him all the bleedin' time?

He was walking up towards Inns Quay, the Four Courts looming ahead of him. The building usually looked forbidding but today the sun was sheening the brickwork, lighting up the copper dome of the rotunda. He'd visited the courts as a kid with his school and he remembered the statues above the portico were Mercy, Wisdom, Justice, and bizarrely Moses. There was another one too. What was it? Ah yeah, Authority. But those austere figures were too high up in the ether to help him now. Gerrity had swallowed them up and smothered or stolen their powers. He was the dispenser of justice now, the only one who could offer Neville any mercy, the one true, Catholic, apostolic authority.

Theo pulled out his phone.

CHAPTER EIGHT

"Howya, Grace. It's Theo. Listen, can I talk to your mam? Sorry, I don't have her number and I need to ask her something bout work. Are you with her?"

"Theo, how's it going? Yeah, sure. We're just out shopping. Gimme a sec, I'll find her for ye. She's around here somewhere. What's the craic?"

In the background, Theo could hear the muted babble of people spending money they didn't really have, hangers clicking on and off rails, bags rustling, some kind of annoyingly twinkly muzak. No point telling Grace anything until there was something to tell. She wouldn't have a clue what he was talking about. For her, Neville was the smart college boy. She must know he smoked hash and maybe she knew about the cocaine – she might even do a few lines herself – but that'd be it. The two of them had been floating in their little love bubble since they met, so he hadn't seen much of them. Neville had his lectures, Grace had her exams and he'd been busy pushing the new supply out. He'd drifted away from his friend. Took his eye off the ball and look where that had got them.

"Same old, same old," he answered, moving closer to the river and away from the Saturday morning traffic building up along the quay.

"Maybe I'll see ye later? Neville was saying something the other day about an open-air concert in Phoenix Park tonight. I think it's some young bands, from round our place, so probably not much talent, but it could be fun if the rain holds off? I haven't heard from him today though?"

There was the merest hint of a question in her voice, an early-relationship query too shy to fully stake its claim.

Theo made a non-committal grunt.

Grace didn't push it.

"Anyway, I'll talk to ye later. Let me grab Mam."

Theo waited, feeling awkward. He'd be the last person Deirdre'd expect a call from at the weekend although they got on well at work, chatting away through their break times, each seeming to have found the right-sized person for a particular-shaped gap in their lives.

It took a while but eventually Theo began to tell Deirdre about his family and childhood over there. Only snippets at first but she was a good listener, mainly because she knew nothing about Rwanda. Because of this, she didn't probe the big picture, happy instead to discuss just what he told her. She asked him about Clément – what he looked like, did he play football, did he pick on his younger brother? And about Angélique – did she cry a lot in the night, when did she take her first steps, did he remember it? And she asked him if his mother was a good cook and whether his father played games with him. It was as though Deirdre was the missing link between there and here. She was effortlessly able to achieve the magical fusion that the counsellors had failed to deliver. He was even more comfortable talking to her than to Jim and Sheila. It was another disloyalty but no less true for that. Jim and Sheila had known too much to be able to see things like Deirdre did and, in any case, they'd had a different job to do. They had to make him feel at home in those first awful years and they knew that for that to happen, he needed to forget the Before. Today, the Before no longer threatened his Now. It was no longer a zero-sum game and so he could allow his memories in. The act of talking about it all seemed to be igniting new circuits in his brain as well, closing the circle on the whole process.

114

During their chats, Deirdre told him stories of her kids, sharing her worries about how she treated them, about whether she was being fair. She told him about her childhood, her mother's cancer, her angry, absent father. After Theo told her of riding his wooden scooter down to the village through the banana plants and past the avocado trees, sending white and yellow butterflies exploding skywards from the long grass, she described the stony fields, full of twisted ferns and crusted cowpats, where she chased herons and walked for hours just to get away from the sickness that had come to roost in her home like a cursed owl.

She told Theo that time was no healer because she still missed her mother. She said that one cataclysmic event had coloured all the rest of her life. She told him she didn't know if she loved her father, that she hardly knew the man who was away so much and then there but not there after her mother died. Theo clamped his lips together at this. His own memories of his father were still too raw – she was right about time – and he was worried Deirdre might ask the right questions and then he'd have to seek answers. He wasn't ready to do that yet.

Neville had come up, of course, and Theo had to tell her they were friends. He threw it out quickly, knowing she was about to slag him off. Grace had told them both that night in the pub that her mam had no time for her boyfriend's charming ways.

"She sees right through you," she'd laughed as Neville pulled a long face.

Deirdre never brought Neville up again after that one time but she seemed a little disappointed that Theo should be his friend.

There were other taboo subjects. He never told her about the drugs and she didn't say much about her husband, even though she once took a photo from her purse and held it out, with a strange little-girl shyness, to Theo. It showed a still good-looking man with dark hair and striking cheekbones, but Theo reckoned there was a flinty look to his sharp angles.

Deirdre had hinted that Fergal hurt her, telling without telling. Her euphemisms – "Fergal was in a bad mood last night" or "Fergal lost the plot the other day" – didn't fool him and they weren't meant to. Somehow, Theo realised, he and Deirdre had become the unlikeliest of friends. Secret sharers and secret bearers. Still she wouldn't be expecting a call from him today. Their common world was the restaurant, not out here.

"Theo? You alright?" Deirdre sounded flustered.

"Yeah, I'm grand. Well, sort of. I can't work today, Deirdre. Something's come up. Can you take my shift? I'm supposed to start at one."

"Oh, let me think. Sure, that should be fine. Fergal's out but Grace is around and she can keep an eye on Kevin 'til she goes to work, or Conor can. Should be alright, I guess. Yeah, I'll do it, Theo. The money'll come in handy this weekend as well."

"Great, thanks. I'll owe you one big-time."

He breathed out slowly. Time, he'd won some time. Now, what would he do with it? His mind raced ahead.

"Sorry, Deirdre, what did you say? My mind was wandering there."

"Are you alright, Theo? It's just... you sound a bit weird. You haven't been drinking or anything, have you?"

"Nah. It's just... I've been... I've got a problem I need to sort. I... Something's happened to Neville and I need to find him."

"What do you mean, something's happened? Did you tell Grace?" Deirdre's voice had fallen and there was an edge to it now.

"Not yet. I didn't want to worry her. It's a long story but I think he's in trouble. Maybe big trouble. He's been running with a bad crowd and now he's missing and I think if I don't do something... I dunno, I dunno what'll happen."

"Where are you? At home?"

"Nah, I had to meet someone in town. I'm on Inns Quay, heading back to Merrickstown now."

"We're at the Ilac, not far. Listen, let me come to you. I'll meet you at the Chesterfield entrance to the park. We can take a walk and then I'll get the bus back."

He started to protest – he didn't have time for this – but she cut him off.

"I need to know what's going on, Theo. I'll be the one picking up the pieces with Grace later if that lad has got himself into a mess." She paused, but then couldn't help herself. "I knew he was no good, I bloody knew it."

She almost whispered it and Theo just let the words hang there. What was he going to say? She was wrong and right, but mostly wrong. Neville was good; he just didn't fit well with the world. He was the wrong shape for the slot he'd been given.

"I'll see you soon then," he managed and hung up.

He stood looking at the phone for a minute, then rang Ronan.

He was clutching at straws, he knew, but there was just the smidgen of a chance Ronan might have heard something on the grapevine, or might know someone other than Michael who could get hold of Gerrity. Theo couldn't fathom it but Ronan was dead popular with the young lads around their area. All cut from the same cloth, he supposed.

"Howya, Ronan? Listen, I need a favour. I need to get hold of Gerrity. D'you know anyone who might have his number? And don't say Michael cos that git's being no help at all."

There was a long pause on the other end. The little cur knows already, Theo thought. He stopped walking and leaned on the railings over the river.

"Do you know where he is? Ronan, do you know where Neville is because so help me God, if you do and you don't tell me, I'll swing for you."

"I dunno, I swear."

Ronan sounded frightened and for a moment Theo felt sorry for him, sorry for all of them caught up in this shitstorm. They'd been stupid but that was all. For other people, in other worlds, living parallel lives, being young and stupid was just the punch line of a story you told in the pub after a long day.

"Tell me, Ronan. You know something. That's bleedin' obvious."

"I just heard they'd picked him up last night. I dunno where they have him. I know Gerrity's in town and I hear he's pissed. But that's it. I swear that's all I know, Theo."

"And you don't have a number? For Gerrity? Or one of the other lads around him?"

"Ye know I only ever deal with Michael, Theo. That's the way it works. One contact. You're the one that met Gerrity, you should have his number."

There was a touch of the snide in Ronan's voice now that made Theo clutch the phone tighter to stop himself from throwing it into the river. A shaft of sunlight lit up the gilt on Seán Heuston Bridge. He'd a bit of a way to go yet. He started walking again.

"Thanks for nothing, Ronan. I'll remember this."

"If I hear anythin', I'll give ye a shout."

Ronan was like a child, trying to fix things after the damage had already been done but he'd nothing more to give. Theo hung up. He'd have to figure this out some other way.

Deirdre was already standing under a tree beside the wide avenue that led from the Chesterfield roundabout into the park. She looked small and insignificant among the giant sycamore and oak trees. Why had he agreed to meet her? She couldn't help him. He was wasting time.

"So, what's going on?"

She'd her hands on her hips and a face on her that said she was taking no prisoners.

Theo spread his hands and shrugged. "Can we walk a bit?"

She sighed but led the way. "Let's head down here. It'll take us towards St Mary's and then I can nip out and get the bus. I don't have much time if I want to get back in time to work *your* shift," she said.

"Fair enough."

Side-by-side, they moved deeper into the green, away from the roar of the traffic. The mist had evaporated, leaving just the faintest memory of the early chill, like the hollow left by a lover's head on a pillow. Above the trees, Theo could see the Wellington Monument rising into the blue, a needle on a compass, pointing to a way out. But, if he remembered right, you couldn't climb the obelisk – there was no stairway to heaven there.

"Okay, now tell me, Theo. What in God's name is going on?"

Deirdre was looking up at him. She had to shade her eyes because of the sun but clouds were gathering to the west and a kittenish breeze was playing with the loose strands of her hair. Where to start? How could he tell her just enough without dropping Neville in it?

"Is it drugs?" she asked abruptly.

Theo said nothing. He was too tired to be a smartarse.

"Is Neville dealing drugs? Is the eejit my daughter thinks is God's gift actually stupid enough to be selling drugs in *this* town?" she said.

"How d'you know?" was all he managed.

"I might be old enough to be your mother, Theo, but I've got teenage kids and friends and I don't live my whole life behind a sink washing rich people's dishes. I live in the real world too and I'm not blind. Or stupid. So who's he pissed off then? Another gang? The cops?"

"He's pissed off his boss. A real nasty piece of work. Name of Gerrity."

Deirdre stopped in her tracks. She'd a weird half-smile on her face, but she was also shaking her head and the smile looked like the kind you'd only wear to draw attention away from your tears.

"Not Barry Gerrity?" she said.

"That's the one. How d'you know?"

Theo had stopped beside her but she wouldn't look at him. She was staring into the trees, still shaking her head.

"Jesus, Mary and Joseph," she finally whispered and then she started moving again. "Go on."

The gyres are really wheeling out of control now, thought Theo, and I've no idea what's going on.

"I think he's taken Neville because he thought he grassed him up. But Neville would never snitch, there's no way. And I asked Michael, that's this other guy who I... who Neville knows, and who works with Gerrity, where he was and he just said Gerrity was going to have a chat with him. But Gerrity doesn't do much talking. If he wants to talk to you, you'd better run for the hills."

The words came in a rush and Theo could feel the panic that had been dead-weighting his chest shatter, sending chips of shame, fear and anger through him. He didn't dare look at Deirdre. He didn't know why exactly but he didn't want to lose her respect. Bit late for that now.

"I'm trying to get Gerrity's number so I can, I dunno, tell him that he's wrong, vouch, like, for Nev, but that's the thing. I don't know how to reach him."

Deirdre had been walking ahead, her steps slowing as he talked and now she came to a stop and turned to face him.

"So, tell me this, Theo, because I can tell you're in this up to your eyeballs too – no, don't deny it, I wasn't born yesterday – what makes young lads like you and Neville get yourselves caught up in Gerrity's web? You could've done anything. Two fine bright young men and you're throwing it all away."

Theo just looked at her, standing there, a good foot-and-a-half smaller than him, her slight frame throbbing with fury, her hands out, palms up.

"I dunno. Chances just come along and then you get swept up in it all and it's hard to get out."

It sounded feeble even to his own ears.

"Bollocks to that! You have so many other opportunities, Theo. Look at Neville. Parents both doctors, he's smart, good-looking. And you... you escaped from the killing, you recovered from all of that, and look at you now. You fit in perfectly. You're a great lad. But you're pissing your future away."

She sputtered to a stop, eyebrows raised.

"That's the thing," he said. "I can't imagine a future. I want to but I don't know how."

He paused. He should stop. This was too hard, too dangerous. He'd never had to put what he was doing with his life into words. He'd never even really thought about it that much. It just feckin' happened, right? But here she was again, asking questions, demanding answers. And today was a day of reckoning if ever there was one. He took a breath.

"I don't take it for granted, don't ever think I do. D'you think I don't know I haven't done anything with my second chance? Give me a bit of credit, Deirdre. I'm very, very thankful that Sheila's sister found me outside that camp. I'm feckin' over the moon that a family found me in the bush and taught me how to hide up to my eyes in the mud. For hours, Deirdre, staying absolutely still and listening to the screams as they found other people and butchered them. So, no, I don't take it for granted. For years, after that, I was still just trying to stay alive, trying to get up every day and keep breathing. Do you know how hard it is to do that sometimes? Just to take the next breath? And I did it. But then, I lost my way. I'd survived, I knew I'd made it, and then I didn't know what to do with that. I don't *know* what to do after surviving."

She was silent, staring off into the trees at a clump of red deer, lit up by a sunray like copper pots in a showroom kitchen. She looked at her watch and started walking again.

"Does Grace know what Neville does?" she said after a while.

"I don't think so but you'd probably have to ask her. I guess she knows he smokes weed, like, and does a few lines. Now and then," he said, realising even as he spoke that these little lies were pointless.

"Does she...? Never mind, I'll ask her myself. Jesus Christ, what an unholy mess."

They'd arrived at the park exit. Theo stood, hands in pockets, head bowed. Deirdre walked out the gate, then back to him, her face set.

"Right, I'm going to get you Gerrity's number. Don't ask me how but I think I can. Call him and sort this out. Don't breathe a word to Grace until you talk to me. I've to go now or I'll be late for work. I'll text you with the number later. Alright?"

Theo just nodded. How did Deirdre know Gerrity? How in God's name was that possible? He remembered something.

"D'you know Michael too, Michael Clancy? Only you didn't ask who he was, when I mentioned him," he asked.

Now it was Deirdre's turn to bow her head.

"As it happens, his mother is a good friend of mine. And I'll tell you, Theo, that's part of the reason this pisses me off so much. That woman has done everything for Michael and he's just sunk deeper and deeper. Fair enough, he's got no father but she's been more than enough for him if he'd have the cop to realise it. So yes, you could say I know Michael and he'll be getting a right bollocking on the back of this, mark my words."

She swung on her heels and started to head across the road to the bus stop. But then she turned and came back again, and without a word, she pulled Theo to her, reaching up to stretch her arms around his shoulders.

"You big, black eejit. Get out of all this, will you? This is not why you came here."

And then she really did go.

Theo's phone beeped. It was a text from Precious.
I need to see you. Now.

That was it. No emojis, no kisses, nothing. Not like Precious. He tried to call her but her mobile was apparently now switched off. Dammit. He didn't know if he could face her. He was too wound up. He needed to walk. He headed back into the park. He would head up to the next exit and then get the bus home. If he'd got Gerrity's number by then, he'd call him and take it from there. It was already gone midday. Neville had called him nearly nine hours ago. Nine hours was a long time to be scared. A lot could happen in that time; Theo knew that only too well.

When his father came back from school that April day, the buzzing, rain-thickened heat was already being sucked into the ground to make way for the cooler night air and the stars. His father was flustered. He rushed into the house, straight to the kitchen where their mother was cutting up plantains for supper. Theo was doing his homework at the table in the front room, where they also had an old fridge that was never plugged in because there was hardly ever any electricity, a small TV, again barely ever used, and three small sofas with cream crochet antimacassars. The table was by the window and, just after his father came in, Theo saw Clément running up the hill. He'd been playing football with some lads on the wasteland down near the community hall. His skinny legs were splashed with thick mud. The rains had come early that year.

As Clément drew closer, Theo glimpsed his face. What he saw lifted him out of his seat and sent him racing into the road.

"What is it? What is it?"

He was only seven but he knew something was very wrong.

"Where's Papa?" Clément gasped as he ran past his little brother, never slowing his frenetic pace.

"In the kitchen."

But Clément probably didn't hear him. He was already in the house and Theo remembered thinking he would get a hiding for not cleaning his feet first.

He followed Clément inside but something made him stop in the front room. Maybe he sensed danger, the same way that birds sense storms and fly around them, or elephants and flamingos head inland before tsunamis. A sixth sense for impending horror. He could hear urgent whispers coming from the kitchen, with one word carrying the weight of a curse: *interahamwe*. His father came out then and saw him standing there.

"Theo, we're going for a walk in the bush. All together. It's a new game that Clément thought of. We all have to go now and stay very quiet, as if we were poachers. Shema is coming too. Can you go call him? I think he is in the top field."

His father smiled but even little Theo knew it was nothing more than a bend in his lips. He ran past the bougainvillea bush, round the side of the house and up the rutted path to the field. Shema was there, bent low as he weeded the beds.

"Shema, come," Theo called.

But the old man didn't hear him. He was already a little deaf and so Theo jumped the ditch into the field and, stumbling a little between the rows of sweet potatoes, he made his way to Shema.

"Come, Shema. My father wants you. We are going to play a game, all together."

Theo remembered how badly he'd wanted Shema to smile and clap his hands at the wondrous idea of them all playing together. When Shema's face crinkled into a frown and he threw the weeds he was clutching onto the ground with no care, he was disappointed but not really surprised. Even he could feel the storm coming. Shema led the way, quickly, back to the house, tightly gripping Theo's little hand in his rough, dirty, veined one. Even today, Theo could picture his family standing outside the house as he walked back to them with Shema: his father in a smart white shirt and black trousers, lean and tight like a leopard; his mother in a dress of red-and-green flowers, fastening the cloth that held Angélique around her breasts; Clément standing beside their father, hands by his sides, eyes wide. Behind them, beyond the corrugated iron roof of their house, Theo saw smoke rising from the valley floor, thick and fast and black.

Shema went straight to his father, who put a hand on his shoulder and drew him away to the side of the house. They whispered together. Theo wondered why his father had to secretly talk to Shema. Surely, he should tell all of them if there were particular rules to this game? As he waited for the men to join them again, he could hear shouts from across the river where more smoke was spilling into the sky. The shouts were deep and angry and underneath he thought he could hear screaming. He put his hand in his mother's. She looked down at him and smiled but it was as if she was thinking of something else. The smile was only for him, not for her.

"Let's go." His father was walking towards them. "And remember, Theo, we are trying to be as quiet as possible. We are going to pretend to be... duikers, moving slowly, secretly through the bush so that the leopards never know, okay? Can you do that? Can you outsmart the leopard?"

Theo nodded and his father rubbed his head. But Theo could tell his hand was doing something automatic – just like his mother's face had been when she smiled at him. His father's heart wasn't in his hand, and was he actually shaking?

They walked for hours, crouching low through the tea plantations, rushing silently through the forests, avoiding the roads. Nine hours of fear and silence and knowing the worst was coming because even a seven-year-old knows when a game is not a game.

So, he understood the weight of every second that Neville had endured since he called him. It was something he knew in his bones, acutely and terribly. That night in Rwanda, he remembered his father's voice coming to him in a disembodied whisper from the front of their single file of fear, saying they had to move faster as it was already midnight and they needed to be hidden by dawn.

When he got home, Precious was sitting on the sofa. She was still in his t-shirt and she'd been crying.

"Jesus, girl. What happened?"

He went to sit by her, to take her in his arms, but then he saw it. The shoebox where he kept his stash of coke was beside her. He stopped mid-step; his hands, already outstretched to hold her, fell uselessly to his sides. She raised her eyes slowly to him and he couldn't do it. He couldn't meet her gaze. Like a schoolboy, he hung his head. The next thing he knew she was out of her seat, slamming her fists into his chest.

"You fool! What have you done, Theo? Do you even know what you have done?"

What was there to say? He tried to grab her hands, to hold her but she backed away.

"I don't understand. Why are you involved in this? What do you have to gain?"

The same bloody question. And again, he had no answer. Why did everyone assume there had been some kind of rational decision-making process before he got involved with Gerrity? He'd tried to describe to Deirdre the nothing that led him here. He couldn't do it. He was becoming less coherent each time he tried to put it into words. Sometimes too many words could leach the meaning out of a thing.

Precious was staring at him but he'd nothing to give. She shook her head angrily.

"Okay then. At least tell me how long? How long have you been dealing?"

"A fair while."

Simple questions were easier. He could do the whats and wheres and hows. Just not the why.

"So, you were doing this when we met?"

He nodded.

"So everything is a lie? Our whole life together is one big lie?"

"No, Precious, that's not true and you know it. This is no big deal. No please, listen to me for the love of God."

"No big deal? You fool. What happens if we get raided? What happens if you get caught? You think they won't suspect me? I am Nigerian, Theo. I have a student visa, and I can't lose it. I... my whole life... if I have to leave, I will never get back. I will not be given another chance. You must know that... do you not know that? Do you not understand?"

When he didn't answer, she turned to leave the room. He grabbed her arm. She shook him off, her eyes brimming with tears.

"This doesn't have to change anything, Precious. I only do a little, and… and I'm thinking of getting out of it. I am, I swear to God. I'll chuck the whole thing in if that's what you want."

Even he wouldn't believe himself but, as he said it, Theo knew he actually meant it. It was the only answer. After today, however today ended, he'd have to stop. How? Now that was another question. One thing at a time.

"I can change," he said. "I just need… I just need to get through today, to find Neville, to clear up this shit, and then, I swear to you, Precious, I *will* stop. We can get out, move somewhere nice. It'll be fine. I'll get another job, and we can be together, and then…"

But there was nowhere to go after the 'then'. He knew it and she knew it and for a moment they stood there together, both realising the emptiness of that four-letter word.

He bowed his head and then he felt her fingers around his neck, pulling his head lower so that it met hers. In that moment, the world seemed to stop turning. There was no sound but their breathing, halting and tear-filled. It was like those first seconds after sex, when they'd both come and lay in each other's arms and the world was still and new, and just them, all them.

"Goodbye, Theo."

She shut the door of the bedroom behind her but he heard the creak of the bed as she sat down, and then a low sobbing, slow and inevitable as rain on a Sunday.

He moved slowly to the sofa, put the bags of coke back in the shoebox and then stood there, with the box in his hands. She was right, of course, and he was such a selfish git he'd never even thought about it that way. If drugs were found here, whatever happened to him, she'd be kicked out of the country. It was one thing to be stupid enough to get himself involved but what he'd done to her was beyond thick. He was stupider than Tommy, he was as callous as Gerrity, he was dumber than Ronan. He'd wanted all his life to fit in. Well fuck it, he fit in now, right at the bottom of the pond with all the other scum.

His phone bleeped. He stuffed the box under the couch, and pulled his mobile out of his pocket.

Deirdre'd got the number. He moved towards the bedroom door but what good would that do? Precious was still crying. There was nothing he could say and his own tears would have to wait until later. He couldn't do this now. He'd to call Gerrity and he'd no clue what he was going to say.

CHAPTER NINE

Theo shut the front door loudly behind him and then stood waiting like a fool outside. Maybe when she heard the door close, she'd come after him? He'd give her a minute. He pulled out his fags and lit up. But Precious didn't come out.

So that was it, then? They'd broken up? He didn't even have a chance to say goodbye. Surely, the past months had meant more than this? But then he of all people should know that goodbyes were a luxury most people couldn't afford. In the real world, goodbyes happened when you weren't paying attention.

For a moment, he didn't know where to go. He turned away from the door and then back, looked at his keys, lifted them to the lock, shook his head and put them back in his pocket. He felt like he was becoming unstuck, floating just a few inches off the ground. He could feel the old panic rising so he ran down the steps, fast, and out onto the path. He turned right and realised he was heading for the little park where he had talked with Cara. Jesus, was that just last night? He'd call Gerrity from there. It was as good a place as any.

He sat on the same bench, the willow whispering above him. But daylight had obliterated the magic. He could see the crumpled crisp packets and cans at the base of the tree, the cigarette butts in the grass at his feet.

He dialled the number and held his breath. He half-wanted it to go to voicemail but this was probably the only chance Neville had, never mind that it was a piss-poor chance at that.

He could see Neville's smiling face telling him not to be an old mother hen.

"You were wrong, Nev. So wrong," Theo whispered.

"Yes?"

"Mr Gerrity? It's Theo. We met once, a while ago? I do… I do some work for you."

There was a long silence. Theo tried to imagine what that fake-friendly face was doing. He could hear the big man breathing, slow and regular. There was no other sound: no cars, no birds, no waves, nothing.

"What do you want, Theo?"

"I think there's been some kind of mix-up, Mr Gerrity. I think… I mean, I *know* you've got the wrong man."

"And which man would that be, Theo?"

"Neville. He's a friend of mine, and he… well, I've not heard from him since last night and I thought your lads might know where he is, so I talked to Michael and he said… he said you were having a chat with Neville, and I just wanted to make sure you knew that no way in hell is that lad a grass. There's just no way. I swear it."

"You swear it, do you now?"

Gerrity's tone was flat, almost uninterested.

Theo swallowed, managed to mutter, "Yes."

"I don't like taking people at their word, Theo. It's dangerous in my line of work. You get that, right? I remember you as a smart lad. You're still smart, aren't you? I'm guessing you are. You got my number anyway, so that's a point to you."

Theo didn't dare say anything.

"So this is what we'll do, right? Come and see me. Now. We'll have a little chat. You'll tell me what you think, I'll tell you what I know and we'll see if we can't figure this one out. I like you, Theo, and I like your work. So let's sort this. Come to Quinn's garage. It's on Finglas Road, near Power City. I'll be there in an hour."

He hung up even as Theo started to stammer his thanks.

He stared at the phone in his hands and slowly came back.

130

There was a robin singing somewhere in the willow's branches, trilling a waterfall of melody down to the ground. There were cars on the road behind him, children shouting in a playground somewhere. A plane rumbled overhead. The world was still here.

He willed himself to get up, to head to the bus stop, but he was suddenly overcome by lethargy. It was as though Gerrity had snuffed out the panicked energy that had got him this far. Theo knew he only had this one chance. He had to get up. He had to go to the garage. Move, you eejit, he whispered. Move. But it was like in his nightmares – he couldn't move his legs. He couldn't make his body do what it needed to do. This had happened before, over there, in a field full of butterflies. Then, Theo had known he had to run and keep running. He knew time was short. But he'd been paralysed with fear, just like he was now. And this time he had to run towards his fear.

"Theo?"

He spun round. Cara was watching him from the path, her head tilted. Dressed in jeans and a pale pink jumper and with her hair in a schoolgirl's ponytail, she looked younger than the terrified woman he'd seen huddled on the street just hours ago.

"Cara, howya?"

He started to get up but she was already coming over. She sat down beside him on the bench so that he felt like they'd always been here, together, under this willow.

He really should go.

"How's the head this morning then?" he asked.

"Not too good," she smiled sheepishly. "That's why I've come out. Mam was ranting about me not texting her last night – not that it stopped her from falling asleep. Not a chance. I could've been dead and she would've slept through it, until she was good and rested and could moan about how selfish I'd been to go and die on her."

Theo laughed and despite it all, or maybe because of it all, he let himself feel a moment of pure, inappropriate joy. *Cara*. It meant 'friend' in Irish. There was something about her that nudged the door to tomorrow a little wider. He didn't know what it was, other than a sense that this girl was made to shine and that he was one of the only ones to see it. It made him feel warm inside. He was special because he saw that she was special. That's what it was. That's why she made him smile: she was not what she seemed and she had let him in on her secret. It was a wisp of a thought, but it was enough right now.

"I'm sorry, Cara but I've gotta go. I'm heading over to Finglas, and I... I really need to make a move."

"Right so. I'll walk with ye to the bus if ye like. I was just getting some air, like I said, and the air that way is gonna be as good as any other."

They rose from the bench, sending the robin spiralling into the hedge, its song cut short.

"Actually, that's not really true. I was coming round to your house."

Cara was resolutely looking ahead of her.

"I got your address from Ronan. I was worried bout ye because... well, I heard Ronan on the phone. I wasn't trying to listen, like, but I was in the downstairs loo and I think he thought I was in me room and he was talking. Bout you. And yer friend Neville. He's the one Deirdre's Grace is going with, isn't he? That's what I've heard anyway."

She swivelled her eyes sideways but Theo couldn't meet them. He just nodded. Today, all the scorpions were coming out from under the rocks. He was knackered by it all.

"Anyway, I didn't hear everything but it sounded like Neville was in trouble and you were wanting to do something about it? I don't know who Ronan was talkin' to but I thought I'd just check in on you. Ronan looked a bit scared, like, after the call. He was sorta shakin', like, his hands were trembling. Is everything alright, Theo?"

"Not really. Not alright at all."

"Anything I can do? I don't mix with Ronan's crowd and I don't ask too many questions but I'm not a baby, Theo. I know what he's up to and he's let slip a few times since ye started at The Deep that you're involved too."

There was a silence.

"To be honest, I'm a bit surprised you're into the drugs, Theo. I didn't think you were like that. Like them."

"I'm not," Theo said.

He stopped dead and grabbed her hands, turning her to face him. He knew he looked like an eejit but he didn't care. He just needed her to really hear him.

"I've gotta run now but this should all be sorted in a few hours. I'm gonna get out of this and the last thing I want to do is get anyone else involved. So forget what you heard, Cara. Put it straight out of your head, right? Don't talk to Ronan bout this, don't talk to anyone. There's some bad people… yeah, including me… and there's a situation and we have to put it right. But when that's done, I'm getting out. The drugs, all of it, it's screwed my life up enough already. Precious just dumped me now because she found my stash."

Cara's eyebrows shot up but she didn't say anything. She just stood there, all eyes and flushed cheeks, and he couldn't tear himself away. He couldn't explain why he wanted to make her understand but, suddenly, it was dead important.

"I've messed everything up, Cara. I should never have got in this deep and I should never *never* have let Neville get involved. But this is where we are. I need to get Neville and then, I'm out."

He nearly said, 'I promise' but why would he say that to Cara?

Credit to her, she didn't pull away like he'd lost the plot.

"Will you let me know, later? Please?" she said. "I'll only worry otherwise."

She gave him her number, squeezed his hand and headed off down the road again, her ponytail swinging.

Theo looked after her for a minute, his brow creased. Then a bus creaked to a halt at the stop and he got on.

The garage was right on the road – a one-storey, flat-topped 70s relic with pumps in the forecourt and a sign advertising

133

sales and services. Indeed, thought Theo. What would you call the service he was looking for today? Mercy? Redemption? He wasn't sure where to go so he stood on the forecourt for a few minutes, hoping someone would come and get him. The place looked deserted. Was this one of Gerrity's? It must be, he supposed. Rumour was the big man had a string of garages and warehouses across the city – all part of the supply chain.

A bell above the door rang as he pushed it open. Behind the counter, in front of a wall display of cloths and sprays and Christmas tree air fresheners, there was a young woman with a pierced nose and a streak of purple in her hair. She raised her eyebrows at him but didn't say a thing.

"Howya, I'm looking for Gerrity?"

She gave him a look, slow and appraising. It made him wince.

"Wait here. I'll see if he's around. Who's askin'?"

"I'm Theo…"

He hesitated but he didn't think Gerrity even knew his second name and he definitely wouldn't care.

"Just Theo."

She nodded and sauntered out through a door beside the display. It clanged shut behind her.

What was he gonna say? How would he start? Should he have brought Tommy's knife? Like taking a fork to fight a grizzly.

Then Gerrity was at the door, the girl behind him.

"Come on in here."

Theo's feet moved forward despite the red lights flashing in his head. The girl pushed past and carefully closed the door behind him.

Gerrity was wearing a slate-grey suit and a pale blue tie. He looked every inch the slick businessman but he's in a two-bit garage, thought Theo, and because of that, he looks like what he is. You can fake the look but you can't fake where you are. Where you are is what you are.

Gerrity took Theo down a short corridor into a dingy office.

It had a desk, a swivel chair, a desktop computer, and one window. Through the dirty glass, Theo saw a puddle-stained yard with a car-wash machine, a few broken-down wagons and a big shed, its black hangar door pulled down like a blind. The black Merc parked off to the side must be Gerrity's. Big man, big car. Gerrity clearly didn't deal in subtle.

"So, Theo. You want to argue Neville's case. You don't think he grassed me up? Fair enough. To be brutally honest with you, I'm not that interested if he did or he didn't."

Theo didn't know what to say but he'd the feeling Gerrity didn't expect him to say much anyway. The guy was always on a soapbox. No conversations for him, just monologues. There was an arrogance there that was equal parts breath-taking and ordained.

Gerrity smiled and sat down behind the desk. Theo felt like a naughty student about to get ripped into by the world's most dangerous headmaster. Like every pupil ever anywhere, he shuffled nervously from foot to foot but just about managed to resist the urge to drop his head.

"I like you, Theo. I told you that the first time we met. But there's things you don't understand. So let me tell you." Gerrity leaned back, crossed his stubby legs at the ankle. "You're a survivor so I think you'll get me. You told me you're from Rwanda. We all know what went on there. Awful stuff, dreadful. But you escaped and you're here. Now, you know as well as I do that for you to survive, you had to have something, something that made you different from the others, the ones that died, God rest their souls. You had to have a drive, a hunger to go on. Am I right, lad?"

You haven't a bleedin' clue, thought Theo. He nodded. He wasn't here to explain the world to this eejit. All he wanted was to get Neville and get out.

"So, you should get me more than the others. I need to survive. And make no mistake, Theo, this is a dog-eat-dog world I'm in. I can't afford to go easy on people who cross me." Gerrity smiled, eyes crinkling, lips pulled back. "A lot of

135

people don't get this city, Theo. There's too much myth, too much legend, making us all misty-eyed. But *I* get this city. I get what makes Dubliners tick. Ah, yeah, they're great craic, they're the life and soul of the party, they love a drink, love a laugh. But underneath, they're a bunch of rebels. Always looking for the main chance, the opportunity to put one over on the system. And I'm part of the system now. I earn more than most government departments and that includes the tax office; I employ more people than some parts of the civil service; I am more deeply embedded in people's lives than the state. The state is so busy sorting out the financial apocalypse caused by its *own* rebels that it might as well not be here. So I'm the one they want to get one over on."

Theo dared to look out the window. A white van had driven in and parked by the Merc. A tall, dark-haired man got out, lit a cigarette and stood smoking. He looked familiar but Theo couldn't place him. He was dragging on his fag like his life depended on it.

Gerrity hadn't stopped. Reluctantly, Theo tuned back in.

"So if I'm the state, I need to have the same instruments at my disposal. I collect taxes, I make rules and if you break those rules, I need to deal out appropriate punishments. I wanted to make sure you understood that, Theo. I wanted you to see this from my point of view too. You're valuable to me and I don't want us to fall out about this."

"Look, I appreciate the learning an' all." Theo tried to keep the sarcasm out of his voice but Gerrity's lips tightened. "But I just want to get Neville and get out of your way. You're talking about punishment but if you're the state, like you're saying, then where's your justice? Neville never grassed and whoever told you he did is lying to you."

"I don't think you've been listening, Theo. It doesn't *matter* whether Neville snitched or not. What matters is that people think he did. And I can't have that. I'm only as strong as the fear I create. There's a line as long as your arm of wannabes itching to take my place and the same again who'd shop me to the cops tomorrow. So for me to stay on top, I can't let people think I'm going soft. Can I?"

Theo said nothing, but his heart was racing now.

"Anyway, enough talking. I've things to do and I'm sure you do too."

Now, he was the one layering on the sarcasm. Gerrity rose and walked to the door. He didn't say anything else so Theo just followed him, hating this role of supplicant. They went outside into the yard. The smoker was still there. He nodded at Gerrity and opened the back door of the Merc. Theo saw a young lad in a faded denim jacket in the driver's seat. Gerrity got in and the other man – who Theo now *knew* he had seen before but where? – got into the van and drove out the back gate. What the fuck was going on?

He grabbed the door before Gerrity could pull it shut. To give him his due, Gerrity didn't even flinch.

"I came for Neville, not for a speech, Gerrity. So where the fuck is he?"

Gerrity had the gall to smile and that sick teeth-baring smirk would haunt Theo.

"You're a good friend, I'll say that for you. He's waiting for you – that's part of the reason you're here. Go back out the front, turn right onto the main road, then second right. There's a small park there in front of the church. He's there. I'm sure he'll be only delighted to see you."

He pulled on the door, yanking it out of Theo's hand.

"Don't call me again, Theo. That number won't work and I'll make damn sure to impress on young Michael there that I don't want him giving you any more numbers."

Theo didn't wait to see him leave. He sped through the garage, back onto the main road, and broke into a run. By the time he got to the park, his face was dripping with sweat and somewhere deep inside, beneath the thumping of his heart and the blood rushing in his ears, he felt that nameless dread that seemed to rise from his feet whenever he ran. Even today.

He stopped in front of the church, swivelling his head

frantically, taking in the flat green space, the handful of stunted trees. There was a bench in the far corner and a figure was slumped on it. Theo broke into a run again but when he was nearly there, he found himself slowing down. Because he'd seen Neville's camouflage Converse under the seat and now he heard the low moaning. It wasn't sobbing, it wasn't crying, it was just a low one-note lament. I can't do this, he thought. I can't see any more broken people.

A memory swam to the surface but just as it was about to break the water, it fell away. It was the sound, he'd heard that sound before. Was it Shema? It didn't sound like Shema, it sounded like his father but it couldn't have been. More tricks.

He rounded the bench slowly.

He couldn't see his friend's face. His head was buried in his jacket and sunk into his chest. But he could see his hand, held palm upwards on his knees. Theo retched. Neville's right hand had been reduced to mush – battered, broken. They must've used a hammer and in the middle of the palm, there was a red, gaping hole.

"Jesus."

He sat gingerly on the bench. He didn't know what to do. Neville didn't even seem to know he was there. Theo touched his shoulder.

"Alright, Nev?"

Finally, Neville raised his head. His right eye was swollen shut, there were round burn marks on his broad forehead and on his cheeks, and his nose was bloodied and broken. Through his swollen lips came that awful sound. It was endless. It filled the world.

Theo realised what the sound reminded him of. Neville was moaning the low *ochón* of the professional grief-singers of old Ireland. Keening from *caoineadh*, the Irish for 'to cry'. It was meant to help mourners grieve at a time when life was slow enough to stop the clocks when someone died. Máistear Burke had played them an old example, saying the tradition had died out in the 1950s. But here on this bench, more than half a century later, it'd been resurrected.

"Ah fuck, Neville."

There was nothing else to say. Tears ran down Theo's cheeks and he put an arm around Neville's shivering shoulders. With the other hand, he pulled out his mobile. He called a cab.

"We're going to the hospital. They'll fix you up, Neville. They'll... you'll be alright, now."

Neville, locked in his pain, didn't react. But Theo knew that if his friend could speak, he would tell him he was talking shite. Nothing would be alright now. How could it be?

CHAPTER TEN

Deirdre's phone bleeped.

"Who's that?"

Fergal was sprawled on the sofa, watching the news. He'd barely said a word since he came in this afternoon, racing the van into the drive so fast it made her fear the worst. But he hadn't been drinking. He stormed past her without a word and went straight upstairs. She heard the shower start and then he must've had a nap because he didn't come down again until they were having their tea after she got back from Theo's shift. She'd been let go early – Des said good weather was always bad for business, although in his typically glum way, he'd said rain was no picnic either.

She hadn't dared ask Fergal where he'd been all morning. She picked her phone from the coffee table.

Got him he's bad at the hospital.

She blanked the screen, pressed the mute button and put the phone down carefully.

"Just Dad. Asking how we are."

"Are ye not going to answer him, then? Or is that too difficult a question for ye?"

Deirdre ignored the sarcasm. No job but listen to the mouth on him.

"Nah, I might call him in a while. You goin' out tonight?"

"With what?"

Fergal spat the words at her. Then he sighed like a man who has seen his own future and his hand reached towards her

140

across the sofa. She was huddled in the corner, knees drawn up. She could well imagine what the body language gurus would say. And they wouldn't be wrong. She looked at the hand, lying there, fingers outstretched towards her. It was the same hand that hit her so why did it make her feel this way?

"Sorry, love. I'm not meself. I've a lot on my mind," he breathed.

Deirdre stretched her hand out to meet his or rather it felt like her hand did it off its own bat. Their fingers laced together easily, as they had been doing for years and she automatically began to stroke the base of his thumb with her own thumb, as she had always done. Maybe there was still something to hold onto. I'm like a teenager, she thought, shy and scared. Like I was when we met, but Jesus, the reasons have changed.

Fergal sighed again. He had closed his eyes, head thrown back. It'd been a while since she had looked at him straight on, instead of furtively squinting so as not to catch his eye. Since the night he pounded her, she had avoided looking directly at him, as though he was a too-bright sun. He apologised the next day, of course. He'd come into the sitting room where Grace had tucked her in, begging her to forgive him and blaming stress. She wanted to scream: "Stress, you animal? We're all bloody stressed. We're all shit-scared because you, *you*, lost your job and then *you* come in here and beat me like a dog."

But the scream stayed at the back of her throat. And when he knelt by her side as she lay still curled on the couch and put his head by hers, she reached up and stroked his hair. She couldn't help herself.

"Please, Fergal. You can't do this. The kids… They can't see this. It'll wreck their heads. Grace is raging but scared too, and the boys… they're frightened too now but what if they grow up to think this is normal? D'you want that? Is that what we wanted when we said we'd start a family?"

His shoulders started to shake.

"I'm sorry. I love ye, I love the kids. It's just… I feel so angry, so fuckin' useless. What's the point, ye know? I worked hard, I was doing well, and then it's all just taken away. How am I supposed to stay on the right path when someone has a gun to me head? I ask you."

He'd always been a bit soft, Deirdre thought even as she whispered comfort. He'd always thought the world owed him something. That gave him confidence when he was younger, provided him with the swagger that had attracted her, but the chip on his shoulder hadn't aged well. It made him sound pathetic.

"What'm I supposed to do, Dee? And, I know, I know, I should go easy on the drink. It makes everything worse. Makes me do things I don't mean to."

"You'd no drink taken last night, Fergal."

He didn't say anything to that, just buried his face further into the sofa. She pitied him and she despised him and she loved him all at once. And how could you hold all that in your heart without it bursting at the seams?

After that day, he *did* make an effort. He couldn't totally shut off whatever rage was eating him up though. He still roared so that Kevin stayed late in his room in the mornings, only edging nervously down the stairs once he was sure the van had gone. Conor was barely ever at home, coming back only to sleep and rarely crossing paths with his dad. Grace was busy with her exams, and after that dreadful two weeks of doors slamming, tears and sullen regrets, she got a job at the Liffey Valley shopping centre, as she'd promised. She also spent a lot of time with Neville, though God knows where. Deirdre couldn't fathom why her daughter was so taken with that boy but she supposed he must've something special because Grace wasn't stupid. Then again, she'd not thought herself stupid as a girl either and look how that had turned out.

These days, the house was so tense – doors solidly closed, faces averted, silence like treacle – that Deirdre was glad to get out and go to the restaurant, even though the work was getting harder and the hours longer as the summer rush began.

After he was laid off, Fergal had crashed into a kind of depression, sometimes sleeping for hours during the day. But he'd mostly kept his fists to himself. He went to the pub less but returned more pissed than before so when he did go after her, he only managed a few weak slaps before collapsing onto the sofa, or the floor. Nothing she couldn't handle.

Then he'd started going out most days around midday, returning around tea-time or later. She'd no idea where he was, and she wasn't about to ask. Eventually, last week, he'd said he got some casual work driving for some big import company. He didn't tell her the name and she didn't care. At least he was earning again, though money was still tight. He didn't have to work every day though, so sometimes he stayed in bed or slouched on the sofa, watching Formula One or football. On those days, he was like a rain-cloud pissing on their lives. Or like her dad had been just after her mam died. It must be true then, she'd thought: women really do marry their fathers. We're our own worst enemies in the end.

When Fergal was late coming home, she made herself scarce, sometimes racing up the stairs as soon as she heard the van on the gravel. She'd already be in her pyjamas so all she had to do was jump under the covers and fake sleep. If he didn't find her downstairs, he rarely came looking, instead switching on the telly and slumping onto the sofa, where she'd find him in the morning. Sometimes, he'd be mad then.

"You couldn't have got me a blanket? I'm shaggin' freezing."

She would apologise and bring him tea. Grace watched warily from the corners, a silent lady justice.

Deirdre dared a crooked glance at her phone. There were no other messages.

"Right, I'm going to go up and lie down." Fergal heaved himself off the sofa. "I'm absolutely knackered."

He left, running his hand along her arm as he passed. Deirdre closed her eyes for a moment as the door shut behind him. *He* was knackered? She was absolutely wiped. How long could she keep swinging between tenderness and hate? Was this it? Was she going to be held hostage by these feelings for the rest of her life? That's what Grace didn't get. Deirdre had no other future. Everyone only had the one, in the end. It might not be as simple as making your bed and then sleeping in it, but mostly there were no other bleedin' beds.

She took her phone and walked quietly to the kitchen. She stopped at the bottom of the stairs. She could just see the door of their bedroom. It was shut. He'd be asleep or playing that bloody Angry Birds on his phone. She'd snorted the other day when he told her what he was doing. It was, given everything, hilarious, but he didn't get it, and that made it even funnier so that she left him scowling over the jingle-jangle of his game while she giggled herself down the stairs. She went through to the kitchen and out the back door into the tiny garden, just a single row of paving stones and a handkerchief of yellowing grass. She went to the very edge by the paint-streaked fence and dialled Theo.

No answer but after she hung up a text lit up the screen.

Can't talk in here. Call u back.

It was still warm though the colours were beginning to fade as dusk cast her veil over the shabby gardens and crowded houses. Deirdre always liked the end of the day. There was a soft beauty in it, a kind of forgiveness of light. Swallows darted above her head. She could hear some kids out on the grass in the middle of the estate, playing football. That'd be where Kevin was. Conor was probably down at the slots with his friends and Grace was working. She'd be back soon. Unless Theo had told her. He might've done if Neville was being kept in for whatever they'd done to the poor lad. She shivered. If the last few days had taught her anything, it was that you never really knew what the bloody kids were up to. She wondered if all the mothers and fathers in all the houses around her were thinking the same, wondering where the children were or feeling that slight unease that started as soon as they were able to leave the house alone and that lasted, she supposed, until you drew your last breath. Maybe all those other parents were also in their gardens, making sneaky phone calls. She couldn't see over the hedge around her little patch to know.

Her phone rang.

"Theo, how is he?"

"He's stable now. I'm having to make myself fairly scarce cos I think the doctor is suspicious. He might even call the Gardaí. I told him it was an accident on a building site but he doesn't believe me. It's a crap story, I know, but I couldn't think of anything else on the spot, like. There's a nurse – she's a right sharp one. She's already had a go at me, telling me to cop on and give up the guys that did it. But sure, I don't know who exactly it was."

The words came in a rush.

"How badly is he hurt, Theo?" Deirdre dropped her voice. Theo sounded like he was in shock. She'd seen it before when she worked in A&E. She'd have to keep him calm, ignore the blood rushing in her ears.

There was a pause. She could hear a muffled siren behind him and then a clattering, like something falling from a vending machine.

"They wrecked his hand, Deirdre. Hammered a nail into his palm. He's got fag burns on his face and he's been bashed up pretty bad around the head too. Thank Christ, he's out cold now. They gave him massive painkillers and they've strapped his hand up but he looks bad."

"Have you told his parents? You'll have to call them, Theo."

"I know. I'm gonna do that now."

Deirdre saw a movement in the kitchen. Grace was home. She was standing at the table, putting her flowered rucksack down and frowning at her phone. She suddenly clocked Deirdre and smiled. You poor girl, Deirdre thought.

"I'll tell Grace now. She'll want to come down to him and I won't be able to stop her. I can't leave because Fergal is asleep upstairs and Kevin'll be home any minute, so can you meet her there, Theo? Did you take him to the Mater?"

"Yeah, we're in A&E. I'll wait here until she comes. She can text me when she gets here. Don't tell her too much, Deirdre. No need for her to know every little detail. It'll be obvious soon enough and I've a feeling Nev won't want her to know everything. It should probably come from him anyway."

"Okay, I've gotta go. She's just come in from work."

"Deirdre?"

"Yeah?"

"Thanks, for Gerrity's number. If they didn't know I was coming, I dunno if they would've stopped. I mean, they probably weren't going to kill him but I dunno."

Even though she knew well what Gerrity was, Deirdre realised she was shaking. She looked again at Grace who was coming to the back door. She wanted to run to her and bubble-wrap herself around her so that she couldn't get hurt by anything ever again. How could she have let Gerrity's sick world crash into her own? She'd taken her eye off the ball, or like every parent ever, she thought the ball game was only for other people.

"Did Gerrity do this himself, d'you think?" she asked. For some reason, she needed to know.

"Not himself," Theo said. "Nah, he wouldn't get his hands dirty like that. His lads did it. I saw one, but…"

"Theo, you still there? I think you cut out."

The pause extended so that Deirdre could hear the swallows' electrical chirping above her head.

"Theo?"

"I'm still here. Sorry Deirdre, gotta go."

He sounded different now, wary. Maybe there was someone listening?

"Tell Grace to text me from reception and I'll come and get her."

He hung up.

When Deirdre turned around, Grace was standing on the paving stones.

"C'mere, love. I've to tell you something."

"You alright, Mam? Why're ye out here?"

"I didn't want to wake your Dad. He's gone to bed. Listen, love, I've some bad news. Neville's… well, he's had an accident. It's alright, he's grand, but he's in the Mater. Theo's with him."

For a moment, Grace just stood there, her forehead creased, like she hadn't quite understood. And she hadn't yet because in her world, at her age, accidents were just that, bumps in a road that looked so long no one could ever imagine its end.

"What happened? I've been texting him since this morning and calling but there was no answer. I thought he was just… well, sometimes he can go quiet for a few hours, even a day or two. What kind of accident?"

Looking at her daughter standing before her, all rounded eyes like the toddler she was just a heartbeat ago, Deirdre felt like a child herself. She desperately wanted her own mother. She would know what to do, what to say. I'm still only learning, she thought. And no one ever taught me this.

"I think he was beaten up. His hand is… pretty messed up."

"Why? Who would do that? Sure, Neville never hurt a fly, Mam."

Deirdre just shook her head. Grace had to learn this lesson herself: sometimes there were just no reasons and sometimes the reasons didn't matter at all.

Grace started crying. Deirdre hugged her tight and for once, her statuesque woman-daughter didn't resist. She didn't ask any more questions either and so Deirdre knew she had some idea of what Neville was up to, some idea of who might've done this. But time enough to talk about that later. You always needed more time.

"But he has beautiful hands, Mam. Really lovely hands," Grace sobbed into her mother's shoulder.

They stood there, locked together as excited shouts and angry jeers came to them on the wind from the football game. Looking up beyond her daughter's bowed head, Deirdre saw a pale moon rising, like it couldn't care less.

Neville was released three days later. He went home to his parents and Deirdre could only imagine that conversation. Grace went round to see him a couple of times. They let her up to his room but she said they gave her the dirty eye. They probably thought she was part of the dark world that Neville had – in their minds at least – innocently blundered into. Grace didn't press Neville on what he'd told them. In fact, they didn't really talk about what had happened at all, at least not about the whys and hows. He told her what the doctors had said but he talked about his injuries as though they had surged up out of nowhere. Like a disease that just chose him instead of all the other lads. When Grace came down from his room, Neville's mother, a thin woman with dark hair, greying at the roots and sides, and eyes deep in her skull, asked her: "Do you know who did this?"

Grace mumbled no. The mother didn't take her eyes off hers.

"It's just we realise we know so little about what exactly he was doing and who he was doing it with. We don't know where to start. I mean, clearly, there was some mistake but then, he must've had something to do with... whoever did this? I mean, they wouldn't just do it to a stranger, would they?" Her voice broke and she raised her hand to rub her forehead like she was hoping she could massage some hidden knowledge into life. "Sorry, it's just so bewildering. I didn't even know about you."

It was a plea and an accusation and Grace had no idea what to do with it. So she said her goodbyes.

At home, she told Deirdre that Neville was getting better. There'd been some kind of infection in the nail wound at first but that had been fixed and now he just had to wait for the bones to heal and the scars to fade. They told him he'd probably have problems with arthritis when he got older but that he should regain most of the use of the hand.

"He's not in bed or anything," she told Deirdre. "He just stays in his room. He can't do much but he's reading and listening to music, and he... he doesn't seem that bothered."

Deirdre looked up from the potatoes she was peeling.

"That's a funny thing to say, and you don't seem that sure about it either, love?"

"It's just... well, I suppose I expected him to be angry or scared or something. But he just sits there, like nothing happened. He still laughs and makes jokes and all but I feel like I'm not gettin' him. Like there's something I should ask him, some important question, but I dunno what it is. If I could just figure out the right thing to ask, I feel like he'd tell me what's really going on." Grace stared morosely into the cup of tea she was nursing at the table. "I'm not making any sense, am I? It's just, like, for the first time, I feel too young for him."

She had the same look about her as she did when she was twelve or thirteen and she used to sit at the very same table after coming in from school, going on about girls who whispered when she came by, or ran off to lunch ahead of her, casting unfathomable looks behind them.

She'd grown up so fast, Deirdre thought now, and she'd crashed into the world the same way every young woman had to. There could be no fixing things with lollipops and stickers now, no protecting with kneepads and helmets, just constantly bearing witness. That was the job, right? She'd take what she could get, always.

Deirdre put down the potato, rubbed her hands on the tea towel, and came and sat at the table.

"He'll get better, love. And I don't just mean his hand. He's had an awful shock and I suppose it'd make you look at your life and what you're doing. It'll take him a while to figure it all out. Is he going back to college when he's better?"

"I don't know, Mam. He won't talk about that. He just

goes on about whatever he's reading. This week, it's *The Girl with the Dragon Tattoo,* you know it's the first book in this series that everyone is talkin' about. She's like a detective, but she's kinda bad too, and you don't really know where she came from."

"Have you read it, love?"

"Nah, but I think I will. He tells me bits, it sounds good but really complicated. He has my head in a twist with it. But maybe if I read it, I'll have a better idea of what he's thinkin'? Do you think that could work, Mam?"

Grace's hope was like a hammer on some soft part of her brain.

"Maybe. But, Grace love, he might not know what he's feeling himself." Deirdre took one of her daughter's hands in hers. "He's had a terrible experience. The pain alone. And he must've been terrified, and maybe he still is. So give him some time. He won't be himself for a while. But if," she hurried on, seeing her daughter's face tense, "if *you* think he's worth it, then you stick with him. He needs someone to be a normal friend to him now. So if that's what you want to do, do it, but don't think it'll be easy. He'll be a mess, inside and out, for a while."

Grace didn't say anything but she squeezed Deirdre's hand back – two squeezes, a pause, and then one more. Deirdre played it back to her and smiled.

After Grace, Kevin and herself had dinner – Fergal was out and Conor had said he would eat at his friend's – Deirdre put on her denim jacket and trainers. She popped her head into the sitting room where Grace and Kevin were watching *Fair City*.

"I'm just running out to see Pauline for a quick chat. I'll be back in an hour. Will ye be alright?"

Grace just rolled her eyes. Kevin slithered his gaze from the screen for the briefest of seconds to give her a glazed smile. At least some things were normal, she thought as she closed the door behind her.

It was a breezy evening. She was meeting Pauline down

where the River Liffey ran along the fields behind the estate. There was a little spot there with a bench on the bank, hidden behind some trees so that no nosey parkers could be watching you. They'd stumbled on it years ago when Pauline used to come over from Finglas to visit, and after she moved here, it became their go-to place whenever they wanted to have a quick chat, a quick cry, or a quick rant. It had been well used over the years.

Pauline was already sitting on the bench.

"Hey, Pauline. So where's the fire? Is something wrong?"

Her friend's face was paler than usual and some of her fizz was missing but then she'd not been herself since the whole Neville thing. Deirdre had had to tell her what was going on when she went looking for Gerrity's number but at first, Pauline wouldn't even consider the idea that Neville could be seriously hurt.

"He's my cousin, Dee. Alright, he's a dealer, but kidnapping? I just can't believe it."

Deirdre had pressed her and, finally, Pauline'd got her phone and dialled the number she had for Gerrity, insisting that she'd find out what was going on herself. But the number didn't work and so she'd gone, none too happily, to ask Michael, who was on a rare visit home and playing one of those shooting games on the Xbox in the living room. Deirdre stood at the door, hating herself. It was bad enough that Pauline had to face off with Michael, who was ranting that he couldn't give the number to any eejit off the street, but in doing so, she was also admitting to her friend that she knew all along what was really going on. Friends weren't always supposed to tell you the truth, Deirdre thought. Sometimes you needed them more to help keep your fantasies alive. Deirdre wouldn't be able to do that for Pauline any more.

When Michael stuffed a piece of paper with the number on it into Deirdre's hand, he'd grabbed her wrist hard. There was a new venom in his sullen eyes.

"I spose ye think you're all that now," he'd whispered.

"Won't last. He's a blow-in, hasn't got what it takes. This is no place for part-timers and ye can tell him I said so."

She'd had no idea what he was talking about but Michael was always shooting his mouth off and she hadn't had time then to follow it up. Pauline hadn't heard the rant. She'd stomped off after the initial showdown.

Now Pauline handed Deirdre a Styrofoam cup.

"Ah, thanks love. I could use a real coffee. So tell me, what's bothering you? Is Michael in trouble again?" She had a horrible thought. "He's not gone missing, has he?"

God knows, Deirdre didn't like the little shit but she wouldn't wish what happened to Neville on her worst enemy. Now that she knew exactly how close Michael and Gerrity were, she was even more terrified, mostly for Pauline though. No good was gonna come out of this and Pauline had suffered enough already. There was so much in the papers these days about drug gangs and feuds and shootings. Her father had been ranting about it only the other day when another body turned up in an alleyway on the south side of the city: some teenager killed as revenge for another lad shot last month.

"Wrecking the country, the little scuts," her father had said on the phone. "We'd have driven them out, no doubt. Sure, we did it many times, north and south."

She'd found his fury both reassuring and exhausting. Would people in this place never learn to just live?

"Nah, it's not Michael," Pauline said, slowly. "He's gone and told me something. About what happened to Neville. I think he wanted me to tell ye cos he wants to hurt ye. I'm sorry, Dee, that boy hates you something rotten. I dunno why. I didn't bring him up to be like that, but then, half the time even I don't know who he is." She stopped, shook her head, and then smiled. "D'ye remember when he was small and we brought him and Grace down here in the summer and they paddled in the water, splashing each other, and throwing stones into the pools? And then one time, d'ye remember, he lay down in the water, and pretended to swim, his little legs

152

going up-and-down and his fat arms splashing water all over his face, and he was laughing so much."

Deirdre did remember. It'd been a lovely day, Grace in a pink bathing suit with a polar bear on it, her toddler curls all wild above her head. When had she lost the curls? Must've been around five or six because she had straight hair when she made her Holy Communion. Deirdre remembered struggling to plait it. "Ow, Mam, you're hurting me!"

She'd been so mad but in the end, she looked lovely and when she saw herself in the mirror, with the veil on top, she'd given her mother a big hug, her little hands reaching around Deirdre's waist.

"Anyway, Michael says... he says, he knows who beat up Neville. Swears it wasn't him and I want to believe him, Dee. Okay, he's mixed up with Gerrity – I knew *that* all along but didn't want to admit it – but I don't think he'd hurt anyone. Hasn't the stomach for it. And he was with me most of that day. You saw him yerself."

Deirdre nodded but she wondered if any mother ever could know for sure what her kid might have the stomach for. It was always the cry, wasn't it? "He couldn't have done it, he was a lovely boy." They were all lovely little boys and girls but that was no guarantee of anything. And that was the tragedy of it.

"So who was it?" she said. "Not that we can do anything about it, can we? We can't exactly go to the guards. They wouldn't be interested. They'd be only too delighted to know the drug lads are going after each other. Saves them some work."

"It's not that," Pauline said quietly. "I know we can't do nothing, but... well, Michael says Fergal was there."

Deirdre nearly dropped her coffee.

"Fergal? What would he be doing there?"

"Michael says he works for Gerrity now, driving, what's he call it, oh yeah, driving the product. It's been a couple of weeks, he says, and Gerrity often gets new lads to do the punishments. That's what he called it, a punishment. To see if they're up to it, a kind of test, I s'pose."

Pauline blurted it all out, fast, as if the words had been piling up painfully behind her teeth.

"Jesus, I'd no idea Michael was in so deep. I'm so sorry, Dee."

"Fergal?"

Deirdre knew she sounded like a fool, repeating the word over and over but she couldn't help it. She felt dizzy suddenly. She put her coffee down on the bench and stood up. She paced up and down in front of her friend, who was reaching for another cigarette.

"Gimme one of those."

"Ah, Dee. Sure, you've given up for years now. Ye don't want to start again."

"Just gimme a fecking fag, Pauline."

She walked down to the bank of the river, her head reeling. She felt sick, partly from the nicotine after all these years but mostly because she had no idea what was happening to her life. She bent over her knees, retched, but nothing came. After a minute, she came back to the bench, sat down again, dropped the cigarette, and watched Pauline's black boot grind it out in the grass. Her friend put her hand on her shoulder.

"I'm sorry, Dee. I had to tell ye. Not cos Michael wanted it but you had to know."

"Of course, you did the right thing," Deirdre said, taking Pauline's hand and looking straight into her face. "I should've known it was something dodgy. He's got no fixed schedule, sleeps for hours some days, he's out at night, but not always drinking. I'm an eejit, Pauline. I should've known."

"Sure, we don't let ourselves know what we can't handle," Pauline said and her eyes were red and watery. "Why would we? We can't change this shit so we might as well ignore it as best we can. Like I told ye, I've been doin' it for years, Dee."

She paused, took a breath, then got up to go, checking her watch.

154

"I've got to run, but Dee, I just want to say I'm so sorry. I feel like this is all my fault. This is my family. Gerrity is *my* cousin, Michael's *my* son."

"Don't be daft, Pauline. This is not on you. Fergal is old enough to know better. I just can't…" Deirdre shook her head again. Jesus, could she find no better reaction?

Pauline was still standing there. "D'ye think he knew it was Grace's boyfriend? Did he know she was seeing Neville?" she said finally. "I know Michael didn't. He thought you wanted the number for Fergal."

Deirdre shook her head and she felt her stomach churning again. She'd forgotten that part. She was so focused on the act, she couldn't get past it. But of course, there was this too.

"He might not've," she said, getting up herself but slowly like a granny in a bus shelter. God, she felt so old. "She's not been talking to him for a while now, not since, you know, that night. I haven't told him anything other than the fact that she's going out with an older lad. I don't think I ever even told him his name. Sure, he's never been that interested, and then, after he was laid off, he was that down he didn't speak to any one of us much."

They fell silent. Deirdre watched the water drifting along in front of her. The water would keep running, the sun would keep shining and the rain would keep falling on everyone.

She had another thought and she couldn't believe it hadn't come immediately. "But you know what, Pauline? He might not have known at the time but he damn well knows now. He knows Grace's boyfriend was in hospital, he's heard me talking to her about his injuries. He's sat there like a stone. Not a world out of him. It's like… I have no idea who he is."

Pauline pulled her into a hug.

"I knew he was violent, Pauline, we all knew, but I thought… I thought it was just me. I didn't think he'd hurt someone else, I swear to God. I thought it was just *me*, Pauline."

155

CHAPTER ELEVEN

Theo slowed his stride to match Neville's. They were cruising through Stephen's Green on one of those rare summer days that could make Dublin feel almost Continental. Just as a particular kind of light, in just the right place, maybe catching the eyes or the hair, can make a plain girl shine, the early August sun transformed the city, gilding what MacNeice called the "grey stone, grey water, and brick upon grey brick." The line always resonated for Theo, marking the difference between Dublin and that place of explosive colours that was his first home. The park was packed with kids weaving wildly on scooters, old lads gossiping on benches in the shade, and office workers sprawled on the grass, jackets and shoes cast off, heads thrown back as they greedily sucked up the lunchtime sun.

They came to the pond.

"Let's sit down for a second," Neville said. "It's fierce hot. Look, there's a bench over there."

It had been a few weeks since the beating. Neville's hand was healing and the bruising on his face was almost gone but Theo knew his friend was nowhere near better. There was something amiss in his slow stride, in the hands that trembled like autumn leaves when he lit his fag, and in the emptiness of his eyes. He wasn't even angry, which he'd every right to be.

He'd never snitched, of course. The whole thing was a classic string of cock-ups: Neville had given some student friends the last of his product for a rave they were going to.

They were supposed to pay him after but of course by then they were skint. Then he discovered he'd left no coke for himself, so he'd gone down to one of the open markets and was picked up by the cops. Luckily, his pockets were still empty so they had to let him go but some tosser must've seen him and told Gerrity. That plus the fact that he had no coke and no money was enough. Theo nearly lost the block at the stupidity of it but Neville just shrugged his shoulders, like the beating had happened to someone else. He barely went out now and hadn't said for sure whether he was going to go back to college in September for his final year. Some kind of spark had been extinguished and it made Theo mad. Mostly with himself.

He'd wanted to confront Michael afterwards. To be honest, he wanted to pound his stupid face to a pulp but he knew that'd be too easy – it wasn't really Michael's fault and there was no way he could get to Gerrity. There would be no revenge there, no feel-good resolution. No point kidding himself with fantasies of bumping into Gerrity in a dark alley and smashing his fake smile into the back of his throat. Wasn't going to happen.

Instead, he'd gone to the dingy apartment in Ballyfermot where he always made his payments, thrown the remaining bags of coke in Michael's face, and said he'd never work for Gerrity again. Michael must've known something like that'd happen but he ranted and cajoled and threatened anyway. It didn't matter. Theo was done. It was as though some kind of internal clock had started ticking again as he sat on that bench near Finglas Road, listening to Neville's keening. He'd finally realised how far his life was spinning out of control, and how stupid he'd been to let it get to this point. Or maybe he just hadn't cared enough. In any case, he had to look after his friend now. It was his turn to be the guardian.

Neville was staring out over the water where seagulls were bobbing beside three elegant swans that looked pissed off at having to share with such bowsies.

"So, Michael just let you go?" he asked.

Theo had been filling Neville in as they'd walked around the park. This was the first time they'd been alone together since what Neville insisted on calling The Smashing.

"You'd want to watch out, Theo. Those guys could just as well come after you. You know things."

Theo thought back to the meeting on Ha'penny Bridge when he'd said the same himself, only to be mocked by Michael.

"Nah, I've nothing on them and they know it. In any case, I'm moving out from my flat tomorrow. Going to stay at the old place with Cath for a while, at least 'til I figure out what to do next."

"Wait, she's still in Clontarf?"

"Yeah, still living in Jim and Sheila's place. Remember I told you she'd some kind of breakdown after she came back from Kenya a couple of years ago? She got out of the whole charity business then. Anyways, she says she's delighted to put me up for a while. I didn't tell her anything. She'd only go telling Jim and Sheila and I don't need them on my case as well."

They sat in silence for a while. Theo had the strongest notion that Neville had something to tell him. He kept pushing his hair back from his forehead and he always did that when he was nervous.

"I'm thinking of going away myself for a while. I might head over to London to spend a few weeks with my dad's brother," Neville said after a while.

Theo was surprised and then immediately not. It made perfect sense. Neville should absolutely get the hell away for a few weeks. Gerrity had made it clear his lads would have no truck with Neville any more – he was out of the game for good – but a bit of distance would be no bad thing at all.

"That's a grand idea," he said. "Yeah, bang on. You'll be able to get well lost there for a while. But you'll come back for college?"

Neville grunted. It wasn't clear if he was saying yes or no. Theo decided not to push it. Neville had his parents to go on about that. Not really any of his business either, though it'd be a shame if Neville dropped out. *He* still had a real chance to turn things around. The world would be his oyster once he had his degree, smart lad like him.

"Have you told Grace? Or is she going over with you, for a holiday, like?"

Neville dropped his head and rubbed his good hand over the plaster covering the other one.

"Nah, I haven't told her yet and I'm not taking her. She's got a summer job now and, to be honest, I don't think I'm that good for her at the moment." He looked at Theo. "I don't know what to say to her, Theo. She comes over and I tell her what I'm doing, what I'm reading or the films I've watched, but I can tell she wants me to talk about all this." He waved his plastered hand in front of his face. "But sure, what am I going to tell her? I can't tell her how... I mean, what it was like. To be honest, I'm trying *not* to remember. The last thing I need is to be rehashing the whole thing. I know that I blacked out a fair few times. The lads who did it were wearing balaclavas so I can't say who they were. I mean they were definitely Gerrity's lads. He was there when they took me from the car and chucked me in the room, wherever it was. Inside some kind of garage, I think. At least it stank of oil and paint. But then when they took me out again to... well, to do this... I didn't see him. He might've been there but in the shadows. There wasn't hardly any light. Except for over the table where they had the hammer."

Theo didn't say anything. He'd heard it all before and Neville had made it clear he didn't want any questions asked. He'd not yet figured out what to do with his sudden realisation, while talking on the phone to Deirdre the day he found Neville, that Fergal was the guy he saw in the garage yard. The face had niggled at him for hours but it was only when he was talking to her from the hospital that he remembered the photo she'd shown him one day at the restaurant. He remembered the man in the photo had been smiling, not a bother on him, but it was definitely the same guy.

Theo hadn't said a word to anyone about Fergal, not because he thought he could use the information one day, though maybe that might be a possibility, but mainly because he really didn't know who to tell. He didn't know anything for sure, anyhow, only that somehow Fergal was mixed up in the whole thing. In any case, he hadn't seen Deirdre since she'd given him Gerrity's number. He'd ditched the job at The Deep and was living off his savings now. Des had been furious. Theo felt bad but what could he do? He'd shrugged apologetically, collected his last few euros in a little brown envelope, and left. It wasn't that he really believed Michael and the gang would be looking for him but, if they were, there was no reason to make it any easier than it already was. A fresh start, that's what he needed.

He couldn't tell Neville about Fergal and, anyways, Neville didn't seem to want to know. He just wanted to forget the whole sorry business. Grace could never know. That was for sure. He'd already got the sense from Deirdre that the girl was spitting daggers at her father because of the way he treated her mam. If she found out what he'd done to Neville, Christ knew what she'd do. Putting a spanner in Fergal's relationship with his daughter might seem like the perfect revenge but it would be a mean-spirited act. Theo was fed up of all the pain. He'd had enough.

So he just carried what he knew around like a stone in his pocket, alongside the memory of his father killing Shema. He couldn't keep collecting these things. They'd crush him.

His phone rang. It was Jim. He didn't need this now but fair enough: they hadn't spoken in a while. Jim had every right to be calling him and he'd no right to refuse to talk.

"Gotta take this, Nev. It's Jim. You going to be alright here for a minute?"

Neville nodded.

Theo walked away from the bench, towards the pond.

"Howya, Jim? Everything okay?"

"Hello, Theo. Yes, everything's fine, fine. Just wanted to check in with you."

There was a short pause.

"Cath said you were moving in with her for a while but she didn't say why. So we were just wanting to see if everything was alright, like? You're not in any trouble now, are you?"

A little girl wearing a t-shirt with a picture of a unicorn was feeding the ducks across from Theo but it was mostly the seagulls that were getting the bread, diving in to snatch the crumbs before they even hit the water. The girl was getting angry. She flung the bread as far out as she could but those screeching gulls weren't to be thwarted and the ducks weren't getting much. Good life lesson, Theo thought. You can't always get what you want, little one, and the noisiest, baddest buggers usually get the upper hand.

"Ah yeah, everything's grand. I'm just a bit short of cash this month. I meant to tell you but the furniture store out on the Dublin Road closed down, so I got another gig in a restaurant but that's finished now too."

"A restaurant shutting in the summer? Sure, I thought they'd be taking on staff now, not letting them go. God, things must be bad up there."

There wasn't a shred of suspicion there. Jim was the kind of man who would always take people at their word. Especially Theo, even now when the distance between them was deeper and wider than the 200-odd miles between their little cottage near Lough Eske in Donegal and the pond where Theo was standing. Time and all its handmaidens had stretched the physical gap so that it spanned galaxies.

"How's Sheila?" Theo asked.

He cast a glance over his shoulder. Neville was still on the bench, leaning back now, his eyes closed, as though the walk had been too much for him. He looked tired or maybe not tired exactly. He seemed worn as though the lines around his mouth and eyes had bored deeper into his skin over the past few weeks.

Jim was talking about how Sheila had 'gone mad for the birds', buying binoculars and spending hours down by the lake, taking notes of what she saw, where and when.

"She's like a different woman, Theo. I hadn't realised how fed up and unhappy she was in the city. I didn't notice, I suppose, until she was happy again and then I saw it. Isn't that strange? When you've been with someone for so long and you don't realise they're so miserable? All the time?"

"Sounds like the move is working out great, so," Theo said, ignoring the none-too-subtle plea for sympathy and feeling bad because of it. "I'm really delighted for you. I'll be up now one of the days to check out the new place. Sure, maybe I'll go birdwatching with Sheila."

Jim laughed, that deep chuckle that rumbled all the way up from his chest. There was something in that laugh that always reminded Theo of his father. It wasn't exactly the sound. Maybe, he thought now, it was more his own reaction: the happiness of knowing you'd made the old man laugh. That was surely it. Memories were sneaky like that. They took and took from all your senses so that you couldn't ever be sure whether what you were remembering was real or some kind of alchemy made from the snippets in your mind and the way your brain reacted to them. So that now, listening to Jim laugh, he was seeing Jim holding the phone hard to his ear and also seeing his father laughing outside their house before the rains came that April.

They chatted a while longer. Theo told Jim he'd broken up with Precious. Jim sighed and said, 'plenty of time, lad', and Theo could tell he was sincerely sorry and that moved him, and he thought he really *should* go and see them when all of this had died down and he'd got back on his feet again, with a job that he could tell them about so that they didn't feel like they had wasted all those years reclaiming him from a horror they'd never really understood.

After they said their goodbyes, Theo stood watching the ducks and the swans for a minute. He always felt bad after talking to Jim, or Sheila, though she tended to call less, which his friends told him was unusual. It was generally the other way around. He sighed and pulled out his fags. It wasn't as simple as feeling he'd let them down. More that he had never fully appreciated what they did for him, and maybe all kids felt like that. There probably wasn't a man or woman in Ireland who was fully what their parents had hoped they would be. People talked about the optimism of youth. It was nothing compared to the blind optimism of parents, in his opinion. He'd seen that a lot. Look at poor Neville. Half his problem was that he didn't know how to give his parents what they wanted, and maybe they didn't even know they wanted anything. Expectations. They'd wreck your head.

Theo did love Jim and Sheila but by the time he hit the skids in his late teens, he'd already begun to drift away. He didn't see himself in them, or maybe it was the other way round. In any case, their relationship began to peter out at some point, the way all parent-child relationships must. And after all, they weren't his parents and once he had been granted asylum when he was seventeen, they weren't really obliged to do anything for him though, of course, they did and he stayed with them until he went to college.

He had looked up 'foster' once in the dictionary. He must've been about ten.

Foster – to bring up or nurse, esp. a child not one's own; to put a child into the care of one not its parent; to treat e.g. the elderly in a similar fashion.

It was a definition steeped in negativity and even his naïve child-self got the message. He was a 'not'. It wasn't Jim and Sheila's fault but there it was.

"Everything alright with the auld lads?" Neville asked as he came back to the bench.

"Ah yeah, they're grand. Seems Sheila has taken to the birds. Nah, not like that. She's birdwatching on Lough Eske. Bought binoculars an' all."

Neville laughed. "Sure, there's life in the old horse yet then. Shall we head? I should be getting back. Where you going to now?"

"I'm meeting Cara up at the top of Grafton Street. We're going for coffee. D'you want to come with us?"

"Ah no, I'll leave you two lovebirds alone." Neville smiled. "You were quick off the mark there, Theo. Very smooth. One lady barely out the door and the other coming in the window."

"Get out of it. It's not like that," Theo said, punching Neville playfully on the arm. "Cara and me are just friends. Like the name says, you eejit."

"Right, I believe you. Thousands wouldn't but I do."

They headed towards Fusiliers' Arch and the exit from the park into Grafton Street.

"So when are you planning to head to London then?" Theo asked.

"Maybe next week. I've to sort out a few things first, get some cash, all that jazz. Mam and Dad are not too keen on the idea but they'll come round. My uncle already said he'd be thrilled to have me over. I reckon he thinks he'll be getting free babysitting for his three young ones. And I suppose he might. I'll have nothing much else to do."

"Wouldn't you do some sightseeing?" Theo asked.

"I've been before. When I took that year off before college and went to Australia. I stayed in London for a month at the end. Did the whole tourist thing – Buckingham Palace, Oxford Street, Covent Garden. I even went to Wembley for the first FA Cup final after it reopened, d'you remember?"

"When Chelsea beat United." Theo grimaced. "How could I forget that disaster? Bloody Drogba."

Neville laughed. They had come to the Arch now.

"D'you see that now, Theo? That's another piece of Africa here in Dublin."

Theo stopped and looked up.

"You're mad, Neville. There's nothing African bout that eyesore. It's just another ugly colonial yoke?"

"Yes, and no. It's for the lads of the Royal Dublin Fusiliers. They fought against the Boers in South Africa. That's all their names underneath and those are the battles on the front there."

They moved in closer, ignoring the people weaving in and out of the park under the arch and through the gates on either side. Gates with no walls, Theo thought. Pointless really.

"See," Neville pointed. "Hart's Hill, Ladysmith. Those are the names of battles. Mind you, there were Irish fighting on the side of the Boers too. Including your man, John MacBride."

"The one that married Yeats' squeeze, Maud Gonne?"

"Yeah, the very one," Neville nodded. "He was shot just over at Kilmainham after the Rising. Bet you didn't know about his South Africa gallivanting, did you?"

Theo had to admit he didn't. Neville was always full of these little snippets of information.

"You should be a tour guide, Nev. You could put on a flat cap, thicken up that posh accent of yours, and you'd rake in the cash."

Neville laughed again but Theo thought there was a space where the heart of the laugh should be.

"Maybe I will yet. I'm doing Arts so the world's my oyster. No job or any job. That's our mantra."

They were under the arch now and Theo was mouthing the names of the dead soldiers: O'Shea. Walsh. Young. O'Reilly. He wondered what they made of South Africa. Did they feel as out of place there as he did here or was it different if you were part of something as big as an empire? You could just remake the new land so that it fit yourself, surely.

"Is there any kind of memorial thing in Rwanda for what happened?" Neville asked as they moved on into Grafton Street, walking up the middle to avoid the window-shoppers with their dawdling and drifting.

"There are, a few actually. But they're not like the ones

you have here – statues and arches and the like. One, just outside Kigali, is a church where a few thousand people were killed. They've got all the clothes, with the dried blood and everything, hanging inside on the rafters and on the benches, and then all the weapons – the machetes and knives and other things – are out the front and the skulls and bones at the back. There was a school there too, with a little kitchen beside it, and the walls are still red there because they smashed the kids' heads against them. That's what I saw anyways on the Internet. I guess there's no sugar-coating what happened, so why even try?"

Neville was silent for a moment.

"If you ask me, it's better that way. That's the problem here. We always make out that war and death are somehow glorious. Monuments and statues and pretty gardens as if it wasn't all just blood and guts and horror. You'd get some tourists now who'd be dead excited that you can still see the marks from the bullets fired in 1916 on the arch there, or even at the GPO, or the bit that's left of it. Better the way your lads have done it. Skulls and bones. That's what it really means. Maybe if we put those kinds of monuments everywhere people'd be less inclined to start killing again, less of the Rambo antics."

"You mean scare the bejaysus out of people by showing them what kind of savages they can be?" Theo asked.

"Yeah, that's it. Call a spade a spade and a skull a skull."

They walked in silence for a while. There was a busker in a checked shirt and jeans on the corner of Duke Street, belting out 'Where the Streets Have No Name.'

"Were you scared of dying that time?" Neville asked now and all the ranting had gone from his voice. "Did you think about what it'd be like, you know, when you were out on your own in the bush?"

"I don't think so," Theo said slowly.

He felt like this was the question Neville had been waiting to ask all afternoon. There was a weight to it, like he'd pulled it, roots and dirt and all, from the ground.

"I don't remember much. I know I didn't want to be hurt and hurting was what they were best at. They used guns and grenades, in some places, but the bodies I saw when I was on the run... they were wrecked, cut up, bits missing. Like the whole place had become a giant butcher's shop."

Theo had to stop and squeeze his eyes shut against the images that were flaring into life in the dark corners of his brain. There was no point revisiting them – what purpose did they serve? It wasn't like they could be a deterrent to anything here. Dublin might as well be in a different universe. He opened his eyes and they landed on Neville's hand. Anyway, you couldn't do it to everyone here. You couldn't wipe out say Dublin or Galway or Cork, or in fact all of them, because that's how many people you'd have to kill to even come close to matching what had happened back there, back then. It was inconceivable here, standing on a street corner, in the August sunshine, with a guy singing about a kind of apocalypse that made good music but real bad life.

"I didn't think much about dying, if that's what you mean?" he said now.

"Yeah, I suppose it is," Neville said. "I guess you were too little to think about there being nothing. About the actual moment, I mean. Whether it'd be something you could or could not do."

"What do you mean?"

Theo was lost, his mind half in his own splintered reality and half trying to figure out where Neville was coming from with all these questions. They didn't usually talk about the killing. They had, he supposed, in the beginning, when they were small. He must've told Neville something but he couldn't remember how he'd described it. He hadn't really understood what he'd seen then so God knows what kind of drivel he'd come out with. His memories had grown bigger over the years, swollen by the knowledge he'd picked up over here. For a while there, when he was about thirteen, or fourteen maybe, he had sought out all he could find about the genocide, sneaking off to the library to pour over microfilms of newspapers or to borrow books about it.

It was difficult to read those books. By then, he didn't see himself in the descriptions of those who died, or the words of those who killed, or the prayers of those who survived. He read the books mostly as an Irish boy, but every now and then, a small detail – the smell of dead bodies sticking to the inside of nostrils, the whistling and singing that heralded the arrival of the killers in the morning, or the way the dried mud became like a second skin – would hit him like a stomach punch so that he had to drop the book, close his eyes, and breathe the demons out.

"I just wonder what it'll be like, I suppose," Neville said. "Stopping. Being nothing, having everything you were, all your thoughts, ideas, fears just disappear. Sort of makes a joke of the whole business. Why do we bother when it's all going to be erased as soon as our minds are switched off?"

They had reached the top of the street and Theo had to go right to meet Cara.

"Sorry, sorry," Neville mumbled. "I dunno why I thought you should... it's just when I was waiting for them to take me out of that room and I knew I was for the high-jump, I got all panicky and started thinking of what it would be like to be gone. But of course, you wouldn't know you were gone and that made me more scared so I had, I suppose you'd call it a panic attack, and now I can't seem to shake that bleedin' idea. It's driving me mad."

Theo didn't know what to say. He didn't think much about death or only as pain and loss, not as oblivion. He'd been schooled too young in the mechanics of death, that was the problem. He'd had no time to think about its meaning, just how it would arrive. Neville came late to the idea and so there were more layers for him to sink into. Kids don't think about after, just now.

Neville patted him on the shoulder. He was smiling again.

"Go, go on now. Cara's waiting for you. Don't mind my

blathering. I'm… I'm just… I don't know what I am." He laughed. "But it'll be grand. A break in London will do me good. Yeah."

Theo said goodbye, made Neville promise to call him when he knew what his plans were, and headed off. He'd the uneasy feeling he'd failed his friend again. He should've had something better to say. He should've had some answer.

Then he saw Cara through the window of the café. She was reading a magazine, hair falling over her face. She lifted a page, smiled and tilted her head onto her hand, and there was such perfection in that one simple gesture. Theo wished Neville was with him because somehow he knew that what he was looking at was an answer.

CHAPTER TWELVE

It felt weird knocking on the front door of the house he'd grown up in but then, in some corner of Theo's mind, knocking had always seemed like an odd thing to do. He'd not knocked on anything during his first seven years – he just walked through open doors shouting *Muraho*, as his parents had taught him. He hoped Cath was really okay about him staying. Technically, it was still Jim and Sheila's place but even so. Technically, he wasn't their child any more. He was his own man since his asylum had been granted. That'd been the theory anyhow. It was only now he was realising how big a lie it was. He'd never been his own man. He might never be. His childhood had seen to that. He'd thought he could build a new man, a different man, after he came here. But you could only layer over the past.

He'd only brought two bags. Mostly clothes, some books and his Lynott tapes. He'd have to clear out the flat later but he'd paid the rent 'til the end of August. Precious had already taken her stuff – the wooden mask that used to hang in the hall, the set of small ebony elephants, a few woven rugs in bright blues and yellows. She must've snuck in while he was out because he found her key on the kitchen counter. Such a flat, undramatic end: an ordinary key on an ordinary counter. As he looked at it, he realised he missed her laughter, her confidence, her body, and he felt bad for the way it had all gone down, but that was it. He wasn't heartbroken and that made him feel even worse.

And now there was Cara, and it was too fast, too soon, and so right. She'd stayed the night at his place. A new beginning starting at the very end. He hadn't planned it but after coffee, they'd gone to a pub for some food and then when they got to his place, she'd followed him in and he was so stupidly delighted. She'd got under his skin, for sure. It was her eyes, her face, the way she looked so alive when she was talking to him. He couldn't break the attraction down to its base elements. It was not so much her features as her essence. The Cara-ness of her. When he'd kissed her, she'd kissed back and then giggled and he felt deliriously happy, like a kid at Christmas.

"Theo! I thought ye'd be arriving later."

Cath ushered him in and they stood looking at each other. Every time they met, it was like they both needed a moment to relive that first meeting outside the camp in Tanzania, a tiny pause to dig the memory up, check again that it was real, and then slot it carefully back into place.

"Drop those bags there, come on through," Cath said. "I'll make us a cup of tea and then you can settle in. No need to show you around at least. Sure, I haven't really done anything to the place since Sheila and Jim left. I brought my stuff downstairs and hung a few pictures and set out my ornaments and the rest of the crap I seem to have gathered over the years. I've ethnic-chic'd the bejaysus out of the place."

Theo set his bags down on the purple carpet. He remembered standing in the same place on his first day here. He'd thought his eyes were going to fall out of his head, there was so much to look at: the fancy clock on the wall with its gold hands, so many doors leading to unknown places, the stairs rising above him, the thick-leaved banana plant in a terracotta pot in the corner. So he'd focused instead on the purple under his feet, strange feet in white-and-red trainers that were pinching his toes. He'd stayed by the door, refusing to move while Jim and Sheila stood awkwardly in front of him, saying 'hello', and 'welcome' over and over. They spoke, he learned later, extra slowly and clearly but he'd understood the words no problem. It was everything else that he couldn't get his head around. Starting with the purple carpet.

He peeked into the sitting room – same worn leather sofa, same bookcases but different books, and a new framed black-and-white map of East Africa on the wall over the small fireplace. There was also a thigh-high bongo drum in the corner where Sheila used to have a glass vase with silver-and-gilt-sprayed Christmas twigs all year around.

In the kitchen, still tiled blue above the counters and with the same green lino on the floor, Cath was filling the kettle – a different one, not the cream one he'd wondered at when he first arrived. This one was red and smaller. A single person's kettle, making him think of cheap motel rooms, sad places for lost people.

But Cath didn't look or sound sad, Theo thought, studying her as she pulled two bright ceramic cups out of the cupboard. Her hair was still blonde, even if the roots looked a little pale. She was maybe a bit plumper than she had been but the haunted look she'd brought back from Kenya in 2008 had left her eyes.

That's when she'd moved in with Jim and Sheila and she'd just stayed on when they left for the wilds of Donegal. Something had happened on that last assignment and she'd decided to chuck it all in. Sheila had told Theo, in that low whisper she kept for global disasters or local scandals, that something had happened after the election: loads of people were killed and Sheila said there had been something to do with a church where some kids were burned alive, and that Cath had been nearby, and had got there too soon. At the time, he understood how Cath might have decided that she'd seen one too many churches turned into crematoriums. There was a tightness about her then, a tension that was all effort because she knew that letting go would mean she would fall to pieces.

Then one night, just over a year ago, after Jim and Sheila had gone to bed, he and Cath had opened a bottle of wine and sat on the sofa in the front room, and she'd said she just couldn't do it any more, she'd no more to give.

"I was dead tired, Theo. I mean, I wanted to help, but... I'd started to hate everyone, even the kids who came round the car when we drove into the villages upcountry. They were adorable, of course, all smiles, and they just wanted to touch me and get a few sweets but I just couldn't even smile at them any more. And it wasn't their fault. It was the awfulness of knowing that no matter how many sweets I gave, or how many wells we dug, or how many schools we built, they'd probably still be there, begging for sweets, or plastic bottles or what have you, in ten years time. I was absolutely knackered by the whole thing and don't even get me started on the violence there after the election."

She'd started crying then and all he could do was hold her hand.

"So, what trouble are you in then, Theo?" she said now, putting the cups on the table that Jim had made himself. "It's not for love of Aunty Cath that you've moved back here, is it now? Not so much as a visit for months, and now you're my new lodger?"

"Long story, Cath."

Theo paused. On the one hand, it'd be good to get it all off his chest, tell someone who wasn't involved in the whole sorry mess. On the other hand, Cath was the very one who'd given him the second chance he now appeared to have screwed up. He didn't want to disappoint her, though she probably had a fairly good idea already what he was involved in. The ten years between her and Sheila meant she'd always had a clearer notion of what Theo was up to over the years. She never snitched though and so she had become something of a confidante. His go-to grown-up.

"I got in with some bad people," he said, still debating how much to say. Fuck it, if he was going to tell her there was no point beating around the bush.

"Alright so, the truth is I've been selling drugs, just a little really, for a while now. And somehow, I fell in with one of the big players, well, not with him exactly but with his gang. Anyways, something happened. You remember Neville?"

Cath nodded and slowly sipped her tea. He couldn't tell if she was shocked, mad or just disappointed. There was no going back now though.

"Well, they took him and hurt him because they thought he'd snitched to the cops, which he hadn't. And that was it for me. I told them I'm out. Now, they're a little pissed about that so I just thought it might be a good idea to lay low while the dust settles. That's the long and short of it, Cath."

For a while, she didn't say anything, just kept looking straight at him. Not in a judgmental way but just looking. The silence was getting to him.

"You won't tell Jim and Sheila, will you?"

He was suddenly unsure. When he heard his own confession out loud, it sounded more serious. Like something someone else had been doing. Or maybe he'd scared her. He should've left the whole Neville bit out of it.

She took another sip of her tea and ignored his question.

"Do you really think you're in danger?"

"Nah. Okay, they hurt Neville but I can't see why they'd come after me. It's not like I did anything to them. I gave them back the… stuff and all. I'm paid up and they know I'm not going to the Gardaí. Sure, why would I? I'd only end up in jail too."

"Who's the player?" she asked, twisting a red-green-and-black bracelet round and round her wrist.

Theo felt guilty. Christ, he shouldn't have put this on her. He owed her everything and here he was, causing her more headaches.

"He's called Gerrity. You might have seen his name in the papers. He's never been done for anything but he's sailed pretty close to the wind a few times. Been linked to some rough behaviour but they never get him and they never will. He's too smart, too sure of himself but that's not a weakness like it is for some people. Makes him more untouchable, like some kinda bandy-legged Al Capone."

He was trying to make her laugh, trying to take the sting out of what he now realised sounded more damning than he'd originally thought. Should he get out of Dublin, like Neville? Surely, it'd all die down after a while? It wasn't like he was the only one selling Gerrity's product. Young Tommy, Ronan, they'd all be raring to take his place. And he didn't want to leave Cara now. She was the only thing keeping him tethered, away from all that white space above his head where he'd drift forever if he lost contact with the ground.

"So what's your plan now? You can't hang out here with me all your days," Cath said. "Why don't you move? Go to another town? You could even go and spend some time with Sheila and Jim. They said they haven't seen you in yonks."

Theo nearly groaned out loud. He loved Cath but he didn't want her to start trying to save him again. Nobody should be saved more than once or they'd collapse under the weight of it. But she wasn't done yet.

"I didn't traipse through the mud there in Tanzania and risk my career and do all that endless paperwork, so you could just end up the same as every other good-for-nothing loser in Dublin."

She was leaning over the table now, her blue eyes riveted on his, her mouth tight with disapproval. So, all that quiet before had been her working herself up to this, he thought. Still, he knew he had it coming.

"*You* are one of the lucky ones, you eejit. One of the kids who made it out of the village, and I know, I know," her voice fell now, "how awful that sounds after everything you went through but you got a chance to move on. Theo, you are the only good thing I can be sure and certain I did during twenty long years as an aid worker. Don't you let me down now."

Theo met her glare full on.

"I don't want to let you down but I don't owe you any more, Cath. This is my life. Yeah alright, it's the life you gave me but then the deal was just to fit in. So I have and I am who I am now. Wasn't that what ye all wanted?"

Even as he pushed out the words, Theo wondered where they were coming from. And there was also a voice whispering in his head: 'It's not the whole truth, Theo. You can't just lay this on everyone else. You looked for these bad men. They didn't come looking for you.' Fair enough, but Cath didn't need to know all that. Cath just needed to know that she couldn't save him again and that it wasn't her job to try any longer.

"I've done what I could, what I thought you all wanted me to do. I tried to forget where I came from. I tried to forget it all: the mud, the birds screeching over the bodies, the smell. I tried to forget who I am. But you know what, Cath, maybe you saved the wrong child. Why didn't you pick one whose father wasn't one of the killers? That boy or girl might've made a better fist of this than me. Maybe I didn't deserve to be saved. Did you ever think of that? Maybe what my father did was so bad, I can't be good and I don't deserve this life. Maybe, I'm just like him. Maybe I'm just a weak fucker underneath. Maybe that's our problem here. You took me to a new world, Cath, but I have another world, another past, and another fucking fate stuck inside me, and it doesn't matter how far I run, I can't get away from it. I will always be my father's son."

He was almost shouting now. Cath put down her cup and placed her hand over his.

"What are you talking about, Theo? You told me you thought your whole family had been killed? What are you going on about?"

He'd gone too far, but again, it was too late now to go back.

"I didn't tell you at first because I didn't remember. I wasn't able to figure it out, what I'd seen. Nothing made sense. I'd no home, no family, I was running through the bush, eating bugs or roots, and then hiding in the mud with the others. I was scared and I'd no idea what had happened. I'd no idea why they were killing us all. No child could ever understand that. I don't even understand it now. And then when you found me, you remember, Cath? I didn't say anything for weeks."

She nodded.

"You just followed me around, quiet as a mouse. I kept trying to leave you in the… What did they call it? Oh yeah, 'child-friendly space'. Terrible name. Like there were any child-friendly spaces in that place then. But you wouldn't stay. I'd turn around at some point and you'd be there, squatting, looking at me. I remember the first day you put your hand in mine," she said, rubbing his fingers.

"So, okay. Tell me exactly what you remember now."

He owed her that, at least.

"I've only remembered bit by bit and I don't have the full story yet, but I've enough. We'd been walking for hours, then we were in a ditch. I remember that because I couldn't understand why my father would crouch down in a ditch. When you're a kid, your father's the boss, right? So I didn't understand. And then, the next bits are very… broken. There were lights and shouting. Maybe someone came and found us. I think I was still in the ditch. I must've been because I couldn't see everything. But I saw Shema – I told you about him, the Tutsi who worked for us – he was looking at me, scared out of his wits. And then I saw my father and he had a machete in his hands and it was raised up, against the light, like this. I couldn't see his face, I just saw his shape, and the machete in his hand, and then… well, when I close my eyes even to this day," and he closed his eyes now, "I see Shema's face again, and I know, I *know* Cath, that he's begging me to save him but I can't do anything. And then I'm alone."

He opened his eyes again.

"I never saw any of them again. I must've run away so I don't know what happened. I was scared. Maybe my father killed Shema to save us because the others, whoever they were, would've known he was a Tutsi and killed him anyway. Maybe he thought that if he killed Shema, they'd let the rest of us go, even my mother, even though she was a Tutsi too.

We all had our papers with us, except my mother because hers would've been a death sentence. The tribe you were from was written on your ID card. *Ubwoko*, that's what it was called."

The word came from nowhere. It shocked him, ringing through his head. *Ubwoko*. Reducing individuals to a collective. The first step towards wiping people out. He pushed the word back under all the other words he had buried deep in his mind.

"The killers would've known that my mother was a Tutsi just by looking at her. Once, they stopped us, there was never really any way out for her. Can you imagine what that does to your soul, to know you have to die just because of your race? They say a lot of people just accepted it all, like it was too big to fight. A lot of people didn't even run, they just waited to be killed. Maybe my father realised he could do nothing except save himself."

He stopped. He felt absolutely wrecked. He could hear the traffic outside, a plane heading into Dublin airport overhead.

Cath walked to the back window, came back and sat down. Her eyes were too bright. He tried not to notice.

"Still having the nightmares?" she said.

He nodded.

"I'm sorry. I wish I could wave a wand and make it all go away. You know, I can still see here," and she took his face between her hands, "the little boy who looked up just as we were driving past that day. God, but it was muddy. D'ye remember? I don't know what made me look out the window at that moment and see you but I did. And maybe it was arrogant of me to think I could take you out of there – I've been called a 'white saviour' time and again, God knows, and not in a good way – but I'm still glad I did. And I hope to God you are too." She said the last bit in a softer voice.

"Of course, I am," he whispered.

Without Cath, he would most likely have died, from hunger or cholera or just neglect. But survival wasn't really a noun. It was a verb. You had to keep doing it.

"I'm not going to pretend I know what you're feeling, Theo. That'd be insulting. But I'm trying my best. I *do* get that you are confused and, sure, that's normal for lads your age, I think."

She had the grace to laugh. She came round to his side of the table and put her hands on his shoulders.

"I *do* think though that you need to know for sure what happened. It's no use thinking you know, you need to really know. And okay, you were too young to maybe even understand what you were seeing that day. God knows, even a grown-up wouldn't necessarily have understood. I didn't and I didn't understand what I saw in Kenya either but we're not going to go into that now. What I'm trying to say is there'll be records. They've had all these trials now in those gacaca courts. Have you heard about them?"

Theo nodded. "Gacaca," he said. "The soft grass. Yeah, I've heard of those."

He didn't tell her he'd tried to watch a film on YouTube showing the gacacas at work but he couldn't. The language, the voices, the sounds in the background and the people, in all their realness: it was too much. It spun him around so fast, he didn't know where he was. He'd had to shut the computer down, slamming it closed on the faces that were made up of bits of his own face, and his mother's face, and Clément's, and his father's, and Shema's.

"I've a friend who's been working with one of the international groups monitoring the courts. He's still in Kigali helping the government to archive the testimonies. Let me get in touch with him, see what he says. We couldn't find any record of your family at the time but maybe there'll be new information now. If nothing else, we could try to fill in the blanks. Like you said, there might've been a reason. Do you want me to do that, Theo? Do you think that'll help at all?"

Why not? He nodded.

"And maybe you'd want to consider going back one day, just for a visit, like. They say that can help, going back to go forward." She paused, picked up the cups and headed to the sink. "It's just an idea."

"I don't know about that, Cath. But you're right. I need to do something. I'm not saying going back is the answer, but I'll think about it. Okay?"

He meant it but he knew too that the shrinks weren't always right: going back could just mean going back. He pulled his phone out of his pocket to check the time.

"Damn, sorry Cath, I've got to make tracks. I'm meeting Ca... a friend out at Sutton. Going for a walk."

"A lady friend?" Cath said, smiling now.

She was probably relieved to get shot of him after all that.

"Is it still that Nigerian girl, what was her name? Sheila told me. Was it Pretty?"

"Precious. No, she left me. She found the drugs in the flat and walked straight out. Did me a favour actually. Made me think. The problem is I haven't been doing enough of that for a while, Cath."

"Look, don't be too hard on yourself," she said. "You've done well so far. Others would've crumbled but look at you. You're smart, you've got talents – alright, some of them are not quite legal, but anyway. For God's sake, you're only twenty-two. So you've hit a bad patch. We all messed up. We didn't think there were different stages to this game. Now, you've got to pick yourself up and move on. It's the only way, Theo."

As he shut the door behind him, Theo thought she might have a point. But then again, no matter how far he moved on, he'd still be carrying all of this around in his head. There was no escaping those demons.

CHAPTER THIRTEEN

Cara was waiting on the road outside Saint Fintan's Church, her hair live-wired by the wind that was whipping the waves up like egg whites in a bowl. Every time Theo saw her, he was newly surprised and ashamed again at how plain and meek he'd thought her when they first met. Just goes to show, he thought. Sometimes it's just because you don't look properly.

She'd gone home since leaving his flat and was now wearing a pair of black jeans and a short-sleeved black jumper. She was carrying a denim jacket over her arm. She looked like a song.

"I was beginning to think I was just a one-night stand," she said.

"What d'you mean?" he said, putting his arm round her shoulders and leading her across the road.

"Well, ye were late so I figured you weren't interested any more since ye'd got me into bed."

She was smiling and blushing and so very bloody *dathúil*. He stopped, pulled her to him and kissed her. In that long moment of contact, he felt like a future was possible. Even for him.

"Sorry, I got chatting to Cath and I sort of lost track of the time."

They walked along a path that ran just above the grassy dunes edging the mud-and-sand of the bay. The tide was out and seagulls pimpled the sheened sand-water between them and the sea. The grey mound of North Bull Island curved on the horizon.

"This is a gorgeous place," Cara breathed. "I'd love to have grown up around here. Did ye come down to the beach much when you were small?"

"Jim and I came a lot, mostly on Sunday afternoons. I remember the first time, I was so green. I mean I'd seen the sea before. From the plane when Cath took me from Rwanda, and then on the flight over here from Paris. But I'd never been close to it. I was scared out of my wits by the sound. It must've been spring because it wasn't long after I got here. I remember standing just over there, you see that bend in the road there, and putting my hands over my ears. Jim was cracking up, he thought it was hilarious. I was terrified of everything then. It was all so... weird. I didn't know whether I was coming or going. The other thing that was freaking me out was the salt, the taste of it on my lips. I thought I was going mad."

Cara giggled.

"Don't you start!" he said, pulling her closer.

"Must be nuts to be inside yer head," she said after a while.

"How d'you mean?"

"You're always between two worlds. Like the seagulls out there. You're not really in the water and not really on the sand. Like, you're here but in yer head, you're there too. How'd'ye manage that?"

He shrugged. "I don't really think of it like that. I mean, it's just I *was* there and now I'm here. It's the same for everyone. Like, you were small and now you're big. I bet you can't believe how things were then, compared to now. It's the same idea. You know what they say, 'the past is a different country'. Just in my case, it really *is* a different country as well. I'm the same person now, well mostly. I just talk different, I wear different clothes I suppose, and I eat different food but I'm still the sum of all those parts. We're all just molecules coming together – bits of memory, experiences, things you saw, things you did. Any kid would react the same way, seeing the sea for the first time. It's just it happened to me later and so I remember it and I was shaken up by everything anyways, so it was a bit more… extreme."

"I dunno, Theo. I think you're amazing, how ye have these two stories coming together inside you and you managing so well to balance it all out."

"Come up here. I want to show you something."

He steered her off the beach and back onto the road.

They walked in silence for a while, huffing against the stiff wind. Leaves swirled around their feet. Autumn was already letting everyone know it was waiting in the wings. The world was always reminding you that the present was almost past, he thought. But that wasn't entirely true either. Leaves fell, were trodden on and died but then there were more leaves in the spring. Time circled back on itself, taking you with it even when you thought you were living a linear life. We're all just fooling ourselves, Theo thought.

"To be honest, I don't think I'm managing that well, Cara."

She looked confused but then he saw her cotton on, catching the thread of his thought so it pulled them together. He loved the dance of her face. He could watch it all day. It was like the sea changing colour as the clouds scudded above: grey, blue, then white, then grey again. But underneath, the sea was still the sea.

"I feel like I've come to some kinda crossroads. It's like I fell asleep after my Junior Cert and I've been sleepwalking since then. Maybe it was delayed PTSD."

"What's that then?" she said.

"Post traumatic stress disorder. You know, soldiers get it. It's like nightmares and anxiety and panic attacks and that kind of thing, caused by what they've seen."

"And ye think ye have that?"

"Not really, maybe just a touch. Somewhere along the line, I lost my way. It's like I haven't given a shit about anything for years, well except for making money from drugs, and Precious I suppose, but all that's gone now."

He felt her stiffen through her shoulders.

183

"S'alright. You don't need to worry. I'm not on the rebound. Precious and me were not really going anywhere. She was always going to go home, and whatever I am here, I'd be something else entirely in Nigeria. And I've too many bloody identities already."

They'd reached the cemetery now.

"You've taken me to a graveyard? Are ye messin'?"

"I told you I wanted to show you something. Trust me."

At the gate, a lady in an orange rain jacket was selling flowers. They dithered over the boxes of cellophaned bouquets with Cara pointing out that it might be easier for her to help him choose if she knew who they were visiting. In the end, he bought a bunch of yellow carnations. They passed through the gates.

"So you don't know who's buried here then?" he asked her as he led her straight down one of the gravel paths.

"Isn't Haughey here?" she said. "I think I remember me da saying something about him being buried here. Ye know, he loved him, says Ireland was only great when he was Taoiseach."

"There's many would not agree," Theo said. "But yeah, you're right. He's here. Even the Great Houdini couldn't escape the grim reaper. But it's not him I've brought you to see. Come on. It's this way."

She laughed when finally they stood in front of the grave. There were five or six bunches of flowers today and a couple of photographs, including one black-and-white snap of Phil at his moody best.

"Phil Lynott! I didn't know ye were a fan but by the way ye found this so fast, this is not yer first time comin' here, is it?"

She hugged him happily and they stood there with their arms around each other, the wind sweeping her hair up so that it brushed his chin. He told her the story about Neville and the video, and she laughed again.

"I know. It's stupid," he said. "But everybody needs a hero and it helps if they look like you. Okay, Phil didn't look much like me but he looked more like me than anybody else. And that was enough then. I was grasping at straws, growing up in all-white schools with white foster parents at home. I couldn't find myself anywhere, d'you know what I mean? There was no reflection of me – no pictures on the telly, no people in the news, no people like me in the shop, because there really weren't then. And then Nev introduced me to Phil and it made me think, 'Yeah, okay, I can do this. I can be Irish. Why not?'"

He bent down now and put the bunch of carnations with the other flowers at the head of the simple gravestone.

"I come every August. That's when he was born, so I make my own little pilgrimage every year. Like a good Irish Catholic."

"You'll be on yer knees climbing Croagh Patrick next," she said.

"Nah, I don't like his music as much."

She hugged him a little closer.

"Before my time, of course," she said. "You'll have to play me your favourite songs later."

Standing there, looking out at the sea, and the island beyond, with the sun dancing on the waves and salt on his lips again, Theo felt a door open, letting in the warm breeze of a memory. He was on a hill, his arms around his mother's waist and she was telling him how she used to walk down the track to meet his father in the village below, when they were first married. He could feel his mother's arms in Cara's arms, feel her warmth in Cara's warmth. But he couldn't see his mother's face. Was it gone? He closed his eyes and tried to pull up the whole memory, something deeper than the sensations that were dragging him back. But her face was blank. Her dress was green, she was wearing red flip flops, there was a scent of flowers and charcoal smoke in the air, the sun was hot and below him, banana plants rose along the sides of the track. He could even hear a radio playing music, soft as a prayer in the heavy air. But he still could not see his mother's face. He blinked away tears. He didn't want

Cara to think she'd made him cry. It wasn't her fault that his memories swam so close to the surface and were so quick to leap out of the water and into the bright blue of the now.

"You know, Cath said something just now, bout going back to go forward," he said, turning away from the sea and leading Cara back down the path towards the gate.

He pulled up his collar. The sun had disappeared behind one of the candy-floss clouds that were drifting in from the sea. He was about to put his hands in his pockets but, before he could, Cara had linked her fingers through his.

"She said she had a friend in Rwanda, someone who might be able to find out what really happened to my family. What d'you think? Do you think that's a good idea, or stirring up trouble for no good reason?"

Cara tilted her head.

"I think it's a grand idea," she said after a minute. "I'd hate not to know, even if it's bad stuff or not what ye want to hear. It's like what ye said earlier, about the molecules. Ye need all of them, and all in the right places, for you to be whole. Your memories are part of that. Does that make sense?"

"Yeah, it does. No, really," he said as she fixed him with a sceptical look.

"Can ye find out for sure what happened?" she asked.

He shook his head. "I don't know to be honest. I've never tried. I read a few years ago that they had these courts, they were called gacaca or grass courts because they were held out in the open in the villages. And people could say what happened to them and talk face-to-face with the guys who did the killing. I think they might even have judged people for what they did. But I never looked into it much. I'd been going with the idea that everyone I knew from that time died. It just seemed impossible that anyone would've survived. It was like… like the apocalypse, Cara. Like the end of the world."

"I can't imagine," she said after a while.

"But now Cath says this friend might be able to get hold of the records of some of those courts. Apparently, he followed the hearings and is working with the government now. Cath seems to think that there might be some kind of account of what happened to my family."

"What'll ye do when ye find out the truth? If it really is that your father killed the guy that worked for ye?" she said. "And what'll ye do if there's no explanation?"

What indeed. He'd no idea.

"I already know he did it," he said slowly. "I know what I saw but I don't know why. Maybe I'll never know that but there might be other stuff, like what happened next to him and to the rest of the family. Nobody was able to find out anything about them when I was in the camp. It was like they disappeared into thin air. It's like I've been able to get this far on what I knew already, but now, maybe because I'm older, I think I need the whole story. I need the end, Cara. I need to be able to say for sure what happened. It's like my father's stuck in my head, lifting that feckin' machete forever. I need to know that he put it down. I need to kill him off for myself so I can move on."

His phone rang. He pulled it out of his pocket, detaching the earphones hanging from the bottom as he looked at the screen. No caller ID. He hesitated but he didn't want to be that person, the one who didn't want to answer the phone because he was up to no good. He wanted to be a person who could answer the phone whenever. That was the only way forward.

"Hello?"

"Theo?"

It was Gerrity. Shit.

"What do you want? I've nothing to say to you. I said my piece to Michael. I'm sure he told you."

"He did, he did."

Gerrity's voice had a laugh in it and it maddened Theo. Cara had walked ahead a bit to give him his privacy but she could probably still hear him.

"But it's not that simple, Theo."

187

"Course it is," he said, struggling to keep his voice low and turning again to the sea, away from Cara.

"You're the ones who told me I knew nothing. So what d'ye care what I do?"

Theo paused, leaving room for Gerrity to answer but he waited. He knew he didn't have to rush, the arrogant git. He knew he'd get what he wanted.

"You've left a vacuum, Theo, and you're a smart lad, you know nature abhors a vacuum. So we need to have a chat. You and me."

"Not happening," Theo said, his voice trembling despite himself. "You can go and fuck yourself, Gerrity. Did you seriously think I'd have anything to do with you after what you did? You're thicker than you look, then. And I don't work for thick people."

He hung up. Cara stopped and turned. She looked scared.

He caught up with her and grabbed her hand. *Holding Hands Means That You Don't Need To Face The World Alone.* Where had he read that? Some stupid wall-hanging, probably in one of those tacky tourist shops on Grafton Street. Pure bollocks but he needed her hand in his right now.

"Bad news?" she asked.

"Old news. Don't worry 'bout it. I told you I'm not doing that any more. They can't make me."

The trembling had gone from his voice, thank Christ, but she still didn't look like she believed him. He couldn't blame her. She'd the sense to stay quiet though. She just squeezed his hand.

They walked on a bit. It was cold now and the magic was gone from the sea. It was just water and sand after all.

"What d'ye listen to? Apart from Phil Lynott, of course."

"What?"

He forced himself back to her, away from the maelstrom in his head, where Neville was moaning, Gerrity was grinning and he was holding Michael by the coat on Ha'penny Bridge.

She nodded at the earphones he was still holding in

his hand. He looked at them like he had never seen them before.

"Poetry. I listen to poetry," he said.

And then he fell about laughing at the horrified face on her.

CHAPTER FOURTEEN

Deirdre hadn't confronted Fergal. She didn't know how to. She thought about doing it in public, down the pub maybe? He wouldn't be able to lift a finger to her then. But maybe he'd start bawling instead. Even in her head, where she roared at him, hammered him with her fists and said all the things she'd been holding inside her for months, she couldn't guess at his reaction. She'd no bleedin' clue what he'd do. After what Pauline had told her, it was clear she didn't know her husband from the next man.

She tried to make it real, whispering to herself when the kitchen was empty or when she was having a bath: "Fergal is driving for a drugs gang" or "my husband is working with Gerrity". But it didn't really work. Maybe because the same voice had whispered to her, not so long ago, "He's so gorgeous, I can't believe he wants me" or "We're going to be so happy, we're going to build the best family." She couldn't trust that voice any more. But as she watched Fergal, properly watched him now, it all fell into place and she felt like the world's biggest fool.

These days, they barely spoke, unless it was about the kids, but Fergal didn't seem that interested in them either. Had he ever been? She tried to remember the early years but it was such a blur. She could remember the kids – their laughter, their jokes, the falls, the bleeding, the hospital visits, the endless nights walking around the sitting room trying to rock one or other of them to sleep. But where was Fergal? He didn't appear in these memories. So she tried to remember just the two of them together. But there were blanks there too. It'd been so long since they'd been anything other than Mam and Dad. But if he wasn't really even being Dad? If he wasn't front-and-centre in her memories of the kids, then where had he been all these years and who was this man living in their house, sharing her bed?

She emptied the washing machine and took the basket out to the line in the garden. She pulled out one of Conor's dark grey t-shirts with the name of some band she'd never heard of and pegged it up. Then Kevin's football shirt, then Grace's jeans. Underneath, there was a pair of Fergal's black jeans. She didn't remember putting them in the machine. He must've slipped them in himself. That wasn't like him. He usually left his clothes in a pile on the bedroom floor. He might not be a complete Flintstone, like some of his friends, but he was no New Age Man when it came to laundry.

Then Deirdre had a thought and she felt a trembling start behind her temples and work through to her fingers. She picked the trousers up, glanced back at the house – he was out but you never knew. She might not hear the engine from here with the kids screaming on the green and the sound of the ice-cream van going round the estate like a police car on happy gas. She laid the trousers flat in the basket, her eyes raking every inch. There were some darker blotches below the right knee and then again on the bottom of the legs. He must've put stain remover on first. Jesus, she didn't even realise he knew where the stain remover lived. She sank back, the jeans gripped in her shaking hands.

"Heya, Mam."

Grace came out the door to her.

"S'lovely out here at this time of the day, isn't it? Will I make us a cup of tea and we'll sit out here and imagine we're on a beach in the Caribbean?"

Deirdre stood up, the trousers still in her hands.

"We're a long way from the Caribbean here, love, but yeah, why not? Might as well enjoy the sun while it's here. I'm sure it won't be staying long. But d'you not have to be getting to work?"

She pegged the trousers onto the line and turned her back on them. She wouldn't be hanging laundry in the Caribbean, would she?

"Don't start 'til one today. Hold on a sec, I'll put the kettle on and bring out some chairs. If we put our sunnies on and squint, we'll be able to pretend we're in the Bahamas."

Despite everything, despite the whole shagging awfulness of it all, Deirdre had to agree it was nice sitting in the sun, listening to the sounds of the estate – children shouting at each other, far enough away to be hopeful rather than annoying, cars on the road, a radio playing somewhere.

"This was a good idea, love," she said, smiling over at Grace, who looked to her like a film star, head thrown back, hair loose behind her, sunglasses on, shoes kicked off. How did *we* make such a beautiful thing, Deirdre wondered for the umpteenth time?

"Where are the others then?" Grace asked.

"Conor's gone to Liffey Valley with his mates – you might see him there later, though I doubt he'll be popping into your place."

Grace laughed.

"Yeah, one of the best things about working there – well, apart from the discount, thank you very much – is that the lads mostly stay well away. You get the odd group, giggling and hooting and making a show of themselves but they get embarrassed fast and they're soon out the door again, tails between their legs, red up to the eyeballs."

Deirdre laughed. Grace had done well to get the gig at the lingerie shop – she was too classy anyway for McDonalds or Dunkin' Donuts.

"And Kevin's gone off with Joey and the McCartneys. They're taking them swimming at the leisure centre. And your dad's out, not sure where. I think he's working."

"Ye know it makes me mad when you call him 'yer dad'. I'm not bleedin' responsible for him. Don't put that on me, Mam."

Grace was half-joking and she smiled to show it but Deirdre made a mental note. She had to stop calling him that. But naming him was only half the problem. If Grace knew... Jesus, she must never find out.

"How's Neville getting on in London? Did you hear from him since he left?"

Grace's mouth tightened and she sat up straight.

"Not a peep. But he only left yesterday, I suppose?"

There was a nervous hopefulness to the question that made Deirdre want to take her in her arms.

"Where's he staying again?"

"He's somewhere around, where did he say it was, Queen's Park, I think. He didn't give me an address, he was really vague about the whole thing, Mam."

There was a pause. Deirdre felt like Grace was asking her another question but she couldn't fathom what it was.

Grace sipped her tea, looked at her watch, opened her mouth, shut it and sighed.

"I just don't know what to do, Mam. His phone's off. He's not answering his emails. I don't have a number for his uncle. Something about the whole thing feels off."

"He might just need some space. I'm sure he'll be in touch as soon as he's settled," Deirdre said, wondering just how wrong she might be.

Maybe Neville just didn't want to see Grace any more. Lord knows she'd been hoping for long enough that they'd break up but she hadn't wanted it to be like this. She'd thought he'd grow out of Grace, move on to other, older ladies, in the fullness of time. She hadn't expected him to drop her daughter so suddenly, leaving her clutching her phone, her eyes sneaking to the screen every few minutes, her finger worrying the volume button, just in case it had been muted accidentally.

"Have you checked if his parents have heard anything?" she said.

Grace shook her head. "They don't like me and besides, I don't want him thinking I'm totally useless. He'll go mental if he finds out I ran to his parents. I think they're half the reason he wanted to get away. It's not that they were mad about what happened. Not really, not the way *you'd* be. He said they don't work like that. Actually, what he said was they're not programmed for that. But they were driving him nuts with their *hurt silence*. That's what he called it. He said he couldn't bear the way they kept looking at him, like they really wanted to understand how he messed up so badly."

The sun slid behind a cloud.

Grace took off her glasses. "I suppose I need to start getting ready."

She bent to get the cups and Deirdre stood up too.

"Don't mind about that. I'll tidy up here. You go and get yourself fixed… but Grace…"

Her daughter turned back from the door where she was slipping her flip flops back onto her feet. Her face was bleak, the eyes a little too wide, the mouth a little too fixed, as though she was trying not to cry.

"Neville's a big boy, Grace. He'll have to figure this out himself. Don't worry. I'm sure you'll hear from him soon. He'll call one of these days and then it'll all be grand. You won't feel it 'til he's back here and all this… this madness will be long forgotten."

Grace smiled, nodded and headed inside. Deirdre would've preferred it if she'd actually called her out on the drivel she'd just spouted, but what else was she to say? Forget him? Plenty more fish in the sea? He was always too old, too posh, too wasted for you? Maybe if she was a really good mother, that's what she would've said. But wasn't being a good mother also making sure you stayed talking to each other, even if it meant lying sometimes? Where was the line?

She looked at her watch. She'd better get a move on.

Theo was standing under the same tree she'd been waiting under a few weeks ago when he'd asked her for Gerrity's number. He'd said he needed some air and Phoenix Park was handy for her. She'd always liked this place and it held its extraordinariness for her even after all these years. It was true what they said: your childhood shaped you and how you reacted to everything afterwards. Because hers was spent in a place of endless, wild space where you could wander at will as long as there were no bulls in the fields and no grumbling old lads moaning about this being their land, she loved this manicured piece of green right in the heart of the city.

"So, how are you filling your days, Theo? Now that you're no longer living the high life at The Deep?"

He came to her and wrapped his arms around her. She was surprised and it took a second for her to lift her arms and hug him back. But then she did so happily, recognising her own need in some self-conscious corner of her brain. She hadn't been held by a man for a while so she gave herself up gratefully to the warmth, the feeling of protection. Then she felt stupid, like some kind of low-rent cougar, so she stood back, laughing to herself and shaking her head. Look at the cut of her; so starved for affection, she was hugging any lad off the street. But she really *had* missed Theo. They'd had a great time together at work. He took her out of herself with his soft voice that opened all these other windows on the world. She could talk to Theo about everything. He wasn't family and he wasn't an old friend forced to see her present through the prism of her past. She was just Deirdre to him, someone he worked with, someone he chatted to. Not Deirdre who'd once been, even if she said so herself, a looker, who married 'the catch', who had beautiful children but who ended up like one of those bitter, mutton-dressed-as-lamb Tiffanys or Kellys in some gritty, depressing soap.

Maybe this was why women her age had affairs. Just to get shot of it all. To drop all the baggage and run down the road, like a child, arms wheeling, nowhere particular to go and no bedtime in sight.

Of course, she didn't want an affair with Theo. Her life was screwed up enough as it was and he was young enough to be her son. But she did need him in some way. Isn't that just the weirdest thing, she thought looking up at him now.

"I'm keeping busy, Deirdre." He shrugged his shoulders and then laughed. "Ah, who'm I kidding? That's not true at all. Sure, I'm doing nothing. Taking some time out, that's what they say, isn't it? Though I'm not sure it's the right... phrase. I don't know that I had anything really to be taking time out from."

They'd started walking, both stepping onto the grass as if obeying some kind of signal, moving away from the road and the paths, the traffic and the people. It was grey and overcast, and Deirdre remembered there was rain forecast. She should've brought her umbrella.

"I'm idling, Deirdre, that's what it is. And I've moved in with my aunt, just in case."

He was a little ahead of her thanks to his long stride but she reached forward to put a hand on his arm.

"What do you mean, 'just in case'? Do you think Gerrity will come after you now?"

She pulled him to a stop.

"And what does that mean for Grace, Theo? Is she in danger?"

Was this why he'd wanted to meet today? Did he want to warn her? Christ, she thought, I just want this all to be over. I want Neville gone from our lives, I want Grace in college, I want Fergal... But she realised she didn't know what to do with him. What was the answer there? Would kicking him out solve anything? The thought was like a sudden punch in the gut. She'd never let herself think it before, even in the dark, soundproofed rooms of her head.

Theo pulled his arm away and put both his hands on her shoulders.

"It's alright. They won't touch Grace. Trust me." He started walking again.

There was something in the way he said it. He knows, she thought, hurrying after him. She hadn't been planning to say anything to Theo about Fergal. No point burdening him with this, and besides, she didn't know how he would react. On the bus here, she'd reminded herself that she didn't really know what Theo had done for Gerrity either, apart from what he himself had told her. She didn't think he was violent but if she could so misjudge her own husband, what else could she be wrong about?

"Because of Fergal? Is that what you mean?"

"You know?"

It was his turn to stop now. If anyone were watching them, she thought, they'd be wondering what kind of fools they were, taking a walk in fits and starts. Theo was staring down at her but it wasn't just shock. There was wariness there and in the way he'd slammed his hands into his pockets. "I swear I only just found out the other day," she said quickly, lowering her voice as a middle-aged man jogged past them.

"I'd no idea, Theo, no idea at all that he was working with Gerrity. And he wasn't, until he lost his job. It only started then. I still don't know what exactly Fergal did, to Neville I mean, but I know he was there. Michael told Pauline, his mam. She's the one I got the number from. She's Gerrity's cousin. Shit Theo, I don't know how all this came together like this. I feel like we've been caught in some web that somebody else has been stretching around us all this time and we didn't know. We were sleeping through it all."

Theo had started walking again. They were crossing the grass now in front of the Wellington Monument. Shame you couldn't go up it. Deirdre felt like things might look clearer up there, she might be able to see a way out. A handful of people were lounging on the steps below the obelisk. A group of lads, all around Conor's age, were having a kick-around on the grass. Full of piss and vinegar, she thought, with their swagger and absolute certainty that everything was going to be fine, world without end, amen. Fair play to them. There was time enough yet for them to find out.

They climbed a few steps and sat down. Deirdre looked

past the lads playing football, out into the trees as Theo told her how he'd seen Fergal the day he went to get Neville from Gerrity.

"Have you talked to Fergal? About what happened with Neville?" Theo asked.

She shook her head. "How would I even start? 'Hey Fergal, did you hammer a nail through Grace's boyfriend's hand the other night by any chance? Ah you did, okay right, just wanted to be sure, like'."

She gulped a laugh. She couldn't help it, and thank god, Theo smiled.

"I don't think he knew who Neville was. Before. But he damn well knows now. He knows what happened to Neville. That's another thing, Theo. He hasn't said a word. He hasn't even looked uncomfortable. You'd think he'd feel a need to say *something*. Or maybe he really thinks he's the boss and whatever he does is just his own business. It's like he really doesn't care any more what we feel or think. What I feel or think."

She took a breath. After holding it all in for so long, it felt great, and awful, to let it out. She'd needed to tell someone and she hadn't wanted to bring it up again with Pauline. It'd just make her friend feel worse than she already did. At the same time, saying all this now, to Theo, meant it really was happening. Things really were falling apart.

"What's there to say to him?" she continued. "If he did that, if he really did hurt Neville and wasn't just hanging around, one of the gang, but even then... Whatever he did, he was there. I feel like I didn't ever know him at all. I didn't know he'd end up beating me but this... This is another level entirely. And if I don't know him, I don't know if the kids are safe any more. I thought there were limits. I always thought it was just me because of the way I annoyed him, but it's not just that, is it? I feel like everything has been a lie. What do you do with that?"

She glanced over at Theo, who was staring down at his hands.

"Remember, I told you about losing my family in Rwanda. I told you I'd run away with them and then they got lost and they were killed. It's not really true."

He was speaking slowly and he wouldn't look at her.

"Or rather it is and it isn't. We did run away. But then something terrible happened. My father killed a guy who worked on our farm. He was a Tutsi, like my mother. My father was a Hutu but he wasn't with the others, the ones doing the killing. They were mostly Hutus too but my father didn't agree with what they were doing. He just wanted to get us all out of there. He was educated. He must've known they were talking shite when they said everyone needed to be killed, calling everyone cockroaches and the like. So I don't know why he killed Shema, that was his name. I can't really remember all the details of how it happened, or what came next. All I have is this image of my father lifting a machete over his head and Shema lying on the ground, absolutely terrified, and then that's it. I'm alone and I know everyone's gone. I don't know how I knew it but to this day, I remember that awful certainty that there was nobody left. I remember standing there in the dark *knowing* they were all gone. I thought I knew my father. I mean I was only a child but I knew my father as much as any child does. The father is always the hero, right? And then in one moment, he wasn't, he was a killer. I wasn't old enough to understand, never mind put words to what I had seen. Maybe that's why I only have bits of the thing in my head. How can you remember what you can't name? But those bits are all I have left now. I can't go back to the way I thought of him before. I can't remember anything without knowing what happened after. It's like having a box of photos that you've spilled coffee over. You'll never be able to clean them. They just have to stay as they are."

He pulled out his fags and lit up.

"So I get what you mean about betrayal and living a lie. It fucks you up."

They sat in silence for a while. The lads had tired of the

football game and were now sprawled on the grass, sharing a two-litre bottle of coke and bursting into raucous laughter every couple of minutes.

"Maybe the answer is forgiveness?" Deirdre said, pulling her coat tighter as a gust of wind came bowling round the edges of the obelisk.

"I've no one to forgive," Theo said.

"You can still forgive them even if they're gone. And Theo, memory can be a sneaky liar. If I only trusted my memories, I'd be hard-pressed to find anyone to love. It's like I can only seem to hold onto the bad stuff. The good stuff doesn't stick. I'd top myself if I believed my life was just the memories that stick out the most. Jaysus, I'm freezing suddenly. Let's move again, can we?"

They got up and headed deeper into the park.

"I dunno if I can forgive Fergal but maybe I need to try. If I can't, fair enough, and even if I could, he'd still have to change or he'd be on his own. But maybe if I don't try, it'll doom us both," Deirdre said.

"You can't tell Grace, though. She'll never forgive him," Theo replied.

"I know. That's fine. I don't hate him enough, even now, to do that. Anyhow, it's not Grace's job to save Fergal. She can move on and out and build her own life. I need to save Fergal, that's my cross to bear. Not that I see myself as a Mother Teresa or anything, God forbid, but I suppose saving him could mean saving me and keeping the family together and holding on to the little we have. I don't think I can learn to be anything different at this stage, Theo."

She paused.

"You're a better person than me, then," Theo said. "I'll never forgive Fergal or Gerrity or Michael. The whole lot of them. You didn't see Neville, Deirdre. He's not right even now. It's like someone has switched off the lights."

She didn't know what to say to that. She felt a right bitch now for bad-mouthing Neville but the past was the past. She discreetly checked her watch. She had to be home soon to get things in order before she headed out to the restaurant to do a couple of hours of washing up. She'd been working a few extra shifts every week since Theo'd left.

"Listen, Theo, I should probably start making tracks. It's been lovely to see you."

But Theo was staring at his phone. It'd just beeped and as he read the message, his whole body seemed to freeze. She was about to say something but then he looked up. Jesus, he was scared, scared shitless.

"Yeah, right so. I've to go too," he said, soft as a smothered scream.

He hugged her again but quickly this time and ran off, heading towards the gate they'd come in, his long legs eating up the grass so that in a few minutes he was lost among the trees.

CHAPTER FIFTEEN

He dialled her number. No answer. He kept trying as he ran, his heart thumping, his breath ragged. Just before he got to the park gates, he stopped. Because he didn't know where to go. He didn't know what to do. His blood was rushing in his ears. He checked the text again.

Cara would like to see you. Having a great time with us.

No caller ID but no matter. It was Gerrity. It had to be. His mind was blank with panic. He started walking again, slower now. He was on Conyngham Road. Left or right? Who could he call?

There was only one person in the end. One man pulling all the strings.

"Theo, I thought it might be you."

"You bastard, Gerrity. You've made a big mistake now. Let her go, or… I swear to God, I'll end you."

"Is that right? I tried to make you see sense, Theo. I told you, you're either with us or against us, and if you're against us, this is the kind of thing that is going to happen. Again and again."

Theo tried to breathe, tried to think of an argument that could persuade Gerrity. But all he could think of was Cara's hands wrapped around his and then her hand palm-down on a table under a bright light, and her screaming as a hammer fell. Other images flashed behind his eyes. Broken bodies, split skulls, bloodied arms, Neville. Jesus, no.

He stopped, leaned against a wall and closed his eyes. He felt dizzy.

"What d'you want? If I give you what you want, will you let her go?"

"Depends, Theo. Depends if I can trust you. Are you going to see sense now and fulfil your obligations to us? There are bags here with your name on them and I've no one else to sell them right now. I've clients telling my crew that they're waiting for you and they can't find you. That's not good business, Theo. And you know me, I'm a businessman to my core."

"You are in your hole. You're a common thug and one day someone will come for you and break you, just like you've done."

"Big words, Theo. But I think you and me, we're beyond words now. Action is what's called for. So, I'll see you soon? D'you remember that pub in Sandymount, where we met the first time? I'll be there at 5."

He hung up.

Theo pulled the phone from his ear. It was nearly four now. He could get a bus from D'Olier Street but he'd be cutting it fine. Gerrity probably knew that, knew how long it'd take from this part of town: he wanted to control everything, even time. Theo spun around and clattered into a young lad, spitting apologies over his shoulder as he legged it towards Croppies Acre Memorial Park.

"Watch yerself, ye shaggin' ape," the lad shouted at him. "Why don't you go back home to the jungle?"

If only I had time, Theo thought. With the rage on him, the young lad would've ended up in the river.

He'd one thought as he rushed down the street: "I have to get Cara. And then we are getting the hell out." He'd no idea how to do either but the words echoed in his head so that he couldn't think of anything else. He weaved through the people sauntering along the river, all taking their sweet time to meander through their normal lives. Lucky bastards. I'll never have it, he thought. I'll never have that ease. The comfort of knowing that life is going to be fine, a few ups and downs maybe but overall pretty fine. I'll always be running from something. And I'll never get away.

On the bus, he sat hunched by a window, twisting his phone round and round in his hands. What would he do if they hurt her? He knew he should come up with a plan but his brain was like a broken record, stuck on that question. It was as though it offered some kind of protection. If he thought there was still a chance they wouldn't touch her, then they wouldn't. It was like praying for a miracle. You were always really praying to yourself, willing yourself to believe there was a chance so you could keep going. Fuck, why hadn't he got a gun? He'd shoot Gerrity in the blink of an eye now. Then he remembered Ronan. Would he know they'd taken his sister? Theo dialled. No answer. He closed his eyes as the dial tone rang out. Leave a message? What could he say? What could that eejit do in the end? He'd never even met Gerrity, didn't know him from Adam. And there was no time to get a gun. The clock had run all the way down.

Gerrity was sitting in the back of the pub, at the same table where they'd met all those months ago. Same smug gob, same stupid smile. Theo stormed across the wooden floor, slamming into the empty tables and chairs, his fists balling. But then he got to Gerrity and he knew there was nothing to do. Gerrity might be sitting alone but his lads would be nearby. If Theo so much as raised a finger to him, he wouldn't make it out the door again so he stood there, arms held out uselessly from his sides, feeling like a plank.

"Where is she?"

"Take a seat, Theo. Let's be civilised. No need to be rushing. Nothing's going to happen to the wee lass, what's her name again? Ah yes, Cara. Don't suppose a lad like you knows what that means, do you?"

"*Dún do chlab*," Theo muttered but he knew there was no way Gerrity was going to shut up. The bastard was loving this.

His hands felt heavy in his lap. Now that he was here, now

that the rush was over, he felt knackered, but more than that. He felt as though his soul had been drained and left wrinkled and parched in front of this man.

"So you do have your *cúpla focal* of Irish then. Fair play to you for that. I never liked learning it at school. Dead language for deadbeat people always looking behind them for the glory days."

Gerrity took a sip of the pint in front of him. He put the glass down carefully, steepling his hands under his chin.

"We had to get your attention, Theo. We're like a family and we don't like losing a family member. We helped you and you can't just turn your back on us now because you're pissed off. It doesn't work like that. Not in this family. Sure, I hear you're an orphan so maybe you didn't realise. I want to make it all very clear to you now so we don't have any more of these unpleasant misunderstandings."

The bastard had all the cards. Maybe Theo had always known, deep down, there was no easy way out of Gerrity's world. Life wasn't a series of doors, leading to ever more interesting rooms. You stayed in the same room but it got bigger and fuller and sometimes, if you were lucky, you could hide behind the furniture for a while. But you were still in the same feckin' room.

"You know nothing about me, about my family, about anything," he said now, leaning over the table so that he was inches from Gerrity's face. He knew he should shut up. This wasn't going to help Cara, or make it easier for himself. But he couldn't stop. He had no gun, no knife, not even a stick. But he had horror in bucket loads and if Gerrity thought he was the only one dishing it out, he was going to show him how wrong he was.

"You think you can scare me? I've seen things that would make you cry, yeah even you. You sit here, big man in your little pub, running what you think of as your empire. But you're just a blip, you mean nothing in the end. You're petty and small and that's why you're taking it out on the weakest. You didn't have the balls to take me, did you? You took Cara, she's just a teenager. I know your type and in the end, you're just a low-life. You have one over on me now but you mark my words, you'll regret keeping me around. I'm not scared for me. Every day is a bonus already and if I told you the half of what I've seen, you'd never sleep again. You're just a thug. Same as the thugs minding your car, selling your gear on the street. Same as me, Gerrity. It's just a matter of luck that you're sat there. You might think you rule the world but the world is bigger than your little corner."

Through this tirade, Gerrity stared straight into Theo's eyes. Theo had to hand it to him: he wasn't easily intimidated.

"Oh, I know the part luck has played in my life, Theo," he said. "Probably not as big a part as in yours but still. I grew up poor, laughed at by the other lads for my broken shoes and my hand-me-down clothes, not even kids' clothes, mind, I was wearing grown-ups' clothes, rolled-up trousers, t-shirts five sizes too big. I made myself. I didn't have a saviour to come and get *me* out."

"You're breaking my heart," Theo muttered.

"Oh I'm sure you had it worse. Mud hut, was it? Barefoot walking miles to school? Yeah, we've all seen the pictures. We've all sung the Live Aid songs. But you're in my city now, boyo, and you'll abide by my rules. You wanted to be part of this place. Well, you are now. There's always a price to pay for the life we want. You wanted money, or prestige, or to be one of us, right? Well, I'm the piper and you have to pay, just like every other dreamer."

Gerrity was right. Theo might not have knocked at this door but he'd still walked through it when it squeaked open before him. He'd no one to blame but himself. It wasn't money or prestige though, and not even because he thought it would help him fit in. He wasn't that dumb. I just didn't not do it, Theo thought. That's all it was.

"So, d'you get the picture now?"

Gerrity drained his pint. Thirsty work being a sanctimonious son-of-a-bitch, thought Theo. He nodded.

"But only if Cara is okay, if you haven't hurt her. I want to see her now, or I swear to God…"

Gerrity burst out laughing then, shoulders shaking, hands on his knees, rocking back and forth.

"I can't do that," he managed to sputter.

Theo jumped up, leaning over the table, his hands reaching for Gerrity's throat. He heard fast, heavy footfalls behind him. He didn't even turn around. It didn't matter. He would kill him if Cara…

"Hold your horses. Sit the fuck back down."

Gerrity had stopped laughing now. He looked over Theo's shoulder, raised a finger and the footsteps moved away again.

"I can't do it because she's not here. She never was."

Theo sank into the chair. What was going on? He'd called her, she didn't answer.

"See the thing you don't realise, Theo, is that I control everything already."

It was Gerrity leaning over the table now so that his face filled Theo's world. He could smell the beer off his breath.

"Even what's in your head. I can make your reality. I can get inside your brain and move all the bits around."

He laughed again.

"That's what real power is, Theo. That's what you need to understand."

Theo knew he'd had enough words from Gerrity to make sense of the situation. They just all seemed muddled, they wouldn't get in line.

"What d'you mean? She was never here?"

"Of course not. We're not savages," Gerrity said and Theo winced at the emphasis on the last word. "I just needed you to understand what you had to do. You see, you might think my power resides in my money, or my guns, or the guys around me. But that'd be wrong. I told you before. It's fear. That's the most lethal weapon I have. The Gardaí are scared of me, the politicians are scared of me, my guys are scared of me, and now you're scared of me. And I didn't even have to do anything."

He sniggered, and for the space of a heartbeat, Theo glimpsed the boy with the too-big clothes and the chip on his shoulder.

He stood up abruptly. He wasn't going to listen to any more of this.

"You have no idea what's inside my head, Gerrity. And from me to you, I wouldn't fuck with that stuff. You never know what might happen. You think I got into this to make some kind of gain? You're wrong. I got into this because I had nothing to lose. That's a subtle difference that should bother you."

"Michael will call you to set up a meeting. Be ready," Gerrity shouted after him as he stormed out the door, bursting into the afternoon sunshine.

Theo legged it down the road, fury driving him forward, but when he got to the corner, he had to stop and sit on a low wall outside one of the identikit houses with their big cars and trimmed lawns. He pulled out his fags. His hands were shaking. Gerrity was the puppet-master, pulling strings all over the city, dragging him to Sandymount, making sure Cara didn't have her phone, creating horror out of nothing. This time. Because who was to say he wouldn't take Cara next time? Any day of any week, he could pick up Theo's life and smash it to pieces like a plastic toy. Just like *the men with a single purpose* had done when he was seven.

It's like I never learned anything, he thought, and the voice he heard was a little voice, speaking in another language. He looked up and down the road – closed doors, a man in a flower-framed garden raking the leaves that had fallen from the oak trees lining the street, a boy on a bike doing wheelies for himself, a woman dusting a windowsill upstairs.

He'd been had alright. He'd thought all this difference – the clothes, the houses, the cars, the stuff, stuff, stuff – meant everything was different in Dublin. I didn't cop that it means nothing, that life is still disposable here, he thought. That all this is no guarantee that you can control anything. I learned that over there only too well but it isn't supposed to be like this in rich places, is it? I thought a person, an actual body, was something here. I thought it could only be broken, smashed, ripped apart over there. But they can rip you to shreds, body and soul, here too. He saw a curtain twitching in the house across the road. A white-haired lady's face appeared. She was frowning. Time to go.

He went straight to Cara's house, boarding buses automatically, sitting in a daze, registering nothing around him until he was standing at her door and realising he was drenched because it was raining, and it felt like it always had been. Ronan pulled open the door. His eyes widened when he saw Theo.

"Surprised, you prick? Let me in," Theo said, pushing past him.

"Cara, Cara!" he shouted up the stairs.

Cara's mother came out from the kitchen.

"What's going on?" she said. "You're Theo, aren't ye? What d'ye want with Cara?"

"I just need to see her. It's... I need to see her right now. Is she here?"

He addressed this to Ronan, who was still standing by the door, as if he didn't know whether to shut it or run out.

"Where's your phone, Ronan?" Theo asked.

"What? What d'ye mean?"

"Just tell me. Where is it?"

"Here. Only I must've forgotten to charge it. It's dead," Ronan said, pulling it out of his pocket. He had the sense to look guilty, at least.

"D'you have Cara's phone as well? Just tell me," Theo said.

Ronan looked like he might start to cry but he managed a nod.

"Gerrity tell you to take it?"

Another nod.

Theo was aware of the mother still standing at the door to the kitchen. He didn't know how much she knew about what Ronan was up to and he didn't care if he'd dropped him in it. Maybe she could pull her son out. None of his business. He'd enough problems.

"Theo, what are ye doing here?"

Cara was at the top of the stairs, hair loose around her face. Even standing above him, she looked as though this box of a house was making her smaller. Like Alice in Wonderland, her head should be sticking out of the window, arms out of the doors. She was too... everything for this place.

"C'mon, we're going. I need to talk to you," he said, already turning around and heading for the door.

"Now, just wait a minute." It was the mother. I don't have the time or the energy for this, Theo thought, but it wasn't her fault. She was just doing what good mothers do.

"Where d'ye think you're going with my daughter? What do you want from her?"

"I just want to have a chat. Cara and me... we're good friends, we've been working together at The Deep and I just need to have a word with her. It's nothing to worry about, honest."

Theo kept his voice soft, reasonable. There had been too much shouting today. He walked back to her, looked her straight in the eye, and said: "I just want to talk to her."

He couldn't tell if he'd scared her or reassured her but she looked up at Cara, still on the stairs, and slowly nodded. For a split second, he saw the scene through her eyes. He saw himself, looming over her, face wet with rain, coat dripping on her old brown carpet, and behind him Ronan still holding the door. His brain was pounding with the guilt of everything that had brought him here. He was the tip of Gerrity's spear, pushing into this hallway. He had to go.

"Give her her phone," he shot at Ronan as he walked past.

Ronan pulled the phone out of the back pocket of his baggy jeans and gave it to Cara. She looked at it like she'd never seen it before. She started to say something but Theo grabbed her arm.

When they were out on the road, he filled her in. She was quiet for a while but just hearing her breathe, hearing her footsteps beside him, was enough for now.

"So you're gonna start selling again? But ye said ye'd get out, Theo?"

"And I will," he said. "But I have to do this now. I don't have a choice. That's the point, that's the hook he has me on. What else can I do?"

He looked down at her. Her face was dripping, her hair hanging like a beaded curtain around it. She might be crying but he couldn't tell. She put her hand in his and they walked on. The sky was low over their heads and the rain was soft but it was the kind of rain that made you think you'd never see the sun again.

"Where are we going?" Her voice was muffled.

"I dunno," he said. "We could go to Cath's for a while? She said she was going out this evening. I'll make you something to eat and then I can bring you home later, if you want. You know, I'm a superhero in the kitchen too."

But she didn't laugh this time. Gerrity had stolen her laugh and Theo felt his free hand balling into a fist at the thought. He didn't want to bring Cara back to her home tonight. He didn't want to let go of her hand or lose the warmth of her by his side. If she was what Gerrity had over him, she was also the only thing stopping him from toppling over, from crashing and burning. Call it love, or hope, or maybe pure need right now but he knew this girl was his salvation. She is real and this is real and Gerrity can't change it. He's not in my head, he can't be in my head. We'll figure this out and there will be a place for us afterwards. I've died before, my world has died before, and I'll be damned if it'll happen a second time, he thought.

211

It felt like night already with the low clouds pushing the tepid light out of the sky. The world was dripping and whispering. Car tyres hissing, footsteps sucking the slick paths, rain sliding softly down his face.

"We'll figure this out, Cara. I promise. This is not it, not the way it will be. I just need some time and then we'll start all over again."

"Ye can't blow everything up and then rebuild it, Theo. It doesn't work that way," she said. "You're dreamin' if ye think there's a way out. If there was, we'd all be taking it. We'd all be rebuilding ourselves, our lives. Making them what we want them to be. Sometimes ye just have what ye have and ye just have to get on with it."

He turned to her, took her face between his big hands.

"You're wrong, Cara. I've done it before. I've been dead and now I'm alive. Really alive now, with you, for the first time. We can build our own world, together, this time for us. All of this," and he took his hands from her cold, wet cheeks, and threw them out, taking in the street, the rain, the cars, the grey and grey and grey, "all of this is just one version of what can be. It's not real. Sorry, I'm not saying it right."

He took a breath. He needed his best words.

"It's not the most important thing. It's just geography. A place. Places change. We are more than just the place around us. This is not us. We're more than what we are here."

And there it was, just a tiny flicker around her lips and then her smile. He felt like the champion of the world. *He,* Theo, had brought that smile back. Okay, so he might have to go back to dealing for a while. He might have to flatter that git, make Gerrity think he was the boss again. But inside, he, Theo, would know he was Cara's smile-maker. Gerrity's just a breaker. I'm a maker. I make smiles and I can remake my world too.

CHAPTER SIXTEEN

In a flickering room in Clontarf, Theo and Cara sat together on a leather sofa, a brilliant red Kenyan shuka weaving their legs together so that in the half-light of the television, they looked like a double-bodied sea nymph rising from a coral-coloured ocean. They talked softly, laughing at half-jokes and half-sentences, kissing, taking time to discover the everything that was their togetherness as shadows rippled across a map of East Africa on the wall.

In Merrickstown, Deirdre had just washed up after dinner. She wiped the wooden counters in the over-bright kitchen, flinging stray spoons and forks into the sink. Conor and Kevin were upstairs, Fergal was out, and she was going to watch a film with her girl. Everything was perfect in this moment, she thought. Sometimes, the smallest things could be enough to fill you with an intense feeling of joy. It must be something to do with routine and place and maybe that little bit of fatigue at the end of the day that slowed you down just enough to feel the good. She put the cloth on the side, went to the fridge, took out the bottle of white wine and poured herself a large glass. It would relax her, and later, when she started to worry about when and how he would come in, it would hopefully knock her out before all that became a problem. In the sitting room, Grace was already slotting the DVD into the machine.

"C'mon Mam, leave the kitchen. It'll be the same tomorrow," she yelled.

Deirdre poured her a glass too and carried them both through.

Grace budged up to make room for her on the sofa. Her phone was in her hand. Still waiting for news from London then, Deirdre thought. She held out the wine, sat down and snuggled up to Grace, making her daughter laugh and fake push her away.

Conor poked his head around the door.

"What ye gonna watch?" he asked.

He was trying so hard to seem like he didn't care that Deirdre had to stop herself from jumping up, folding him in her arms and tickling the boy out of the man. But it was too late for that now. He had to be the man-boy he thought worked. There was no other way.

"*He's Just Not That Into You*," Grace said, without looking up.

"Fuck's sake," said Conor, shaking his head.

"Nobody asked your opinion. Why don't ye go back up to your cave and play your little boy computer games," Grace shot back.

Conor held up his middle finger, and then, hesitating just a heartbeat too long for Deirdre not to notice, he left and thumped up the stairs.

"When did you two stop being friends?" Deirdre asked.

Grace grimaced and rolled her eyes.

"No, I mean it, love. When was it? You used to be great pals, you had such laughs together when you were eight and he was five. He worshipped you. You were his hero," she said.

"Ah Mam, get over it. And by the way, no one says 'pals' any more. He's been a moody brat for years now. Can't be doing with his sulking and face-pulling. Let's start the film or you'll be asleep before the end as usual."

She grinned at her mam, they clinked glasses and Grace pressed play.

"Anyway, we'll probably be friends again someday. Don't worry bout it. It's all normal."

Several miles to the north, a man in a black donkey jacket was striding along the canal on legs that seemed too short for his broad torso.

"Harvey! Harvey, c'mon here now," he called to the Labrador criss-crossing the path ahead of him like a furry ping-pong ball, dragging all the light of the dying sun into its honey-coloured coat. Harvey stopped suddenly, barking out at the water, and the man nearly tripped over him.

"Jaysus, Harvey! What ye looking at, boy?"

The man edged closer to the water, bending to soothe the agitated dog. The light was fading but there was just enough to see that the shape in the middle of the canal was a man, face down, hands by his side, gliding slowly out of the city. The stocky man pulled his phone from his pocket with shaking hands. But just before he dialled the police, he paused to make sure and to pay his silent respects. Even the dog quietened and, for a moment, they both stood silently watching the faceless body slide across its own Styx as the sun gave up its hold on the edge of the world and slipped below.

Theo and Cara were heading up to his room. Cath would be back soon and although she wouldn't object to Cara staying, Theo didn't want any third party bursting the fragile cocoon they had woven around themselves tonight. This evening was for them alone. Their hopes, likes, dislikes and all the atoms that made them up were popping around them like champagne bubbles.

The phone rang and he had to go back into the sitting room to get it, leaving Cara to climb the stairs on her own. By the time her bare foot hit the upper landing, the cocoon had been ripped open, the bubbles had burst and the storm that would lift him away from Cara was already raging around them.

After he hung up, he stood still, staring out the window. The pool of light under the street lamp outside the gate showed a circle of silvered uneven paving stones. It was as though everything else had disappeared behind a curtain of rain. Maybe it had and maybe it should.

Neville's mother said they'd found the body – she didn't say his body, or Neville – in the canal at Blanchardstown. She

215

didn't know how long he'd been there but the Gardaí seemed to think it was a suicide. The words came meshed in tears. She was going to the morgue now. She just managed those bleak details before she started sobbing, deep wordless moans that crackled through the phone into his ear and down into the dark place where Theo hoarded all the other crying. He didn't say anything. He couldn't. Her grief left no space in the world.

He sank onto the sofa. All the questions he'd wanted to ask her fizzed in his head, pushing the truth back. But Neville was in London? Did they make a mistake? It couldn't be his friend. Why would he be in Blanchardstown? Neville could swim, couldn't he? So what? He stepped over the edge and did nothing? Just let himself go, deeper and deeper until he answered the question that Theo couldn't help him with: can I do this? Can I become nothing?

Cara was calling his name and then he heard footsteps on the stairs and she was beside him, and he was gulping and sobbing and telling her that Neville was dead. As she held his head on her shoulder, his whole body shuddered as this new pain rushed along the dried tracks already worn into his soul. Those trails would always be there, waiting for the next downpour of grief.

"I thought he was in London? Are you sure, Theo? They might've got the wrong lad. It can happen," Cara said. But her eyes were wide and her face was pale and he knew her words were the kind of desperate prayer that never gets answered.

He lifted his head from her shoulder.

"I didn't see him again after he said he was leaving. I thought he just wanted to be on his own, get us all out of his head for a while. I should've checked. I should've known he was not alright."

He looked again at his phone, called up his messages, because you never know and sometimes you could miss one, but there was no new message from Neville. He could feel bits shearing off him like shards of ice. He was shivering. He leant into Cara, breathing deeply from her hair, needing her warmth, her breath on his neck. A tear fell onto his hand. She was crying too. He put his arms around her.

"I should've known, Cara. He was acting all weird last time I saw him. We were in Stephen's Green and he was asking me if I'd been frightened of the moment, like the exact moment when life ends, you know, when those things were happening in Rwanda. I didn't really understand what he was trying to get at. He said he'd been so scared when Gerrity's lads took him, so terrified imagining the end of it all, that he'd had some kind of panic attack, and now he couldn't stop thinking about it. He couldn't stop thinking about not being here."

He stopped. A siren squealed outside, its initial blare descending until it was just a hole in the silence. Somebody else's world was ending.

"I didn't know what to say to him, Cara. To tell you the truth, I didn't think about dying back then. I only thought of the pain. I was seven and I didn't want to be hurt. I saw what they did and that's what scared me. It was that simple. And I didn't want to be alone. But Neville, once he knew the fear, he couldn't shake it off. He wouldn't have wanted to live with that fear, marking the days off 'til the end. Neville didn't know how to sugarcoat life for himself. That's why he did the drugs, why he took risks. He was always looking for the thing that would explain the point of it all and then when he thought he was going to be killed, I guess, he decided there was no point. That was the secret. I think once he knew that, he could never unknow it."

He fell silent. The tortoiseshell clock in the hallway ticked them into a new reality. Theo closed his eyes; he was sitting in the long grass, watching the golden orb of the sun rise above the waving tips. He was cold then too but instead of a clock ticking, the crickets were clicking out his life, their chirping counting seconds that even his seven-year-old brain recognised were finite, so that he knew he should do something, go somewhere, hide, before the chirping stopped. But there was nowhere to go and nothing to do so instead he sat, picked petals off the wild flowers growing low and safe in the grass' shadow, and listened and wondered where everyone had gone.

"Do you want me to make you a cup of tea?"

Cara was wriggling out of his arms, lifting him gently back into his own body. He sat up straight. She was right. He had to pull himself together. They couldn't stay here crying all night. Cath would be back soon.

He nodded, hauled himself off the sofa and followed Cara into the kitchen. The fluorescent light sputtered into life, the initial fizzle freeze-framing the scene so that Cara's silhouette became a shadow on his retina. She suddenly turned to him, her hands freezing above her head where she was about to open the cupboard to get the cups.

"Has anyone told Grace?"

Theo felt his heart sink. Bad news must travel. You couldn't stop its rush through the world. In his own grief, he'd forgotten Grace but Cara was right. Grace was in the path of the wave. Neville's mother probably wouldn't even think of it, not with the state she was in.

"I'll go over to her place now. I don't think I should tell her on the phone?"

He knew it was not really a question. Cara knew too.

"D'ye want me to come?"

In the harsh light of the kitchen, Cara looked pale and tired, like a child who should've been put to bed hours ago. Bad enough she had to put up with his grief and her own sadness. She didn't need any more of this tonight. The days to come would be tough enough.

"No, you stay here. Tell Cath what's happened and where I've gone. I guess I'll be a couple of hours at least. I dunno… maybe she'll want company or maybe she'll just want shot of me. I'm part of it, you see. Part of the whole mess."

"Okay, but only if ye're sure. I'd be happy to, well not happy, but ye know. Only I don't know Grace that well, definitely not well enough for this."

"Don't worry. This is not on you, Cara. I'm just sorry I got you mixed up in it all. But I'm not sorry I have you here with me. I don't know what I'd do if you weren't. I think I'd just run and run until there was no ground left under my feet. You're what's keeping me here, Cara. You're the ground I'm standing on."

She put the cups down and came over to him.

"That's a big bleedin' responsibility," she said, trying to smile. "I'm not sure I can bear the weight of ye, ye big eejit. Ye'll need to find some surer ground."

She wrapped her arms around his waist, leaned into his chest and, for a moment, they just stood there, hearts drumming into each other. Finally, Theo pulled away.

"Listen, I'll be back soon. Cath knows you're here so just tell her what we know when she gets in. If there's anything else, I'll give you a bell later."

Outside, it was chilly but the rain had finally eased. Theo headed for the bus stop. If there was no bus soon, he'd hop in a taxi, if he saw one. But Sunday night was a bad time to be looking for a cab in this town, especially if you were a black guy, even now. He remembered standing outside a club near Merrion Square with Neville, a few years back. They'd both started college, they were both still single and had been on the pull. No luck that night though so they were aching for their beds. It must've been after 2 am and the queue was at least twelve-deep ahead of them. Neville was smoking a joint – he always smoked in the street, like he was daring the Gardaí to catch him. For a moment, Theo thought about asking for one for himself. It'd take the edge off of the cold and trim the minutes off the wait they were in for. He'd be able to zone out of this queue with its squabbling, stumbling, half-naked ladies, lads blown up on beer like helium balloons, all big and squeaky, and the young lad in front of them who was just one stomach-churn away from dumping his night on the path. But he'd recently quit the drugs and he didn't want to go back.

"Jesus, it'll be daylight before we get home," he muttered.

"D'you know what, I'm going to chuck in the studies and set up a taxi business," Neville said. "Clear demand, good earnings, as long as the price of petrol doesn't skyrocket."

Neville's face was flushed, from the cold, from the night, from the weed. He was happy in himself at that moment. All the wrinkles had been ironed out and he was in the zone.

"The zone just got too small for you, Nev. You were always pushing too hard at the boundaries," Theo whispered now, sending the words, too late, into the sky.

Who knows, he thought. Neville could just as well be there as anywhere else. The idea offered a kind of ancient comfort, though Theo had never been very religious. His parents were Christians and he remembered once going to an outdoor mass, somewhere near Kibungo, with his mother and Clément. It must've been before Angélique was born. There was a small red brick building that might've been a school. He couldn't remember. Another one of the tiny questions that grew like lichen off the big ones in his head and no one ever able to answer them. The congregation sat on benches on the grass – there were way too many people for the tiny building, whatever it was. The altar was set under a white awning and everyone was singing. He could hear the tune in his head, but the words weren't there. Just the rise and fall of the music, a meaningless melody echoing through his body. He started humming along and didn't even notice he was crying again.

The film had finished and Grace had gone up to her room. Deirdre was watching the late news and finishing off the wine. It'd been a while since she and Grace had watched a film together. What with the exams, and Neville, and her job, there just hadn't been a lot of time. She stretched her feet out on the sofa, flexing her toes. The room was dim, lit only by the lamp in the corner, a wedding present from her father.

In this light, you could almost imagine it was a fancy room, Deirdre thought. You couldn't see the stains on the carpet and the dark took the sting out of the gilt twirls on the cream wallpaper. She hated that pattern. Fergal had chosen it when they first moved in, giving in to his delusions of grandeur, as usual. She'd been wanting to change it for years. But then one day, she'd realised it didn't matter. Changing it would mean nothing, except that it would no longer be there. So Deirdre just let it go. It felt like dropping a heavy bag down onto the kitchen floor after struggling home from the supermarket in the rain. The relief.

She did the same with her idea of putting a coat stand in the hall and her plan to put more shelves in the bathroom for the bottles that cluttered up the narrow windowsill. Maybe it was because she'd turned forty in January. She hadn't thought about it much at the time but now, it was as though some kind of fatigue had set in. Or maybe it was just the realisation that, even looking on the bright side, she was halfway through her life and time was no longer on her side, if it ever had been. Since her birthday, she'd been waking more and more in the night to thoughts so bleak it felt like they might crush her so that the end might be right there, sparing her at least from the rest of this dark night and all the other finite, dark nights that were ahead of her. She tried to remember how she had lived before, when she didn't ever think of death. She'd forgotten how to do that. It saddened her more than the realisation that she would never now learn the piano, scuba dive on a coral reef, or join the mile-high club.

The presenter was talking now about how Ireland's Pakistani community was raising money to help their relatives cope with the effects of the recent floods over there. Imagine, 10,000 Pakistanis living in Ireland? It was amazing how little she knew about her own country. Deirdre didn't know any Pakistanis, though maybe alright there were a few lads going to Mount Temple. It was terrible to see all those little houses being swept away, corrugated iron roofs just lifted off by the water, and then the people standing on the roofs of the few concrete buildings, waving up at the sky. Who was going to rescue them, she wondered? Not the TV crews filming their misery, for sure.

The back door opened with a bang. Shit. She'd been so absorbed she hadn't heard the van. She lunged for the remote, turned down the volume and waited. She'd planned to be in bed by the time he came in. She wouldn't get past him now without him seeing her. She should close the door between the kitchen and the hall in future – he often came in the back door now. Why the hell hadn't she already got into the habit of doing that? She picked up her phone. Just after eleven. Damn. He'd taken off early, no word of explanation, just up and off out the door, and then the crunch of gravel under the wheels. If he'd been in the pub since then, there was no telling what mood he'd be in. She'd have to risk running upstairs. He might have his back to her, he might be at the fridge. She slipped off her trainers. She might be lucky.

Deirdre was not lucky.

"Where the hell do you think you're going? Running away from your own husband, are ye?"

She froze and turned. He was standing in the kitchen doorway and, even from here, she could tell he was drunk. It was in his stance: arms too carefully by his sides, feet planted on the ground like they would never move again, torso swaying, and head pushed into his neck like it was too heavy.

"I didn't hear you come in. I'm away off to bed. It's late," she said.

She tried to stand tall, she tried to keep her voice low, to stop the fear and panic from squeaking out from under the words.

"Why don't ye stay and talk to me? Why don't ye ask me where I've been? Sneaking off like that. Too good for me, are ye?"

Jesus, she was tired of this. Tired of creeping around like a mouse. As drunk as he was, he was right. She was a mouse in her own home but she wouldn't stand here and talk to him tonight. They'd done this too many times before and there was nothing new in the world to say.

"Don't be stupid, Fergal. It's a long time since I bothered

to ask about your day. You probably have good reasons not to tell me. Who knows what you're up to, right? That's how you want to keep it and that's fine by me. Why would I ask you? If you get pissed off, maybe you'll take a hammer to me too. So yeah, I am too bloody good for you and I'm going to bed. Alright?"

Deirdre didn't know why she'd mentioned the hammer but it was too late now. Maybe he was too far gone to notice? She turned and put her foot on the stairs but, for a drunk, he was fast. She didn't so much hear him as feel the weight of him pushing through the air between them and then his hand was in her hair, dragging her back into the sitting room, where he slammed on the light so that all that dim perfection was blasted to hell.

He flung her from him and she stumbled on the rug in front of the fire, falling and scraping her hands on the hearth. Not again. She straightened up. So this was it. This was how it was going to happen.

"What do you mean take a hammer to ye, ye hoor? What do you mean?"

He was whispering though. He knew the kids were upstairs. Whatever he might think about her, he wouldn't want them to know this, she thought. She could have her say tonight but it'd cost her.

"You know damn well what I mean. I mean Neville. I mean your own daughter's *boyfriend*. What the hell happened to you, Fergal? What happened to you that you sank that low? Gerrity, for fuck's sake."

He stood there, mouth gawping like a gormless baby bird.

"You think I'm stupid, you think that you can pull the wool over my eyes day in day out. But I know what you're up to, I know who you're running around with. Now, let me go the hell to bed."

She tried to get past him but he pushed her back.

"Oh yeah, ye know so much do ye, smart arse? How d'ye think we'd put food on the table? The clothes on yer back, the booze ye drink, schoolbooks for the kids? The fucking mortgage, right? Where d'ye think all that comes from?"

His face was twisted into a sneer.

"You're a right Miss High-And-Mighty, aren't ye? You can stand there on your mountain top, but ye haven't a clue what's going on. Ye think I wanted to do this? There was nothing else on offer, Dee. Nothing else on offer, and then, just when ye think ye might be alright, as long as you don't get nabbed, there's something else to do. And now ye can't say no. Now, you're in."

He fell silent and turned away but this wasn't enough for her. His excuses would never be enough for her again. There was no going back. She could feel the pity drain out of her. It was as though time stopped as she looked at him – she saw him now and as he had been. Those memories she couldn't find before, of him laughing with the kids, walking with her in the park, dancing in some dive, they all rushed through her mind, the only things moving in this frozen bubble but still they weren't enough. It was like the wallpaper all over again. She had to let this go. There was no time left for this.

"I can't do this, Fergal. I can't be with you now."

He didn't turn around.

"You've done too much. That's all. You've changed or you've dropped the mask you used to wear, whatever. I don't know. All I do know is that I don't want to be with you the way you are now. And I don't believe any more that you can change for the better. We're done."

She started to walk out but, as she passed him, his fist caught her on the temple so that the blow echoed dully in her head even before she felt the pain. She rushed for the door but he grabbed her waist. They grappled silently for a few minutes. He was unstable but still strong and she couldn't break free. She couldn't get to his face because he was behind her. He was trying to kick her legs from under her, to bring her down, but he couldn't connect. For the briefest of seconds, and despite her fear, she saw how ridiculous they must look. How ridiculous they had become.

She felt a mad burning to be done with this. Above his heavy breathing and grunting, she could hear footsteps on the landing upstairs. She gave a final tug, heard her jumper rip, and then she was out the door. She could've made it to the top of the stairs, she could see Grace standing up there, eyes wide, a high-heeled shoe clutched like a knife in her hand, but then the doorbell rang and they were all stuck there, like actors who've forgotten their lines, frozen in the spotlight.

Her eyes locked on Grace's, she shook her head and went to the door. She could feel Fergal hovering behind her.

"Theo! What...?"

There was something in his face, something about the way his mouth was set, or maybe it was his eyes, too bright? He looked like he'd been crying. Or had it been raining? Stupidly, she looked out beyond him as though all the answers were up in the cloud-filled sky. Afterwards, no matter how many times she played the scene over in her head, she couldn't decide whether she would have been able to stop it all if she'd known how to name what she saw in Theo's face.

"I need to talk to you and to Grace. Can I come in?"

"No, ye fucking well cannot."

Fergal was right behind her. She turned to look at him. He was raging but there was fear in his face too. Of course, that's why... he'd seen Theo before. He'd seen him the day Neville was hurt, when Theo went to the garage. Fergal knew who Theo was and what he did. She could hear Grace coming down the stairs, she could hear the blood rushing in her ears, she needed to stop all these pieces coming together.

Theo pushed past her into the hall. He stood in front of Fergal. Grace was halfway down the stairs, still holding the shoe, her fingers white around the stiletto heel. Theo looked from Fergal to Deirdre.

"You been beating her again, have you, Fergal?"

"What are ye talking about? Get outta my house, ye dirty black, before I make ye."

But Fergal didn't move. He was a couple of inches shorter than Theo and he wasn't so drunk that he couldn't see he'd be on the losing end of this one. Theo didn't move an inch.

"I think the best thing would be if you go back there to the kitchen, make yourself a cup of coffee, and let me talk to Deirdre and Grace. I have nothing to say to you. You don't want me to talk to you. Not today."

Theo's voice was like a knife in the air.

For the tiniest fraction of a moment, Deirdre felt relief. Fergal would get out of the hallway, Theo would say whatever he had to say, and this disaster would become just another evening. Move, ye thug, she whispered under her breath. For God's sake, move.

Fergal stepped back alright but only to better point the gun that had appeared in his hand.

Deirdre screamed and the scream echoed through Grace's throat.

"Get upstairs, Grace," she shouted. "Get upstairs now! Nobody comes down, go."

She chanced a look up the stairs although she didn't want to take her eyes off Fergal for fear of what he'd do if she stopped willing him still. Grace was staring at her dad, her mouth still shaping the scream. Deirdre mouthed 'Go' again and her daughter turned and ran.

Theo hadn't moved.

"D'you think you're a big man because you have a gun? I know what you did. But you didn't need a gun then, did you? When you wrecked Neville's hands? Or maybe you were holding the gun on him, maybe you just watched while the others smashed him. It doesn't matter. You were there, you carry the same responsibility. You and Gerrity and every fucker who was there that day. You all killed him."

It took Deirdre a moment to register what Theo had said. She couldn't take her eyes off the gun. Where and when? How long had he had it in the house? She raised her eyes to Fergal's face. He was adrift, confusion and drink making him look like a puffy-faced cartoon character.

"What d'ye mean? We sent Neville back to ye, ye punk," he spluttered.

"Only for him to top himself by jumping into the canal."

Deirdre clasped a hand over her mouth. Theo was breathing heavily now. He half-turned to look at her, mouthing his apology. He hadn't wanted to tell her this way.

Fergal made his move. He launched himself at Theo, raising the gun as if he was going to hit him in the side of the head. Deirdre fell back against the door, slamming it shut. She might've screamed, she didn't know. Theo's hand shot out, grabbed Fergal's wrist and pushed the older man back. They tumbled to the floor, Fergal's drunken weight pulling Theo down on top of him, his free hand flailing, wrenching the gilt mirror off the wall and onto the ground where the glass smashed and the wood splintered. Deirdre started forward. That mirror had been her mam's. She had to get it out from under them, out from the feet that were now grinding the wood to pieces.

The gunshot echoed like a thunderclap, dull, definitive. It stopped everything. The men were still on the floor. Deirdre couldn't move. Then slowly, Theo pulled himself up. He had the gun in his hand and he was looking at it as though it had bitten him. He looked down at Fergal and back at her.

"I didn't... Oh God, I didn't..."

Footsteps upstairs and then they were all there. Grace, Conor and Kevin, looking over the banister at Fergal, his blood draining into the carpet from a hole in his stomach with splinters of gilded wood like water skaters on a cherry-coloured pond.

CHAPTER SEVENTEEN

Theo woke by degrees. He opened his eyes, registered the peaty nothingness above him and the pale square of a window to his right; he heard the lonely bleat of a seagull and then an answering blare from an invisible donkey. Below these rogue soloists, he could make out the thrum of the sea. His mouth was dry, his stomach was empty and he needed to pee. His feet were uncovered and cold, and the heavy blankets encasing his torso smelled of turf smoke and a universe of rain. He lay still, swivelling his eyes around the room until he remembered – he was with Deirdre's father.

He rolled onto his side. The bed creaked under him and the noise seemed to set off a chain reaction of other squeaks and groans, rippling out from his bed through the rest of this strange safe house by the sea. He brought his watch to his face: 6.35 am. When he pushed his arm back under the covers, the shape of the numbers, digital anchors for this new unreality, stayed hanging in the air. He closed his eyes and tried to ignore the swelling of his bladder. He wondered what was happening back in Merrickstown but his imagination couldn't get beyond the fight in the hall. Was it really just over a day ago? Maybe he could reason himself into the future. Wasn't that what words were for: naming things into existence? Right, okay so. I shot Fergal. He's probably dead. Deirdre probably hates me. Grace too and the boys for sure. What now? What next? But the questions just echoed emptily in his head, finding no reply, until the din drove him out of bed. His whole body groaned as his feet hit the floor. The cross-country cycle had taken it out of him. Every muscle shrieked its disapproval as he shuffled to the window, hands outstretched, moving like a man at the bottom of the sea. His breath caught in his throat: he hated not being able to see, he hated the dark but that word was too soft, too balanced. Dark, lark, park. The Irish word was better: *dorcha*. It sounded like the sour call of a bogeyman. In Theo's experience, the dark always meant the dance of the bogeymen.

Last night, he'd swapped the bare bones of his story for a cup of tea and the promise of a bed. Sitting on a three-legged stool, in front of a turf-fired range, where a black-bottomed kettle hissed, he told the old man about his drug dealing, about Gerrity, about Neville, about Grace and about Fergal. He told him how he'd met Deirdre in the restaurant, and how she helped him find Neville. He didn't speak of Cara, or of how Fergal beat Deirdre. No use maligning the dead and Cara was his treasure, to be hoarded and protected for fear that she too would be taken permanently from him if he brought her into the light. Her, he kept in the dark, his talisman against all the monsters.

Séamus didn't say much. He shook his head a little when Theo told him that Fergal had started working with Gerrity and his eyes narrowed when he heard about Neville's hand and how Neville was Grace's boyfriend, but he must've known Theo was at the end of his tether and he kept his tongue in his head until the end.

"I'm sorry about your friend," he said, getting up slowly and taking the cups to the back kitchen. "And I'm sorry for poor Grace. She's a lovely lass. But I'll tell ye, I never liked that Fergal and Deirdre will back me up. Can't say I'm completely shocked. Always thought he had a nasty streak of weakness in him. A man like that won't hold the line when things get tough. Anyway, ye look wrecked. Ye can sleep in Deirdre's old room. I keep it for guests now."

But he faltered on 'guests' as though even he knew it was too obvious a lie.

Theo pulled back the curtains and lifted the net ones underneath. The window gave onto the front garden and beyond the road to a bay hewed from stone with a frame of sand. The sun was rising behind the hills to his left, spilling light like liquid mercury. Silver water licked lazily at the metallic sand.

A movement caught his eye. Séamus was walking, back bent, along the beach. He had a stick in his hand and he stopped every now and then to look out over the placid water. Silver land and sea, dark rocks and solitary man. Like a tableau made to capture the essence of loneliness. Theo felt like a voyeur but he couldn't tear his eyes away. If there was sorrow, there was also some kind of elemental hope in the scene, something eternal. He let the curtain drop, picked up his shoes and went out of the room, looking for a bathroom.

He got as far as the sand before Séamus heard him and turned. Theo nodded – he didn't want to disturb this unfurling world with words – but Séamus still glared at him and then pivoted back to the sea. Theo walked to the edge of the water, his trainers gouging deep holes in the damp sand. It's all real then, he thought. If I were dreaming, I wouldn't leave footprints, would I? All at once, the sun hauled itself over the hills, washing the water with a thin sheen of gold as though it were exhaling gold dust after its climb. As though brought to life by this light-breath, two seagulls whirled overhead, mewling as they twisted along invisible sky-roads. Theo became aware of other sounds – the cascade of a robin's song, the punchy drill of a wren.

"You're awake then?" Séamus threw the words across the three yards between them. No need to answer, thought Theo. Why were the Irish so fond of questions that were not questions? Questions that were already wrapped around the answers, like shiny papers on chocolates. If you'd the paper, you'd the sweet as well. It was as if everyone on this island suffered from chronic uncertainty so that even the most obvious fact had to be confirmed, as often as possible.

"Yeah, needed the loo."

"Not remorse twisting your guts and poisoning your sleep then, as the priests say? Maybe you're harder than you seem."

It was the first time Theo had heard anything like approval in the old man's voice.

Séamus started to walk up the beach, back towards the house. Theo shivered but he didn't want to go back yet. The sea had hypnotised him with its implacable swaying, rocking his mind so that he let go of the now. And then he remembered that Neville was gone. He'd never see him again. That's what Neville had meant that day on Grafton Street. He understood it all now, in a way he hadn't when he was seven and others left him in the same way. Then he'd been confused, death and danger were everywhere and it was all too monumental to be understood. Now, he knew what death meant. He would never see Neville again. It was as simple as that. This was the other side of the nothingness Neville had obsessed about. Nothingness there and emptiness here. Two sides of the same coin that his friend had tossed. We both lost, Theo thought. We were both always going to lose.

"C'mon then, or are ye going to stare at the sea all day?"

Séamus' voice cracked across to him. Theo turned and followed him up to the house and around the back, past a low, open-sided shed stacked with turf and bales of hay. There was a narrow gravel path running along the wall of the house and a bench where you could sit and look out at the field bouncing away to stone walls mottled green with moss. The road ran along the sea to the right of the house, winding back to Galway and through the soggy midlands to Dublin. Would he find Kavanagh's redemption on the leafy banks of the canals if he went back? But maybe you needed to be sorry first. And he wasn't sorry, even if it was an accident. If he dug beneath his fear for the future, Theo knew he'd find a kind of jubilation.

Justice could be delivered, in this world at least. Fergal had it coming. He might not be the only one responsible for Neville stepping off the edge of the world but he played a part. He was guilty of cruelty at worst, and turning a blind eye at best, and it was only right he paid a price. Theo was sick to death of people doling out horror and then walking away, like comic-book villains strutting off as burning buildings exploded behind them. *I didn't mean to kill him but that doesn't mean it wasn't the right thing to do*, he reasoned. *After all, he's the one who pulled the gun. I was only defending myself.*

But he knew no court would ever believe him, a young, drug-dealing African who had gone off his own bat to the dead man's house. Never mind that the gun was Fergal's. Never mind that he'd had no intention of confronting Fergal, that he'd forgotten what Fergal had done in the awfulness of wondering how to tell Grace that her boyfriend was dead. None of that would matter. His notion of himself, and his notion of how others would see him, were like cats in a sack. They'd always been fighting, or at least since he got to Ireland and came to realise that there were two versions of himself: what he was and what other people saw. Since then, he'd held both in his mind – even as he worked to bring them together by softening the edges that made him so foreign – because he knew that his reality would never be the whole picture. He could never escape the other version of himself, so better to keep it front-and-centre. This time that external gaze would be all that counted and there'd be no saviour in a white car coming for him.

Inside, Séamus was sitting at the table, hunched over a cup of tea and a plate piled with thick pieces of soda bread covered in strawberry jam. He nodded to Theo to sit down. The radio was on but low so that Theo couldn't make out the words. There was a small telly on a counter in the corner, a relic from the 80s from the look of the knobs on it, a picture of Jesus with an electric sacred heart burning red on the wall, and a single birthday card on the windowsill. It showed a champagne bottle popping glitter. *Have a great year!* There was something heartbreaking about its cheerfulness here.

They ate in silence, which suited Theo fine. He was starving.

"So why didn't ye go to yer own people? Someone must've brought you up here, wherever ye came from in the first place," Séamus said as he finished his bread and lit a fag from a packet on the table.

"My foster parents are in Donegal. Moved from Dublin last year."

"Ye could've taken a bus there as well."

Theo pulled his own fags from his pocket, lit up and squinted through the smoke at the man on the other side of the table.

"I wasn't really thinking straight at the time. I just wanted to get out. Deirdre said to come here. I guess she thought it was out of the way enough to be safe. And I didn't want to get Jim and Sheila involved. They've done enough for me already."

Séamus chuckled.

"But ye didn't mind dragging Deirdre's family deeper into yer mess?"

"Other way round," Theo shot back. "Your family got me into this in the first place. Well, your son-in-law did. He pulled the gun on me. And he helped push Neville over the edge, whatever part he played."

Séamus harrumphed. He stubbed out his cigarette in the white ceramic ashtray on the table and stood abruptly. Theo had hoped he might be about to give him some advice, tell him where to go, what to do now, how to turn the clock back on this unholy fuck-up. Deirdre had said he used to be in the IRA. He'd have some notion about dodging the law, surely? But he walked right past Theo into the back kitchen.

"Right, put yer shoes back on, we'll head out. I'm not sitting here in the kitchen, drinking tea and gossiping like an old woman all morning. C'mon."

The last thing Theo wanted was to go hiking in this wilderness. He'd to make a plan, figure out what he was going to do. But Séamus was already stuffing his feet into his mud-covered wellington boots. Theo sighed and rose stiffly to follow him. There was no way he was sitting alone under the sacred heart lamp in this sad kitchen.

They headed out onto the road, retracing the route Theo had taken the night before. Séamus went ahead with a slow, determined plod, hands joined behind his back. The sun was well up now and the sky was cornflower blue but a band of clouds was already pushing in, speeding brashly into the blue void and trailing shadows across the land. After a while, Séamus headed off on a track that cut across an open stretch of bog. He balanced expertly on the narrow paths of hard sod between the mounds of purple heather, yellow furze and tufts of long, soft grass. Theo paused to catch his breath and pulled out his phone. No signal. That figured. He was nowhere now, off the grid. The old man was fit, he'd give him that. They'd left the road well behind now. Blue-hazed mountains rose over the edge of the horizon so that Theo felt like he was being watched from all sides. A lark exploded from the heather in front of them, soaring higher and higher, its pure song falling to earth like diamonds onto a glass table.

As they trudged across the squelching bog, Theo found himself relaxing. You couldn't even imagine Dublin out here. It might as well be on another planet, especially on a day like today. He felt like Dorothy must've when her spinning house crash-landed on the wicked witch and she stepped out into a Technicolor world. He'd never been to Galway before and he'd always thought of the west as a drenched, sodden wasteland, full of crazy culchies who spoke Irish in thick accents. He'd never thought it could be beautiful. Even Séamus, stomping hunchbacked ahead of him, couldn't drain the colour from today.

An hour or so later, they came to a lake, an oval of startling deep blue. Séamus sat on a tuft of heather and moss. He motioned to Theo to do the same.

"This is far enough. We'll head back in a minute. How's yer head now? Clearer?"

Theo was about to snap a retort but the old lad was right. He nodded.

"So, d'ye know much about the history of this place? No? I thought as much. Ye see those reeks of turf there? On the other side of the lake?"

Theo nodded again. The tightly packed triangles stood dark against the all-seeing hills that shaded from blue to silver-grey as the clouds spun past the sun.

"During the war, the real war against the Brits, Irish fighters used to hollow them out and hide inside. My dad was one of them, God rest his soul. Those nights in the reeks gave him a dreadful cough. It kept at him 'til his dying day. But the reeks were good places to hide other things too: guns, any kind of contraband, really. I used them myself back in the day. I've probably a few guns I've forgotten in reeks round here," he chuckled. "D'ye have turf where you come from?"

"I come from Dublin. So no."

"No need to get yer knickers in a twist," Séamus said. "I'm only asking a civil question and mind, ye're happy enough to sleep in my house and eat my food so you shouldn't be getting all hot and bothered over a few little questions. I know you've come from Dublin *now*, but where ye grew up, did they have turf there?"

Theo shook his head. "I grew up in Dublin mostly. But if you're asking where I was born, I was born in Rwanda. I came here when I was seven."

"Ah, so that's where yer from."

Theo shook his head but he didn't have the energy to pull that piece of nonsense apart. What did it even mean? And what could it really tell you at the end of the day? Did everyone here believe in geography as destiny? As though the place you were born determined who you were. Better

235

to ask: what have you seen or where have you been? If you really wanted to know a person, surely these were the things to consider. Theo couldn't reduce himself to 'where are you from?'. It could never be answered. It *should* never be answered. It didn't expand your knowledge, this question. It was a reduction, a way of hollowing you out with the spoon of the interrogation mark.

Séamus pulled a plastic bottle of orange squash from the pocket of his misshapen jacket, took a swig and handed it to Theo. It was too sweet but just what Theo needed after trekking across the bogs. He took a gulp, watching a flock of sheep grazing on the other side of the lake. Someone had splashed blue-and-red paint on the animals' backs so they looked like carnival creatures, all dressed up with nowhere to go.

Séamus followed his eyes.

"Did ye have sheep in Rwanda? Were ye farmers?"

"No, my father was a teacher but we grew tea and maize and sweet potatoes. We didn't have any sheep though."

He knew he was building his own box now for Séamus to put him in. African, foreign, different. No matter that he spoke English, no matter that he was on the run from a Dublin drug gang, no matter that he spoke Irish better than Séamus' own daughter. And sure, there was some truth in the box. It just wasn't big enough.

The sun slipped behind a cloud and the grasses growing out of the lake curved and bowed like ballet dancers as a gust of wind sallied out of nowhere. Shaggy cloud-shadows scrabbled across the mountains. Aside from the wind, and the distant burble of birdsong, it was so quiet.

"I come here to this lake a fair bit," Séamus said, rubbing his hands together. "Ye know, there's a legend goes with this place. They say a beautiful girl threw herself into the lake rather than marry the rich man her father had chosen for her. She was in love with a poor boy, ye see, but the father was having none of it. Nothing much ever changes, does it? Money

236

rules. Anyway, the story goes that you can whisper your darkest secrets into the water here and they'll be lifted from ye and kept safe down below there, just like the poor girl's love for the unsuitable boy has been kept safe underneath all these years."

Theo said nothing. He just sat staring at the water, thinking of Neville and the secrets he took with him, as the wind traced its fingers across the surface.

"It doesn't have a name on the map. Most of the lakes round here don't, there's too many, but my dad used to call this one *Loch an Cháillte*, for the lost girl, her lost love, and the secrets we could lose in here."

"Did you bring Deirdre to this lake when she was a child? I don't remember her talking about it."

The words slipped out before Theo could screen them. It was the silence: it let you think, and then your mouth took over. Séamus looked surprised and then put-out.

"Did ye talk a lot, then? I thought ye just worked together. I thought, maybe, Deirdre felt sorry for you. She's always had too big a heart, that one."

"We're friends, I suppose," Theo said slowly. "We talked a lot, about everything really. She's a good listener, not nosy like a lot of people, not looking for an angle, just because I'm black, like. She told me a bit about growing up round here, her mam, walking in the fields, that kind of thing. So I just wondered if you'd ever brought her here."

Séamus was staring at him now and Theo could see the harder man inside the old one, the man who spread silence through his home like other people spread laughter. But then he coughed, lowered his head, and there was something about the way his hands hung huge, limp and dark-stained on his knees that made Theo think the old man might've been looking for the laughter too down all those years.

"No, I never brought her here. Nor her brother, Cian. This has always been my place. I told my secrets here, and made my atonements, and that was nobody else's business."

"So what am I doing here?" Theo said.

Séamus stood up.

"I thought ye might like to dump yer own secrets in here before we head back. It'll lighten your load. You're not the first to have killed a man or to have told the lake about it. The deaths at my hands, I've dropped them all in here. Even the ones that had to happen, the people who couldn't be saved, the ones who wanted to die, whether they knew it or not."

He took a few steps towards the water, stumbling a little on the uneven, soggy ground.

"My Sarah's secret's in there too. I suppose Deirdre told you about her mam's cancer, how she was taken from us? I bet them's the words she used too: taken from us. That's what we say, isn't it? Sarah wasn't taken though. Nobody could take that woman, she was strong as an ox in her own way, even at the end. No, she wanted it and I always tried to give her what she wanted. God knows, I didn't always succeed but I did try, even at the very end. So, that was another thing for me to throw in here."

He was at the very edge of the lake now. Slowly, he bent down, put his hand in the water, and then rubbed his glistening fingers over his face.

"This is my rite of forgiveness. I've no time for the church. If I want absolution, this'll be the only place I come. Sarah didn't blame me. She begged me to end it but then, of course, ye always wonder was there a last-minute change of heart? But there's a moment, a second really, when it's too late for that. And when that moment is gone, ye can ask the question no more. I'll have to live with never knowing."

He straightened up again and there was a sheen on his mottled cheeks.

"We'd our problems through the years, alright, but I think I did right by her when it really mattered. I had to believe that anyhow, just to get through the days. Some days were harder than others. I know the kids suffered but I did what I could. That's all we can do and the sooner we realise it the better.

Mind you, that secret stays here," he said, wagging his finger at Theo.

"Even if ye do get back to Dublin, back to Deirdre, you'll not breathe a word of what was said here. Now, I'll leave ye a minute in case ye have anything to say. This is the only help I'm able to give you, lad. What happens next, well, that's your problem. But maybe you'll deal with it better if ye name your faults here and let them go."

He started walking back the way they'd come, heading into the sun, so that he became his own shadow.

"Mind you, they also say that if ye drink from the lake, ye'll be rich, and that hasn't happened to me yet," he shouted back. He laughed and shook his head, never slowing his step.

This is bleedin' ridiculous, Theo thought. He'd nothing to say here, he didn't want or need absolution. He needed *a* solution, a way to get back his life. Séamus was clearly losing the plot and no wonder living out here on his own. He might not even know what he was talking about. He was well old after all. What did he mean by doing right by his wife? Wasn't that always the way cancer patients died? An overdose of painkillers from someone who couldn't bear to see them suffer any longer. Still, Séamus hadn't said anything about pills and he did have the look of a man who might find it in himself to hold a pillow down over the face of someone he loved.

Theo was about to get up and follow Séamus when another gust of wind made the water shiver. A flock of crows exploded from a bunch of thin trees in the distance, cawing, wheeling, a murder of movement. In the quiet, Theo could hear the grasses rubbing against each other and suddenly he was back in the swamp, buried up to his eyes in the mud. Around him the papyrus was swaying and now the rain had started and the soft plops drew a curtain over the distant sounds of whistles and whooping and machetes being banged on trees and screaming. Theo squeezed his eyes and spun back further, to the roadside and the ditch where he was crouching with his family. There were the lights he had seen a million times and could never explain. There were the voices that would forever remain disembodied, set free from man and meaning, and there was his father, his arm raised, the machete solid as a shadow in a bright room.

Theo could feel the sweat on his brow but he couldn't tell if it was now or then. He was breathing fast but was it here or there? He breathed out slowly, taking the air from the dark place where his memories were stored. This time he did not fight. His fear that reliving that moment would somehow poison him didn't matter any more because the worst had already happened. He had killed, as his father had killed. He'd already fulfilled his destiny so what else was there to fear? Theo let the images flicker on the screen behind his eyes.

There was Shema, eyes wide, lying on the ground. But this time, Theo could see more. His father was standing over Shema, as he always was, but now Theo could see the tears running down his face, and he saw that his father wasn't looking at the older man on the ground. Theo followed his father's eyes into the dark and out of the frame that had held this image until now. His father's eyes took him to his mother, held tight by a tall man in a stained blue t-shirt and torn khaki trousers. The man had a knife to her neck and there was a string of dark blood already slipping onto the flowery cloth that covered little Angélique. His mother was trying to fold herself around the baby at her breast. The man tugged her arm, trying to break the human cocoon. His hair was matted, his eyes were huge, the whites shining like moons.

Theo heard a voice now, but it wasn't the tall man. It came from outside even this expanded frame. And suddenly Theo recognised it. It had been echoing in his head for years but he'd never before been able to distinguish the words. The voice was wrapped in the sour smell of stale beer and the sharp, metallic scent of blood. It had always been speaking Kinyarwanda but this time, as though someone had turned a tuning dial in his head, Theo heard and understood the words.

"Thomas, we know you. You are one of us. But you know,

this man, and your woman, they are cockroaches and you know what we have to do to the *inyenzi*. You can join us, run with the *rubanda nyamwinshi*, be part of the great majority as we take back what they have stolen from us. We will overlook your weakness in marrying one of them. You were bewitched, we have seen that elsewhere. It can be understood. But the zeros must be exterminated or they will take what is ours, as they have been doing all our lives. Thomas, you must choose now. This woman, and the beings with two heads, these snakes you call your children, they have no future. You can have a good future. We are all becoming rich now, we have food in our bellies, roofs on our houses, we have clothes, radios, cooking pots to take home every day."

As the voice rang in his head, Theo saw his father flinch again and again as though the words were physical blows. He did not loosen his grip on the machete, it stayed above his head, but his shoulders dropped, and his head sunk into his chest as though someone was letting the air out of his body. And now he realised why he'd thought he recognised Neville's moaning that day on the bench. It wasn't just the keening tape at school. He'd heard it before that – it was the sound his father had made as he stood there, knowing everyone would die. It was the sound of the most terrible fear, the most terrible pain, and the most profound helplessness.

Now, Theo's eyes fell on Shema again. He was looking straight at him and his mouth was moving and the need to understand what he was saying made Theo's whole body arch and ache. Then it came.

"Theo, run! Run boy, get out. Go!"

Shema wasn't asking for help. He had never been asking for help. Little Theo wanted more than anything to run. He could feel the horror of what was coming like a cold hand on his small neck. But he couldn't move. Or could he? Sitting on a tuft of heather, at the edge of a lost lake, Theo breathed deeply again, willing the story to end and not end. He had never come this far but how much further? He squeezed his

241

eyes and there it was: the end of everything. His father's arm fell, the machete thudding dully onto the ground; his father launched himself across that impossible space between him and his wife but Florence's lifeless body was already collapsing, blood spurting from her neck. Theo heard the thud of clubs breaking Shema's bones, one by one, as the old man screamed. Then above it all, his father's roars, grief and pain and fear woven together to make a sound that had echoed, unknowable, in Theo's head ever since.

He opened his eyes. His face was wet and his chest was heaving. The sun was gone, the lake was still, the mountains unmoved. Theo stood up, went to the edge of the lake, dipped his hand in the water, and washed the tears from his face. Then, he turned and followed Séamus' dwindling figure back across the bog, stumbling like a man woken from a deep sleep. He'd nearly caught the older man up when he realised there was one person, one voice, still missing from his recovered memory. Where had Clément been?

CHAPTER EIGHTEEN

Deirdre could never quite remember the sequence of events that night. It was like when she drank too much and her brain turned off, clocking out discreetly and taking itself off to bed while her body partied on without it. She hadn't drunk that much before Theo arrived at the door but maybe her brain thought she'd had enough trauma for one day and decided to blur the details to save her sanity.

For several hours, she completely forgot that Fergal had been about to lay into her again. It was only much later, when she was sitting in the squeak-filled, over-bright hospital corridor, twisting her hands, that she noticed the grazes and remembered falling in front of the fireplace. That was also when she remembered what'd happened to Neville. It seemed unthinkable but, until that moment, she had forgotten he was dead, forgotten that *that* was why Theo came to the door. All through the long hours of Fergal's surgery she tried to piece the night back together, sifting through the mess in her head for a corner piece that would hold it all together.

Pauline had arrived at the same time as the ambulance. While the paramedics tried to stop Fergal's bleeding, Pauline tried to pull Deirdre back into herself.

"Go," Pauline whispered. "We'll be fine here. Just go. And Dee, when the Gardaí come, listen to me now. When the Gardaí come, and they will, just cry and say you can't talk to them, that you're too upset. Do that whether… whatever happens. They'll probably come here too but I'll handle them."

"But, the gun? What'll we do with it, Pauline?"

"I'll get rid of it. For now. I'll hide it. Don't worry, Dee."

Deirdre didn't remember much of the ride to the Mater, just the banshee-wailing of the sirens setting her teeth on edge, threatening to scream her out of herself again. She hunched on the chair near Fergal's head. A stocky female paramedic sat next to her, checking Fergal's pulse, tapping machines and adjusting the tentacles of tubes that had sprouted from her husband's arms and face. Deirdre knew she should feel distraught at the sight of Fergal bleeding out on the gurney, but she didn't and she was sure the paramedic knew this. It was in the way she grimly avoided Deirdre's eyes.

At the hospital, someone took her to a bleak corridor, sat her in a plastic chair, and gave her a hot cup of tea but she didn't have the energy to drink it: to lift and tilt and swallow. It seemed like too much. She just sat with the cup in her hands, watching nurses and doctors speed-walk past, listening to the coughing and moans from the recovery rooms, feeling the endless ringing of a never-answered phone jangle through her bones.

At some point, as night gave way to day, she called her dad. She'd to try a few times before he answered. He didn't have a mobile, of course, so he'd have had to get out of bed. The image of him stumbling on bare feet through that dark, cold house almost set her off again. She told him what had happened, more or less: that Theo was on the way, that it wasn't his fault, that he needed help, and that she'd thought of her father because... she hesitated. "Because I panicked, and I knew you'd know what to do, Dad."

Her father hardly said a word but his questions hung unspoken in the space between them. She told him she'd call when Fergal was out of surgery. His only comment came then.

"That young African friend of yours better hope he makes it. There'll be no mercy if a white father-of-three dies after being shot by a black. Not in this place."

The blackouts, or brownouts, or whatever you'd call the

crumbling of her brain, stopped at some point during the hours of waiting. It was as if the sheer boredom stifled her panic, dulling her brain back to its normal rhythm. The doctor, an austerely pretty woman who looked like she hadn't slept enough since med school, came and said Fergal's liver had been damaged and there was a build-up of acid in his stomach that had to be treated. They'd know more in a few hours. She asked Deirdre to stay because the Gardaí wanted to speak to her. Deirdre nodded and the doctor left, padding off to become an always-shadowy bit player in some other personal drama that would mark her forever. Deirdre had seen and done it all before – she knew that reassuring smile too well and the sympathetic listening look you wheeled out for the questions that really couldn't be answered – but now the brutality of being on the other side took her breath away.

As she waited, she silently recited what she knew. Theo had shot Fergal but Fergal had pulled the gun. Neville had killed himself. Theo had gone to her dad's, maybe. Fergal had tortured Neville, maybe. If Fergal survived, she would never let him back into the house. No ifs, buts or maybes. That question at least was answered. But the bigger one – did she want him to survive? – that question was still out there.

Some time later, two guards came to see her. They didn't look much older than Grace and they towered awkwardly before her as if waiting for her to take the lead. A nurse found them a little office to talk in. Deirdre told them what'd happened, leaving out all the stuff about Neville and Gerrity and drugs. It didn't take long and it didn't make much sense but she was too tired to care, and she could tell they weren't too bothered either by the whys and wherefores of a brawl on a shabby estate. She said she thought Theo must've worked with her husband but she wasn't sure. She said what'd happened was an accident and that she, for sure, didn't want to press charges. She couldn't speak for her husband but she didn't think he would either. She didn't know where the gun had come from. She didn't think her husband had one but she might not have known. She'd no clue where Theo had gone. She didn't know his last name and this much was true because she couldn't for the life of her remember it. The two young lads didn't even try to hide the knowing looks they tossed between them. She'd clocked them staring at her grazed hands. She hated being all they expected.

"It was nothing more than a scuffle," she said wearily. "It just got out of hand."

Never had a truer word been spoken, she thought, as she watched the Gardaí leave the room, boredom, disinterest and a kind of pitying scorn coming off their jackets like steam. They were as glad to go as she was to see them off. She doubted there'd be much follow-up, though they said they'd be back to have a chat with Fergal when he was able to talk.

Afterwards, she called Pauline, who said the kids were fine and not to worry. She'd stay until Deirdre got home, whenever that was.

"But, Grace? How's Grace, Pauline? Can I talk to her?"

"She's been in her room since last night. She won't let me in, Dee. I don't think she'll come to the phone. Leave her be. She's had a lot to deal with and sometimes it's better to be alone. We know that. She's a big girl, she'll get through this in her own way. Just stay there and worry about Fergal. I've got it here."

So Deirdre wandered the corridors, bought coffees in a shop where get-well cards were stacked beside mass cards and sank into the no-hours rhythm of this halfway house for life. When the doctor, paler now, her lines more pronounced, finally came to tell her that Fergal would make it, she just nodded. She no longer had the energy for relief. Unsure if she even felt it. Somewhere, in a dank basement beneath her consciousness, a version of herself had been weighing how she would live without him, how long it would take the children to recover, what she would say to them, how she would make widowhood work. The doctor pushed a strand of hair from her face, her eyes fixed on Deirdre's. Deirdre knew she was not playing her part, the doctor knew it too, but in the over-bright corridor where nothing could be hidden, the two exhausted women folded this knowledge neatly and put it away. What good would come of shaking it out? The dust would only blind everyone.

Fergal was still groggy when they finally let her see him. From the neck up, he looked no worse than he did after a heavy night out. She tried to concentrate as the doctor talked to her about dressings and exercises and time off work, but the words were like flies buzzing around her head, never settling. She fixed her eyes on Fergal's face, looking for a sign that he'd changed, that this crazy night had somehow reordered him too. He looked like he was sleeping. The doctor finally left her, pointedly pulling the chair closer to the bed on her way out. Deirdre squeaked it back to its original spot. She wasn't going to weep at her man's bedside for the trouble he'd got himself into. So she sat and just looked until Fergal's eyelids flickered and he was back. She felt the air leave her body.

"Dee, oh thank Christ."

His eyes filled with tears and he reached his hand across the loose-knit bedspread towards her. Deirdre didn't move. This is our rock bottom, she thought. This is where it ends. And just as she had let the wallpaper go, and the coat stand, she breathed slowly and got ready to let Fergal go.

"I'm glad you're okay," she said, standing up. She wobbled but steadied herself against the chair. He still had his hand out. He thought she was coming to him.

"I'm glad you're not dead because that would make the kids sad and I don't want to break their hearts, Fergal. But I think that might be the only reason I'm glad and isn't that a terrible thing? I've been watching you, wondering what I'd feel when you woke, and then you opened your eyes, and do you know what I felt? Empty. You've been stretching me like elastic for years now, pulling me back and forth, making me love you, and hate you, and wish you dead, and wish you'd

247

buy me flowers. But I'm not doing that any more, Fergal. We're done."

She started for the door. She was determined to go but even so, she knew there was just the tiniest breath of a chance hovering over the five steps between the chair and the door. She wanted to be strong, she needed to be strong, but her eyes couldn't leave him yet. He dropped his hand to the bedspread and his eyes, bleary and bloodshot, locked on hers. He was trying to piece together his own jigsaw. What had taken her hours, he was trying to do in the time it takes to walk five steps. The sand ran out and he fell back on his anger.

"Fair enough. Then fuck off. Ye nearly got me killed, you bitch. You and your monkey boyfriend. What's that all about then? Cradle-snatcher now, are ye?"

The words punched holes in Deirdre, making her gasp. But what stopped her in her tracks were the tears running down Fergal's face.

She closed her eyes, took a deep breath and pulled up one of the clearest images from the night before: Grace, Conor, Kevin and Pauline standing on the doorstep, pale faces blue-rinsed by the spinning lights of the ambulance. Grace had wrapped her arms around Kevin and there were tears running down his cheeks. Deirdre thought he was sobbing but she couldn't be sure from where she was sitting in the back of the ambulance. In any case, she couldn't take him in her arms to soothe the sobs out. She had sworn then that this would be the last time her husband would tear her into strips. No more.

She took a last look, taking the time to recognise Fergal's need, to remember everything he was and was not, and then deliberately stepped away.

"I've tried, Fergal. God and all the angels know I've tried. I've made excuses for you, I've loved you even after you hit me. I stayed because I still thought we might be able to fix things so that we could make the life we'd promised each other. But enough is enough. I don't trust you now and I am too tired to start trying to get to know you again. I'll call your mam. She'll take care of you. Don't come home when they let you out. I won't let you in. And Grace may very well kill you."

The fatigue hit her as soon as she stepped out of the hospital into a light so bright it skewered her eyes and her head. Everything looked too fresh, too obvious. People were heading back to work after lunch but the jester sun and the playful, light breeze held them back, slowing their footsteps so that they seemed to glide like pastel-coloured swans. A heady bouquet of ice-cream, suntan lotion and lunchtime wine perfumed the air.

Deirdre texted Pauline to say she was on her way but then decided to walk to Blessington Park before catching the bus. She needed the air. God knows where she'd end up if she got onto a bus in the state she was in. She called her dad to tell him Fergal was alright but there was no answer. He must be out. I wonder what he does all day? She'd never really given this much thought, content with the certitude that he would be there after the news at nine whenever she made her semi-regular phone call. Wasn't it mad how one day people could be your all and then you ended up being fine with not knowing what they were up to at any given moment? How long until she didn't care what Fergal was doing? She wondered where Theo was. She'd tried to ring him a few times but his phone must be off, or dead. She'd no idea how he would get to her father's place, but there were buses, and you could still thumb a lift in some places. Mind you, might not be that easy for a six-foot-plus black guy. She didn't know. She'd never asked him about that side of his life, the reality of being black here. She supposed she thought it'd be embarrassing, for both of them, but maybe she should've tried.

Maybe that's the thing that makes this life so hard, she thought. Maybe they should teach that at school – looking and living through other people's eyes. It'd be more use than the bloody Venn diagrams that nearly drove Grace to distraction these past weeks.

She was in the park now and she quickened her step. It was cool under the trees at the edge of the reservoir. She passed a young mother, pushing a toddler in a buggy. The woman had a coffee on the go and bags under her eyes. She looked exhausted. A mallard waddled through the fence onto the path and the mother stopped and crouched down beside her son, pointing and smiling.

"Look, it's a duck, Brendan. A duck. Yeah, that's right. Quack, quack. That's the sound ducks make."

Deirdre felt tears well in her eyes as she drew near the woman. It was the goddamn simple beauty and ticking tragedy of it all. Love and hope and laughter, the promise of a future, and all these things already being in Deirdre's past. But these are the only things we really need, she thought. Nothing really: a duck on a path in a sunny park.

"Are ye alright, there?"

It was the young woman. Ah God, I've been talking out loud again, Deirdre thought before she realised that she'd tears running down her cheeks. There was a tightness in her throat that was making it hard to breathe. The little boy was still saying, "Duck, duck" but in a flat voice, like he knew the fun was over for now. He stared impassively at Deirdre, as though he knew too that it was her fault.

"Yeah, I'm grand, not a bother. Thanks for asking."

Deirdre hurried past, wiping her face with a tissue.

When she got home, Pauline called to her from the kitchen. Deirdre stepped around the stain on the carpet in the hall and sat at the table in front of her friend. Pauline poured her a cup of tea. They didn't say much. They'd both learned that sometimes there was just too much to say. Pauline told her that the kids were were okay, shocked but okay. They were glad their dad was going to be alright but they hadn't slept well and were all in their rooms now, kipping.

"Are ye taking him back?"

"No."

Pauline gave her a hug then, pulling Deirdre into her chest

so that she could finally let go. When Deirdre had cried herself dry, she went to talk to Grace but her daughter wouldn't open the door of her room. She could hear her crying and she couldn't stop herself from kissing her hands and placing them on the door as if she could send her love through the wood.

"Darling, just let me talk to you," she begged, over and over.

The door stayed closed.

Later, Kevin stumbled down the stairs. Deirdre clung to him, stroking his sweaty hair, kissing his head, spilling all her love and fear onto the one child who would still bear it.

"Dad's going to be fine now but he'll have to stay in hospital for a while, and then... then we'll see."

It seemed to be enough. Or maybe Kevin already knew that was all she could offer and that's why he didn't ask any more questions. Maybe he was already old enough to see her limitations. Conor came down a little while later. She gave him the same speech. He shrugged his shoulders and poured more cereal into his bowl. But his eyes were glazed and his lips trembled.

Deirdre sent the boys off to their friends and then she and Pauline scrubbed Fergal's blood out of the carpet. Neither said a word so that the dull scrape of the wire brushes on the carpet was the only sound in the whole house and maybe in the whole world.

Afterwards, Deirdre told Pauline to go home. She laughed.

"Why would I go home, Dee? There's nothing for me there."

She set Deirdre up on the sofa, tucked a blanket around her and ordered her to sleep.

Later, the doorbell rang, dragging Deirdre from a dream-free doze. She listened. It wasn't the police.

The sitting-room door creaked open.

"Sorry Dee. I wasn't sure if you were awake. It's Neville's mother."

Pauline's head disappeared and a small woman with huge

eyes in a face drained of colour came in and walked slowly over to the sofa.

"Hello, I'm Lisa Mulholland."

She held out her hand. Deirdre stood and shook it.

"I'm so sorry for your troubles, Mrs Mulholland…"

There was no way to go forward so Deirdre stopped. Lisa nodded and dropped her head.

"I'll get us all some tea," said Pauline, disappearing into the kitchen.

"I'm sorry I didn't call before," Lisa said. "I suddenly remembered that I should tell Grace about… what happened and then I just walked out the door to come here. I didn't even think of calling. I don't know why. I knew where you lived and I came. I needed the air, I suppose."

Deirdre looked at the small woman standing in front of her. All our dead leave these shadows walking the earth, she thought.

"Is… Is Grace okay?" Lisa asked.

There was no answer to her question or at least not one that Deirdre could give, so she just let it be.

"You must be exhausted," she said. "Such a dreadful thing. I just can't imagine."

Lisa sat down, pulling her beige trench coat together over her knees. She was wearing crumpled black trousers and trainers and there was something forlorn about the outfit. Deirdre felt as though she would never have worn it before Neville died.

"It's like the clocks have stopped," Lisa said. "When the police knocked at the door, when I saw them through the glass, the clocks stopped for me. I don't think they'll ever start ticking again."

She looked at Deirdre but this was another one of those statements that had no reply.

Pauline came in with the tea, handing out the cups and then sitting in a chair near the window as though she could sense Deirdre would not be able to handle this sorrow on her own.

"I knew, in that moment, I knew that he was dead. It's not that I was expecting it. He'd said he was going to London with his friends, that's what he said. But I think I always knew, in some part of me, that he was not telling the whole truth about that. You always know when they're lying, don't you? But we can't call them out on everything, can we?"

She looked at them both, her head swinging left and right, her eyes beseeching them for the fragments of absolution she would spend the rest of her life seeking.

"To be honest, I thought maybe he'd gone to Spain, or even Morocco. I don't know. Somewhere he could get high to escape from it all. I knew Neville, you see. I think he thought I didn't but I did. It made me sad that he didn't get it. I wanted so much for him, but still, I did know him as he was. And I still loved him. I just don't know why he couldn't see that. Why he didn't know that it made no difference."

"Pauline says we only see what we know we can bear," Deirdre said, nodding at her friend. "Maybe Neville didn't want to see himself as you really saw him. Maybe he needed to think that you saw him differently. Maybe that was something he needed to lean on. I don't know."

Lisa sipped her tea. Her hands were shaking.

"I thought after what happened to his hand, he might change. I hoped that's why he was taking a trip, to sort of mark an end to all that. I wanted to believe it."

She looked straight at Deirdre now.

"I feel like everything we've done has meant nothing. Our whole lives, every minute where we thought there was reason and hope and a future, it was never true. We were always travelling to this place. None of the rest was real. I see that now. *This* was the only reality, waiting for us every moment of every day. And the worst thing is, I don't think there was ever anything any of us could've done to change it."

The sunlight came softly through the window as if it too knew it must tread gently in this room. It must be late afternoon, Deirdre thought. Everything was quiet. Then the ice-cream van's jingle exploded outside. They all jumped. They'd forgotten the world.

As the noise died down, Lisa spoke again. "I found this letter in Neville's room. It's for Grace. I might've found it sooner, if I'd thought to look, but… It must've been on his pillow and then it slipped down, and I was lying there last night, and… Anyway, I found it and I wanted to give it to her."

She held out a plain white envelope. It had *Grace* written on the front in black biro. What could Deirdre do but take it? Was her girl strong enough for this? She remembered the first love letter some uppity lad had given Grace when she was just nine. Her little girl had bawled and made Deirdre take the letter away. She'd told her to burn it, she didn't ever want to read it but it was still upstairs in a box, pencil love fading day by day.

The door creaked open and Grace came into the room. She was wearing her pyjama bottoms and a sweatshirt Deirdre had never seen before. It must be Neville's. It was navy with the name of some US university plastered on the front. Grace wouldn't normally be seen dead in something like that. This is how we lose our kids, Deirdre thought. I didn't even know there were bits of him here. I didn't know about that sweatshirt.

Grace went to Lisa and shook her hand. She kept her head bowed, mumbling her condolences into the ground but then, her eyes betrayed her, landing on her mother's face, despite herself. She ran over, fell to her knees, and buried her face in Deirdre's lap.

"I'm so sorry, my darling," Deirdre whispered. "I'm so very, very sorry."

There were other words and they would have to be spoken, but not now. Not in front of this other mother, who was grieving her son, and who didn't know and would never know what really happened because it wouldn't make any difference.

"Lisa found this letter. It's for you from Neville. Take

your time. You don't have to read it now, darling, if you're not ready," she said, even though Lisa was leaning in and her desperation was terrible to see. If it were my son, I'd want to know now, Deirdre thought. Grace took the letter but she never raised her head and she made no move to open it.

Deirdre looked over at Lisa and mouthed, "Sorry".

Lisa nodded, put her cup on the table and stood up.

"I'd better be off. Owen will be wondering what I'm doing. I asked him if he wanted to come with me but… he's not very strong at the moment. He's been on sedatives since we found out. I don't think he wants to wake up most of the time."

Grace looked up.

"Please stay. I think you should read this too. It's the only bit of him we have now. I'm not gonna keep it to myself, Mrs Mulholland. But can I have a look on my own first?"

Lisa nodded and sat down again.

Deirdre took Grace's hand in her own. It was still so small.

"Do you want us to go outside for a second, love?"

Grace shook her head, stood up and walked to the window. She stood staring out at the lawn and the hedge and goodness knows what else, until there was the sound of paper tearing. Deirdre had to look away. It was too hard to see Grace's bent head, the vulnerable white of her neck and the trembling in her shoulders. But Grace was bearing this so she must too. She'd brought her daughter into this world and so she must stand beside her as long as she breathed. Lisa's head was bowed. She'd her own cross to carry, no longer a witness to her child's pain, unable to help any more. Grace turned back to the room. Her face was suddenly swollen and red, as if the mere touch of these new tears had melted the mask she'd put on to hide the ravages of the last hours.

She handed the note to Lisa and came to Deirdre, dropping her head onto her mother's shoulder. Deirdre pulled her close.

Lisa read, out loud as though she didn't believe she could be permitted to keep the words for herself: "Grace, I'm sorry for doing this and for not being able to tell you why.

It'd never make sense. But just know I loved getting to know you and being with you. We threaded our lives with beautiful moments, a gorgeous necklace of good times. That's all that really matters. For me, this is as good as it gets. I can't go on, every day, waiting for the string to break. I can't do that, Grace. But you will and you'll have more moments to hang on your necklace. I'm just glad they'll be beside the ones we made together. I love you and I'm so sorry I never learned how to live, Neville."

Grace let out a sob that reverberated through Deirdre's arms and into whatever it was that made up her soul. She held her girl as tightly as she could. Lisa was crying quietly, her tears falling onto the letter until she noticed and dabbed them off gently with her fingers. She folded the letter back into its envelope.

Outside, the ice-cream van was coming round again to tempt kids with late-afternoon treats. The children squealed as they ran to it. The same thing would happen tomorrow and all the tomorrows until the kids went back to school. There was no other way.

CHAPTER NINETEEN

The bus slalomed gracelessly through the blind bends of the road heading west, past sheep grazing in purple heather, wind-flayed bungalows surrounded by twisted evergreens and headlands stretching cat-like into the sea. Deirdre's eyes were closed but she was not sleeping. She had left Dublin early and even though the opening of the motorway last year made the cross-country ride less of a tractor-filled obstacle course than in the past, she was tired now as she got closer to home. She couldn't sleep. It wasn't that she was reliving the horror of the last few days. She just felt too utterly empty to summon the energy to switch off.

She sensed the arrival of the bus in the town; people began to fold their papers and gather their bags, filling the air around her with the twittering and rustling of anticipation. She opened her eyes. The bus was labouring up the hill from the little port to the main street. It was a monochrome afternoon, dense clouds scudding across the sky, squeezing the light out of the air, casting a dull sheen on the choppy sea. She'd walk to the house. It was only about two miles and now that she had made it here, she was, of course, doubting her decision to come. Typical, she thought. Rushing all this way and now dragging my feet. Homecomings were always like this for her. Whenever she made the trip down from Dublin as a student, the anticipation that propelled her out of her digs tended to evaporate by the time she hit the River Shannon. The optimism that things would be different this time could only carry her halfway across Ireland it seemed, or maybe it was because the force field of her new life only reached that far. Any further west and she was back to being the girl she had been, no longer immune to the slights that hurt her then and could still sting now.

She hoisted Grace's rucksack onto her back and started walking along the main street, past the shops that seemed to shrink a little more between each visit. She'd take the sea path. It was longer but it'd be light for a few hours yet. Her dad knew she was coming but she hadn't given him a fixed time and he was unlikely to be worried. It was rare that he was in when she came home. It was as if he didn't want to seem too excited, too needy, so she usually found herself pushing open the back door only to find the kitchen empty, the kettle sizzling on the range, the clock slowly ticking out the seconds until she could leave again. Usually, it was just the ghosts who greeted her. Séamus always turned up around five minutes later. She guessed he watched her arrival from some corner of the fields, hidden by one of the trees he had planted to keep out prying eyes, hat pulled low, stick in his hand, motionless as a stone. They were an odd family, for sure.

She was glad when she'd made it through town. She didn't want to be stopped by any of the old lads or ladies who might remember her and start at her with their questions. Especially not today. Usually, it'd be no bother to lie. Sure, that's what everyone did all the time. The 'I'm grands', 'Not a bothers', and 'Can't complains' that were like the diesel in Ireland's engine, keeping the country going even when the road had run out. But today, she knew she wouldn't be able for the charade. There was just too much other shit in her head and she was terrified she might blurt out something mad, like 'My husband's in hospital with a gunshot wound' or 'I'm just down to visit my dad whose sheltering a Rwandan, on the run from the cops and the drug gangs." That would send a fire raging through the invisible gossip networks that were the only kind of wifi in this part of the world.

She'd got as far as the beach now and slowed her pace as she stepped off the tarmac onto the track that ran just above the drifts of pebbles. The grass had no give, it was hard under her feet. As a child, she'd preferred to wobble her way across the stones, deliciously thrilled by the prospect of falling or wrecking her shoes and getting yelled at when she got home. She'd be unlikely to see anyone down here now, or only tourists anyway. Locals didn't really go in for walks along the coastal path, although maybe things had changed, she warned herself. One of the problems with coming home was that her eyes never seemed to be able to go beyond the patina of the past. Half the time, she didn't register what was really in front of her. She was like a defective computer that wouldn't save the changes you made to a file. There was just the original – the view from her eyes as a child. The font size changed but the content never did.

The wind was getting stronger and there was the promise of rain on it. Pauline used to laugh at her whenever she'd said that she could feel the rain coming.

Pauline had been a life-saver these last days. She'd pretty much moved in with Deirdre, cooking for the kids, tidying, doing all the things that Deirdre couldn't face doing any more.

"You're stuck and ye need to get unstuck," she'd said. "You don't think things will ever be normal again, we never do. I certainly didn't after Peter walked out. I thought the world would end cos my world had ended. We think we're so important, don't we?"

And she'd let out a smoky chuckle.

"But life goes on, Dee. What other way is there?"

Deirdre stared out at the seething sea. There was a cormorant standing on a rock, wings spread to dry. It looked like a feathery crucifix. What did her dad call them? *Cailleach dubh*. Black witch. She shivered and hurried along. Whatever Pauline might say, the rain was on its way. She checked her phone. No signal. It was hard to believe there were still places in Ireland where you could fall off the grid, but it made sense that her childhood home would be one of them.

For the first time in days, she really was alone, apart from the cows in the fields, staring at her over the swaying clef-heads of the ferns. For a wild moment, she wondered if she could take off over the walls, run away into the mountains, start again on her own with a simpler life. Then she thought of her kids, suddenly, with a rush of guilt. It had been years since she had forgotten them for even the windowpane of time it took to create a daydream.

She started walking again, pulling her thin denim jacket tighter around her. Cara would probably be trying to get in touch. She'd been spending a lot of time with Grace since she'd turned up at their door, an hour or so after Lisa left, white as a sheet with an older woman Deirdre had never seen before. The woman said she was Theo's aunt and then corrected herself. "I mean, I'm the sister of his foster mother. Can we come in?"

They all sat down awkwardly around the small kitchen table. Deirdre hadn't realised that Cara and Theo were an item. She'd never really gotten to know Cara – she couldn't see what Theo saw in her but then what had she seen in Fergal? There was no knowing what really went on in other people's heads or hearts. Apparently, Cara had texted Grace when Theo hadn't come back in the morning and found out what had happened.

"I spoke to him a couple of hours ago. I think he was on a bus. He said he couldn't talk much but he was on his way to your father," she said, wide eyes raking Deirdre's face for confirmation. She was too young for this. Deirdre told her she'd got a text too but nothing since.

"I'm half out of me mind because he was so upset about Neville, and now... Are the Gardaí after him? D'ye think they'll be looking for him?" Cara said.

"I don't think so, though to be honest, I don't know for sure," Deirdre said. "They don't really care about working class lads kicking off against each other and I'm guessing they already know that's what this was, in a way. You can see their point. I'm fairly certain Fergal won't press charges. Not in his interest to have the Gardaí digging into things. And Pauline got rid of the gun, so it's hard for the cops to follow up on that."

She looked up at her friend, standing arms folded like a rebel guardian angel by the back door. Pauline hadn't told her what she'd done with the weapon and Deirdre had no intention of asking. The police had searched the house while Deirdre was in the hospital but Pauline said they were like teenagers, looking without bending their knees.

Cara's eyes didn't leave Deirdre's face, though Cath shifted awkwardly in her seat. She's still getting used to it all, Deirdre thought, looking at the older woman. She's still fixing these new lenses over her eyes, poor thing.

"I can't get through to him now," Cara said, pulling her own phone from her pocket and holding it out, as though she thought Deirdre would be able to press a button and dial her into whatever dimension Theo was in.

"There's no mobile network where my dad is and that's just how he likes it," Deirdre said, trying to smile. Nobody else did.

They all fell silent. Grace came in. She hugged Cara and they disappeared upstairs.

Cath picked up her bag, stood to leave.

"Thanks, Deirdre. I've to go now. Can Cara stay with you for a while longer? She's that upset I don't want to send her home, still without knowing. And maybe your dad will call when Theo gets there?"

"I doubt I'll hear from him tonight now," Deirdre said. "But I'll call him tomorrow. Sure, let Cara stay the night. It'll be some comfort for Grace too."

She walked Cath to the door, side-stepping the place where Fergal's blood had leaked into the carpet. They hadn't managed to scrub it all out so she'd put a rug over the brown stain but it was more than she could do yet to casually walk over it. She'd had to throw out a few cushions and a pair of curtains over the years when her own blood had been spilled. She couldn't throw the carpet out though. Jesus, those CSI types would have a field day in her house with their ultra-violet, blood-detecting light. The place'd light up like a Christmas tree.

"Can you forgive Theo? For what he's done?" Cath hesitantly said on the doorstep.

Deirdre stared at her. She'd forgotten that not everyone knew the full story. Time to come clean even if it was to a woman she'd only just met. The road would be long so better take the first step as soon as she could. If Fergal was to stay gone, to stay away, she had to be able to name what had happened to her, why she'd kicked him out.

"Fergal's been beating me for years," she said slowly. "I'm not sorry at all he got shot. Got what he deserved if you ask me. I've told him not to come back. So really, Theo did me a favour. I don't think I'd have had the courage to leave Fergal on my own. I wanted to, I'd even decided to just before Theo arrived but I'm not sure I would've gone through with it. Even though I knew what he was, what he'd become, I couldn't make the break. Ah, I won't bother you with it all – it's the same old story everywhere. Thinking he'd change, worrying about the kids. It's stupid, I know. I'm like every woman ever. It's always the same clichés. Trouble is it doesn't make it any less real."

Cath put a hand on her arm, left it there for just a second. It was so spontaneous and so discreet a gesture, Deirdre could feel herself beginning to unravel. She blinked hard.

Cath was halfway down the path but then turned and walked back to Deirdre. She looked like she was puzzling something out.

"You know, Theo's a good lad, really. I know, he messed up getting into the drugs and all but with what he's been through… well, it's no surprise. I don't know how much he told you but he'd to be so tough at such a young age and he saw terrible things, unimaginable things that'd have us on our knees. That *have* had me on my knees. He's always just been trying to fit in. Same as we all did. But I think we put too much on him. We thought fitting in was just a thing that you did and then it was done. It's never done, is it? And then he's never really known what happened to his family and I don't know why we didn't cop that that would be a problem. We should've been on that, looking for answers too. But the whole thing was so awful, so incomprehensible. It was too hard to look at the individual stories. Even Theo's, even after we knew him. It's difficult enough to process the numbers, to accept the scale, without having to recognise each individual's nightmare. You get so bogged down in asking, 'How could anyone do this?' and 'What makes people kill their own neighbours, butcher kids they grew up with?' that you forget to ask 'What happened you, what happened to your family?' I don't blame my sister or Jim but *I* should've known better. I thought I was great – giving Theo a second chance by getting him out. But he never asked for a second chance, and I, of course, just assumed life here would be better and that would be enough."

Deirdre stayed quiet. She wasn't really sure what Cath was talking about but it was clearly important to her.

"I think Theo does a great job living in the middle space," Cath said. "I suppose we all do it to one degree or another, don't we? Even if it's just that little area where what we thought would happen and what happens overlap. Isn't that where most of us are?"

She smiled, gave Deirdre's arm a final squeeze, and headed off.

The sea path had taken Deirdre all the way to her father's house, finally running parallel with the road. She knew a place where the stones were low and she could hop over easily. It was still the same. She climbed over, landing hard so that the gold dust from foxgloves growing on the verge scattered into the air and onto her shoes.

As she crossed the road, she saw Theo sitting on the front

wall. He'd his earphones in and his eyes closed. She stopped, unsure, suddenly shy. What was she trying to do here? But there was no going back now though.

She was nearly upon him when he opened his eyes. For a second he looked scared but then he pulled the earphones out and jumped up to give her a hug.

"Deirdre, you're a sight for sore eyes. I was that sure I'd never see you again," he said, his voice too high and too full.

"Why? I told my dad to tell you Fergal's okay."

Theo's eyes widened.

"He didn't die? I thought I'd killed him. There was so much blood, I thought there was no way he could make it."

"No, he's still in hospital but he's going to be alright. His liver was damaged but they operated. He's going back to his mother's when they let him out."

Theo listened, all the while shaking his head.

"I didn't kill him," he said when she finished but she couldn't place the tone: it was somewhere between relief and regret, maybe.

Deirdre caught a movement at the front window – a figure pinned between the light from the kitchen out back and the window in front, just the shape of a man gliding around the edges of his life. She turned and sat on the wall beside Theo. Her dad would come out to her when he was good and ready.

"Cara asked me to come, Theo. She wanted me to tell you that it's alright, that you can come back. The Gardaí aren't interested, Fergal's not pressing charges and she's desperate to see you. Cath is worried too. Come back, Theo. Sure, there's nothing for you here."

"I dunno, Deirdre. There's still Gerrity and his lot. What if they come after me or after Cara? I'll never be free of it all."

Deirdre didn't have an answer to that and so they fell silent, listening to the waves smash on the sand and the shrieking of the gulls. It was getting dark now, the last of the light gathering on the rim of the sky. The sun flared suddenly, as if to tease them with a late reminder of what could've been if only it could have been arsed earlier to push through the clouds. She'd been wrong about the rain.

"And I'm not sure it's true there's nothing for me here, Deirdre. This place has worked some kind of magic on me," Theo said. "And your dad, he's been good for me. He doesn't give a shit but maybe that's what I need right now. And you can tell, he's a hard man, with all the baggage that brings. It's like I'm being forced to think about what happened here. Really think about it. And I'm remembering things. And part of that is because of your dad. He took me to a lake out on the bogs and something happened. Something good, really good. I always thought my father killed Shema, our worker, but I was wrong. At the lake, it all came back. Or maybe I'd never really forgotten it. It's just I'd only been able to see part of the picture. That's why I thought my father had killed someone."

He fell silent, blinking hard.

"And now, because I know that my father didn't, it's like someone's given me back my right to be happy, to travel my own road. I'm not cursed after all. It sounds daft, I know, but I thought I had to somehow pay for what he did, that his sin was mine and that was just the way it had to be. But if he didn't kill anyone and only tried to save us, then it doesn't have to be like that. I can just be, or try to be, the person I am now in this place. Maybe even in any place?"

He paused, and the wonder of that idea made him smile.

It was a lot to take in and he'd been babbling like a child so that Deirdre felt like her head was only just catching up with her ears. But there was no denying Theo looked happier than she'd ever seen him. Maybe there were other beds for them after all.

"We all have the right to be who we are, Theo," she said. "I think I'm just realising that myself. Maybe the things we think are holding us back are just in our heads."

"Maybe," he said. Then he frowned.

"But there's one thing still missing, even after everything I remembered down here. I don't know what happened to my

265

brother, Clément. I saw the others, I've remembered what happened to them, but he's not in the picture. I mean, he is, he has to be, but maybe I didn't even see that bit at the time. Maybe I can't bring back the memory because it's just not there. Maybe whatever happened to him happened in the dark, beyond the places I could see. But someone must've seen something, someone must know something. He was real, he was there, and I want to know what happened. It's like my brain's been lying to me all this time and now it's lying again, cutting him out. So, I'll not come back yet, Deirdre. And not just because of Gerrity. I might even head up to Donegal, spend a few days with Jim and Sheila. But tell me, how's Cara now? And Cath? And Grace? How's Grace coping?"

Deirdre filled him in but she didn't mention Neville's letter. He'd need to read that himself, if Grace would let him. That comfort, if comfort it was, was not hers to give. Then she felt rather than heard her father at the door behind them.

"You've arrived then?"

She turned. It'd been a while since she'd seen him and he was more stooped than she remembered. He used to fill that door, but now the light from the bulb in the hall spread all around him so that he looked frail and otherworldly. She couldn't see his face in the gloom. She squeezed Theo's hand.

"I'm going to have a word with Dad."

"No worries," he said. "I'll probably take a little walk down the beach myself."

He planted his hands on the wall and lifted himself off, a jaunty move that belonged to a younger boy on a different wall. He smiled.

"I'll not be long."

Inside, he was stoking the fire in the range, sending a fine coat of ash into the air around him. She saw the birthday card she'd sent him two months ago on the windowsill. No sign of a card from Cian. The kitchen looked neglected, like her dad. The last rays of the sun spotlighted the thin film of dust on the windowsill and on the counters. The lino hadn't been brushed, never mind polished, in yonks and there were dirty plates and cups all over the table. She put down the rucksack, shrugged off her jacket, and started piling the dishes together, taking them out to the sink in the back kitchen. He gave her a look but said nothing.

"How are you, Dad?"

He grunted.

"Not too bad, considering the mess ye dropped me into."

"Yeah, sorry about that. Like I told you, I panicked, and you were the only one I could think of who could handle this. I thought Fergal was going to die, you see. I thought Theo would need to hide."

"Hiding's not always the answer."

Deirdre started running water into the sink. No washing-up liquid, of course.

"What do you mean by that?" she asked. "And why didn't you tell him that Fergal was okay, after I told you? And what the hell is this business of a lost lake or something?"

Séamus harrumphed. He was sitting in the armchair by the fire, chewing his lip, head lowered but eyes watching her every move.

"There's fresh tea there in the pot. Pour us both a cup, won't ye?" he said.

Deirdre sighed. When her dad didn't want to talk, there was no moving him. Sure, let him stew. She was in no rush now. She went to the cupboard for the cups and every movement – her steps across the room, the way she reached to the bottom of the cupboard to open the door because the handle had fallen off years ago, the taking of the tea towel off the rail on the range to hold the handle of the stainless steel teapot – was a recollected one, of the now and from the then, smoothly switching her onto well-worn tracks.

When he'd had his tea, and after he'd switched on the news, and after he'd watched silently for a few minutes, her father decided he could speak. He muted the box.

"I didn't tell him straight away because sometimes ye have

to confront the worst of what ye are. Sometimes, ye need to look right down into the black and see your reflection. It's the only way to know who ye are and who ye are going to be."

Deirdre said nothing. She was that afraid he'd stop. For a moment, they sat, looking straight at each other, the steam off the tea rising around them, the flickering of the telly and the dying rays of the sun sending dust motes swirling around their heads. Part of me has always been here in this kitchen, Deirdre thought, surprised.

"That lad is lost, ye can see it in his eyes. I've met plenty like him. None of them black, mind you, but lads who felt left out of the world, lads who weren't sure where they belonged, what their place was. I watched some of those lads pick up guns, or make bombs, or just throw stones. Of course, they believed in the cause. We all did.

"But now, the way things are, everything settled today, peace mostly, ye wonder what was really driving us all those years. What drives anyone to step off the road and into the grass? It's not always just about the cause. It's personal too. Ye get caught up in something that takes ye over because, maybe, sometimes there's not enough of anything else to tie ye down. So off ye float. Wasn't necessarily the case for me, but there was an element of that, not knowing how to be. Not knowing how to be a good father, a good husband, especially after yer mam was gone. It was easier to adopt some higher calling than just to be stuck with what I was, found wanting, useless."

Her father sighed.

"I took Theo to *Loch an Cháillte* because it's helped me deal with the stuff I've done. I know the legend's just blather but it's been some comfort to me and that's not to be sneered at these days. I'll take ye out there tomorrow, if ye want."

Deirdre nodded.

"I've a thing or two to tell ye there too," he said, shuffling towards the door. "Then, we'll see."

As he passed her, his hand hovered just above her hair, so

that the movement of the air became a caress that he could not bring himself to give. Deirdre froze but he didn't stop.

"Goodnight, Sarah," he called from the hall, and she knew it wasn't a mistake.

You're still here too, she thought. Of course, you are.

Deirdre sat a while longer in the darkening kitchen. She felt restless, almost excited. Somewhere in the back of her mind, tiny, translucent ideas were coming to life, thin stalks stretching and fleshy leaves unfurling. She looked out the window and saw Theo on the beach. He was flinging pebbles into the waves and there was a looseness and joy to his throws that reminded her of Kevin. Tiny buds pushed through the leaves, opening like a symphony. What if she came back? What if there was a new life here? What if she decided, on her own, to rebuild her dreams here, in her father's house? It was such a delicate thought, so fragile, that she barely dared breathe as she looked on it. Too early to pick these flowers but they were there now and they would grow and tomorrow she would check them again.

CHAPTER TWENTY

It was the smell that got him first. As soon as the plane doors opened, it crept in, seeping into pores, sliding down noses and throats. It conjured up sticky heat, thick soil filled with sprouting seeds, rain-soaked earth and saturated, hot air. Theo closed his eyes as the people around him jostled to be the first to get out. Phones beeped, voices rang too high after hours of silence, joints creaked. He breathed deeply, and the smell switched on lights in his brain, bringing the sweet taste of plantain to his tongue and tingling his skin with the remembered caress of hot rain. It awoke other darker memories too but these he refused, picking and choosing like a child in a sweet shop. A tall man in a smart cream jacket toppled towards him, his hand shooting out at the last minute to stop his fall.

"I'm sorry," he said.

"That's okay," Theo replied.

It was a few seconds before he realised that he'd spoken in Kinyarwanda. He listened. Most of the voices around him were speaking in Kinyarwanda. He'd been understanding everything but he hadn't registered what he was listening to.

It'd been five weeks since the shooting, since he'd fled Dublin on a bike, ended up by a lake with an old man, and finally unlocked that room in his head. He'd stayed with Séamus for a few more days after Deirdre arrived, then headed to Donegal, where Jim and Sheila were waiting, as they would always be waiting for him. He wasn't sure what Cath had told them; Jim's eyes were misty when he picked him up at the bus stop and Sheila held him a little longer than usual on the doorstep but they didn't say anything about what had happened. That evening, while they were sitting outside watching the sun dip behind the mountains around the lake, Cara called. Jim brought the phone outside and handed it to Theo.

"Theo, they've arrested Gerrity."

Theo walked into the garden, where inky shadows were smudging the day's sharp edges.

"For Neville?" he asked.

"No, no, not for Neville. Not even for drugs, would ye believe. Or not directly. It's to do with some lad's disappearance last year. Deirdre said his name was Billy Mannion, from Blanchardstown? Maybe ye didn't know about it? Michael told Pauline there's some CCTV footage of him getting into a car with Gerrity the night he disappeared. Apparently, someone came forward with it last week, and that led to more cameras, and then they found his bones, scattered around a field in Wicklow. Seems Billy's family's been working this whole time to find out what happened. Michael thinks Gerrity's going down hard for this. He's getting out too, heading over to England on the ferry, so Deirdre says."

Theo was silent.

"D'ye hear me, Theo? You can come back now, he's been arrested. He's not going to be worrying about you. He's got bigger problems. Please, come back. I miss you. Cath misses you. Ye can't keep running just for the sake of running. I'm here, I need you."

Theo turned back to the house. Jim and Sheila were talking in low voices, trying not to listen. They just wanted him to be okay. That's all anyone wanted for him, all he wanted for himself. Maybe it was time to stop trying to outrun the shit in his head.

"Listen, I'll even let ye play your poetry podcasts to me," Cara said. He let himself laugh and it felt like a new beginning. So he'd gone back to Dublin and he and Cara had walked again to the cemetery in Howth and laid yellow carnations on the graves of both of Theo's heroes: Phil and Neville.

Now, he was here.

Cath had said a guy called Martin Sebiroro would meet him at arrivals. He worked in the genocide archive and Theo would stay with him for a night and then they'd travel together to Kibungo. Cath had arranged everything. She said Martin had said he would try to dig out whatever information there was before Theo came, but he couldn't guarantee anything.

"What have you got to lose?" she'd said, Cara nodding beside her.

How could he explain that he didn't know and that this unknowing terrified him? What if he didn't recognise his home or the place where his father had died? It had taken so much time and effort, his whole life, to pull the pieces together; he didn't want to shatter the reflection now by chucking sticks in the pond. But then there was Clément. He was still there, earnest and silent in Theo's head, demanding a reckoning.

Kigali airport was all sharp angles and gleaming floors. Theo couldn't remember what it had been like when he left but he'd definitely come through here then. He remembered being on the plane and Cath bending over him to do up the seatbelt. An absurd gesture after all he'd been through in the previous months. He should've had a seatbelt for life. When the plane started down the runway, his whole chest swelled with terror so that he could hardly breathe. He was so scared, they were going too fast, they were going to die. Then there was the moment, between the tarmac and the sky, when it felt like everything had stopped, even time, and he thought he was already dead. Which made sense because he thought the air hostesses had to be angels; they were so clean and perfect.

Martin was holding a sign with Theo's name written in red capital letters. He'd written the full name: *Théoneste Mukansonera*. Those twenty letters sang so loudly he felt his face becoming hot. It was like seeing his name in a book or in the newspaper or hearing it in court. It was startling. Like I've stepped outside myself and I'm looking in, he thought.

He greeted Martin in English. The tourist he felt he was.

"Welcome," Martin replied. "Welcome home."

They stood for a minute. Martin, a thin lad in a neat, short-sleeved checked shirt and black slacks, looked steadily at Theo, his smile stretching across his lean face, his head bobbing. Theo didn't know what to say. He shifted his sports bag from one hand to the other, breaking the spell.

"Let me take that," Martin said. "My car is outside. Follow me."

It was already dark but the air was warm and heavy with the heady scent of the flowers growing around the terminal and the bitter tang of airline fuel. Theo shrugged off his jacket, pulled a water bottle from his rucksack and drank deeply.

"I think you do not recognise this place?" Martin said as he pulled open the boot of the car. "Of course, this airport was only renovated in the last years, so it has changed very much."

"I left when I was seven," Theo said as he got into the car. "I don't remember much of anything. I don't think I'd ever even been to Kigali, except for when I left."

Martin nodded.

"Your accent? It is what? You do not sound like…"

"Like you? Nah, I don't, do I? My accent is Irish, well, Dublin really," Theo said, reaching for the seatbelt.

"I didn't know they spoke different in Ireland to how they speak in England," Martin said. "Of course, I have never been to either place so how should I know?"

He drove silently until they were through the barriers and onto the main road, heading into the city.

"It will take only about twenty minutes to get to my house. It's a pity you cannot see now, but tomorrow when we will go to Kibungo, you will see how pretty Kigali has become."

Theo nodded. "So Cath said you might've been able to find out something about my brother, Clément? Did you have any luck?"

273

Martin didn't take his eyes from the road, even though there was barely any traffic.

"You have just had a long journey. You must be tired. You have waited many years. What is one more night?" Now he finally turned, and Theo saw that his smile was still wide but thin. Still, he was right: Theo was exhausted and the truth could wait one more night.

Kigali *was* pretty, Theo thought as they drove back through the city just after dawn. Pretty was the perfect word for the bright colours, the tree-fringed streets, the conspicuous order. Even the motorbike taxis seemed to obey the rules better than the average taxi driver in Dublin. Everywhere Theo looked he saw reflections of himself and realising this, he couldn't imagine how he had ever coped in a place where his image was so absent. I'm invisible here, he marvelled, as they sat at a busy crossroads, watching a man with mattresses piled high on his head weave through the motorbikes and cars. I'm just a lad in a car. I don't mean anything else. It was exhilarating.

Martin said it would take about two hours, maybe three, to get to Kibungo.

"Why are there so few dogs on the streets?" Theo asked as they drove through the city. "I'd to get a rabies shot before I came because the doctor said there were loads of wild dogs in African cities."

Martin shook his head and Theo couldn't tell if he was amused by what he said or just by the idea that this big Rwandan beside him had had to get shots to come home. A vaccination to protect him from his own place. But maybe it wasn't such a mad idea after all.

"It is true there are very few dogs here. You see after the killing, there were many bodies in the street for many days because those who could have claimed them were lying dead beside them or too scared to come out of the bush or the swamp or the tiny holes they were hiding in. So the dogs got a taste for this new meat. And then, when we came to stop the killing, we had to get rid of those dogs." He said it so matter-of-factly that Theo felt his shock was somehow indecent.

After about an hour, they stopped at a roadside kiosk for coffee and thick slices of fresh baguette. They sat on iron chairs around a rickety table under the shade of a mango tree.

"So you never left Rwanda?" Theo asked Martin as he spooned coffee granules into his cup and then added boiling water from a giant red thermos. The cups were china with gold leaf around the chipped rims.

"No, no, I did." Martin replied. "In fact, I was born in Tanzania. My parents fled Rwanda in the 70s so I grew up there. Then, I joined the rebellion and came with the fighters into Rwanda in 1994. We fought our way to Kigali and actually I also came to Kibungo at that time. Hmm, yes."

Above them, some bright blue starling-like birds were fighting noisily in the tree. The road was quiet, only the occasional truck passing, some with sacks of coffee tilting precariously over the edges. The sharp scent of the beans tickled Theo's nose. Each truck left a film of dust on the already grey leaves by the roadside. Must be the only things they don't clean in Rwanda, Theo thought. Even here, they're not going to wash the leaves.

"I don't remember the fighters coming to Kibungo but we might've already left," he said. "We took off just after the whole thing started, and then my father and my mother and my sister were killed at a roadblock. Our worker, our friend, Shema was murdered there too. He was a Tutsi."

"You are not a Tutsi?" Martin posed it as a question although he must know the answer. Theo could understand why. Some things could never be simple now, he supposed.

"My father was a Hutu, my mother was a Tutsi, so I guess that makes me mixed race? Or what do you call it here? Maybe they told me once, we must've talked about it, I suppose, but I don't remember. My memories are not the clearest."

"You are Hutu," Martin said. "Your ethnicity comes from your father. That is how it has always been. But you are also

275

a *rescapé*, a survivor. You know, we cannot speak of ethnic groups here any more. We have done something so terrible because of those divisions that those names have to be wiped off the face of the earth. Of course, we still know who and what we are and we still know what we did but we are trying to become something more. To build, you know, you must first knock down the old house."

"That makes sense," Theo said. "But what if there's nothing left to build on, or build for?"

"But there is," Martin said. "Look around. We are still here."

They sat in silence for a while.

"So, maybe now we can talk about Clément," Martin said. "I was asked by your friends to find out what happened to him, if it was possible."

He picked up the laptop case he'd placed carefully on the table and pulled out three or four pages in a plastic folder.

"These are for you. I did not find anything in the gacaca archives. But I did find these." He paused, opened his mouth as if he were about to say something else, and then shut it again.

"I will be in the car."

He gulped down the last of his coffee and headed across the car park slowly, like a man who has done a lot of walking in his time and prefers to minimise the effort whenever he can.

Theo picked up the folder and opened it. A photograph of Clément – older, a little thinner around the jaw but still recognisably his brother – stared out at him. He was wearing a grubby white shirt and short trousers, his head was shaved, there was a rosary hanging round his neck, and his eyes were narrowed, the way he used to squint when he was angry, chasing Theo around the house for eating the last mango or for teasing him about some girl at school.

The next page gave his name, his date of birth, and age. It said he was fifteen. This was a Clément Theo had never met. The paper was dated 1997. It was stamped *Gitarama Prison*.

It took Theo a few minutes to understand what he was reading. It was a photocopy of Clément's death certificate. He turned back to the first page, searching that familiar and strange face for a goodbye, a sense of its own destiny. It stared back, hostile, angry, dead.

The paper listed Clément's parents as unknown, birthplace unknown. It did give his surname. Cause of death was given as complications from suffocation. Theo wouldn't have been able to understand the original French but someone had scrawled the English translation above the typed words. Suffocation.

Theo exhaled, long and slow. He'd never believed there would be a tearful airport reunion – not really, not much – and that's why he hadn't pressed Martin for whatever he'd found yesterday. If Clément wasn't at the airport, he was dead. Of course, he was. He looked at the next page. It was a photocopy of a handwritten note. It was Clément's writing. Unlike his face, his eyes, it hadn't aged. It had frozen at the moment when his childhood had died.

If I told you everything, I would never stop. The beginning was the death of my parents and my sister. We were trying to flee our village near Kibungo. But we were stopped by the interahamwe. They said my father could join them, as he was a Hutu, but that we children and my mother must die. My father did not join them. He was beaten to death. My mother's throat was cut and my baby sister was also killed. But that I do not want to describe. They came to cut me with a machete but I begged them to let me join them. I cried and they laughed and then they said yes but I must prove myself. Our worker was with us. He was a Tutsi. They said I must kill him. They had already beaten him but he was still alive. They gave me a masu. I looked for my brother, Théoneste, because I did not want him to see what I would have to do. I could not see him. I hoped he had got away. So I killed Shema. Or at least I tried. I beat him on the head and he bled but I think I was not strong enough, so I hit him again on his forehead but still he moaned. The others laughed at me, calling me 'boy' and 'weakling'. I tried again, but still Shema moved. Then the leader, he came and brought his machete down on Shema's neck. I have never seen so much blood, it washed over me, into my eyes, even my mouth. But then Shema was still because all of his blood was gone. I stayed with that group for many weeks. I got better at killing so that I would not cause so much suffering each time. I was taken near Kabgayi by RPF soldiers. They brought me here to Gitarama. I am sorry for what I did and many times, I see those I hurt when I close my eyes. Luckily, there is no space to sleep in the cells here because we are so many, so I do not often close my eyes.

That was it. No signoff, no goodbye, as if Clément had more to say but ran out of time. The handwritten piece was not dated. Theo turned back to the picture. I ran, he whispered. I ran away and left you. I didn't even try to help. I turned my back on you.

There was a lump in his throat but he could not cry. This was beyond tears. He read the letter again, slowly now, stopping every now and then to look straight into his brother's eyes.

"I'm sorry," he said at last. "I couldn't even remember right. I couldn't keep your story alive. All this time, I've been rehashing lies. I've let you down in so many ways. All that time, I was whinging about school, and kids in the playground, and your breath was being sucked out of you here."

The face on the page did not change. It would never change now.

In the car, the radio was turned up high, a jaunty, salsa-like melody sashaying across the empty car park. When Theo got in, Martin started the engine and they pulled back out into the road. They drove for nearly half an hour before Martin spoke.

"I am sorry it was not good news about your brother. But I hope you can find some comfort in the truth. I have been collecting stories of sorrow for more than five years now and it is difficult work. I feel as though I am a collector of tears, so many people cry when they speak of that time. But afterwards, they often say how much it has helped them, just being able to speak."

Theo swallowed hard.

"Do you know where my brother is buried? Is it at Gitarama?"

"He must be buried there if he is buried anywhere although I do not know if the grave will be marked. There are so many graves from that time that, if we marked them all, this would be a nation of gravestones."

"I'd like to go there. I'd like to look at the things he looked at. Can I do that?"

Theo turned to look at Martin.

"We can try. It is on the other side of Kigali. But I must warn you, Théoneste. It is a bad place even today. At that time, when your brother was there, there were thousands of *génocidaires* packed into tiny cells, no room to sit, or lie down, only to stand on feet that swelled, feet that rotted so that toes even fell off. It was a place for the guilty but then so many of us were guilty. Your brother was just one and an unlucky one because he was caught when so many others escaped. But even today, that jail is a place of despair, a place that reminds us of the worst we can be."

Theo thought of Clément's feet. He had their mother's small, shapely feet while Theo took after his father. But Clément was fast, running up the hill from school or chasing the ball into the corner when he played football with the other boys on the dried-out patch of ground behind the community hall in the village.

"I'd still like to go," he said.

Martin nodded.

"I will take you but you know, you may not find answers there. This is a country of questions or maybe just one question. Why? We will never be able to answer this but even to ask it is to acknowledge the importance of trying to find an answer. *Umugayo uvuna uwugaya uwugawa yigaramiye.* Do you know what that means?" Martin asked.

Theo shook his head.

"The blame hurts the one doing the blaming, while the blamed person is enjoying life. We want to enjoy life now, so we have learned not to blame and we have learned to live with the open question. It is the only way. It may not be the same as forgiveness but, without it, there can be no future."

They drove a little further, passing villages strung out by the road like beads on a rosary. Straw-roofed huts and brick homes with corrugated roofs grew like mushrooms on the terraced mountains above valleys carpeted with thick banana plants and patches of tilled, red earth.

"We are coming to Kibungo now," Martin said, turning down the music. "Do you recognise this place, Théoneste?"

Nothing had looked familiar so far but now as one-storey, pastel-coloured buildings, with iron grates around the windows, began to congregate on either side of the road, something began to stir.

"Are we coming to the market? Something tells me it should be just on the right now?" Theo asked.

"Yes, that's correct," said Martin, sounding proud.

They passed rickety tables stacked with tomatoes, bananas and avocados. There were piles of colourful basins on the ground, a mountain of Timberland-type shoes, and piles of knickers on a piece of plastic sheeting.

I've been here, thought Theo.

"My father bought me a pair of shorts here," he said slowly. "They were light blue, like football shorts. I had to try them on over my school trousers. We came straight after classes and my father bought me a Fanta. Yeah, I drank a Fanta, just over there, on that wall."

The memory exploded all at once, a blast of sound, taste and colours that changed everything. I know this place, Theo thought.

Martin parked the car on a patch of open land just beyond the market.

That's when Theo's feet took over. He didn't think, he didn't reason, he just went. As he walked, he automatically gravitated to the shade beneath trees and awnings, weaving easily between the oases of cool. This is not me, this is just my body, he thought, amazed. My body knows where it is going.

"I'm going to walk to my house. It's not far from here, I think. Okay?" he threw over his shoulder.

"We can drive. It will be cooler for you than walking in this heat. You will get very tired," Martin said.

I never got tired before, Theo thought, striding forward.

They pushed through the crowds, past a stall piled with batteries, Nokia phones and radios. There was a narrow lane leading from the market, out into the fields beyond and up the hill.

Theo led the way or rather his feet did. This path was in his blood. Little things leapt out at him. He knew, before he saw it, that a tree on the right would have a fork in the trunk that you could just about reach from the ground. He stopped by it. The fork was now at chest-level. He grinned to himself.

I got big, he thought.

Martin seemed happy to stay behind him, refusing to adapt his regular pace to Theo's skipping, stop-start canter.

After a while, Theo noticed the silence and he stopped to let Martin catch up. There were birds singing, insects whirring in the long grass on either side of the track, but nothing else. No shouts, no cries, no laughter and no radios. This was not how it had been. Theo's ears were in on the joke now too, racing ahead of his mind, uncovering a long-buried playlist, but there was no echo outside in the real world.

"Why is it so quiet? I don't remember it being this quiet?"

Martin plodded towards him. He slowly took a white cloth handkerchief from his pocket, opened it, and wiped his face.

"Everyone left the village after. The houses were burned and the crops were destroyed and so the *rescapés* preferred

281

to move to new houses that we built by the roads. Nobody wanted to live in the village any more. There were too many ghosts, too much pain. And they felt it was safer to be by the road."

His words seemed to be swallowed up by the eerie silence.

"You lost family members?" Theo asked.

Martin nodded.

"But that is not all of it. Here we say: don't ask me to tell you everything because then I will never stop talking. But I will tell you this. We came in from the east, we pushed down through villages and towns and swamps, and what we saw made us so angry that sometimes... sometimes anger makes you do things. I killed many people. At first, it didn't bother me. I was very, very angry. I had seen things no man should ever see. So when we came upon the killers, we showed them no mercy. And some of them were teenagers, like your Clément. But maybe sometimes we did not have time to be sure. And we were not God, so we should not have carried out these final judgments. I regret many of my actions. I regret them every day because when I hear the stories of the survivors, I see myself. Not in them, in the others."

"For ages, I was dead certain my father was a killer," Theo said. "And I thought what he did was on me too. Maybe because I ran away and survived. I got out and had a new family in a country that was like a bleedin' dream. I felt guilty and I felt I owed some kind of debt because of what my father did. And then, just a couple of weeks ago, I remembered. I remembered what'd really happened, and it was like I was born again. I was so bloody relieved that we were clean. All of us. Now I know what Clément did but, to be honest, I can't take it in really, because I have no memory of it. So it's not real to me. I only see him as he was, a boy, my big brother."

"Keep that in your heart," Martin said. "Nothing should change that. Your brother was what you remember, but he was more also because he had to be, he had no choice. You cannot blame him, you must forgive. You must go on and the only way we can do that is if we learn to live with the horror. We can't always forget it, forget what was done to us, what we did to others, but we must try to forgive them and to forgive ourselves. We must think of those times as another life, separate from this one, an after-life that for one time only, in a world gone crazy, came before the life."

He put his hand on Theo's arm.

"We must be nearly at your home?"

Theo nodded and headed off up the track again, swatting the flies away with an arm that remembered the gesture all too well.

The village was deserted. Many homes were gone. Their straw roofs had burned so easily after their owners had run to the bush, or even sometimes before. Theo found his house quickly. The corrugated iron roof was gone, the walls were crumbling, and there were weeds growing through the stones. The bougainvillea bush was still there though, the flowers pink as a scream. He went inside. The rooms were empty. The furniture, curtains, pictures, everything was gone. It was as though no one had ever lived here. He went into the kitchen. They had even taken the taps from the sink and the pipes underneath. In a corner, there was a bundle on the floor. He picked it up. It was his mother's apron, the one Clément had bought her from the market one Christmas. It was blue and red and green, flower shapes and spirals weaving around each other. He lifted it to his nose but she was gone. It only smelled old.

He walked out the back door. A few feet away, a calabash lay in the grass. The neck was broken but the rest was intact. The smell of banana beer lingered, just, or was it in his mind?

"Our... Shema used to drink beer from this," he said, lifting it carefully and showing it to Martin, who was silently following through the house.

"Up there, you see, past the trees. We grew maize and sweet potatoes and some tea. I used to go up there with Shema, I'd watch him pick the tea. I guess I was a lazy bastard, even then."

He laughed. Martin didn't say anything.

The fields were overgrown now, the tea bushes dead, but the mountains rose up just the same behind them, the sun was just as hot, and the air was the same, going into his same lungs. Maybe it's just me, he thought. Maybe what I am is just me, wherever I've been. As long as I breathe, I will carry all these places with me. That's who I am. That's where I'm from.

There was something else in the grass. Theo bent down. It was his scooter, intact, forgotten, not valuable enough to be taken.

He turned to Martin.

"This is mine. I rode this, here, when I was seven. This is mine. Jesus Christ, it's still here."

Theo sped down the slope. He closed his eyes and he could feel the red dust rising from the ground to tickle his nose. The wind was pulling tears from his eyes and he was going so fast the sun couldn't lay its hand on him. His own shadow couldn't keep up as he flew through time and space and all the dimensions, going faster and faster until he felt like he was finally outrunning himself.

ACKNOWLEDGEMENTS

My deepest thanks to Tom Chalmers, Lauren Parsons and the team at Legend Press for giving me another chance to get what's in my head onto paper and, most importantly, for setting a deadline. I am especially grateful to Lauren for her superb editing and guidance.

The lines from 'Epic' by Patrick Kavanagh are quoted from *Collected Poems*, edited by Antoinette Quinn (Allen Lane, 2004), by kind permission of the Trustees of the Estate of the late Katherine B. Kavanagh, through the Jonathan Williams Literary Agency. Thank you very much.

The extract from Louis MacNeice's 'Dublin' is quoted from *Collected Poems*, published by Faber & Faber, through the David Higham agency. Thank you so much.

Thank you to my parents, Máirtín and Máire, for teaching me to be curious and to never give up, and for letting me disappear for hours to chase herons through the fields. Thank you to Martina, Gearóidín, Máirtín, Esther, Máirín and Antaine for bringing so much laughter into my life. And for driving me, everywhere.

Writing is a lonely endeavour. It's a cliché but, like all the best ones, it's true. Thank you to Francis, Sue, Ann and all my extended family and friends for your unwavering support through the launch of my first novel. Your kind words and generous praise made all the heartache seem so worthwhile, I decided to do it again.

As ever, this book is dedicated to two inspirational young

women: Lucy and Rachel. Thanks, girls, for holding off on getting a puppy until I'd written a first draft, at least.

Finally to David, my ever-faithful first reader and the poor soul condemned to listen to my mid-novel ranting every time: You have my undying gratitude and love.

COME VISIT US AT
WWW.LEGENDPRESS.CO.UK

FOLLOW US
@LEGEND_PRESS